Forever ♥ Loved

Sarah of Swan Point

CYNTHIA WEST ABBOTT

ISBN 978-1-64300-229-3 (Paperback)
ISBN 978-1-64300-230-9 (Digital)

Covenant Books, Inc.
11661 Hwy 707
Murrells Inlet, SC 29576
www.covenantbooks.com

CHAPTER I

James West
London, England
1764-1765

"We'll tell them we found it on the ground," James West whispered to his friend, as John came out of the darkened shop carrying the heavy, red-hooded cloak.

John Hussey flashed a quick, sly smile at James and nodded. "Now to see if we can get someone to pawn it for us tomorrow. Someone's got to know we took it, or it's all for naught."

The two young men spent the rest of the cold night shivering inside the vacant building they had found three nights before, less than a mile from the clothing shop in the Cloisters, West Smithfield, in the heart of London near the Thames. The low stone structure was empty except for their individual sacks that contained all they owned in the world. John started a fire with a little kindling, and James mentioned the possibility of tossing the newly acquired cloak into the small blaze for additional warmth.

"You want to destroy the evidence? Feeling guilty, are you, James?" asked his friend John. "You wouldn't just be destroying the evidence, you know? You'd be burning up our ticket to America."

James West nodded. Knowing that did not diminish the waves of guilt that washed over him as he thought about his mother and father back in the Welsh village of Manorowen he had left just two weeks ago. He could envision his father turning the pages of the family Bible and reading aloud to his wife and children gathered around him, not to mention his parish priest of the Episcopal church they frequented, speaking on the topics of sound morality. "Thou shalt not steal," echoed in his brain until it almost drove him daft.

I didn't steal the cloak, James consoled himself. *This John Hussey fellow stole the cloak. Broke into Mr. Jackson's shop, and stole it. It wasn't I who stole the cloak.*

Those insistent thoughts brought no real peace to sixteen-year-old James. He was going to be charged, found guilty, and sentenced to at least seven years in America. That was the plan.

It was not always the plan, however. James curled up in a ball trying to stay warm inside his thin, worn surtout coat. He slid a little closer to the flames.

"You want to put this cloak on? It should provide a little more warmth," John said to James, tossing him the stolen red cape. "And the hood will keep your head covered. I've got this heavy cardigan on under my coat."

James sat up, holding the coat up by its hood, and said, "We want to sell it or pawn it. I haven't bathed since the day before I left home. No one would want to buy it after smelling me all over it!"

"I don't think that's going to be a major issue, Master West," John said with a laugh. "We stole it after all! What do we care about the odors Mr. Jackson will have to get rid of?"

James wrapped himself in the red cloak and pulled the hood round his head, almost covering his face. He used his sack as he had the last few nights as a pillow, missing once more the goose feather pillow from the bed he shared with his younger brothers, Joseph and William.

Joseph and William, Cecily and Jane, his mum and papa— what were they thinking about now, now that he had left without even saying farewell? Francis, his oldest brother, had bid the family a fond farewell in 1758, almost seven years ago. Francis had even sent three letters from America, from the colony called North Carolina. The first letter had not only told them that he had arrived in America but also that he had wed a woman named Christian Talley. The next two letters contained the news of sons, one per letter: James, born in 1761, and Charles, born in 1763. It was now late 1764, and no further news had come their way. In all three letters from across the ocean, Francis had included a message to James to consider America "if in need of a true adventure."

Underneath his head through the sparse articles of extra clothing in his sack, James could feel the book he'd brought, a book he had read several times. It was a copy of Daniel Defoe's *Robinson Crusoe*. Defoe's tale was alluring and filled James with such ideas of adventure like those Francis had hinted at. He imagined himself on a ship to America, reading on deck by daylight while smelling the salty seawater and hearing waves lap against the sides of the ship. Perhaps they might find themselves shipwrecked upon some exotic island and meeting interesting people as Crusoe had done.

Just before slipping into a deep slumber, James remembered just over two weeks before, the day the resolve had settled into his heart instead of just his mind and imagination. He had been out dutifully slopping the hogs on his family's farm, weary from the tediousness of the routine. He had dropped his bucket, gone into the house and retrieved a few things, placed them in this large leather pouch, and had headed down the path that led away from the village of Manorowen to the next village on the coast, a little place called Fishguard. From there, he had sought passage on a small boat and sailed around to London. His plan had been to seek further passage by agreeing to work aboard a ship and earn his way to America as Francis had done.

The trip to London had almost made him change his mind or at least made him wish he had taken the extra time to walk or hitch a wagon ride for the nearly two hundred miles to London. The waters had been rough, and the little fishing vessel on which he had gotten a lift had almost gone down in an enormous storm that had frightened even the old, seasoned fisherman who had welcomed him aboard for the companionship.

Growing up a little over a mile from Fishguard, James had been out on the water numerous times. His mother's brother Joel and his family lived in Fishguard and made a living off what they pulled up out of the waters. James and his cousins had had grand times boating and fishing. As a matter of fact, the last outing he had had with his older brother Francis had been a trek to see their uncle Joel. On the mile-and-a-half walk down there, Francis had shared his dreams of going to America and had planted so many images in his mind of what it was going to be like to sail to the young country that James could scarcely sleep the first few nights after Francis had left. He had listened closely as Francis and Uncle Joel discussed the different prospects and means and ways of getting to America. Francis had saved some money, and Uncle Joel had given him the name of a relative in London who was a partner in a shipping company and had been happy to have Francis aboard to work in order to pay for passage.

That is what I should have done, James thought. But Uncle Joel had died two years ago, and there was no one to help James find an easy, sure passage to the new world of America. His plan had been to arrive in the shipyards of London and find the same shipping company that had taken on Francis, explain his relationship, and promise to be as hard a worker as his brother had been. Plus, he had hopes that the veteran fisherman who had brought him to London might vouch for him in that regard.

However, when they had docked in London, Captain Rafe—as the old sea salt had asked to be addressed—at once walked away from his boat and James without saying a solitary word, and James had gazed about him astonished at the size of the crowd gathered for various reasons. He had thought about looking for someone who seemed to be in charge of a ship to ask about a job opportunity but had been distracted by a "parade" of prisoners chained to each other and headed for a ship in port waiting to take them somewhere. Some folks swore oaths at them, and some taunted them, but most just watched.

Someone very near him had said, "That's one way to get to America, right?" James had turned to see for the first time John Hussey also watching the long line of criminals heading to one of the ships in port. That had begun their discussion of petty larceny and the penalty of being transported to America for seven years and the development of the plan they had carried out to steal the cloak.

When James awoke just after daybreak, John had already been out and gotten some bread and cheese and two apples for their morning meal. James was very certain John had stolen the food, but he was so hungry, he found himself thanking God that his newfound friend was a good thief, as he said a silent prayer asking that God also bless this stolen food.

"I found a place that I think will take the cloak," John said, his mouth full of cheese. "But as I lay awake last night, it came to my mind that we need to wait a day or two just to make sure Mr. Jackson realizes the coat is missing. He's got to get word out so folks are on the lookout for that red cloak you're now wearing."

James spoke through his disappointment, motioning around the cold bare room, "I was surely hoping that last night would be our last here."

"My mum's uncle ran a little pawnshop not too far from here. I know about these things. Mr. Jackson will get word out the coat's missing, and when we take it in to pawn it, the owner will look at any notices they've gotten and know if it's stolen or not," John explained.

"Are you sure we can get sent to America just for taking this thing?" James asked, plucking at the red cloak he was still wearing.

"Stealing is stealing. They send them by the boatloads to the colonies. London wants to be rid of its common thieves." John was quiet a few moments then continued, "You know, James, it's not going to be easy. You may hate this nook we've found, but you'll probably be dreaming of it after a few nights in jail. And I know the life of a convict servant is a tough one. We'll basically be slaves to whoever buys us, you know that, right?"

James nodded and said, "But they say when one gets to America, many escape and make a life of their own. That's what I'm counting on."

"Yes, that's my hope as well. It's got to be better than living on the streets here and scrapin' to get by." John had told James little pieces of his story, but he seemed to be more in need of talking this morning since the deed was done, and now it was just a matter of killing some time.

"Where's your family?" James asked him.

"The last of 'em have been in the churchyard for months now. My mum and my sister took sick and died with the fever in early spring. The winter before that, my brother Stephen died of the same.

He was twelve. My father passed on two years before that. After he died, Mum took us all to live with an aunt outside London, but we never had much to eat. Auntie Jane was old and had a dried up garden and a pitiful cow that didn't give much milk. My mum was already sick when we got there, and she didn't feel much like helping Auntie Jane. I took on some work, mainly helping out on the docks, but it didn't amount to much. And when my auntie passed a month ago, I just took off. You know one of the reasons I spoke to you the other day when I saw you in the shipyard is you look a bit like my brother Stephen. He had a head full of dark curls just as you do. And you looked a bit lost. You don't look like you're sixteen, you know. More like fourteen."

John was nineteen and was taller and broader than James, but both young men were on the scrawny side. Just shy of six feet, John was taller than James by about five inches. His long sandy hair framed his face and neck like dirty straw under his hat.

James ignored the comment about his slight stature and his boyish looks and went on, "So you are alone in the world now? No other family?"

"It's just me."

For a few minutes, James sat and contemplated taking John and heading back to Manorowen so he could taste one of his mum's delicious chicken stews and listen to one of the stories his father would tell while smoking his pipe by the fire. It hurt his heart to think of being only nineteen and having no family left in the whole entire world, and James felt the sudden urge to share his with his new friend.

As if John were reading his thoughts, he asked, "Does your family know where you've run off to? Do they know what you're planning to do?"

"They certainly don't know about my stealing to get to America. But I think they have been expecting this. I've talked often enough about wanting to follow Francis to the colonies. But I'm certain they thought I would at least say a proper farewell. My uncle got Francis a job with a shipping company. We've gotten three letters from him. He's in Granville County, in the colony of North Carolina. He landed not too far from where that group disappeared there all those years ago. But he moved inland near the Virginia colony and has become a farmer. He has a wife and two sons that we know of. I plan to find him. I know he will give me a small piece of land, and I can eventually buy it from him and start my own farm. He just speaks so highly of that place in his letters. He's not near the ocean, but he's near a river they call the Tar River. He's farming cotton and tobacco and doing very well at it."

"How many slaves does he own?" John asked, tracing a line in the dirt floor with his forefinger.

"None, I don't think. I can't imagine a man as kind as Francis owning a slave."

"From what I hear, once you get over there and start a plantation, slaves are part of the whole process." John picked up his apple core and tossed it across the room.

"I don't think his farm is that big a place as needing all that. His last letter spoke of a lot of hard work and raising his sons to help him out on the farm. That's what I would like to do." James wanted to add his feelings about going to America and being part of this new land and experiencing great adventures, maybe even a confrontation with a native or two, but he felt he couldn't vocalize such things so that John would understand his feelings. It seemed rather like the fancies of a schoolboy, and he didn't want to seem foolish to his older friend.

By midmorning, they decided to go to a pawnshop just to see if a notice had been sent out. The worst thing that could happen was they would pawn the cloak and have a little money to get through until John could steal something else. Mr. Jackson's shop had been easy enough to break into.

Not too far from the pawnshop John had found while out procuring their morning meal, the two of them spotted a woman standing on a corner. "You know, we can't just walk into the pawnshop ourselves. We want to make it seem as if we are trying *somewhat* to avoid capture," John said with a grin as they approached the lady.

"Miss," John asked, extending the cloak toward the woman, "do you know where we might sell this cloak we found? We are very hungry and need a bit of money. Do you know someone who might purchase this garment?"

She walked closer and took the cloak from him and inspected it. "Nay, I cannot sell it for you, but I know of a pawnshop that perhaps would take it. You might not get much for it, but I know someone who just might pawn it for you. Found it, you say?" she asked doubtfully. The boys nodded.

"Stay here for a bit. I will see what I can do. If I do get him to pawn the thing, I want a little something for helping you, you hear me? You can watch me. I'm only going into that shop there," she said, pointing across the narrow street and heading that way with the hooded cape in hand.

The boys watched her enter Lane's Pawnshop, and within a few minutes, a young errand boy left the shop at great speed. Soon, a constable walked briskly toward the store and entered through the doorway with the young lad who had left in such a hurry now on his heels.

John grinned at James and shook him by the shoulder, "I think we've been found out! Mr. Jackson must have sent notice 'round this very morning!"

James and John looked on as the woman came from the shop shouting and waving her arms in their direction. "There they are! Those two lads on the corner!"

The boys were accosted by the woman leading the way pointing at them, followed by the constable and a man they assumed was the pawnshop owner. Even the young errand boy came out to observe the confrontation.

The shop owner waved a paper and the cloak, saying, "Mr. Jackson just sent this advertisement within the last hour to be on the lookout for this exact cloak! Now what have you boys got to say for yourselves?"

The constable stepped in and said, "Now, Mr. Lane, I'll do the questioning here if you don't mind. Now, lads, where exactly did you say you got this cloak?"

James was amazed by the theatrics of his new friend as John immediately began a very dramatic denial.

"Sir, please, we are alone in the world, my little brother and myself! We are cold and starving. We meant no harm! We found this in the street late last night like some woman had merely dropped it off her arm by accident! We just asked this lady if she wanted to buy it or if she knew of someone who might buy it. We are very desperate here, sir!"

"We will let you share your story with a magistrate in a week or two, that's what we will do!" growled the constable.

Jail was every bit as awful as John had said it would be. It was cold, but not as cold as they had experienced in their abandoned building, and the gruel they were served daily made James long for some stolen bread or cheese or fruit. It was a noisy place, and many men were hauled in for public displays of drunkenness. Some would come in and sleep it off, while some men came in ready to swing at the first person they saw. John had to jump in several times to protect his "little brother" and himself and even went to court with a black eye and swollen cheek after one brawl just before their court date.

The constable should have said a *month* or two, for the next time James and John saw the cloak, the woman, and the pawnshop owner was in court on January 16, 1765, over two months after the theft. Their hearing took place at the Old Bailey, London's grand three-story courthouse that had been renovated in the last decade. All the prisoners whose cases were due to be heard on that date were penned into the bail dock, a porch of sorts surrounded by metal walls topped with sharp stakes to prevent anyone from trying to escape. Many of those waiting had been housed at Newgate Prison, and James found himself feeling grateful that he and John had only been held in a small, local jail.

When their case was called, they found there were two others present: one was Mr. William Jackson, the clothing shop owner, and the other was a lady who worked for him. The judge was His Honorable William Stephenson, Lord Mayor. The attorney assigned to the case asked Mr. Jackson to the stand to tell of the circumstances since he was the chief plaintiff in the matter.

"On the evening of November 1, I had a cloak stolen from my shop in the Cloisters, West Smithfield. 'Twas a red-hooded cloak valued at four shillings. The next morning, as soon as I spied it was missing from the storefront window, I sent an advertisement out to the local pawnshops to be on the watch for such an item. Mr. Lane came across it at his shop on Purple Lane and stopped it," said Mr. Jackson.

A clerk, sitting near the judge, produced the red cloak.

"That seems to be the very one," Mr. Jackson testified.

Mr. Lane was called to the stand next and verified Mr. Jackson's story. "On the second day of November, about eleven in the morning, Mary Davis brought me that very cloak, and having read the advertisement, I stopped it and sent my boy to fetch a constable."

Mr. Lane vacated the witness stand and was replaced by Miss Davis who seemed to be enjoying her day in court. She began her testimony thus, "Those two prisoners there approached me with that cloak and told me they'd found it. They wanted me to pawn it for them. I was more than a little suspicious, so I took it to Mr. Lane. He immediately stopped it as he'd just been notified to be on watch for this item."

The last person to the stand for the prosecution was Miss Elizabeth Waklin who identified herself as an employee of Mr. Jackson. "Yes," she declared. "I placed that very cloak in the window, and it had lain there for several days before it was taken."

James was very nervous to be called to the stand next in his own defense; he had so hoped that John could go first. But he found himself fidgeting in the seat and responding to the lawyer's inquiry as to his role in this theft.

"I was coming along with this young man," James said, pointing to John, "and I found the cloak on the ground and picked it up. We saw this lady"—he was now pointing to Mary Davis—"and we asked her if she could sell it for us, as we needed money, and she said she couldn't sell it but she would pawn it for us."

John was the last called to testify. "I was on an errand for my father," he explained, "and as I was coming down Holbourn, I saw that cloak lying against a post. My friend there took it up, and we went and asked that lady to pawn it for us."

At this, the constable who had been the arresting officer at last spoke up, "Your Honorable Lord Mayor, the story this young man gave me on that very day was that they were brothers and they were orphans, and now he says he was on an errand for his father?"

His Honorable Judge William Stephenson clapped his gavel and, with very little emotion, spoke the words both John and James had been waiting weeks to hear: "Guilty as charged."

CHAPTER 2

Sarah Bowman
Swan Point, Charles County, Maryland
January 1765

$\mathcal{S}$ ixteen-year-old Sarah Bowman found herself peeking through her closed eyes lowered for the family prayer before dinner that evening. First, she observed her father as he continued on in his praises and gratitude for their many blessings. He had not even begun to ask God for what they stood in need of. Her older brother Edward fidgeted a little in his seat, and his face showed impatience, and Sarah was fairly sure his thoughts were somewhere other than the family prayer. Four-year-old Priscilla had her eyes shut tight, but her chin rested on the table in front of her. Her hands were in her lap, but she was slowly and rhythmically smoothing her smock from her thighs to her knees, waiting for her father to be done. Sarah hesitated to look toward her mother, as she did not want to see her wiping away tears during the prayer again. She found it comforting that though her mother's head was low to her chest, tonight she had managed to control the weeping that they had all witnessed in the last few weeks.

The two empty chairs, the cause for all their sadness, were still without eleven-year-old Timothy and two-year-old Hannah, both of whom had succumbed to the sickness that had afflicted their entire family at the beginning of the winter season. Except for the loss of two infants before she or Edward were even born, Sarah's family had not had many encounters with death. She had not been around to watch her parents grieve the stillborn babies, but seeing their grief in the last few weeks was painful indeed.

It's been painful for us all, Sarah thought. *Dear God,* she began her own prayer inside her heart as her father at last finished his lengthy supplication, *please help us all learn to handle this emptiness, this permanence of loss. Bless my mother that she can one day soon smile again, a genuine smile, not the false one that attempts to hide the hurt in her soul.* Now Sarah's eyes were closed again in earnest, and Edward elbowed her in her side.

"The prayer is over, Sarah. Were you not listening?" he said grinning at her.

"Children, do you have any idea whose birthday it would have been today?" asked Peter Bowman, as they began eating dinner.

Edward shook his head, but Sarah answered, "I think this would have been Papa's birthday."

"You are right," said Peter. "My father, Daniel Bowman, if he were still alive, would be eighty-five today. I miss my father and my mother," said Peter. "They came over here from England sixty-five years ago, in 1700, when they were newly married." Peter reached over and took his wife's hand. "Your mother's family was already here. The Simpsons came in the mid-1600s."

Judith added, "My mother just loved living here. I think she thought it was very romantic living in a place called Swan Point."

"Isn't it true," asked Sarah, "that Captain John Smith named this place?"

"Indeed," answered her father. "Apparently, he saw thousands of the birds wintering on the shores of Cuckold Creek and named it then."

When dinner was over, Lucy, the family's servant, came in to clear the table. Sarah jumped to help her. Lucy Wade had been such a blessing to the whole family in the last few dreadful months of sickness and death, and it was amazing to them all that she had not contracted the influenza that had assuaged them all.

In her late thirties, Lucy Wade was the granddaughter of William Wade, the first of the indentured servants Sarah's grandfather, Daniel Bowman, had purchased when he started the family tobacco farm.

Purchased—Sarah's father hated that word. Peter Bowman was a kind, gentle, God-fearing man who had very strong feelings about the whole idea of humans purchasing other humans. He had been outspoken on the subject all his life, even having disagreements with his father.

When their time of servitude was completed, Daniel Bowman had told the Wade family and their offspring that they were free to go, but they had asked to stay and work on the farm at Swan Point. He gave them a piece of land, and they not only had their own gardens and small tobacco crop, but they also helped both Daniel and then Peter with their crops. They were paid for their help, and they stayed on.

One of William Wade's sons named Robert had built a nice home and was doing well with his own crop of tobacco, while the others still lived in refurbished cabins built originally for the indentured family. A couple of William's daughters had married and moved in with their husbands' families, but Lucy, the daughter of the oldest of William's sons, had never married and had always been close to the Bowman family. She had worked for them ever since Sarah could remember.

The Wades were white and from England just as the Bowmans were. Sarah's father liked to point out: "The only difference between us and them is we came from a family a little more blessed in England, and my parents had land we could sell to pay for passage here to America and money to buy land here. The Wades had to work to pay for passage. They worked on the ship and then had to be sold when they got here. They are blessed that it was my father who bought them and not some cruel taskmaster."

Daniel Bowman had bought a few other indentured servants while on trips to Baltimore from time to time through the years, and he had even once taken on two convict servants who were cheaper to buy than indentured servants. One of his friends who captained a ship talked him into it, but he sorely regretted that decision when one of the two men attempted to rape one of William Wade's daughters. Both men escaped before the guilty one could be punished, and Daniel Bowman decided he would rather pay a little more for indentured help than ever take on another convict servant. Once his father died, Peter Bowman made a vow to never buy another human; he paid men, many of whom were from the Wade family, to work on his farm.

Overall, Sarah's family had been blessed, notwithstanding the recent deaths of her younger siblings. They had escaped, for the most part, the recent war between the French and the British by living on this little peninsula on the Potomac. Her father had served with a local militia, but the only thing Peter Bowman's regiment dealt with was helping to feed and house a group of British soldiers who regrouped near Swan Point for a few weeks.

Sarah and Edward were educated as both their parents were literate and made sure the children learned to read and write. The Bible was not only a source of faith for them but also was the main primer for their schooling. Her mother had brought a few books from England, and Sarah had read most of them several times.

When Sarah wasn't helping Lucy and her mother with the housework and chores, she would slip away and write. She was passionate about recording her feelings and the day-to-day occurrences there on Swan Point. Her father often teased her that his greatest expense for her upkeep was paper and ink. She would have loved to spend more time in the midst of the lovely natural scenery of their home, but the threat of attack by Indians or wild animals kept her close to home. Sometimes, she would accompany her eighteen-year-old brother Edward when he was armed and out hunting for game or fishing, and under his protection, she got to see a little more of their beautiful peninsula and was inspired to write about it, sometimes even in the form of poetry.

The place Sarah loved to visit the most was a lovely clearing nearby on the banks of Cuckold Creek. It was about halfway between their farm and the Wade's place. Sarah and Miranda Wade, Edward's sweetheart and Sarah's dear friend, liked to meet there and talk for hours. Miranda enjoyed watching Sarah draw. It was also here that Sarah helped Miranda learn to read and write when they were younger. Miranda was grateful for Sarah's instruction because she was now able to write love letters to Edward.

By lantern light that evening, Sarah sat at the dining room table and turned in her journal, a burgundy, leather-bound volume given to her by her parents on her sixteenth birthday, to continue what she had started writing earlier in the day about the deaths of Timothy and Hannah. Sarah was driven by a desire from deep within, an almost panicked feeling or fear that her little brother and sister would be forgotten if she did not make a record of their existence. Her father had promised them all that he would see to it that the plain large rocks that currently marked their graves would be replaced by etched stones once winter was over. But even then, years from now, Sarah thought, would anyone even care that they had lived on this earth for their short little life spans?

About two-year-old Hannah, she wrote, "Her hair had grown long around her face and down her neck, and she had auburn-colored ringlets, natural curls. Her eyes were a bluish-green, and she had a small dimple in her chin. Her lashes were very long, and I am sure, had she lived, she would have had many young men seeking her attention."

Sarah paused and then began to sketch Hannah's face just below the writing. She wasn't a bad artist either, she thought. At the very front of her diary, she had done a beautiful drawing of a swan. Her mother had made quite a fuss about how lifelike it was and what a talent Sarah possessed. Above the swan picture, she had done a title of sorts in a fancy script that read, "Sarah of Swan Point."

On the page beside the one of Hannah's image, Sarah wrote of Timothy, age eleven: "His face was framed by dark curls, and he had a smattering of freckles on his cheeks. His eyes were a blue-gray. Timothy loved to pretend he was a soldier, not a British soldier, but a colonial militiaman, marching about with a stick upon his shoulder ready to aim and shoot at a Frenchman or an Indian. We have a brake of woods next to our house that became his encampment, his fort, from which he assaulted approaching imaginary enemies and in which he held in bondage all those he captured." Sarah then sketched Timmy in action, "musket" by his side, curls on top of his head. Under the picture, she wrote, "Timothy Simpson Bowman 1754–1765." Below Hannah's sweet face, she wrote, "Hannah Abigail Bowman 1763–1765."

She heard a sudden gasp and found her mother right behind her, gazing over Sarah's shoulder, clutching her throat as she choked back a sob. Sarah jumped up from the table and grabbed her mother about the waist, and together, they wept in each other's arms.

When her mother could speak, she said through tears, "Oh, my dear heart! What a precious thing you have done! Thank you, Sarah!" She stood in front of Sarah and stroked Sarah's long auburn waves with one hand and, with the other, wiped the tears from Sarah's cheeks.

"Oh, my daughter! I am sorry," Judith Bowman said in a voice broken with tears. "I have forgotten that you must be suffering even as I am. We all miss them very much! But how dear of you to memorialize them!" She sat down, wiping her own tears, to look again at the drawings. "What a gift you have, Sarah!" She also read Sarah's words and sighed, "Thanks to you, we shan't forget them."

Her mother looked shamed a moment and said, "You are probably wondering how a mother could ever forget her own child. I can't. But details, over time, these things can escape the human mind. Doing this, drawing them, and writing about them, it helps, does it?" she asked her daughter.

Sarah nodded. "And I promise you, I shall improve. I will get better and draw more and more pictures of them. Perhaps Father can make frames for them, and we can put them on the wall."

"Oh, Sarah. I have been so miserable. And I still am. I am grieving so deeply in my heart for my little ones. But this helps ease the hurt. Thank you, darling."

She pulled Sarah into her lap as she used to do when she was little, and Sarah, relishing the moment, put her head against her mother's neck. "I love you, Mother. We are going to survive this. We are still a family."

"With God's help, we can survive this, Sarah. And such a daughter He has blessed me with. I am thankful. I love you too, darling."

Sarah kissed her mother's cheek, took her book, and headed upstairs to the room she shared with little Priscilla whom she found already asleep under layers of quilts. When her eyes became acclimated to the darkness, Sarah could discern the outline of her sister's face. *Four years old but still such a sweet face of a baby*, Sarah thought. *God, I love my family*, she prayed silently. *Please bless those of us who are left that we may ever remember Thee*. And Sarah's last thoughts before she fell asleep were, *Tomorrow, I shall be sure to draw Priscilla. Bless us, O Lord, that we may be remembered as well.*

CHAPTER 3

James West
London to Baltimore
January 1765

A t the Old Bailey courthouse, sentences were being issued for the day's hearings. The throng around the outside of the building had doubled in size since the court had ended that day's session. To keep from bringing the prisoners back into the courtroom, judgments issued by His Honorable William Stephenson were read aloud outside the gate of the bail dock for all held there to hear. The rowdy crowd, both inside and outside the holding area, grew silent as the following decisions were delivered.

"Transported, for fourteen years, one: Alice Roney. Transported, for seven years, twenty-two: Mary Felton, John Foster, Joseph Davis, Richard Inez, Frederick Young, James West, John Hussey, Alexander Connell, John Wallis, Moses Lawton, John Morris, Thomas Hackley, Mary Vander, Morris Pierce, John Saverin, Catherine Clark, Catherine McFarley, Joseph McFarley, John Saintree, Nicholas Langham, Christopher MacDaniel, and Francis Farrell." The bailiff paused briefly then continued his reading of judgments.

"To be branded, one: Daniel Williams." Several in the crowd cheered raucously. "To be whipped, three: Amelia Green, John Adams, and Sarah Turner."

This news brought about more shouts from a growing audience. A branding and three whippings. The citizens of London gathered outside the Old Bailey considered this a worthwhile way to finish out the day. Not as pleasing to watch as the seven executions that had taken place Wednesday last, but four punishments to serve as entertainment would provide enough of a thrill to see the guilty have justice meted out and would perhaps serve as a deterrent to potential lawbreakers among them. The four to be corporally punished and publicly humiliated tried to hide among those in the bail dock but were found by the other guilty parties and pushed toward the gate. Two officials of the court were already heating a branding iron to be used against Daniel Williams, convicted of trying to steal someone's cow. The remaining guilty persons sentenced to be transported to America were required to watch from behind the iron posts of the bail dock as the penalties were carried out. While waiting for the branding iron to reach a hellish temperature, others were busy tying to the whipping posts the three found guilty that day of prostitution and the sale thereof.

"See how you like being lashed, you sorry whores!" one woman's voice called out.

Another shouted, "Hell's going to hurt worse and last a lot longer!" The whole group of Londoners gathered by the bail dock cheered in a frenzied manner as if watching a grand sporting event. They grew louder with each sharp emblazoning of the whip.

By the time Daniel Williams received the hissing brand of the iron on his forearm, the group had become less engaged, the mood almost anticlimactic, but a few cheered anyway. One voice chided, "Teach you to try and steal someone else's property!"

James closed his eyes in repulsion at the whole painful scene. It made him almost grateful that all he had to endure was an embarrassing parade to the docks. He could not bring himself to imagine what conditions were going to be like aboard the ship transporting them to America.

James found himself praying silently as the group of twenty-three were chained together and marched down the streets of London toward the shipyard to board the vessel that would take him to see his brother Francis in America. People lined the sides of the roads and taunted and jeered the prisoners with harsh words and hurtful phrases.

Lord, thou knowest what this kind of humiliation feels like. I don't mean to compare myself to Thee, Lord, but I am grateful to know You led the way before me. Please bless my family as they learn of my fate, and keep them safe in my absence. Forgive me, Lord, for doing these acts that led me to this place. I promise You, if You will help me to arrive unharmed in America, I will devote myself to Thee, and I will be a light to others that they may knowest of Thy goodness and mercy.

James did not even look toward John, though he knew and was thankful that the two of them were chained together in a group of six. Being part of this "parade" was actually welcome, except for the loud, rude reactions of those gathered to watch because they were finally out of the jail cell they had been crammed in since November. This January day was cold and biting, but again, welcome for its fresh air.

James and John knew only a few details of their journey. They would be on board the ship in a cargo hold for three to four months. They knew the ship's name was the *Tryal*, and they knew they were to land in Baltimore, in the colony of Maryland. James was grateful also that he still carried his satchel on his back; it had been searched and found to contain just a few pieces of clothing and a book, and he and John both were allowed to keep their remaining scant possessions.

The *Tryal* was taking some supplies to the colonies but would pick up an enormous load of tobacco and cotton once in Baltimore to bring back to England. This ship typically dealt with both cargo and slaves, though there would be none on board except themselves as convict servants and several indentured servants. They heard rumors that they, being such, were at the bottom rung of human servitude. African slaves were treated cruelly but were economically worth more in America and received only slightly better treatment, at least on board the ship. A captain wanted all the money due him for the delivery of slaves and would go to greater lengths to preserve African human cargo. Indentured servants were lower in value and were treated a little less favorably, while convict servants brought very little money at all and were barely fed and kept alive by a captain and his crew.

James said farewell to the fresh air they had enjoyed on the walk to the docks, for as soon as they neared the *Tryal*, there was a stench that stifled their breathing. It seemed to be a combination of human sweat and waste combined with rotting sea life and the wet wood of the ship. He could already hear the swearing and oaths of the crewmembers making this voyage. On board, there were lists to check and papers to be signed.

James and John looked at each other for the first time when the group was taken below to the hold area where they would be kept: a dark space that was only about four and a half feet in height, making it impossible for even someone as short as James to be able to stand. Here, the stench was at its worst. For a few moments, they could see their temporary home as the door from above was still ajar, and a little light filtered in. Once closed, the area grew as black as night. The few women were to be kept in a separate location, and they were all informed that in groups of six they would make an occasional visit on deck to empty their used pots and to walk about a little.

They at last departed in the early morning hours, and several of the men in the area where they were being held grew horribly seasick. The group had not eaten since they had had a little gruel early before going to the Old Bailey the day before, and at last, about six hours into the journey, they were brought stale bread.

John's voice sounded near James's ear. "How are you faring, little brother?"

"I'm all right," James replied. "I'm not letting myself think of the fact that even if I were unchained, I could not stand upright. The thought almost makes me a bit daft." He tried to laugh a little, but even to James's own ears, it sounded a bit misplaced here in this malodorous blackness. Someone nearby heaved once more and lost the little bread he'd eaten.

On the third day of the voyage, it was James and John's turn on deck. They, with the four other men to whom they were chained, were almost blinded by the glaring sunshine that greeted them above. John and James held the pots to be emptied and quickly were led to the side of the ship to carry out the awful task. The six were kept together and required to walk around the deck several times. At first, it was not easy as James felt the sharp needles of returning circulation in his feet, and he almost tripped. The two men who were leading them by the longer chains that bound all six together held whips and did not hesitate to crack them if they moved too slowly. On their third circuit around the deck, suddenly, someone called out, "West! James West!" John nudged James as if he had possibly not heard. James lifted both of his chained hands.

"Here, sir," James responded.

"Captain would have a word with you," growled the sailor. And with that, a key was produced that freed James from the group of convicts.

James glanced back at John as he was led away. It was the first time the two had been parted since they had met, and James wasn't certain he liked being taken away from John. Sensing that James needed his approval, John nodded as if his consent meant something.

James was led into the captain's chamber and was surprised to see the man lying in his bed under the covers in a nightshirt. James thought that this man in no way resembled the captain of a ship but seemed more like someone's sick, elderly grandfather.

"Here's West, sir," the sailor said, and he was curtly dismissed with a movement of the captain's hand.

"You have your possessions with you, lad?" the captain asked. He turned to lie on his side and propped himself up on his elbow. James nodded and brought his bag around to the front.

"Here, sir," James said, holding up his satchel for the captain to see.

"Empty the contents here on my bed," the captain said, patting the space in front of him. James did as asked, and two shirts and a pair of socks and pants fell onto the mattress along with his volume of *Robinson Crusoe*.

"It's true then, the rumors I'd heard. You have a book on board, and it appears to be one of my favorite tales from my boyhood days," the captain said, picking up the book and looking at the binding. "You read, lad?"

"Yes, sir," James replied.

"Boy, do you have any idea how long almost four months is upon the ocean? Especially when one is down in one's back? You will be required to sleep with the others at night, but I expect you to be here every morning to read your book aloud to me. Is that understood? And you are not to say a word to the others with you that I am incapacitated. Is *that* understood? My crew is aware, but I do not care to share my plight with a group of convicts. In exchange for keeping me entertained, you will receive extra rations—better rations."

"Aye, captain. Thank you, sir," James said with an appreciative smile. *Thank You, Lord*, he prayed in his heart. "When shall I begin?" James asked.

"You may start tomorrow," the captain answered him. "I'll send for you in the morning."

James knew that disappointment must have shown in his face. He had truly hoped to start that very minute. James also had several questions for the captain but was not brave enough to ask. The first one was, what *was* he supposed to tell John and the others? Another question was, could the captain not read on his own? Couldn't he have simply asked to borrow his book? And, what *was* the captain's name?

James was led back to the dreadful cargo hold where they were kept. He had decided not to say anything to anyone, including John, about his new assignment, for what if the captain forgot about it or changed his mind? When John asked him in a whisper what the meeting with the captain was all about, James didn't want to lie, so he told his friend, "He searched my bag." The truth. Well, perhaps a half-truth.

Another question came to James over the course of the day and into the night. How did the captain even know about the book? No one had checked his bag since they had arrived on the ship. He and John had not spoken of it at all. The only other time he'd had to empty his satchel was in jail. All he could imagine was that the records from jail, including a list of their belongings, must have followed them to the ship. James finally slept after praying that the captain would not forget to send for him the next morning.

The sun was just lightening the gray sky when James was called for the next day. Someone stood at the door of the cramped hold with a musket, as another made his way in with a key to free the lad. James was taken a bit roughly up to the captain's doorway and almost shoved inside by the man who was armed.

The captain was still in bed but propped up on several pillows.

"Morning, lad. Breakfast should be here anon."

"Good morning, Captain—" James's voice trailed as he had no idea the captain's surname.

"I am Captain Duggar," the older man said. James stood next to the bed looking around a little aimlessly, not certain of where or if he should sit. Captain Duggar pointed to a low stool and motioned for James to move it closer and to have a seat there. The door to his quarters opened, and a member of his crew stood there with a tray. He brought it in and placed it on the bedside table. James's mouth watered at the smells that filled the room. There were two plates, and each contained a small bowl of pease porridge, a rather large slice of ham, and a thick piece of dark bread. James could tell by the scowl directed at him as he was given his plate that this crewmember was not pleased to be serving a convict a captain's breakfast.

James took the fact that the captain was consuming his meal as a cue to start his own. James tried not to gobble his food as quickly as he desired so as to savor it and make it last, but it was difficult to do. He thought of John and felt a pang of guilt, so when the captain turned to the tray to retrieve his cup of tea, James took that opportunity to place a third of his bread and a piece of ham into his satchel by his stool on the floor. He hoped the captain would not ask to see the contents of his bag again but knew it was worth the risk if he could share his bounty with his friend.

"Come pour your own tea," the captain ordered. James could imagine that in his younger years, this captain was an intimidating figure on deck. He clearly still commanded respect as the crew obeyed him when asked to feed a young street urchin in his own cabin.

As they finished their tea, Captain Duggar began to speak, "Boy, this is very likely to be my last voyage. I don't think I can tolerate many more days upon the sea. It's my back, of course. If my back were still working properly, there is no doubt I could continue for many years as captain of a ship. I still have the mental acuity to manage such a task." He paused and simply glared at James as if he expected him to say or do something. Finally, he spoke again, "Tell me about yourself, son."

James thought for a moment and said, "I am James West. I'm from a small Welsh village called Manorowen. My brother Francis left for the colonies years ago, and I want to go join him there."

The captain smiled just a little. "You're not really a thief, are you, boy? I know you are the youngest convict I've ever had on board."

"I am nearly seventeen. I will turn seventeen on board this ship. I helped to steal a cloak from a clothing store, but it was the first thing I have ever taken as such. I really am not a thief."

"Where did you get your education?" the captain asked.

"From a village school established by our priest a few years ago. Several of us in my village have taken advantage of his willingness to teach us. All my brothers and sisters have done so. I come from a fairly large farm, and my parents read and write as well."

"Your parents gave you their blessing on your adventure, I take it?"

James shifted uncomfortably on the small stool. "Not exactly, Captain."

"I see."

"They knew I dreamed of going to America, but I just left suddenly one day, so I am sure they were surprised by my disappearance."

"And grieved as well, I am sure. Before you leave this ship, I expect you to write them a letter, and I will make sure it gets to them."

"Yes, sir, and thank you, sir."

"Now," began Captain Duggar, "I want to revisit my boyhood and have you read this wonderful tale of *Robinson Crusoe*."

"Begging your pardon, sir, but do you not know how to read?" James asked rather timidly.

The captain chuckled a bit and admitted, "My back is not the only problem I have, lad. My vision is not like it used to be. I can barely see to read and sign papers and such. But I used to pass many an hour on a long voyage reading books and newspapers. I will, when we dock, have a member of my crew buy a copy of the *Maryland Gazette*. Of course, I won't have you to read it for me, but on deck, with more light, perhaps I can make out the main stories. Anyhow, commence with the tale of *Robinson Crusoe*, Master West."

James began to read, nervously at first, then began to get into the story, but he had to admit, there was not enough light in the cabin to easily make out the words. He read several pages and came to a rather tedious account in the novel, and as he read, he suddenly heard soft snoring coming from the bed. *I have read the captain to sleep!* he thought. James stopped mid-sentence and wondered, *What am I to do?* He was not free to slip out of the cabin and roam about and look for his way back to the hold where the others were. So he decided to read silently past the rather boring passage and find where the dialogue began again. He marked the page by folding down the corner and waited to see if Captain Duggar would wake and remember where he'd left off.

James was startled by a loud snort and reopened the book when the captain asked, "Boy! Why have you stopped reading? Pray continue."

James started at the part of the new dialogue, and the captain seemed content to hear the familiar story continued. When James reached a certain point in the book, Captain Duggar stopped him.

"I had such a thing happen to me once, lad. It was a maiden voyage of a ship called the *Trinity*. We endured such a storm on that voyage! I don't think in my history of sailing I have ever encountered such gales!" He stopped, remembering for a moment, and then continued telling his own story. James became so enrapt with Captain Duggar's real-life tale that he completely forgot about Defoe's book open on his lap.

It was probably close to noon when the reading session was brought suddenly to a halt by the captain. "More tomorrow, young man. And I will see if my crew can arrange a comfortable place for us to sit out on the deck. I know the light in here is not sufficient for reading. If you keep that up, you will lose *your* eyesight as well. We can't have that."

With that, James knew he had been dismissed for the day. He waited while a crewman responded to the ringing of the captain's bell and followed him back down to the stinking dungeon of the ship.

As he was chained up again next to John, his friend immediately sniffed the air.

"Is that ham I'm smelling, little brother?"

When James opened the satchel and gave John the piece of bread and ham, John snatched it and ate before asking where it had come from. One of the men chained with the boys suddenly became very upset and contentious.

"You're feeding ham to your brother? Where have you been, West? Where's our extra rations?"

The man turned and raised his chained hands to strike James, and John head-butted the irate prisoner. "You leave my brother alone!"

They began to scuffle as much as their bonds allowed. James joined John in the fray, and they all three wound up with bloody lips and noses. No one was coming to stop them, so they finally stopped on their own.

Another man from across the cramped, dark room called out, "Where have you been, Baby Face West? Whatcha been doin' for them extra rations?"

James felt compelled to speak up, so he said, "I've been asked to do chores on deck. I'm just helping out a little."

"Why you?" one convict asked curiously and angrily. "You had better be about getting us all extra rations, or we're going to make your time down here hellish."

James leaned back against his bag and wiped a trail of blood from his nose along his sleeve. John drew close to his left ear. "Next time, just get the extra bread. Forget the ham."

CHAPTER 4

Sarah Bowman
Swan Point, Maryland
March 1765

Peter Bowman took his wife's hand in his as he broached the subject he knew she dreaded discussing. He patted the top of her hand clasped in his lovingly and reassuringly as they strolled up the path to their home.

"Now, Judith, we need to start making plans for Sarah's future. She is a lovely girl. I know we do not have the advantage of London society nor a proper way to debut our daughter to available gentlemen, but we must make plans for her nonetheless."

"Peter," his wife began, "as you say, we are not in London. But I want you to remember how you and I met. We grew up here in Swan Point. My family was from a neighboring farm just like the one your father established here. We were not forced to marry. Ours was not an arranged union, and I don't think we should plan to do that for Sarah."

He kept his wife's hand in his as he led her up the four steps to the large covered porch of their home. The two ended their walk around the bay by sitting on the cedar bench he had crafted some years ago. He placed his arm about the shoulders of his dear companion.

"We may not have been forced to marry, Judith, but we certainly were introduced by our parents and given many opportunities to become acquainted," he said with a smile.

"There are not many more families here now than there were then, especially since some have chosen not to return when they went to the forts up north during the war," she said.

"Well, let us look at the possibilities. There is the Moran family two miles south of us. They have one son who is about Sarah's age. They are very devout Catholics, however. From our parish, we have the Matthews further north, about three miles away. I know Jacob Matthews. He is a fine man, and he has two sons just a few years older than Sarah. Their farm is only slightly larger than ours, and they only employ indentured servants as my father used to do, though I have heard he is thinking of expanding and buying slaves."

"What about one of Miranda's brothers?" asked his wife. "Edward is marrying Miranda, although you are not in favor of that so much."

Miranda was the daughter of Robert Wade, the son of William Wade, the servant Peter's father had bought years ago. Robert was the son who had made quite a success of his farm on the land given to the family when their servitude had come to an end. Miranda was a kind, lovely girl; she and Edward had known each other all their lives.

"Do not misunderstand my motives, my dear. I am thankful that my son has found a woman for whom he cares deeply. I am not so bothered by the issue of class differences, if you will. There is nothing wrong with being from a hardworking, God-fearing family. I just want more for Sarah," he insisted. "She is so bright. I would love for her to be with people whose children have had a classical education, people who value learning. I don't think Edward's Miranda has ever been taught to read or write. She will be a fine farmer's wife, however."

"I just don't know how much Sarah will allow us to tread upon such an intimate part of her life," Judith told her husband. "She is very tenderhearted. She has very deep emotions on such topics as relationships, and I doubt she would want us to interfere in something as important as choosing a mate."

"She is just sixteen. We have a little more time to think on it." Her husband was finished speaking on the subject for now, though in his mind, he was planning a visit to Jacob Matthews' farm.

At breakfast the very next morning, Peter Bowman took his seat at the table after returning from overseeing the early chores. He included in his prayer that morning a little sermonette thanking the Lord for his lovely wife and stressing in his prayer how important it was that Adam was given Eve as a helpmeet, and how thankful he was, and how grand life was because he had found his own lovely helpmeet. When he was done, Sarah saw Edward as he looked down at his hands in his lap, and then he turned his head toward his sister and gave an impatient rolling of his eyes. She could not help smiling at her brother.

Her father began, "Mother, I have decided to go pay a visit to Jacob Matthews' farm. We have not been visiting as of late, and I think it would do you good to go on a carriage ride. We are having some warm early spring weather here in March, and I would love to have you accompany me to see them. They were kind enough to visit us and bring food right after—the children passed."

Sarah wondered how long it would be before a reference could be made to the loss of Hannah and Timothy, and it did not feel as if someone had thrust a knife into their chests. All eyes focused on Judith, surveying her reaction to the mention of her little precious ones.

"I think I am in great need of fresh air, and a ride in the carriage would be wonderful." She smiled an almost genuine smile in Sarah's direction. "And, Sarah, let us plan to make an apple pie or two to take to them."

Her father said, "Tomorrow then? Edward, could you please plan to oversee things here in my place? Your mother, Sarah, Priscilla, and I plan to be gone most of tomorrow."

Sarah knew she had no voice in the decision to go visit the Matthews family. She enjoyed spending the afternoon in the kitchen with Lucy and her mother as they baked three delicious apple pies. They enjoyed one pie after dinner that evening while the other two were wrapped in cloths to take to the Matthews.

The Bowmans left home a couple of hours after sunrise, and though there was still a bit of winter chill in the air, the sun shone warmly upon them as they made their way northward. Priscilla had brought along her rag doll, and Sarah wished she had thought to bring something to pass the time. She chose instead to daydream and allow herself to be mesmerized by the scenery.

Ever since the war and even before so, travel always produced some nervousness. One never knew when a raiding party of Indians might spring from the woods that lined their path. Sarah could see her father's rifle lying within reach just behind where he and Judith sat at the front of the wagon. But Sarah knew some folks had been attacked because the natives wanted to take their weapons, wagons, and possessions, so the open visibility of her father's gun was both comforting and disconcerting.

Sarah became a little anxious from her thoughts and decided instead to concentrate on the view. She and her sister were in the back of the open wagon, and Sarah leaned back so that she could look up into the sky that was laced with a few white clouds. She often had thoughts about the enormity of the world and was amazed to consider just how big it all really was and felt gratitude to God that He had created such beautiful things to enjoy. She closed her eyes and said a silent prayer of thanks.

At last, the Matthews' farm appeared in the distance. They reached the fields first on either side of the path and saw groups of workers beginning to break up the land for future planting. Some were pulling up old plants and stalks still hanging onto the land where tobacco had been harvested months before. Sarah noticed, as she was certain her mother and father did, that among the field hands were about ten or twelve African slaves, mostly men and boys, but one or two women. The workers did not stop their labor, but they did glance at the Bowmans as they drove by.

Not long after they passed the field-workers, they could see a rider galloping toward them on the back of a beautiful solid black horse. He brought his mount to a stop as he approached the Bowmans in their wagon. Mr. Bowman slowed his horses and greeted young Garrett Matthews. He was Edward's age, and they knew each other from Trinity Church.

"Mr. Bowman!" he called out.

"Master Garrett! Is your father home?"

"Yes, he is somewhere about the property. I'll find him and let him know he has visitors," the young blonde man told Sarah's father. He gave a nod and smile in Sarah's direction, and she found herself blushing. He continued, "Abigail's on the porch, and mother is in the house, I'm sure."

"Thank you. We would appreciate it if you'd ride on and announce us."

He rode swiftly back in the direction of the house, while they continued at a slower pace in the wagon. When they finally pulled up into the front yard, Sarah could see her friend Abigail seated on the large veranda with something in her lap. As they climbed down from the wagon, Mrs. Matthews came through the front door, and she and Sarah's mother greeted each other warmly. Sarah remembered the pies and retrieved them from the wagon from under a folded quilt. Mrs. Matthews leaned over and kissed Sarah's cheek and thanked her for the pies. While the two ladies went into the house followed by Peter Bowman, Sarah and Priscilla joined Abigail on the front porch.

"Oh, that's lovely needlework," Sarah said, praising the fine lettering on the off-white linen cloth pulled taut in a wooden hoop. "What's it say?" she asked Abigail.

"It's a wedding gift for my brother Andrew. He and Martha Burkett are marrying next month. It says, 'As for me and my house, we will serve the Lord.' Father has ordered a frame for it. I'm almost finished. I just have to do 'serve the Lord,'" Abigail said smiling at Sarah.

"From the book of Joshua," Sarah noted. "That certainly is a perfect gift for a married couple to display in their new home."

The girls engaged in conversation concerning the different works of embroidery they had both done, and then Abigail shared with Sarah the details of the upcoming wedding. Sarah lost focus on Abigail's last few words as her brother Garrett rode into the yard on his horse again. He did a few maneuvers to show off his horseman skills, and Abigail smiled and pulled Sarah by her arm so she could whisper, "I think he is trying to impress you, Sarah!"

Garrett dismounted, tied the reins to the railing of the veranda, and joined the girls, sitting on a chair facing the bench they shared. He had heard the last of his sister's details about Andrew's wedding, and he added a few details of his own. As the conversation waned, Garrett asked Sarah how she felt about the impending Stamp Act. Sarah had heard her father discussing that and other taxes levied against the colonies and felt as strongly as he did that it had to end.

"I worry that the weight of all the taxes together could hurt our family farms," Sarah told both Garrett and Abigail.

They nodded and Abigail spoke up, "I worry more about having another war. We were *with* the mother country in war just a few years ago, but I feel things could turn suddenly, and we might be fighting them in order to be free of so many taxes!" Abigail exclaimed.

"I'm afraid you could be right, sister," Garrett said. "I would be willing to fight. I am hearing more and more men say we can no longer withstand the pressure of being told what to do by England, especially when they do not allow men from the colonies to go represent our interests."

"Talking of war with two beautiful young ladies present?" The three of them turned suddenly to see Andrew standing in the doorway of the large veranda. He came out onto the porch and sat in the last chair available next to his brother Garrett.

"It's not very appropriate to discuss war and taxes with women, Garrett," Andrew said.

"I just heard you and Martha discussing the very topic the other day!" said Garrett in his own defense. He hated it when his older brother made him feel humiliated.

"Martha is to be my wife very shortly. We can speak of such things. At your ages, you should be conversing about books, the weather, or—" Andrew's voice trailed off.

"The wedding," said Abigail with a smile. "We were just talking about the wedding too, Andrew. We are very excited about it." She turned her comments to Sarah. "Mother has had a very lovely pale pink gown made for me to wear. Would you care to see it?" With that, Abigail gathered her needlework and led Sarah into the house. Priscilla, doll in hand, followed the girls inside.

While admiring Abigail's lovely dress, the girls could hear through the open window that their fathers had joined Garrett and Andrew on the front porch, as their voices were raised with emotion.

Jacob Matthews was speaking of his current situation with buying a group of slaves from an auction in Baltimore recently. Sarah's father had not yet jumped in with his disapproval but was letting his friend speak before saying anything.

"I've had to hire an overseer," said Mr. Matthews. "Not so much because of the recent acquisition, but I think I've created issues by having indentured servants and adding four convict servants, and now I've got these fourteen new slaves. They just don't get along, and I am not a hard man. I've never had to use much force with my servants before, but this is my livelihood, and I've got to make it work. There are fights among the indentured servants who do not trust the convicts, and then there is great hatred for the new slaves I've purchased. There are language barriers, and it gets very contentious at times. So I hired a man out of Annapolis to run things. He's making great progress, but he's had to resort to staying armed and carrying a cudgel. I am thinking of getting rid of the white servants and buying more slaves."

Sarah was not on the porch but could just imagine her father's expression. She heard him begin, "I must say, Jacob, I don't understand how you do it. I cannot understand how a man buys other men. I believe God is the Father of us all. I do not think human beings should ever be thought of as property."

"Now see here, Peter, your own father bought servants."

"And I argued frequently with him on the subject."

"Peter," Jacob Matthews interjected, "there have always been men enslaved by other men at various times in history. It is just the way things are. Now here in the colonies, if you want to be successful in the area of farming, you must have slaves to do the work!"

"That is a mighty high price to pay for success, I must say," said Sarah's father. "I believe I would rather hire people as I do and be able to sleep at night with a clear conscience than having literal blood on my hands for mistreating fellow human beings in order to have a successful crop of tobacco or cotton."

Abigail's father ended the conversation by saying, "You are a strange and unusual man, Peter Bowman." Abigail seemed not to hear the conversation and made no comments, but there was an awkwardness that settled between the girls after that.

The two families shared a meal early that afternoon, but conversation was a little uneasy after the one on the subject of slavery. Only the two mothers seemed to be unaffected and continued to speak warmly to each other. Sarah was glad her mother had had this opportunity to spend the day with someone as loving and kind as Mrs. Matthews. At last, Sarah and her family said their farewells and left the Matthews' farm later that afternoon.

As the sun began to go down, Sarah huddled with Priscilla under the quilt in the back of the wagon as the air grew brisk. Sarah had a great deal of time to think over her father's words and his beliefs. She felt in her heart that her father was right. Slaves were human beings as well. From what she knew, these people were taken by force from their homes in Africa, brought to America to work under the whip, and were even separated from their families. Sarah tried to imagine how painful it would be to be taken from her family. The deaths of Timothy and Hannah were very recent reminders of how painful loss could be.

Later that night, after Sarah and Priscilla were sleeping, Judith and Peter held each other in their own bed, and Peter told his wife, "I would not want my Sarah to be part of such a family."

Surprised, Judith said, "I think the Matthews are a very loving family. Jacob and Mary love their children and just want what's best for them, just as we do, Peter. I believe they are kind, God-fearing people just as we are."

"Judith, I know I'm kind of a strange being to live here in the colonies and not to believe in slaveholding. Maybe I just think things too deeply. You know it hurts my heart when I have to hunt animals for skin or for food, but I think God just made me that way. I am always thinking, 'What are they feeling? What does it feel like to have your life snuffed out? What does it feel like to have your freedom taken away? How would I feel if I were taken captive? Or you, or one of the children?' I'm sorry, Judith, but I can assure you that you will never be the lady of a large cotton or tobacco plantation. I am content with what God has blessed me with, and I pray you are as well."

In response, Judith kissed her sweet husband on the cheek and wished him a good night and said a silent prayer of gratitude for her blessings.

CHAPTER 5

James West
En route to Baltimore via the Tryal
Early May 1765

For many days, James read to Captain Duggar on deck in the fresh open air. All the crew now knew that James was entertaining the captain by reading *Robinson Crusoe* to him, and that led to the young man being taunted, not only by those working on the ship, but also by those with whom James slept incarcerated at night. He only slipped John bread now, and James noticed that even his friend seemed to resent his partial freedom. One of the prisoners grew sick and eventually died, and all the prisoners were taken on deck for the burial at sea. The captain had dressed, and he conducted the service, brief though it was.

When James at last finished *Robinson Crusoe*, the captain had his eyes closed. This was one of the days he did not feel like leaving his cabin and was under the covers. James closed the book and looked quietly at the captain.

Captain Duggar was not asleep, however, and he opened his eyes and said, "Thank you, lad, for reading to me. It has been a joy to hear the story again one last time. James, would you do me a great favor, young man?" It was the first time he'd called James by his given name and not Master West.

"Yes, Captain. What can I do for you?"

"Come over to my table here next to my bed, and open the bottom drawer."

James did as he was asked. Inside the drawer was a Bible. James took it out and placed it on the bed next to the captain.

"I would like it if you would read me your favorite parts of the Bible. I know you have told me that your father read to you from it often. You must have favorite stories from its pages."

"I do, sir."

James noticed the Bible looked old but not worn. He flipped the pages and first went to the story of Elisha, the prophet in 2 Kings, chapter 6. He read of the battle facing Israel. Then he read verses 15 through 17, "And when the servant of the man of God was risen early, and gone forth, behold, an host compassed the city both with horses and chariots. And his servant said unto him, Alas my master! How shall we do? And he answered, Fear not: for they that be with us are more than they that be with them. And Elisha prayed and said, Lord, I pray thee, open his eyes, that he may see. And the Lord opened the eyes of the young man; and he saw: and, behold, the mountain was full of horses and chariots of fire round about Elisha."

"So, lad, do you think we have angels warring for us whom we cannot see?" asked Captain Duggar.

"Aye, sir, I do."

"You are a grand reader, my boy. Do you know where to find the story of Jesus healing the lame man?"

James turned to the New Testament and found an account in the gospel of Luke in chapter 7 in which the followers of John the Baptist witnessed Jesus healing many. The captain listened patiently and then said, "I want the story of the man who had to be lowered on his bed through the roof of the building in which the Lord was teaching. I think it is elsewhere in Luke."

James perused the pages silently looking for the story and found it just two chapters ahead, in chapter 5 of Luke. He read it out loud, and the old man smiled.

"I remember hearing my grandmother read that story to all her grandchildren when I was just a boy. My father died when I was only two, so I do not remember him. But we moved in with his widowed mother. She was very educated and proper, but she loved to read the Bible to her grandchildren. I remember when she shared that story, I could visualize in my mind those men lowering his bed through the roof and marveled that Jesus healed him from the palsy. He took up his bed and walked out of that place! Can you just imagine the astonishment?" The old captain almost chuckled in wonder.

It was at that moment Captain Duggar's head of crew came into the chamber without so much as a knock.

"Captain! We have an urgent matter! One of the women on board, Alice Roney—the other women have sent word that she is in labor! She is in great pain!"

James could tell from the reactions of the two men that no one even knew the woman was with child. James had heard no rumors of it at all.

"Send word that the women will have to assist her in giving birth. We can do nothing," he said, sinking back onto his pillow. "Keep me updated." To James, he said, "Turn to Psalms, Master West. Read to me from the Psalms."

James turned to the twenty-third Psalm and began to read, "'Yea, though I walk through the valley of shadow and death, I will fear no evil. Thy rod and thy staff, they comfort me.'"

The women, there were six in all, were in a small cabin near the captain's, and even with the door to the captain's chamber closed, James and the old man could hear the shrieks. He bade James to continue his reading. About half an hour later, the same crewman returned to inform Captain Duggar of the birth.

"The babe is stillborn, sir. It was not yet her time. The mother is not doing well."

Captain Duggar motioned for James to close the Bible. "Have them ask the poor woman what she would have us do."

James was hoping he would not be dismissed to go below until he had found out what they were to do with the babe.

When the man returned a few moments later, he told Captain Duggar that the women had wrapped the baby's tiny body in a blanket and that Alice was holding onto it weeping. She had asked that she, and she alone, be allowed to bury her baby at sea the next morning when she had the strength to rise and walk.

Captain Duggar nodded his approval. "Kindly let me know when she is ready to do that on the morrow."

James went below, and the crewman was so distraught by all that had happened that he merely escorted James to the hold door and did not bother to manacle him with the others. James slipped the extra bit of bread from that morning's breakfast to John. He tried whispering to him about what happened, but of course, all heard. James had to repeat the story so all the men could hear, and even though there was some chatter, most were silent.

James stayed unshackled and slept a little more comfortably, but he was also disturbed by the thoughts of the poor woman's dead baby and the knowledge that she would have to toss the small body over into the ocean in the morning.

Before daybreak, James slipped out of the cargo hold while the others were still sleeping. He curled up in a space of the deck between the captain's cabin and the one where the women were kept. He kept watch until in the gray of dawn, he saw Captain Duggar emerge fully dressed, and at the same time, poor Alice Roney came from her cabin wearing a long, dingy white shift. She was still holding the infant who looked like a tiny doll swathed in a blanket. She was accompanied by another woman, who was holding her up to keep her from falling. At first, Alice walked silently to the ship's side with the other lady walking next to her grasping her by the elbow to steady her. The sea was very calm and glassy. Alice pulled away from her friend and spoke to her and the captain, crying out, "Stay back!" James watched as this other woman and the captain each took three steps backward. Alice Roney's pale figure moved to the edge of the ship's railing, and using what was probably the last strength she had left in her body, she leapt mightily and flung both herself and her stillborn baby into the ocean.

James watched as both the captain and the other woman ran to the railing gasping in horror, looking at the bodies submerging knowing there was nothing they could do.

"Let me call for help!" The captain turned to leave. "We have got to try and save her!"

The woman grabbed his arm. "Save her for what? For her fourteen years of servitude in the colonies? For a lifetime of memories of the son she lost?" The woman looked at the captain directly in his face and said, "If it weren't for my husband in the prisoner hold below, I would cast myself in after her!"

James appeared from his place of hiding and helped the captain to his cabin. James was worried about him as he saw him struggling for breath, and he had to help the man to his bed.

"James, my boy. It never entered my thoughts that she would do such a thing! Did you see?" He was still breathing very hard.

"Aye, captain. I saw. It is not your fault, sir! You mustn't blame yourself."

"Lord, forgive me," the old man cried. There were tears on his cheeks.

James tried to console him, but the man continued, "No, son. I have much to be forgiven for. I have lived a life not always in keeping with God's ways. I have hurt many people in my life. I have lived with a lack of concern for others. I have done unspeakable things!"

James sat and held the old man's hand.

"You have humbled yourself, Captain. You have asked to be forgiven. It is all any of us can do. The rest has been done for us."

"Is it really that simple, boy?" The old sea captain was still weeping.

"I don't think there is anything simple about being a mortal, sir. But I am amazed at what the Lord can do for us in His mercy. Even when we don't deserve it. But it's true. All He asks is that we have a broken heart and a contrite spirit. I think you've had that change in your heart, sir."

Word spread quickly throughout the ship of the demise of Alice Roney and her baby. Captain Duggar, who had no idea he had a husband and wife aboard his ship, made special arrangements for the McFarleys—Catharine and Joseph McFarley—to have a private meeting. He felt that only a husband could console his wife at a time such as this. And as despondent as the woman was, he did not want to be responsible for two suicides on his watch.

A day or two from Baltimore, Captain Duggar called James to his cabin. This time, he was up and dressed. As the two breakfasted together, the captain said, "I have not forgotten. I have paper over there on my desk. You are to write home and leave me your father's name and how he can be found. I will see to it he gets it."

So when their morning meal was over, James went over to the desk, picked up the quill pen and paper, and began to write: "My dear parents, I pray you will forgive me for causing you great concern. I am on board a ship to Baltimore in the colony of Maryland. I am almost in America, and I plan to find Francis. I pray for you and ask that you pray for me as well. I will love you for the rest of my life and hope to see you someday in the great hereafter. Your loving son, James." He folded the paper and wrote both his parents' names on the outside of the paper along with the words: "The village of Manorowen, Wales."

He turned to thank the captain and stood to pick up his satchel and felt a heaviness that had more than doubled the weight of the bag. He opened his mouth in question and disbelief, and Captain Duggar smiled.

"I guess there was no way for me to conceal my gift so that you would not know it was in there."

James opened his bag and found the Bible tucked in with his few other things.

"I don't know what to say, sir."

"It's going to be a burden to carry around, I know. But I hope it will lighten your load to have it with you. It will strengthen your shoulders, young man, and I know that it will strengthen your heart and mind. Thank you for all you have done for this old sea captain. I am forever in your debt."

James reached out his hand to shake the one offered to him, but as he did, the captain pulled him to his chest in an embrace. Then he released him but spoke to him with his hands upon both of James's shoulders.

"Lad, I wish I could do more to see to it that you have an ideal situation when we go ashore. But understand, I have no control over your fate. I have a feeling, though, that you, like Elisha, are surrounded by angels to aid and assist you in your noble desire to find your brother."

Later, James read the note written on the inside cover of the Bible. "To Master West. Never forget your voyage to Baltimore for I know I shan't. I pray you will remember me when you read this. I also pray that it may bring you comfort, as you have brought me comfort. Fondly, Captain Trenton Duggar."

When the *Tryal* arrived in the harbor of Baltimore, the crew and all the passengers on board were still very somber following the tragedy of Alice Roney and her baby. James and John stayed together in their group of six, but not for long. They were all separated and sold in various auctions, but by some miracle, James and John were sold together and purchased by a man from a plantation in Lower Cedar Point in Charles County, Maryland.

As they were once again shackled together, James smiled at John. "We are headed south. I am almost there." He then prayed silently, *Thank You, Lord, for Your many blessings. Please continue to bless me as I seek Francis. And, Lord, please watch over Captain Duggar.*

CHAPTER 6

Sarah Bowman
Swan Point, Maryland
May 1765

$\mathcal{S}$ arah's father kept his promise and paid someone to carve Timothy's and Hannah's names and dates into granite tombstones to mark their graves. This brought some comfort to the whole family, and Sarah loved to sit by them and read and write. On this beautiful spring morning in early May, Sarah was tending to the flowers she and her mother had planted a few weeks before. She had watered and weeded the little cemetery, knowing that the two rocks in this small patch of land by their house marked the graves of the stillborn babies her parents had lost in the first few years of their marriage.

Death is such a devastating reality of life, Sarah thought. *Father, why is this kind of pain necessary? Why must innocent children die? Our entire family got sick. Why am I still alive, yet Hannah and Timmy are gone? How will we ever get over losing them?*

As she cried and pondered the loss of her sister and brother, Sarah suddenly felt words come into her heart as an answer to her questioning. *Oh, my daughter, Timothy and Hannah are more alive now than they ever were on earth.* This response, which Sarah knew came from outside her own being, startled her, and she gasped, suddenly stopping her tears. *And you will know them again someday.*

In gratitude, fresh tears came as she whispered audibly, "Thank You, Father!"

As she brushed away tears and stood to leave, she was taken again by surprise when she saw someone galloping onto their property on a black horse, and Sarah knew it was Garrett Matthews. She watched as he dismounted and tethered his horse to a tree. Seeing her, he walked over and greeted her.

"Good morning, Sarah!" he called out, smiling cheerfully.

"Garrett, good morning to you as well. Is everything all right at your home?"

"Yes, Sarah. I came to speak with your father. Is he here?"

"Yes, I'm sure he's in the fields," she answered.

"Well, I know I should ask him first, but I've come to ask if he will let you accompany me to a luncheon on the grounds at the parish. It is following a concert in the church by Mr. Dexter's wife. Our whole family will be there. Have you heard about it?"

Sarah felt her face flush, and she stammered, "I—I would love to go, Garrett. But of course, Father will have to give his approval."

Trinity Parish, which both families attended, was about halfway between their homes. The church had only recently acquired an organ, and Mrs. Dexter played it beautifully. Sarah knew there would be a social gathering in conjunction with it and that she and her mother would surely cook and bake for the luncheon.

Garrett leaned against a tree with his arms folded, staring down into Sarah's green eyes and asked, "How is your family doing?" He motioned toward the small cemetery, and Sarah understood the polite question.

"We are coping. Some moments are more painful than others. My parents are very sure in their faith, and they rely on God and trust in Him, but some days, that is not enough to take away the pain of the loss. I do not know what people do who do not have faith in God. Death is painful enough when you do trust in Him," Sarah finished.

This was the first time Sarah had had a conversation alone with a male not in her family, and she suddenly became concerned if her father were to see them alone in this brake of woods. She began to walk toward the house, and Garrett followed. She called out as they entered the front hallway, "Mother, Garrett Matthews is here."

It was her father, however, who appeared from the dining room.

"Garrett, lad, how are you? How is your family?" Peter Bowman greeted the young man. It was obvious her father had been working alongside his hired field hands.

"I apologize for my appearance," Mr. Bowman said. "As I'm sure you are doing, we are busy keeping the new plants watered. It has been dry of late."

"Yes, sir, we are watering as well. Father has had the new servants digging a ditch from the waters of the inlet to his fields. It is hard labor," said Garrett.

"We are about to have our midday meal, and I hope you will join us. What can we do for you today?" Sarah's father was very kind and hospitable.

"Well, sir, I am sure your family is aware that we are having a concert followed by a luncheon at the parish next Saturday. I came all the way here to ask if I might escort Sarah as my guest."

Sarah watched as surprise registered on her father's face. He looked at her to gauge her reaction to this. In an instant, he could tell she was not surprised but was awaiting his reaction. He looked back at Garrett.

"Well, I am certain we will be attending as well, so we plan to be there. You may escort her once she arrives." His voice trailed off, and Sarah found herself wanting to laugh at her father's awkwardness. "I cannot stop you from spending time with her once she is there."

"Yes, sir," said Garrett, blushing. "I guess perhaps I am asking you if I may call on your daughter in the future as well."

"Let us see how things go at the luncheon, shall we?" Mr. Bowman responded. Sarah could not believe her father's attempt to put fear into the young man or at least uncertainty. It was not like her father to seem even the least intimidating. After all, there weren't that many young men in these parts to come calling on her.

"Of course," Garrett said, looking a bit uncomfortable.

Peter Bowman gestured the two young people to join him in the dining room.

"Lucy," he called out, "we need another place setting at the table."

After they ate and enjoyed polite conversation with the men talking of tobacco and cotton and Sarah and her mother saying little, Judith Bowman said to her daughter, "Perhaps you and Garrett would like to sit on the porch and talk?"

The two of them did as she suggested and strolled out to the cedar bench her father had built. Her parents often sat there and talked for long periods of time.

"I am not so sure your father likes me," Garrett said as he sat.

"He is just getting to know you, Garrett, just as I am." She smiled.

"Our families have been in church together since the two of us were born."

"Oh, I am aware of that, and so is he. I am just his first daughter to come to an age of being courted, and I suppose he is a little protective."

"I can certainly understand that," he said, smiling over at her. Ironically, the two spoke mostly of Andrew and Martha's wedding that took place in April and also of the wedding of Sarah's brother Edward and Miranda that would occur in June. Garrett at last stood to leave and politely offered Sarah his hand to help her to her feet.

"I've enjoyed my visit today, Sarah, but I must be going. I look forward to seeing you on Saturday."

"I feel the same, Garrett. Thank you for your visit. I pray you have safe travels home."

As he was still clasping her fingers gently in his, he quickly lowered his head and brought her hand to his lips. "Until Saturday then."

"Goodbye, Garrett."

Sarah blushed deeply, watched him ride off, and turned to go into the house.

For Saturday, Sarah and her mother baked two pies and made a tureen of delicious chicken stew. Priscilla, Sarah, and Miranda sat in the back of the wagon with the food. Her parents rode up front as usual, and Edward followed on horseback. Edward and Miranda were also going to speak today to Father Callahan about the upcoming wedding, which they'd decided to have at the Bowman homeplace on the covered front porch. It would be a small, simple wedding with mostly family present. Having been playmates and dear friends since childhood, the girls were as close as sisters already.

As they approached the church, Miranda poked Sarah in the side teasingly as the first person they saw was Garrett standing expectantly just outside the chapel doors. There were others setting up long tables outside under the trees. Everyone was placing their dishes on these tables, which kept the linen tablecloths from blowing away. Dish cloths covered the food and hopefully would keep insects away during the concert recital.

As everyone gathered in the church, Sarah entered on Garrett's arm. They could see and feel the parish members smiling in recognition of their courtship, nodding and poking each other and pointing out the courting couple with delight. The two sat not far from the back on a wooden pew with Garrett sitting closest to the aisle. The doors in the back were left open so that a cool breeze could enter.

After Mrs. Dexter played her fourth hymn and paused for their polite applause, there was a brief moment of silence before she started playing again. Sarah saw Garrett's eyes widen and his face suddenly at attention. He turned to her, excused himself, and left the church. Within a couple of minutes, Mrs. Dexter's fifth hymn was interrupted by two sudden blasts of gunfire. Many of the men jumped to their feet and ran out of the open church doors. They found Garrett holding someone's gun he'd gotten from the nearest wagon and saw two large black bears disappearing down the path next to the chapel. One of the tables of food had been upset, and the food was in disarray on the ground. Some of the men pulled the table upright and began to salvage the dishes that could still could be eaten. The others returned to the sanctuary to inform the ladies of the attack on the food and told how Garrett had saved the other table from the hungry bears. The concert was clearly over, and the women exited to go see to the chaos, chuckling to themselves about how they should have known better than to leave the food unguarded.

Sarah walked outside to see Garrett, surrounded by the men, clapping him on his back, praising him for his heroics. He looked up and saw Sarah and smiled. They soon left the lad alone, and he and Sarah met out in the churchyard.

"Our hero," Sarah said grinning at Garrett.

"Oh, it was not that brave a feat. I'm just glad I spotted the gun so as to frighten them off."

"How did you hear them?" Sarah asked him. "I was next to you, and I heard nothing."

"Bears make a very distinct low growling sound, especially when foraging for food. I have heard it on occasion, once when I thought I was going to be the meal!"

Sarah laughed.

The women of the congregation were glad to see that there was still enough food to feed the crowd of about forty-five parishioners. The Bowmans' chicken stew and pies were spared and consumed along the other savory, home-cooked dishes. Garrett and Sarah sat and ate on a blanket he'd brought along and placed under a large oak tree. They made small talk as various folks came up throughout the meal to congratulate Garrett on a job well done.

When it was time to depart for home, Garrett walked Sarah over to her family's wagon and, in front of everyone, gently kissed her hand again. He helped her into the back of the wagon where Priscilla and Miranda were already waiting. Once she was seated, Garrett reached over into the wagon taking her hand once more.

"You'll be hearing from me soon, Sarah!"

"Goodbye, Garrett! Thank you for a lovely afternoon."

Priscilla and Miranda teased Sarah all the way home about her newfound love. Miranda at last embraced her and told her, "Sarah, you know I am only sportin' with you! I know how you are feeling, my dear! Perhaps we should make the wedding next month a double one!"

Sarah was in her room that evening writing in her journal about the afternoon. She was thinking of the next words to write when her father suddenly stood in her doorway and asked permission to come in. She quickly closed her book and turned to face her father.

"Sarah," he began, "I would love to have a word or two with you."

"Certainly, Father."

She had watched her father's reaction all afternoon and had seen him praising Garrett and laughing and talking with the other gentlemen about Garrett's bravery and quick thinking.

"Sarah, my dear," he started, taking a seat on the edge of hers and Priscilla's bed, "I think Garrett Matthews is a fine young man. I have always respected his father. But I want you to know my concerns. I know you have heard me discuss from time to time my feelings on the idea of, well, the trafficking of slaves. I am aware that many men here in Maryland own slaves, yet many do not. I was opposed to my own father buying indentured white servants. Sarah, it has always been a very sensitive subject in my heart, the way humans ought to treat one another. Something inside my heart hurts when I see anyone mistreated. I remember accompanying my father to Baltimore once, and I saw slave auctions with my own eyes. I witnessed the brutality that was used against them, before they were purchased and afterward. These men and women are *not* animals, but I certainly saw them treated far worse than animals are treated. I knew then I could never own a slave or any human being. I believe it grieves our Father in heaven to see any of His children mistreated by His other children. As you know," he continued, "Garrett's father has recently acquired not only a group of African slaves, but has taken on an overseer as well, whose job it is to keep these slaves in line. He must whip them and bring them into submission! They did not ask to be brought here and treated as such! They were taken captive and dragged from their homes and families! I feel these plantation owners, maybe even all of us, will pay a price some day for these deplorable actions," he stated, clearly impassioned on the topic.

Sarah waited quietly for him to finish. She loved her father and admired his pacifist nature. She knew that was one of the reasons he chose not to move his family to a fort during the recent war. He knew going to a fort would require him to be part of the large militia there and to kill any Frenchmen or Indians who attacked them, though she was certain that being part of the small militia here, he would have defended them against attack, if it had become necessary. She also knew some men were harsh with their wives and even harsher with their children, and she was grateful for the gentle natured father that God had blessed her with.

"Sarah, I will not forbid you to marry Garrett if that is what you choose to do. I am also opposed to interfering with other people's free will. But I just wanted you to know it saddens me to think that you might become part of a family who owns other humans.

The wife of a slaveholder must also become skilled in disciplining the slaves under them. I have heard other men speak of how they had to harshly reprimand their own wives and sons and train them to be brutal to their slaves. It is only greed that leads to such action! And power! One man's assertion of power over another! And I am obviously in a small group of men who thinks that this is offensive to God!"

The emotion in his voice softened a little, and he went on, "Sarah, remember there are families around us who choose to not own slaves or cannot afford to own them. You have other choices. You are not engaged to be married yet. I know Garrett and his family could provide some of the finer things in this world, but I ask you to consider a higher purpose. Imagine yourself as the wife of a slaveholder, and think on how you might handle that. I feel and have always felt that you, my daughter, have a heart akin to mine. Pray on it, sweet Sarah."

"Father," Sarah finally spoke, "as you said, Garrett has not asked for my hand in marriage yet. I promise you I will think on what you have said. Perhaps Garrett feels as you do. Maybe he has a heart that is as soft as yours." A smile played on her lips as she said, "After all, today, he only shot that gun to frighten those bears! He could have massacred them there in the churchyard!"

She and her father laughed. "Yes, I guess that proves he has a kind side!" he said as he stood and leaned over to kiss his daughter's cheek. "Sleep well, Sarah, and don't forget to say a prayer. I love you, my child."

CHAPTER 7

James West
Charles County, Maryland
May 1765

James awoke with a severe headache. He was sleeping on the dirt floor of a rickety cabin, and he remembered immediately that he was on the plantation of Thomas Orr. Orr had purchased both him and his friend John Hussey and four other convict servants two days ago in Baltimore, and late yesterday, they had finally arrived at this huge tobacco farm in Lower Cedar Point, Maryland.

James had not had anything to eat since he had had breakfast with Captain Duggar in his cabin two days earlier. He knew that was the cause of his headache, that and severe thirst. He lay back down weakly and dozed off again, only to feel John shaking him awake.

"James, my brother, they are bringing food. Wake up."

James sat up and rubbed his forehead and his neck slowly but vigorously.

"I have got quite a pain in my head, John. I feel dreadful."

"We both need to eat. We both look pretty scrawny, if you ask me," John replied.

A loud, stout man stuck his head in the cabin. "Did you not hear the bell? You must eat before you go to the fields."

"I think my friend here is very ill," said John, pointing to James who was still holding his head in his hands.

"Well, that is just awful, isn't it? He's expected to work even if he's out there purging his guts in the middle of the rows. He came cheap. We can replace him just as cheap and throw him in a ditch somewhere."

James was thinking that he wished that they *would* throw him in a ditch somewhere, as it would make it so much easier to start his journey to North Carolina.

"Could I just bring him his food?" asked John.

"Get out here both of you! You eat in the yard with the others."

The two young men stepped into the light of dawn and saw several tables spread out under large oak and maple trees. They could smell food that seemed quite desirable, and they both perked up. The slaves sat at two tables, and the white indentured and convict servants sat at the other two. The two kitchen servants who had brought all the food out took their places with the others at the slave tables. James and John slipped into available spaces along the benches of tables for the white servants.

They had been prepared for a meal of gruel or corn mush but were pleasantly surprised to find plates of baked biscuits and molasses to go with them. There was hot coffee to drink. James glanced over at the tables filled with slaves, and their meal appeared to be the same.

An older worker seated across from John seemed to read their thoughts.

"Orr feeds us pretty decent, but 'e expects 'ard work. Don't slack up. Right now, we're plantin' tobacco. There's two 'undred acres we got to get done, and we're getting a late start as it is. They got a nice-sized vegetable garden that you will be workin' in some of the time. There's some fruit trees too. Don't get no ideas when stuff starts coming in of taking anything, and you'll be all right." He threw a look at John's most recent black eye that was almost healed and said, "And no fightin'. Mr. Orr's overseer is Mr. Morris, and if you get into fights, 'e's got a cowskin that'll tear your 'ide."

After they finished eating, the loud, stout man came back over to James and John and the four other new men. "Tonight, when you're done in the field, I need to see the six of you. I got to get your names writ down and your clothes issued to you. My name's Hank Walters, and I'm in charge of you. Mr. Morris is in charge next, and then we all answer to Mr. Orr. They'll bring a little food and water to the fields about midday, and tonight we eat again right here unless it rains. If it rains, we go to that covered porch up there by the kitchen and eat."

The sun pounded down on them most of the morning and afternoon as James and John helped sow the new tobacco plants. They soon developed the knack of knowing just how far down to go with the planting stick; too far down wasn't good, but not far enough, the plant wouldn't take root. Even with the repeated bending and stooping, James's head got better instead of worse. He figured the biscuits and molasses had done the trick.

That night, both James and John were tired down to the marrow of their bones. Just as James was sitting and rubbing his throbbing feet, Mr. Walters came into their cabin with an armload of clothing and a sack of stockings and shoes. He also had with him a ledger and a quill pen and ink. All six of the new workers were housed in the same crude shack.

"Come meet me at the tables," Walters ordered.

The six followed along. "Sit on the ground, and go through these shoes," he said, dumping out pumps of different sizes. They looked fairly new, and the men began to try on shoes and discard the ones that didn't fit and traded off until each had a pair they could wear. They began the same procedure with the white Oznabrig shirts scattered over the tabletops.

"Go bring your possessions, and prepare to strip naked," ordered Walters again.

They went to the cabin and got their bags and things and reported back to the tables with all their worldly goods in hand. James had purposely left his Bible and copy of *Robinson Crusoe* in the cabin.

"Now strip down. I have to record your names and write down a description of you. I need to see any scars or birthmarks. If you run away from Mr. Orr's, we put advertisements in the newspaper, so if you're caught, you can be easily identified. Is that understood?" The six men nodded.

Walters continued, "Dump out your old clothing, and lay it with your new. I have to make a record of anything you might be wearing if you take off from here."

They all sat naked on the ground until they were called up. James paid attention to the other men's names as he wanted to learn who they were. The first man up was named Roger Alley. He gave his age as twenty-five, or so he thought. Mr. Walters checked him carefully and spoke out loud as he wrote, "Missing one front tooth. Long sandy brown hair, a birthmark on left ankle." He recorded his clothing and shoes.

"You next," he said, pointing to a rather large man. "Name?"

"Thomas—John Thomas. I am thirty-two, and I come from Liverpool."

"I don't care where you come from! All they will need to know if you try and take off is where you took off from. Come here and let me check you out. No scars. Dark brown hair and looks like brown eyes. You're about six feet tall, my height. Those your clothes?" The man nodded. Walters jotted down his belongings.

The next man was John Maund, but he said he also went by the name of John Philpott, his mother's last name. He was about twenty-one years of age with dark hair and was just a little taller than James. As he answered Mr. Walters' questions, they all detected a speech issue, and Walters wrote down and read aloud, "Speaks with a lisp."

James shook his head in amazement at all the Johns in the group. Even Mr. Walters almost laughed when John introduced himself.

"John Hussey, sir," he said with a smile. Walters wrote down that *this* John was nineteen, had sandy colored hair, and gave a detailed list of his clothing.

The next man was named Samuel Street. He was in his thirties, he said. He had rusty-colored hair and a reddish complexion. Mr. Walters noted a scar over his right eyebrow and also recorded his few pieces of clothing.

He turned to James, who was still seated unclothed on the ground. The others had begun to dress.

"So, lad, I have a Roger, a Samuel, and three Johns. Your name doesn't happen to be John, does it?"

"No, sir. I am James West."

"And your age?"

"I just turned seventeen."

Walters continued to write and read aloud. "You have dark, wavy brown hair, and your eyes? They look gray to me. No markings?" James shook his head and turned around in a slow circle so Mr. Walters could clearly see his bare body. He pointed to the remaining pile of clothes on the table.

"Two white shirts, a pair of leather breeches, and a light-colored surtout. And you are about five and a half feet tall. Get dressed."

He closed the ledger and stood up from his seat. "I need to remind you again that you are in a fairly good working situation here. No trouble out of you, and you should not have any trouble brought down on your backs. Is that understood?"

The men nodded in agreement, gathered the rest of their things, and headed to their cabin. Before James entered, John pulled him aside and whispered, "Any thoughts as to when you plan to take off?"

"Not this week anyway. I've got to think it through. Will you consider coming with me?"

"What have I got to do here except plant this man's tobacco?" John grinned at him.

Two nights later, as they were going to sleep again after an exhausting day of hard labor, James could hear the other two Johns whispering in low voices. The one named John Thomas explained to the other one, "My cousin is here in Maryland, not too far from this place. His name is Robert Wade. His father and mother came here years ago as indentured servants, and they did their seven years. Their owner liked them so well that he gave them land. William Wade was my mother's older brother. His son Robert took his piece of land and has started his own tobacco and cotton farm."

"Ith that where you are headed when you leave thith playth?" lisped the one named John Maund, alias Philpott.

"Yes. My cousin sent me a letter months ago with directions to his place. His farm is only about twelve miles south of here."

James's ears keenly heard the word *south*. Right now, they were located near the banks of the Potomac River, and just across that river lay the colony of Virginia. And Francis and his family lived just south of the Virginia-North Carolina line. James continued to lie still as if he were in a dead sleep. He did not want the men to know he had overheard them. Maybe he could confide in them his plan to go south as well, and they could help him escape.

The next day was Sunday, their day off, and James sat out under the large oak that hung over their ramshackle cabin. James had his Bible in his lap and was reading from the book of James on the subject of faith, specifically about faith that does not waver. He thought about Captain Duggar's words that he felt James was probably going to be assisted by angels in finding his brother. James knew he must have a great deal of faith if that were going to prove true. He then closed his eyes in silent prayer, and when he opened his eyes, he saw standing against the side of the next cabin over a slave, a young man, about twelve years of age. He was watching James intently. James met his gaze, smiled at him, and waved hello. The boy turned away immediately as if he were burying his face in the wall. James closed his Bible and stood and walked over to the young man.

"Hello there!" he said softly. "What's your name? Do you speak English?"

At that, the child dashed around the corner and into his own little hut. James turned and walked back to the cabin and continued to read God's Word.

Later that afternoon, James took his Bible and walked down the path to the creek that ran by the plantation. He was not told he could not go. He was not leaving. Anyone could see from any vantage point he was simply walking farther out to enjoy the early summer evening and to read in peace.

As he finished the twenty-third Psalm, he looked over by the creek bank and saw the same fellow who had watched him earlier from outside his own cabin. The young man had a cane fishing pole he was baiting. James closed his Bible and placed it on the ground where he sat and got up and walked over to the boy.

"Hello there," James spoke kindly. "Do you speak English?"

He nodded but didn't glance up from his pole. He cast its line out over the water and sat down on the bank.

"Mind if I join you?" The young man said nothing, so James took off his shoes, sat down next to the boy, and slipped his feet into the cool water.

"My name is James. I just got here. How long have you been here?"

Without looking up from his view of the creek, the boy said, "I was born here. My name is Calvin."

"It is a pleasure to meet you, Calvin. I am from England—Wales actually. I have never worked on a plantation. My family has a farm, so I am used to garden work, but I have never planted tobacco before now. Is your family here?"

"My mama works in the kitchen, my sister helps in the house, and my daddy works in the fields. Mr. Orr let us stay together."

"Well, that's a good thing."

They were quiet for a few minutes, and at last, Calvin said, "That's a mighty big book you got. You read?"

"Yes, it's a Bible. The captain of the ship I was on gave it to me."

He looked over at James for the first time. "I never knowed a servant that could read. How did you figure out how to read?"

"I went to school since before I was your age. How old are you?"

The boy shrugged, pulled up his pole, and tossed his line back out into the water.

"I don't know how old I am. Last I heard, my mama say she think I am eleven."

"Do you know how many eleven is?" asked James.

Calvin shrugged again. "Not certain."

James took a stick and drew eleven lines in the wet sand by the creek counting each one aloud. "You've been here eleven years. You were born here," he said, pointing to the first line. "And a year is a spring, summer, fall, and winter, and then it starts over. You've been through eleven years."

"How 'bout you?" Calvin asked.

"I just had my seventeenth birthday in February." James added six more lines and counted from the start up to seventeen. "Do you know your letters?" James asked him.

He shook his head. James went and retrieved the Bible and sat back down with it in his lap. "See? These are called words. They are made up of letters." He recited the alphabet for Calvin. "The letters that spell my name are"—and here he drew in the sand again—"JAMES."

"Do you know the letters in *my* name?" the young man asked, placing his pole on the ground next to him. He slid over and made space for James to write more letters.

"I am pretty sure your name is spelled like this—CALVIN," James said his name again, starting with the *C* and underlining each letter as he pronounced it.

Calvin stared at the word and smiled.

"You know," James began, "there are some great stories in this Bible. One of my favorites is the story of a man named Joshua. He and his men, with God's help, marched around a city until it fell."

"My mama talks about God. We go to church sometimes with Mr. Orr's family. We go and sit in seats kind of up some steps, away from the white folks. I like to hear the songs. Can you read me a story from your Bible?"

James turned to the story of Noah's ark, and Calvin nodded as he read seeming to have heard it before.

"You not just makin' up them words? That's what them words really say?" Calvin asked.

"Yes, sir. Those are the real words. Calvin, I tell you what. How about next Sunday, that's today, the Lord's day on which we do not work, we meet here by the creek bank, and I could teach you your letters and numbers. I could teach you how to read from this book. And if you like, I have another book. It's a great adventure story called *Robinson Crusoe* about a man who gets shipwrecked."

"What is shipwrecked?"

"It means the ship got broken up in a bad storm. They were washed up on an island. That's a small piece of land completely sur-rounded by water."

"I know about islands," Calvin replied. "We got islands nearby. My papa has a brother who lives on one. He has to take a boat with his master to get over here to Maryland."

"You are already a pretty smart lad, y'know?" James smiled at him.

Suddenly, both of them turned when they heard a shout. It was Mr. Walters, the loud one in charge.

"Hey! West! What in the bloody blazes are you doing?"

James and Calvin went running to meet the man, James carrying his Bible and Calvin, his cane pole.

"We are chatting is all," James said with a smile. "I was showing the lad his letters and reading from the Bible to him."

"You were *what*? Are you really that stupid, West?" Walters said with pure animosity dripping from each word.

"What's the harm in that?" James asked, puzzled by the man's attitude.

"You really are new to this place, ain't you, lad? You are not to even *speak* to the darkies here on this plantation. You work side by side with 'em, eat with 'em, but you do not speak to them! And trying to teach one to read—that's a whipping offense! And I intend to see you get taught a lesson."

He grabbed James by both arms from behind, forcing him to drop the Bible to the ground, and pushed him along back up past the cabins and up to the large barn. Calvin followed them out of pure fear. Calvin stopped at his cabin as they passed by it and sat on the stoop crying. There was enough commotion with James yelling in his defense and Walters screaming oaths at him that everyone came out of the servants' quarters and out of the farmhouse. When Mr. Orr saw what was going on, he called for Mr. Morris, the overseer, whose job it was to mete out the punishment. Walters was busy removing James's shirt hastily and tying him to the whipping post inside the barn when Mr. Morris arrived. Without even asking about the offense, Morris was rolling up his shirtsleeves preparing to start the whipping. He went for the cowskin, finally inquiring as to what the boy had done wrong.

"This bright young lad was teaching Zach's boy to read!" Walters informed him.

"I didn't know it was wrong!" James insisted, his voice breaking. "I did not know!"

"Well, the seven lashes you'll get from me will guarantee you won't forget again!" said Mr. Morris, practically spitting out the words.

James could hear John Hussey shouting out, "No! No!" as the other two Johns held him back and prevented him from approaching the barn.

There was no getting away from the stinging of the long whip, and James only winced with the first blow, trying to be brave. But the second and third came so quickly behind the first that he found himself screaming from the intense pain. Mr. Morris took a great, sick pleasure in drawing out the last four lashes so that the agony from each registered deeply, like a warped savoring of slow bites of food. James was weeping pitifully and was left tethered to his place of torture for a little while. Finally, Morris and Walters untied him and let him lay bleeding in the dust in the doorway of the barn. At last, Walters took him up and almost dragged him back to his cabin, shoving him roughly inside and throwing his shirt in after him. He fell into John's arms and looked up into his friend's eyes, and they gazed at one another's tear-streaked faces.

"We never should have come here!" John sobbed. "What happened, little brother?"

James drew in his breath and began to explain, "I was simply at the creek, and that little fellow was there from the cabin next to us, and I was showing him his letters is all."

James's words were cut short by screaming and yelling from the cabin beside them. Above the shrieks of Calvin's mother, his father could be heard, pleading, "Let me whip my own boy! He's my boy, let me do the whipping. I promise I'll whip him good."

From the way the sounds carried and his mother kept crying, James and John knew Calvin was being dragged to the barn. "He is old enough to know better," Walters yelled at Calvin's distraught parents. "And if he don't, now's the time to learn." His mother and father

were forced back into the cabin by other slaves, who were simultane-
ously trying to console them.

"Oh, God, no!" James cried out, clapping his hands over his
ears, new tears surfacing. He could not bear to hear the screams coming from the innocent young man as he too was whipped inside the
barn. James lay on the ground inside the cabin, continuing to weep
and trying to stop the horror from entering his ears and reaching his
brain and his heart. "He didn't do anything!" James sobbed, as he
rocked himself on the ground.

The other two Johns and Roger and Samuel kindly vacated the
cabin for a while and sat out in the fading sunlight under the tree
and left John and James comforting one another in the little shack.
It was so quiet, James could hear Calvin sniffling next door and even
heard his mama's voice alternating between crying and singing softly
to him.

At last, James sat upright, wiping the last of his tears, and said
softly, "John, we've got to leave. We've got to get out of here!"

After it was completely dark, the other four men came back into
the cabin. John Thomas was the first to speak.

"I have a cousin only twelve miles away. That's why I'm here.
His name is Robert Wade. He lives at a place called Swan Point, and
he will not turn us in. All six of us should go tonight."

The lisping John interjected, "No, not tonight. They'll be
expecting uth to run off tonight. I thay we work one or two more
dayth, make 'em think we are over it, and then we'll take off. Can
you do that?" he asked James. Roger and Samuel were in full agreement with the plan.

The next morning, after not much sleep from being in pain,
James stepped out of the cabin and almost tripped over his Bible,
lying there in the early sunlight, next to his shoes, both retrieved
from the creek. He stooped to pick them up and glanced over and
saw Calvin's eyes peeking through the window. James nodded and
smiled at him and hugged the Bible to his chest in gratitude. He
mouthed the words, "Thank you."

They were going to escape. After all, he had angels assisting in
the noble cause.

CHAPTER 8

James and Sarah
Charles County, Maryland
May 1765

The lash marks on his back made it difficult for James to work in the fields, but he managed to keep working as if he never intended to leave this place. The most hurtful thing, however, was seeing Calvin laboring out in the fields as well, knowing that he was in pain too. James was grieved as he knew neither Calvin nor he deserved the punishments they got. He longed to meet with Calvin and to apologize for his own ignorance and to thank him for retrieving and returning his shoes and his Bible from the creek.

The plan for escape was only whispered once among the six of them. All six were leaving together but minutes apart. They were going to slip out one at a time in the middle of the night and disappear by way of the creek, staying close to the woods. All were told how to get to Swan Point in case they never found each other en route and how to ask for and find Robert Wade, John Thomas's cousin. They did not know the area well enough to plan a place to meet between there and the Wades.

James was to be the first to slip away in the middle of the night. John Thomas and John Philpott were to leave next, separated by about five minutes, followed by Samuel and Roger, with John Hussey being last. The reason for leaving with time in between departures was to increase the chances of most or all of them sneaking out. If only one was caught, they would not all be caught together. If only one was caught, the others might be successful in leaving the Orr plantation, or perhaps they all would make it out. They knew if they stayed close to the shore yet remained hidden in the woods, they would eventually finish walking the J-shaped, twelve-mile path that would lead to Swan Point.

After two days of working in the fields following his whipping, James was tired, but his heart pounded over the prospect of leaving. He packed everything he had in his satchel and sat in the dark next to where John lay on the floor. None of the six men was asleep.

"I guess this is it, brother," John said, giving James a gentle pat on his shoulder. "If I don't find Swan Point or if I get caught, best of luck in finding Francis."

"I am in your debt," James said to his friend. "I would not be here now if not for you."

"Remember," said John Thomas. "Head to the creek, and follow it down to the riverbank. Stay along the river, but stay just inside the woods. Best of luck, lads."

James stood to go, and John Hussey rose and embraced him. "We'll meet at Swan Point," he said.

James slipped out into the night and followed the path down to the creek where he had talked with Calvin three days before. It was very dark, and his feet got wet as he had a hard time following the creek yet keeping his feet out of the water. He ran and stopped every so often behind a tree or tree stump and listened carefully for the sounds of anyone who might be following him. There were no footsteps, no barking dogs. Finally, he came out of the trees onto the bank of the river and continued moving, hugging the line of woods, yet staying within sight of the water's edge.

After traveling for what seemed about thirty minutes, James found an ideal hiding spot, a ravine just inside the woods, and he was able to pull a large loose branch to cover himself. He found this large, deep ditch by accident. He tripped and fell into it headlong but managed to roll when he hit the bottom and did not get injured. He lay there, not moving and listening to hear if anyone was following him. There were only sounds of the night in the woods.

James actually dozed for a few minutes, hidden in this hole. He was awakened by the sound of voices, and for a few seconds, he worried these voices might belong to people from the Orr plantation searching for him, but he suddenly recognized John Philpott's lisping words.

James stood in the ravine, and only his head was above the ground. He knew it was too dark for them to see him, so he called out in a loud whisper, "Psssst. Hey! It's me, James!"

"James! Where are you, lad?" asked John Thomas. By following the sound of his voice, the two were able to see James below ground and helped pull him up to the top and set him down.

"Any word on John and the others?" he asked, deeply concerned for his friend's welfare.

"We haven't heard from any of them," answered John, the lisper.

At that moment, from far off in the distance was the sound of gunfire. One, two, three, four shots rang out. It was far off, and they heard no sound of horses galloping or dogs barking.

"Down in the ditch!" said John Thomas. Before he jumped in to join them, he grabbed a couple of loose branches to use as cover. They heard only two more shots then nothing.

James was shaking and whispered, "You think they chased them on foot? Maybe they just fired warning shots as they were fleeing, and they got away!"

"Not sure," replied John Thomas, "but I don't think it's safe to stay here. We need to keep moving. The more distance we put between us and the searchers before daybreak, the better."

James hated going on without knowing about his friend John Hussey, but he knew John Thomas was right. They had to keep moving and get as far as possible from the hateful people on the Orr plantation. But James was worried about John. What if he'd been shot? What if he was lying injured back there in the woods somewhere? James and the other two men moved forward, walking all night as quickly as the darkness and the woods would allow. James, however, had a very heavy heart.

When he was so tired and felt as if he could not take another step, James was surprised by a voice in his head. He felt as if he heard John's voice, speaking to him clearly, "Go on ahead, little brother. You have to find Francis. Be brave and keep on toward freedom." It was such a clear, sudden feeling that tears flooded his eyes and spilled onto his cheeks, and he was thankful the other two men could not see him crying for his friend.

By daybreak, they had probably walked six or seven miles, so they knew they were more than halfway to this place called Swan Point. They continued the pattern of following the bank of the river yet staying inside the woods that lay within sight of the water. They were headed south.

They found themselves starving since they had had a meager meal the night before. James had been hungrier, but he realized then that hunger is hunger. When you are barely being fed, two days of starvation felt the same as four. He was astonished when John Thomas stopped them in a brake of woods where there was a carpet of pine needles and pulled out a small loaf of bread and broke it into three pieces. He never said where he got it, but James was thinking, *I wonder if this man is a thief like my John.* He knew he must have gotten the bread from the Orr kitchen. Their cabin had been close to the building set apart from the house. James said a silent blessing, *Lord, I don't know how he managed to get this bread, but know that I am grateful for it. Bless us in our journey that we may find freedom. Bless John Hussey, Lord. And Captain Duggar, Father. And Calvin. Bless Calvin.*

As they ate, John Thomas told the two of them, "Today, Orr will send out an advertisement to the paper." It brought to James's memory when John explained the advertisement that would go out with the theft of the cloak. People did not like having their property disappear.

"It will give our names, what we look like, what we might be wearin'. We need to decide now on other names that we need to know and call each other from here on out. What name do you want to be called, lad?" he asked, looking over at James.

"I will be Duggar—Trenton Duggar," James said in honor of the captain. Then he realized that others might know that to be the name of the captain who brought him over. He changed his mind with a shake of his head. "No, Francis Duggar." The two men repeated it. John, the lisper, decided if they got stopped, his name was Henry Glover.

"That wath my uncle'th name back in Manchether."

"I will be George—after our wonderful, kind king back in the mother country," John Thomas said, his voice heavy with sarcasm. "George Albert."

The three escapees spent a few minutes practicing their new names, and then they headed south to find Swan Point and the Wade farm.

It was early afternoon when they reached what they thought must be near the location. It was a small farm, and "George" approached the white field hands lugging buckets of water to newly planted tobacco.

"G'day," he began. "I am George Albert, and I am looking for Mr. Robert Wade's farm."

The servant to whom John Thomas spoke shook his sweaty head and pointed farther south.

"Wade's about a half a mile down that way. This is Master Bowman's farm."

"Much obliged, sir," said John Thomas.

The servant gave an irritated snort.

"Come, gentlemen," he said, motioning to "Henry" and "Francis."

The last half mile seemed to go on forever. Finally, they came to another large field of tobacco being watered and tended to by a different set of servants. Past the fields was a two-story farmhouse crafted from hand-hewn logs. There was a separate kitchen, a smaller log building behind the house with smoke coming from its chimney. John Thomas asked James and the other John to stay on the path while he went to the door of the farmhouse to see who was at home from the Wade family. Watching from the road, the two young men were relieved to see the woman at the door warmly greet and embrace John Thomas and welcome him inside. James sat down in an exhausted heap on the path, taking his satchel from off his shoulders. He hoped this would mean water to drink and a good meal to eat and soon.

Soon indeed, John called for them, and they picked up their satchels and entered the farmhouse. James thought he would weep just from being in a place someone called home. It was clearly a place of love and caring, just seeing the charming and simple but comfortable decor. The neatness spoke of care and concern, and the smell of bread made them feel satisfied and happy. John obviously felt safe here as he used his own name and introduced them using their real names. Word must have spread of their arrival, as the door opened and in walked a tall, older man who embraced John Thomas with a huge grin on his face.

"My cousin! It is so grand to see you! All are well back home? Meggie," Robert Wade told his wife, "this my aunt Rachel's youngest son, John! I told you I had the letter from him! You surely have the family looks, lad! You favor my father William. I know you don't remember any of us as we left long before you were born, but I would have known you were family if I saw you in a crowd!"

They had kindly offered all available chairs to the three weary escapees. More family came in to join them, and they were introduced to Robert Wade's children, including his daughter Miranda, who was about to wed Edward Bowman from the farm next door.

"Peter Bowman is a wonderful man," Robert told them. "His father bought my father William and family as indentured servants. But by the time Peter's father passed away, we were freed and living on land the old man had given us. Peter does not believe humans should own other humans."

"We passed his farm," John Thomas began. "I saw no slaves, but I saw what looked like indentured servants, though."

"No, he doesn't own a one. Some were perhaps my own nephews who work for Bowman, but he hires them. I have two brothers who live nearby, and they work for him or for me. We live in peace here."

"We just spent a few days on a plantation north of here in Lower Cedar Point. They do not live in peace there. They whip their slaves and their white servants as well. It was just a temporary stop so as to get here," said John Thomas.

James noticed that John seemed to be leading Robert to think they were just indentured servants, not convicts who had broken the law to be here. James decided if John wasn't going to mention it, he surely would not.

John did say this much to his family. "We had to escape to get here. You may be seeing advertisements in the paper about us, but I know I can trust you not to turn us over to the authorities."

"Absolutely not! We would never do that!" Robert Wade said, embracing John again. "Now, Meggie, these gentlemen look famished! Please, if you could warm that wonderful stew and slice some of that bread for them!"

James couldn't believe it as they were invited into the dining room and seated at the table. It felt marvelous to be treated as a real flesh and blood human again, he thought. While waiting for the food to be warmed and served, Robert and John Thomas discussed sleeping arrangements. Robert insisted on his youngest sons sleeping in the barn, at least for a night or two so that their guests could have beds to sleep in. One of his sons reminded James of John Hussey; he was about his size and build and with the same straw-colored hair. It made James sick in his heart to not know of his friend's fate.

Robert told them that one of the cabins that were closer to the Bowman farm was empty. It had been refurbished through the years, but it might need to be spruced up a bit. They could have use of that cabin, and its location would make it possible for them to work on either farm—the Wade's or the Bowman's.

Fatigue set in, and James found himself nodding off at the mention of cabins and beds. The meal was the best James had ever eaten in his life, he insisted, and they all but cheered when Meggie brought out apple pie. Their satisfied appetites only increased their tiredness, and soon, they were shown three beds upstairs. John Thomas told Robert that they had worked in the field all day the day before and then had not slept but traveled all night in the dark. Tomorrow, they would head down to the vacant house and see to getting it cleaned and ready for habitation.

Miranda Wade walked to the Bowmans the next morning so she and Sarah and Judith Bowman could discuss the details for the wedding. Judith was a wonderful seamstress and was making her future daughter-in-law's gown, and it was time for an updated fitting on that.

As Miranda stood in front of Judith trying on her lovely cream-colored dress, Sarah sat on her mother's bed smiling and fingering the cloth.

"Miranda, you are going to be so beautiful!"

Judith said, as she stepped back to look at the almost finished gown, "Meggie should have come with you to see this!"

"Mother is rather busy helping with our houseguests. A cousin of father's has arrived, and he has two men with him. They just came from England. They landed in Baltimore and were bought as indentured servants, and they just escaped the plantation where they were to work."

"Where were they?" asked Judith.

"Some tobacco plantation in Lower Cedar Point. They got away and walked twelve miles to get here. The other men who escaped with them got shot."

"Oh my!" Sarah exclaimed.

Sarah's mother put the last pin into place in the hem of the wedding gown and stood up. "What are they planning to do here?" she asked Miranda.

"They will go to work for Father and for Mr. Bowman if he needs them."

"Where did your mother put three more people in her house?" Judith wanted to know.

"One of the cabins near your property is empty, Father said, so he's letting them stay there. The one on the other side of the clearing on Cuckold Creek. That way, they will be close to both farms. I hope you don't mind," Miranda replied.

"Those cottages haven't belonged to us since Peter's father was alive. Your father is free to put whomever he pleases there," Judith said smiling at Miranda.

"Mother and Father are helping them set up their household this morning—taking beds, tables, and chairs over. There were some used beds in our barn. Father was so glad see his cousin. His name is John Thomas, and he is Father's Aunt Rachel's son. Father says he looks just like my grandfather William."

Judith asked her how old the three gentlemen were.

"John is in his early thirties, but the two with him—one is probably a little older than Edward, and the other looks to be younger than Edward."

Sarah threw in, "Well, now they are free from being indentured servants. I've heard the colonies are trying very hard to get the mother country to stop sending over indentured servants and convict servants."

After a midday meal, Sarah announced to her mother that she was going to walk Miranda halfway home. "I think I'm going to take my book, pen and ink and do some sketching or writing, Mother, if that's all right with you."

"Yes, darling, just don't lose track of time."

"I won't," Sarah said, kissing her mother's cheek.

The girls left arm in arm, laughing and talking again about the wedding. Edward had popped in to share their meal and to steal a brief kiss or two from his sweetheart, so Sarah was teasing Miranda about her future husband.

Sarah and Miranda said their goodbyes and parted ways on the path that led to the Wade farm, and Sarah strolled into the woods to her favorite clearing that overlooked one of the most beautiful parts of Cuckold Creek. Sarah always imagined that this was the spot where Captain Smith must have seen the swans *en masse* that inspired him to name this area Swan Point.

She sat on her favorite flat rock by the water and was about to take her ink bottle and quill pen from her pocket when she suddenly saw a head emerge from the surface of a deeper part of the creek several feet out. It was a human head, and the person was rising slowly, his back to her. At first, all she could see was the back of his head, dark hair dripping wet and curling up on his neck. She watched as he came up, his back still turned to her. After his hair, she saw his strong bare shoulders, and as he stood up to his narrow waist, the first thing that caught her attention were several perfect stripes on his back, clearly marks created by the force of a whip. She must have gasped aloud as she stood up from the rock because the young man, startled, spun around in the water to face her, still in water to his waist.

His mouth flew open in surprise to see her there, and she turned and ran away from the clearing. He was not sure she heard him call out, "I'm sorry, Miss! I didn't know anyone was around!"

James dried off using his worn shirt and retrieved his clean, white shirt hanging on a nearby bush and put it on, followed by his breeches, tucking the shirt inside.

He couldn't shake the image of that poor girl's shocked face at seeing him bathing in the creek. *It wasn't just a shocked face*—he smiled—*but a lovely face. A lovely face framed by a great deal of thick, reddish brown hair.* James felt the stinging of his still fresh wounds underneath his shirt and remembered she had seen his bare back first. *She had to have seen those marks*, he thought. He knew she wasn't one of Robert Wade's daughters as he had met all four of them. He assumed she was from a neighboring farm, perhaps the Bowman farm. Maybe he would get an opportunity to meet her and apologize at some point.

Sarah ran home breathlessly with her heart still pounding. She finally stopped only when she reached home and flopped down in the little graveyard. She lay in the grass, trying to regain her composure. It was embarrassing to know she had accidentally walked in upon a strange young man bathing, but she was deeply disturbed by seeing the lash marks. *Only mean, evil servants would get whipped*, she thought. But the face she had spied as he had turned suddenly to her was anything but mean. *He was boyish and angelic*, she remembered. *He reminded me of Timothy if he had lived to be that age.*

CHAPTER 9

James and Sarah
Swan Point, Maryland
June 1765

S arah did not see that young man again until the day before Miranda and Edward's wedding the first Sunday in June. He came with everyone from the Wade household that Saturday to help set up tables and benches on the front lawn. The couple was going to come down the aisle created by the seats and benches, ascend the front steps of the porch and be united in holy matrimony by the priest of Trinity Parish, Father Michael Callahan.

The porch was decked with flowers, and mother's blossoms in the yard were just so beautiful for the occasion. Everyone was in such a festive mood for the wedding.

The families had been close for years, and though they were not related at all, it was clearly going to be a blending of two households who held each other in high regard.

Sarah walked over to check on the cemetery to see that there were no weeds around the flowers there and just to visit her siblings who were missing from the festivities. She was kneeling by Hannah's grave when she heard a voice, a familiar one. The last time she had heard this voice, it had called out, "I'm sorry, Miss! I did not know anyone was around."

She stood to greet the young man who was now saying, "I had hoped to meet you at some point to apologize for startling you a couple of weeks ago. My name is James West."

Embarrassed by the memory of having seen him bathing, Sarah blushed and said, "I'm Sarah Bowman. I guess *I* should be apologizing to *you*. I did not mean to intrude upon your bath," she smiled shyly.

"I think it was one of those accidental things when the timing was just wrong." He grinned back at her with a quick wink.

"So are you enjoying your stay at Swan Point?" she asked.

"Very much so. Even though I am working hard on the Wade farm, it's much more pleasant than where we were."

"Miranda told me you came from England to Baltimore."

"Yes, a very long journey. But there is a very important reason why I'm here. I'm on a mission of sorts."

Her expression showed true interest, so he continued, "I'm looking for my brother. He came over to the colonies a few years ago. Except for three letters, my family never heard from him again."

"Is he in Maryland?"

"No, he's south of here, in North Carolina—Granville County, North Carolina. He married a girl named Christian Talley, and last we heard they had two sons, and then we heard nothing else."

"So when will you go there?" Sarah asked.

"Right now, I'm working to save money to go. I want to be able to purchase land there and build my own farm."

"Like a plantation?"

"Oh no. More like this place or the Wade place. I will *never* be a slaveholder," James declared with vehemence.

Sarah looked at him more attentively, remembering her father's words. She also recalled the cruel stripes on James's back, and now she truly knew that James was very far removed from her original thoughts concerning a vicious, evil servant. Now she wondered more than ever what this gentle, kind young man had done to warrant lash marks on his back.

"I saw and experienced enough on the Orr plantation to ever want to subject someone to that type of treatment. It's not human the way some of them treat their slaves and servants," said James.

At that moment, Sarah saw Garrett Matthews gallop into the yard on his horse. They had seen each other two or three times since the day of the social at church when he saved the luncheon with his bravery against the two bears. He spotted Sarah in the cemetery talking to James, alit from his horse, and joined them quickly.

He approached with, "Hello, Sarah," leaning over and kissing the top of her head.

The look he gave James was a clear message of "Back away, she belongs to me." It was James who extended his hand to Garrett.

"Hello, I'm James West. I'm with the Wade family, friend of the family rather."

When Garrett didn't say anything in return, Sarah said, "James, this is Garrett Matthews from a neighboring farm. We attend church together at Trinity Parish."

"I'm from the Matthews Plantation," Garrett clarified.

Sarah could feel the tension coming mainly from Garrett who seemed to be intimidated by James's very presence. James, however, seemed to be oblivious to the fact that he was a source of intimidation to anyone.

James then said, "Well, I had better go finish helping with the setup. It was very nice meeting you, Sarah. Garrett." With a tip of an imaginary hat and a sweet grin, James was off.

Garrett told her as he leaned against the large oak there in the tiny graveyard, "Sarah, you should learn now that it is not wise to socialize with the help. That indentured servant had no right to come up to you to make conversation."

"He is no longer an indentured servant."

"Everybody knows the Wades have always been and will always be nothing but indentured servants."

Sarah felt angered at Garrett for the first time ever. She could not believe how pompous and condescending he seemed. "First off, he is not a Wade. But the Wades are now landowners and have been for quite a number of years. And my brother Edward is marrying a Wade tomorrow, as you know!"

The two did not speak for a couple of minutes, and Sarah had her arms folded angrily. Finally, she went on, "You know, Garrett, as Christians, we should never consider ourselves above another human being. We are all equal in the sight of God."

"Then why did God make us so unequal?" he asked snidely. "Why do humans come in so many forms and classes? Some are born with money and become educated. Some are born into poverty and must rely on servitude to stay alive. Since the beginning of time, there have been classes of people enslaved and held in lower esteem than others. It is not my fault that some were born in such dire circumstances! My father owning slaves, for instance. He is keeping them alive. They were taken from a place where they had to deal with tribal wars and living like animals to this place where they are fed and taught proper behavior. We even take them to church and teach them about God."

Sarah did not like this argument, and she was certain Garrett was merely repeating words he'd heard his own father say in defense of slavery. But she felt she must stand up for how she felt and how she was taught. And the image of the stripes on the back of that sweet James West was still so clear in her mind.

"Does your father use a whip on his slaves?" she dared to ask.

"No, of course not. That's why he has hired an overseer. And *he* only has to use such punishment if they become disobedient."

"Well, I think slavery is wrong. My father refuses to own slaves. He does not believe in it."

"And, Sarah, dear, I'm afraid your father will never have much in this life. He won't be able to leave a legacy to you and Edward and your families."

"I think it's more important that my father can sleep at night without a guilty conscience, and he will be in heaven for the kind way he has always treated all humans!" With that, Sarah stomped out of the cemetery and went into the house. She stood at the window and watched Garrett untether his horse, leap into the saddle, and ride away clearly upset.

The day of the wedding was heaven-sent. The sky could not have been a more beautiful shade of blue. There were not any puffy white clouds, just an occasional wisp of white for a gorgeous wedding day backdrop. The flowers still looked lovely from the afternoon before. Sarah's mother Judith and Lucy had been up baking most of night with some help from Sarah and Priscilla. Sarah and Priscilla wore sky-blue gowns for the wedding, and her mother's gown was a pale green. Edward had gathered flowers for his Miranda to carry as she walked with her father Robert Wade up the path to the front porch. All the Wades were there. Even their visitors—John Thomas, John Philpott, and James—were wearing clean white shirts and dark breeches. Sarah could tell Meggie or maybe one of her other three daughters had trimmed James's hair from off his neck a little, and Sarah thought he looked so handsome. The Matthews family had been invited, but only Garrett's parents came to the wedding.

The ceremony was touching and filled with kisses and smiles as the two families became one. Sarah loved the happiness she witnessed, but she got a little emotional thinking of her brother leaving their home. He and Miranda had been building a farm closer to the Wade's property, and it was ready to be moved into, though there were other things that would be added in the weeks and months to come, such as a barn and one day a separate kitchen. For now, Miranda would cook for her new husband from their own fireplace. The important thing was they had a new home of their own.

As the crowd gathered on the lawn to celebrate with tasty pies, pastries, and little tea cakes, Sarah was touched on the elbow and turned to see James standing there. He smiled at her.

"I don't think I've ever seen such a lovely gown. You look beautiful, Sarah," he began. "You must be thrilled to have such a sweet girl as a new sister-in-law. I think the world of Miranda. I'm very happy for both her and Edward. Both your families remind me a great deal of my family back in Wales."

"You are Welsh?"

"I am. From a little village near the coast called Manorowen. My brother Francis and I used to walk to the seaside village called Fishguard. My uncle lived there with our cousins, and we would help them fish. I miss my family."

"They must miss you dreadfully! How did you ever get them to agree to such a journey as you've taken?"

James hung his head just a bit. "I didn't. I ran off. I was so determined to come over here and find Francis. But I did write them a letter. The captain of my ship made me write it, and he promised to have it delivered on his return."

"So did you work on board the ship to earn passage over?"

"In a manner of speaking." James did not like lying and even felt guilty with half-truths. But at this point, he had no intention of telling Sarah about John Hussey and the cloak and his time in jail. That was in his past. Now he was a hired farmhand, and soon, he would be a landowner. *Oh,* he thought, *if only John could be here to enjoy this freedom I've found. If it weren't for finding Francis, I could be content to stay here at Swan Point forever.*

The next evening after spending all day cleaning and putting everything away from the wedding, Sarah left to go to her favorite clearing. She had such a need to record all about the wedding and finish the sketch she had started of Miranda and Edward while it was still fresh in her mind. She had done a little sketch of Priscilla in her gown with flowers in her hair. Her mother had seen it and was already making such a fuss over it.

As Sarah sat on the flat rock overlooking the water of Cuckold Creek, she thought about the last time she was here, when James had surfaced in the water. Before the she knew it, she was sketching what she had seen: James from behind, standing waist deep in water, his hair curling and dripping on his neck, and the stripes on his back. As she gazed at what she'd drawn, she felt tears filling her eyes. *God allowed me to see that for a reason,* she thought. It had certainly moved her. He was probably healing now. He probably needed someone to put liniment on his wounds. She found herself wishing she could comfort him in that way. She felt so deeply about James already and not in silly schoolgirl fashion. He just had such a sweet spirit about him, she thought. She remembered her father's wishes for her that she could meet someone who despised slavery as much as he did. Garrett was certainly not that person, and she disliked the rude way he had treated James two days earlier.

She sat tracing the lash marks she'd drawn with a slow movement of her fingertips. She was more than startled to hear his voice call out to her and to see him standing in front of her.

"Guess our timing is a little bit better today," James said, greeting her with a smile.

She shut her book quickly to prevent him from seeing what she'd drawn. She now wished she'd not sketched it as she would be horrified for him to see such an inappropriate image. She had no immoral intention, she knew, but it was such a personal image that he would probably wish she had not seen or drawn.

"Mind if I share this rock with you?"

"Of course not," she said sliding over.

"So when is your wedding to Mr. Matthews?" he asked with a half grin.

Sarah blushed deeply. "Garrett Matthews and I are *not* engaged to be married."

"I just assumed since he was so glad to see you the other day." This time, James chuckled a bit.

"I think he *thinks* I belong to him, but it's not true. We've been together to one or two social events, and I am certain now that he is not the person for me, especially with the way my father feels."

"How's that?"

"My father does not want me marrying into a slaveholding family. My father is very opposed to the whole idea of humans owning other humans."

"I must get to know your father better." James smiled again and then asked, "What makes him so against slavery?"

"I think it's because my father is a God-fearing man and he believes we are all His creatures and that one is no better than another."

"That's a very good reason," said James.

"He also witnessed something." Sarah could not believe how easy it was to open up to this James West fellow. "He was in Baltimore once with his father, my grandfather, and they actually saw a slave auction taking place right off a ship. He saw whippings taking place," she said gently, knowing that this was literally a painful subject for James. "He and his father disagreed even on the subject of buying indentured servants. My father said he could not do that either."

James suddenly changed the subject. "So what's in your book there?" he said, nodding to the volume in her lap.

She clutched it to her chest, hoping he would think it was so personal he would not dare ask to see inside of it. "It's just where I write down my thoughts," she answered. "Kind of like a diary or a journal, but sometimes, I write down other things I find that I like, such as my favorite Bible verses or some of my favorite poetry or quotations."

"Oh, it's your commonplace book!"

"My what?"

"You've never heard of a commonplace book? Father O'Brien back home taught us about them. He made us keep one. He was not just my priest but my teacher as well. He started a school for some of us."

"James West, you are a most interesting young man," Sarah said smiling. "I don't think I've heard of an indentured servant who is educated."

"Blimey, girl, I read and write and everything!" he joked.

She laughed and he continued, "I have books with me on this trip. I brought along Defoe's *Robinson Crusoe*, my favorite adventure story, and I now have a very nice Bible. On board the ship, the captain found out I could read and that I had a copy of *Robinson Crusoe* with me. He was mostly confined to his cabin with a back ailment, and he had me come read to him almost every day. Then before we arrived in Baltimore, he brought out his Bible and had me read some from that. The day we arrived in port, he gave me his Bible to take with me. And I left a letter for him to take back to deliver to my parents. He was on his last voyage, he told me." James gazed at the water lost in thought and memory. "He was a very good man."

"Sounds like he was a fine man," Sarah agreed. "So you didn't feel alone coming over here? You kept company with the captain of the ship?"

"I wasn't alone at all. I had my friend John Hussey with me. We met in London. He was planning to come to America too. We just became, uh, servants together." James did not want Sarah to know that he was a convict servant as he was already feeling a great deal of shame about that fact. "We were purchased together and went to the Orr plantation together. But I am fairly certain he was shot trying escape. I got away first, and the others followed. We didn't all leave at once as we knew if we went together, we could all get caught together. This way, some of us got to escape. I heard the gunshots, and he and the other two fellows never followed us, so I'm pretty certain that they may have lost their lives to help us escape. But I'm praying he was just injured and somehow got away."

Sarah said, "It's so hard to lose someone you care about. I just lost my brother and sister a few months ago."

James sat upright. "No! I'm sorry! How did it happen, Sarah?"

"We all got sick with a fever. Timothy and Hannah didn't survive."

"How old were they?"

"Timothy was eleven, and Hannah was just two. I wrote about them in my book. I also drew their pictures. I'm an artist. Well, I am *attempting* to be an artist," Sarah said. "My mother seems very impressed," she said smiling.

"Do you mind if I see?" he asked.

Sarah cautiously opened the book back some pages to the entries about Timmy and Hannah. She showed the pages to James but held tight to the book.

"Sarah Bowman, you are amazing! How lifelike they are! You will never be able to forget what they looked like as long as you have this." He read the words that described the children. "Very touching. It must have been dreadful losing them. I take it they are in the family graveyard we talked in before?"

"Yes, along with the two babies my mother lost in the first few years of her marriage." She showed him the Sarah of Swan Point page, and he was equally impressed.

"You could work for a printing house and illustrate books, girl!" He hugged his knees to his chest. "I wish I could draw. If I could draw, I would draw my folks. I'd draw Captain Duggar, John Hussey, Calvin."

"Who is Calvin?"

"A young man I met." James said no more about Calvin.

"So, James West, how old are you?" Sarah inquired.

"I'm seventeen!"

Sarah smiled and pushed against him a little. "I'm seventeen also!"

"Is that right? What a coincidence. I just turned seventeen on the ship coming over. February the sixth."

"I just turned seventeen in April, on the fourth."

"Happy belated birthday, Sarah!" he said reaching over, placing an arm around her shoulders and pulling her to him, kissing her cheek.

"And happy birthday to you, James. So sad you spent it without your family on board that ship." Then she asked him, "What was it like aboard the ship? I was born here, so I've never been on the ocean."

"This ship was called the *Tryal*. They were bringing supplies to the colonies and a load of us… servants. I'm not sure I ever want to be on another such ship. Perhaps one day, I will write about it," he finished.

The two were quiet and lost in thought again, but suddenly Sarah realized it had grown dark. The lovely sun earlier spreading its golden rays on Cuckold Creek was now gone, and the woods had grown dark without their being aware.

"James!' she exclaimed. "I must be going home!"

"I will walk you, Sarah." He had to almost run to keep up with her. At last, they reached the clearing to her property. She was moving very quickly, but James stopped and pulled on her arm gently. She shifted her book to her other arm and held it by her side.

"Sarah, my apologies. Time just slipped by. I enjoyed talking to you."

"You as well, James. Thank you for walking me home."

She started to slip out of the grasp he had on her arm when he quickly drew her to him and kissed her softly on her lips.

"Good night, James," she said and ran to the house, her commonplace book clutched to her chest. *He will never see this book*, she thought with a smile, *especially after I have written about tonight!*

CHAPTER 10

James and Sarah
Swan Point, Maryland
June 1765

James and Sarah developed a habit of meeting at their favorite rock on Cuckold Creek each evening when he was finished working and eating. She had added a sketch to her book: a portrait of James. She had worked on it one night when they had met by the creek but finished it later at home. She loved the couple of hours they sat there that evening, talking some, yet she spent most of the time gazing at James as she drew while he looked at her or at the sun going down on Cuckold Creek. She was grateful for the talent God had given her as it made it possible to stare at her own work and see his face even when he wasn't present.

One night while sitting closely together on the rock, James embraced Sarah and kissed her deeply. He then smiled and said, "You know, I am so glad Garrett Matthews comes from a slaveholding family."

"Oh, James! I promise you that is not the only reason Garrett and I did not get along. He is very pompous. My father did not want me to pursue a relationship with him."

"Does your father know you come out here to meet *me* every evening?"

Sarah lowered her eyes. "No, but I don't think he would have a problem with my seeing you. You really do need to get to know him. You have a great deal in common."

"That's for certain. I know we both love a young lady named Sarah," he said, looking deeply into her green eyes.

This was the first time James had said he loved her. Sarah turned and embraced him, and they kissed again. "Oh, James! I do love you too! You have been like someone I already knew from the beginning of time! It's like our finding each other was just meant to be."

"I agree. I've been able to share things with you I never thought I would tell anyone," he said, holding her hand and gently trailing his fingertips along her arm.

"James," Sarah began in a whisper, "I would like to show you something."

She released his hand and pulled the book up from where it was leaning against the rock. She turned slowly, first to her portrait of James. She revealed the page to him, and he stared at the finished product and was amazed.

"It's like I'm seeing into a looking glass! I think you've made me too handsome, though!" He smiled.

She said, "You *are* handsome, James! I thank God for my talent. Because of it, I am able to see you when we are apart." She paused for a moment trying to decide whether or not to let him see the other picture. "Please do not be mad at me, James, but this next one is a sketch that I did of you after I first saw you. It touched my heart. No, it broke my heart."

She turned to the picture of James in the creek from behind, his scarred back facing forward. She didn't know how to read his reaction at first. Then she saw him reach up and wipe away a tear or two as they slid down his cheek.

"I don't know what to say, Sarah," he said, his voice breaking.

"James, I think I loved you from that moment, not out of pity, but out of deep compassion. I cannot imagine what could have happened that made those beasts at the plantation feel they needed to whip you!" She was choked with emotion as well, and her hand touched his face, and her thumb wiped another tear from his cheek.

He sighed, "I'll tell you." He drew in another deep breath. He used the back of his hand to wipe away yet another tear. "On my first Sunday there, the only day we did not work, I was sitting under the tree by our cabin, and I was reading my Bible. I looked up and saw a young man, Calvin. I think I mentioned him to you before. He was a slave child. He was eleven years old. He was watching me. I waved hello and went over to talk to him, and he ran into his cabin. Later that day, I went down to the creek that ran along the plantation to a place almost like this one, and I took my Bible to read. I looked up and Calvin was there, with a pole, fishing in the creek. This time, he talked with me. He asked about the big book, my Bible. Before I knew it, I was sitting on the ground next to him with a stick and drawing letters in the sand. I wrote out my name, and he wanted to know if I knew the letters for his name, so I spelled out—'Calvin.' He got very excited, and I started showing him words in the Bible. I got an idea and suggested we meet on Sundays down there, and I could teach him his numbers and letters. He had a big smile on his face. Suddenly, Walters, the one in charge of us, came upon us and demanded to know what we were doing. I told him very truthfully, as I saw nothing wrong with it. He told me that teaching a slave to read was a whipping offense. He knocked the Bible from my hand and dragged me back up to the barn. I kept insisting I did not know any better, but it was in vain. The overseer, Mr. Morris, came into the barn, and together, they tied me to the whipping post."

James had fresh tears surface, and he wiped those away as well. "The worst part was they whipped little Calvin also!" James paused here to try and regain his composure, but his voice tightened. "I wanted to kill them! I know, Sarah, that I am supposed to love and forgive, but I don't know if I will ever be able to forgive those men for what they did. To me, there must be a special place in hell for people like that who do such things!"

When he put his head down and wiped more tears, Sarah put her arm on his back to console him. She could feel the raised welts still through his shirt, probably toughened scars after all this time.

"James," she asked barely above a whisper, "have you been able to put any liniment on your back to help with the healing?" She was still moving her fingers softly in small circles on his back.

He shook his lowered head.

"Tomorrow, I shall bring some, if you don't mind. I will rub some on your back for you."

"You would do that for me?" he asked.

"Of course, I would! I love you, James."

The two kissed again, and then they got off the rock and headed in the direction of Sarah's home so they could say their goodbyes at the edge of the woods.

The next evening as the sun was getting low in the sky and the shimmering gold from the sun gilded the surface of the water, Sarah and James were back in the clearing, this time sitting on a blanket she'd brought from home. She took out a bottle of liniment she had also brought. James kept his shirt on, but he untucked it, and he lifted it up to his neck. Sarah held her breath as she looked at the scars. They were still very red and raised, and she knew they must still have caused him pain. He insisted they were better, however. She poured a little of the solution into the palms of her hands and began to rub it gently into the long, sore places. He moaned not only because it felt so good to have the salve applied, but also it felt so good to be touched by hands he had come to love.

She continued to massage his back gently, and he finally said to her, "Sarah, I am not just saying this because you are being so kind to me, but I want to marry you."

Sarah stopped suddenly and slid around to face him, her fingers still under his shirt touching his sides. He continued, "I want us to be able, in the eyes of God, to touch each other all the time, every night. I love the feel of your soft fingers on me. I want that forever. I want to be able to touch *your* back, *your* skin."

By this time, they were forehead to forehead, and then their lips came together. Before she knew it, they were deep in an embrace on the blanket with James lying over her, holding her, and kissing her passionately, and her hands were still under his raised shirt, now moving along his back. After a few moments, James sat up breathlessly. "I am taking you back now to your home. You mean so much to me, but I cherish your virtue, and I will not take it before we're wed!" Sarah sat up, torn over leaving him so soon. She hesitated and her face showed her reluctance to end this moment. James stood and said forcefully, "Sarah, here the temptation is too great! I must meet your father so we can marry! I love you, Sarah. I do not want to live without you."

He pulled her to her feet and took up her book, the blanket, and the bottle, and they walked side by side, silently to the edge of her property. Neither could speak as each was reliving the passionate feelings newly kindled.

"Shall I invite you to dinner?" Sarah finally asked. "I will ask to have you over for dinner, say Saturday night. If my parents agree, I will let you know tomorrow night when we meet again."

He shook his head. "No. There will be no more meetings in the woods. Send word to me in writing." He stopped and looked at her. He still seemed shaken. "Forgive me, Sarah. I love you, but I want to do this in God's way. I could never forgive myself if anything happened. I will wait for your written invitation."

He gave her a very quick kiss, followed by another. "Good night, my love."

James gave her the book, blanket, and bottle of ointment and turned and walked very quickly back toward the creek and his cabin.

Sarah walked into the house and was startled to see Garrett and his father sitting in the parlor with her father. She had been so distracted that she had failed to see their two horses tied to a tree in the front of the house. Her father was sitting in his large chair with a newspaper in his lap. She said, "Pardon me," as she passed through. Garrett might have looked her way, but they did not acknowledge her presence. Then she slipped into the dining room so she could listen to their conversation.

"I don't understand why you are bringing this to *my* attention," her father said. "These men are visitors, even relatives of Robert Wade."

"But," Garrett's father spoke up, "Wade is your servant."

"No," said Peter Bowman. "My father had William, Robert's father, as an indentured servant. The entire family finished out their servitude when my father was still alive. It was *my* father who gave them freedom—no, they *earned* it! They are now free men working their own land!"

"That may be," Jacob Matthews went on, "but that doesn't change the fact that Robert Wade is harboring three escaped convict servants! You read the advertisement in the *Gazette* yourself, Peter!"

Sarah almost gasped aloud as she heard those words. *James, a convict?* She began to shake. *It couldn't be true!*

Her father stood, with the newspaper in his hand. He handed it back to Mr. Matthews. "I still say you are talking to the wrong person."

"Have these men worked for you at all?" asked Jacob Matthews. "I know I was introduced to all of them at your son's wedding two weeks ago. I heard them introduced using these same names."

Peter ran his fingers through his hair, frustrated by the truth. "Yes," he finally admitted. "They have been working for me some. I did not know they were convict servants. I was told they were indentured servants who escaped the plantation where they were."

"Yes, the Orr place." Jacob Matthews stood also. "Peter, Jess Richards, who works for the *Gazette*, is a friend of mine. He brought me this copy of the paper himself since I live in the area. He wanted me to be on the lookout for these three."

"Would you like for me to speak to Robert about it, or are you planning to do so?" Sarah heard her father ask.

"I guess I am here because I respect you, Peter, and I thought you should know. But also know this—the authorities have already been notified. They should be down tomorrow or the next day."

Jacob Matthews folded the newspaper and tucked it under his arm, and he and his son left the house.

Sarah felt torn between telling her father everything and pleading with him to protect James and the others or taking off and running to James's cabin herself to let them all know. Talking to her father was going to be difficult as she knew he wanted nothing to do with convict servants after what happened with the ones his father bought years ago. One of them had attempted to rape Robert Wade's sister Nellie. Sarah feared her father would never accept James since he was now a convict.

She knew her father was generally a kindhearted man, but she also knew he would be livid to know that she was now in love with one of the convicts and was planning to marry him! He did not know James as she knew him! He would probably rather she marry a slave-holder than a convict!

Sarah prayed a silent prayer and stepped into the parlor to speak to her father, but he interrupted her, "I'm sorry, Sarah, but I must go on an errand. Tell your mother I am headed over to Robert's. I will be back soon."

Sarah wrung her hands and paced the floor. All she could do was wait. She took her book and things to her room and lay on her bed, praying silently. Little Priscilla came in, and Sarah helped her with her clothes and slipped her nightgown on. Sarah picked up her comb and began to comb through her sister's hair but without speaking or paying attention. Sarah tucked her sister into bed, and when Priscilla was sleeping soundly, Sarah walked back downstairs to await her father's return. Her mother was seated in the parlor now with sewing in her lap.

"Did your father say why he had to go to Robert's so late?" she asked when Sarah told her where he had gone.

"The Matthews were here, Mother—Garrett and his father. Mr. Matthews had a newspaper article. It was an advertisement that said that Robert's cousin John Thomas and the other two are escaped convict servants." Sarah was trying to keep her composure but, at last, burst into tears. "It cannot be true, Mother! I know James. I have gotten to know him, that is. He is a fine young man. He is educated. He is a good Christian."

"I've seen the two of you talking, but, Sarah, the tears? You have deep feelings for him?"

Sarah nodded quickly. "I love him, Mother. He has been treated so unfairly. He loves me, and he wants to marry me!"

At that, Judith Bowman came to her feet dropping her sewing on the floor.

"Sarah! You can't mean that! He is likely to be headed back to prison! You must give up such foolishness!"

"No! And if he runs off, I shall run with him!" she said, falling into her father's chair sobbing.

"You cannot mean that!"

Judith tried reasoning with her daughter, but she was too distraught. The two of them moved to the front porch waiting for her father to return, and Sarah was still crying softly. She was telling her mother how kind James was trying to teach the slave child to read and how he was whipped for it. She told her about James's mission here to find his brother Francis.

"Mother, they cannot arrest him!" she cried.

Peter Bowman rode up on horseback, tethered his horse, and climbed the steps.

"I've spoken to Robert. We've talked to all the lads as well. He did not know that his cousin was an escaped convict servant. They all confessed when Robert confronted them with the news I brought." Here, Peter stopped and sat next to his wife on their cedar bench. He went on, "It seems John Thomas stole a pair of shoes in London so he could come here to be with Robert. John Philpott was caught stealing food because he was hungry. The youngest one, James, was caught stealing a cloak from a clothing store in London. It seems he has a brother in the North Carolina colony, and he is looking for him. Robert does not want anything to happen to any of them, and he is sending them into hiding. He knows to expect authorities here in a day or two. I think he is going to try and bargain with Thomas Orr and see if he can offer him a profit on the three of them. Perhaps Robert can buy them for more than Orr paid for them, and he will be satisfied and drop the charges. I do not think these three are anything like the convict servants my father bought. Did you know, Judith, that young James reads and writes? He has a Bible with him that he reads all the time."

Sitting on the steps, Sarah stopped her tears and sighed with a sense of partial relief. Her mother only looked at her daughter and back at her husband. Sarah closed her eyes praying that her mother would not say anything that would make her father change his new attitude about James. Her mother cleared her throat and said, "I've heard as much. It must have been Meggie or Miranda who told me what a fine young man he is." She smiled at her daughter who returned the smile. Then Judith stood and continued, "Now we can only pray that God's will, will be done and that Robert can get this Orr man to agree to his offer. I think it's out of your hands, husband!"

"Except for the praying part!" He smiled at his wife. Sarah overheard him as he stood and escorted his wife through the front door. "Did Meggie tell you that poor James was whipped at that plantation?"

Sarah followed her parents into the house and up the stairs. Before she climbed into the bed with little Priscilla, she opened her book and, by the moonlight, looked at her portrait of James. What was he thinking right now? Was he thinking as she was that their plans for marriage might not work out? Was he as heartsick as she was? She touched his face that she had drawn. She remembered the touch of her fingers on his back. *I want that forever*, he'd said. Right now, he was in hiding, and she knew not where! She calmed down as she heard in her mind the words James had spoken to her earlier. *I love you, Sarah. I do not want to live without you.* She recalled the ache that she felt as he kissed her. She loved that he desired her but also desired to protect her virtue. She was touched that her mother had not revealed to her father all that she had shared in tears earlier.

Thank You, Father, for letting mother understand me, Sarah prayed. *And thank You that my father has a soft heart that will hopefully grow softer still. And speaking of softening hearts, Dear Lord, bless Mr. Orr that he will take Robert up on his offer.*

CHAPTER 11

S arah slept fitfully, worrying all night about James and his fate with the Thomas Orr situation. She awoke early in spite of little sleep, got dressed, and headed toward the Wade farm on foot. She met Miranda on the path, and her new sister-in-law greeted her with a hug. She had confided in Miranda almost as soon as she and James had begun to meet in the woods in the evenings. Miranda had not even shared her confidences with Edward. Actually, Sarah had been forced to share the truth with Miranda, as she'd walked into the clearing one evening and found James and Sarah sitting together on the rock holding hands and talking softly to each other.

On this morning, Miranda was on her way to see Sarah because she had some news to share. She and Sarah made their way to the clearing and sat upon the rock.

"What word do you have?" Sarah asked.

"You know then? About them being convicts? They confessed to such when your father came with the news last night. Edward and I were at the house."

Sarah nodded. "I had just gotten back from meeting with James here, and Garrett and his father were in our parlor sharing the newspaper advertisement with Father. I'm sure Garrett was smirking and gloating a bit, though I couldn't bring myself to go in there and look in his face. I eavesdropped from the dining room."

Miranda told Sarah, "My father left a few moments ago headed to the Orr plantation. He is planning to offer to buy the three of them for a profit for Mr. Orr. He had sixty pounds with him. He knows Orr probably only paid at most fifteen pounds each. So he is offering twenty each. I just pray Orr is not a spiteful man and will accept the offer." Her family had grown very attached not only to Robert's new found cousin but also to James and John Maund Philpott as well.

Sarah sighed and rubbed her tired eyes. "Let us pray so," she said. "Miranda, James has told me he loves me, and he wants to marry me."

Her dear new sister smiled and embraced Sarah. "Does your father know?"

"No, but my mother does. Do you know where they are in hiding?" Sarah asked.

"No. Father does not want us to know in case we are questioned, we can be entirely truthful in our answer. I am sure it is somewhere on our property or your father's, somewhere close by."

"I hope they are all right. James was so happy being free from starvation and physical punishment, and it breaks my heart that he is having to go back into hiding and possible captivity!" Sarah felt tears spring into her eyes.

Miranda hugged the girl again tightly, trying to console her.

"How is my brother?" Sarah asked. "Does he know?"

"Edward is fine. I think he senses there may be something between you and James, just from the talk he's heard from John. But I don't think he is opposed to the two of you being together, even if James is a convict," Miranda told her. "How did your mother take the truth?"

"I was just so upset, so I told her everything. At first, she was horrified, but as I told her about James being whipped and why, she softened."

"Why *was* he whipped?"

"He was teaching a young slave boy how to read and write. He thought he was doing a good, worthwhile thing, and when the overseers found out, they whipped both him and the young boy!" Sarah began to cry again. "James wept telling me about it!"

"How do you think your father will feel about your relationship with James?" Miranda asked her.

"At first, I could tell he was not happy finding out the truth about the three of them being convict servants. You know, after your aunt Nellie was assaulted by that convict servant my grandfather had bought, my father and my grandfather vowed never again! But when Father returned from sharing the news with everyone last night, I overheard him tell my mother about James being whipped and how he felt the three of them were not like the convict servants his father had once owned. He seemed in favor of Robert making an offer to buy them back from Orr. He even said he would pray about it."

"Your father is a good man, Sarah. And I feel that James is a kind and good young man. He reads the Bible, you know. He only stole the cloak, he says, so he could come to America and find his brother."

Sarah nodded. "I know. Francis. In North Carolina."

"If you marry, will you go with him to North Carolina?" Miranda asked.

"I will. But first, we must pray James's freedom can be bought."

Robert Wade arrived at the large Orr plantation and met with Thomas Orr in his study, and he opened truthfully. "John Thomas is my cousin, and he came to America to be with me and my family. The other two are with him. They took off from my place when they heard of the advertisement for their capture." Robert paused but added, "I do not know where they are now."

Orr looked at him and said gruffly, "I think you are lying. So I take it you are not here to turn them in and receive a reward."

"No, I came to see if I could make a bargain with you and buy them from you."

"I thought as much. You know, I paid fourteen pounds apiece for them."

"So you would be willing to sell them to me for, say, twenty pounds each?" Robert asked.

"I might be. I have already had to purchase more servants to replace them. I had to get indentured ones, so they will cost me more in the long run. I think one hundred and twenty pounds might do."

"One hundred and twenty? I am only prepared to pay sixty!"

"But, Mr. Wade"—Orr smiled maliciously—"I lost six servants the day those three escaped."

"I cannot help that the others ran off as well!"

"The six left together. I was only able to shoot the last three who escaped." Orr glared at him.

Robert Wade was incredulous. "You murdered three men and expect me to pay you for that?"

"In the eyes of the law, they were mine to do with as I saw fit," Orr smirked.

"That is inhumane!" Robert Wade shouted.

"Mr. Wade, if you want to buy the freedom of those lowlife convicts you call family, the price is one hundred twenty pounds. Otherwise, I shall have you arrested for stealing my servants."

Robert paced the study, thinking. He was land rich compared to the rest of the family, and his farm had done well. But he had just invested most of the cash he had in planting his new crop and paying his workers. If he went back and got the other sixty pounds, he would not have anything to live on while waiting for this upcoming harvest.

He turned to Orr. "If I pay you this sixty, will you let me return with the other part of the money?"

"We must get that in writing, Mr. Wade. I assume you can sign your name, or do I need to get a witness or two?"

Robert wanted to punch this pompous man in his face. "I can sign my name, Orr. I am also as good as my word. I will sign an IOU."

As the paperwork was completed, Orr told Robert, "Tell those sorry thieves they better stay in hiding until the last of this is paid. Because if I do not get the rest of the money from you by this date, you will have authorities there by the next morning to take them in!"

James was beside himself and was pacing around the inside of the cave they were holed up in. He missed John Hussey so much. He had grown close to the two other Johns, but they did not seem to see him as a little brother as John Hussey had. He missed Sarah most of all, however. He lay on his blanket and replayed the last scene in the clearing over and over in his mind, and it caused him a great aching in his heart. He recalled the touch of her fingers on his back and the way it felt to kiss her. *She is so beautiful,* he thought until he was almost crazy. He thought of her auburn hair and green eyes and her sweet smile. *Angels will assist you,* he heard Captain Duggar's voice like a benediction being offered upon him. He knew that Sarah was one of those angels who was now in his life. *Lord, You led me right to her! Thank You, Lord, and bless me that this all may be resolved and we can be together! Please don't let her hate me for being a convict. I know I should have told her the truth from the beginning, but I was afraid for her to know. Please soften her father's heart that he may see me for who I really am.*

Later that evening, Robert showed up at the cave with food and more supplies for the three men. He brought the things into the cave and set them down, and the men gathered to hear the results of his visit.

"This can't be good news if you've brought us more food," John Thomas began.

Robert sighed and shook his head. "The man is a heartless brute! I paid sixty pounds, but he wants sixty more!"

"One hundred twenty for three of us? That's robbery! He only paid twelve pounds for each of us," James interjected.

"He told me he paid fourteen!" Robert exclaimed. "And he called *me* a liar! He says he lost six men the night you ran off. That bastard says I must compensate him for the three he shot and killed!"

James clenched his fist and slammed it against the rocky wall inside the cave where he stood. "John Hussey *is* dead then! God, how will I ever forgive those evil men!" His voice broke with emotion.

Robert touched James on the shoulder and continued, "I signed an IOU for the other sixty. I must have it paid in five days, or he will have me arrested for stealing you all. And if they find the three of you, you will be taken to jail, as well."

"Do you have the other sixty, cousin?" asked John Thomas.

Robert nodded slowly but then added, "It is all I have to live on until harvesttime, though. I will have no way to pay you or to pay for other things."

"Well, as for me, if you buy my freedom, I will forego any payment from you and will work for free as long as I can. I will even give you back the little I have saved thus far," John told Robert.

James insisted, "That goes for me as well."

John Maund Philpott nodded his assent.

Robert agreed to go pay the man the next day, but he knew it still was going to make life difficult in his household financially.

"Do you think it is safe for us to leave the cave then?" James asked.

"I don't know. I'm not sure I trust the man. He said to tell you to stay in hiding until the debt is paid," said Robert.

John Thomas told the other two, "Then we will stay here until my cousin returns tomorrow."

That night, James had a very difficult time sleeping. When he did manage to fall asleep, he dreamed of John Hussey. James dreamed he was marrying Sarah and John Hussey surprised him and showed up at their wedding. James was so glad to see him, he wept and embraced him. As he was clutching his friend, someone shot John, and James could feel the wound in his own body. The last thing in his dream was the sound of Sarah screaming hysterically. He awoke the two Johns as he sat up and yelled from his frightful nightmare.

The next morning, Robert passed the Bowman farm on the way to Orr's place. He stopped to talk to Peter about what had happened thus far. Sarah could see her father and Robert conversing in the front yard and nervously paced in the parlor until her father entered.

"Judith"—her father came in to tell his wife—"Robert is off to pay the last sixty pounds for their freedom. Do you know that Orr had the nerve to ask for one hundred and twenty pounds? He insisted that he lost six servants that day and demanded Robert pay for them as well! He admitted shooting the other three and says Robert must pay to replace them! If Robert doesn't pay, he will be arrested for stealing his property! Oh, this is just *one* of the evils of slavery, I tell you! Men who feel justified in murdering humans with no fear of repercussions!"

"And greed is another, so it seems," Judith said, shaking her head.

Sarah was so saddened to hear about the deaths of the other three men confirmed. She had heard James speak so highly and warmly of John Hussey. She knew James had hoped that John might have been only injured and escaped. If only she could be there to comfort him, wherever he was.

She went first to her mother with what she proposed to do.

"Mother, when they are no longer in hiding, may we have them over for dinner? They will be famished and craving a home-cooked meal! Mother," she said, "I want Father to get to know James. I want him to see him for who he really is. Please say we can have them over? All three, and then Father might not yet suspect how much I love James but be warmed up slowly to the idea?"

Mother agreed. "How about tomorrow night? If Robert is able to free them today, it would give them a chance to clean up a bit and get a good night's sleep."

Sarah gave her mother a hug and went to her room. She took out paper and made a beautiful invitation to dinner, just as she'd promised James. He might be concerned or ashamed that she was now aware that he was a convict, and she wanted this to be her way of letting him know she still loved him no matter what.

She walked to their cabin. Sarah had never been there, and she walked up to the tidy front porch and left the invitation just outside the doorsill. Part of her wanted to be there herself waiting with open arms to greet him. But she felt awkward and turned and left.

Sarah, Judith, and Lucy spent the next day roasting a goose and baking two different kinds of pies. Sarah took extra time with her hair and her dress for that evening, donning the lovely blue gown she'd worn for Edward and Miranda's wedding.

When the three arrived, Sarah watched as her father embraced the young men, welcoming them home. Her heart sank a little as James did not seem to be able to bring himself to look at Sarah. It was as she'd feared. He felt shame, and she was worried that he was going to let this affect their plans for marriage. She tried to smile during dinner and engage them in conversation through which her father might see that James was educated and faith-filled, but this whole ordeal seemed to have taken its toll on James's usually convivial personality. Near the end of dinner, it was John Thomas who at last spoke up and thanked the Bowmans for a wonderful meal, and he apologized on behalf of the three of them.

"Mr. Bowman, we feel great regret that we were not totally honest about our being convict servants. You are clearly a forgiving man for inviting us over. But we, all three of us, want you to know that we are sorry we were not open and honest about being convict servants. I guess I was afraid my own cousin might not welcome me into his home. Stealing is wrong, and we all know that. We did what we did only so we could come here to the colonies and start a new life. I, myself, thought of selling myself as indentured, but I was worried that no one would take me on since I have no training. And James there," he said, nodding to the young man, "he did not even steal! The young man he was with, he stole the cloak, but they went along with the punishment together."

Sarah's father cleared his throat to indicate he was ready to reply to their humble admission. "Thank you, John, and I want you all to know I plan to have you continue to work for me whenever Robert doesn't need you. You never wronged me, but I appreciate your honesty."

John hung his head. "I shouldn't be saying this, but I don't know when we will be able to do such a thing. We will be working for Robert for free for a while. He used the last money he had to buy us our freedom. He has nothing left to live on 'til harvesttime. We're even going to give him back what he's paid us so far to make up for what he's done for us."

Sarah and James made eye contact for the first time that evening, and her look was one of understanding, and his was a look of relief that perhaps she now understood his inability to follow through on their plans.

"I had no idea. Thank you for letting me know," Peter Bowman said quietly. They finished dessert, and the three stood to leave. Her father shook hands with each of them and told them, "You have suffered enough. We will work this out."

As they headed out the door, Sarah hesitated and then said, "Father? May I?" Peter Bowman nodded and motioned toward the front door and smiled. Sarah smiled at him and ran out of the door.

"James!" she called after him.

He turned to her and embraced her there under the moonlight. "Sarah!" he breathed into her ear. "I am so sorry."

"I know. And I do not want to hear those words again. Everything is going to be fine."

"Only I can't offer to marry you now. I have nothing for you. It will be a long time until I do. Now we are indebted to Robert for our freedom."

She took his face in her hands and told him, "I love you. I will wait for you as long as it takes."

He kissed her sweetly. "I don't know what I'd do without you, Sarah." He looked at her with sad eyes. "John Hussey *is* dead," he said as if she may not have heard.

She suddenly knew that was another reason for his quiet mood at the dinner table. "That awful Mr. Orr will pay for what he has done! If not in this life, surely in the next!" Sarah said, touching his face gently.

They kissed tenderly. "I love you, Sarah. I meant what I said. I love you, and I do not want to live without you. It just may take longer for me to be able to become your husband."

They kissed again without speaking of when they might see each other again.

Inside the house, Peter Bowman went to his wife and embraced her from behind, kissing her on her ear. "Judith, my dear. It seems you will have to forgive me for breaking a personal oath I made many years ago."

Judith turned around and looked quizzically into her husband's face.

"I think I am about to purchase three convict servants."

CHAPTER 12

*P*eter headed over the next day to see Robert Wade. He had one hundred twenty pounds with him. He found Robert out near a field not too far from his house.

"Good morning, Robert!" Peter said, slowing down his horse as he approached his friend.

"Peter, how are you?" Robert asked, taking the horse's reins as Peter dismounted. He tied the reins to a nearby fence. The two gentlemen walked together back toward the house and sat on the front porch.

"We had the lads over for dinner last night," Peter began. "A very enjoyable evening. They are very apologetic for not being completely open and forthright about being convicts, although in my eyes, what's really the difference between an indentured servant and a convict servant? Both receive brutal treatment and are considered property. I think the lads have learned their lesson. It was kind of you to buy their freedom."

"Well, Peter," began Robert, stunned at Peter's seeming change in attitude about convicts, "to me, the difference is that convicts are guilty of breaking the law. I do not condone theft, and I'm sure you do not either. But there is forgiveness for us all, we hope. You seem to have had a change of heart, Peter. It was difficult for me to find out because, as you know, my sister was assaulted by a convict servant many years ago. I am just relieved to know that my cousin and his friends are sorry for the thefts they committed."

"I feel the same way," Peter Bowman replied. "Robert, I have a proposition for you. I need the use of the lads to work for me, and they say they cannot as they are indebted to you. I am willing to buy them from you."

Robert shot a look of disbelief at Peter. "What? You who vowed to never own another human?"

"Well, they are rightfully yours now, but I surely could use their help. He doesn't know it yet, but I am planning to take on James as an apprentice, teach him carpentry, in addition to learning to be a farmer. I can teach the others as well if they will agree to it. If you are willing to part with them. Maybe they could continue to live in your cabin? I'd be willing to pay you extra for housing them. Say, one hundred twenty pounds?"

Robert realized then that the men had shared his financial hardship with Peter over dinner. He hung his head and said, "I'm sorry. They should never have told you how it strapped me for cash to buy their freedom. I had no idea Orr was going to be such a bastard about the whole thing. Peter, I have land I can sell, you don't have to—"

"Robert, I really don't mind. Besides, I think James West is going to be my son-in-law!" he said with a smile.

He stood, clapped Robert on the back, and handed him the one hundred twenty pounds from his pocket. "And I think they will still have the time to help you on your farm if you need them."

Robert embraced Peter and said gratefully, "I don't know how to thank you, Peter."

Robert went to get the three from the fields where they were working and called them over.

They all gathered under a tree to shade themselves from the broiling late June sun. Robert began, "Lads, this is your new owner." All three, but particularly James, were agape, shocked over the news, knowing how Peter Bowman felt on the topic of human trafficking.

Peter took over at this point. "I know that you know how I feel on the issue, but know this. I have purchased you in order to free you. I would like, however, to know if you would be willing to become apprentices. James, I thought perhaps you could learn the trade of carpentry from me. It's my true love, and I think it is a skill you could benefit from the remainder of your life. That and farming. The offer stands for all three of you."

James was smiling widely at the thought of being much closer to Sarah now. "I'd be honored, sir!" he said.

Peter went on, "The three of you could continue to live in the cabin if you like. I am willing to pay your rent. Finish out your day here, and you two can decide about the apprenticeship idea and let me know tomorrow."

Peter clapped James on the back and bid farewell to a grateful Robert Wade.

James stood there and watched Sarah's father walk away, and he prayed in his mind and heart, *Lord, thou art so good! What blessings thou hast bestowed on me!*

Peter made his announcement over dinner that evening of what he had done. Sarah leapt up from the table and ran and embraced her father. "Oh, Father! Thank you! I love you so much!"

That evening, James walked all the way to Sarah's house, as the sun was getting low in the sky. When he tapped on the door, Sarah was just finishing helping Lucy with the dinner dishes. She saw James and raced out to the porch. They embraced and sat on the cedar bench.

"I take it you know what's happened, what your father did?" asked James.

Sarah could not contain her excitement. "Yes! He told us tonight! I'm so happy, James!"

They sat holding hands and watching the sun head downward over the Bowman property.

"As soon as I think the time is right, I plan to ask your father for your hand in marriage," James told her, and he kissed her gently on the lips. "I love you so much, Sarah. You are my angel, you know?"

"And I love you, James. The last few days have been just awful! I don't know what I'd have done if you had been taken back to that terrible place!" Sarah exclaimed.

"Sarah, I cannot believe that I am truly a free man! I know I should have never become a convict servant. I should never have gone along with such a plan. But it's brought me here—to you. I feel as if God had this in His hands all along. I can almost picture myself being drawn along on a thread, from Wales to London, from London to Baltimore, from Baltimore here—all on a thread—the Lord just leading me along to the one person I was meant to find and to love."

Sarah nodded in agreement. "That makes me think of my mother's favorite proverb: 'Trust in the Lord with all thine heart, and He will direct thy paths.'"

"Indeed," James said, squeezing her hand and kissing her lips tenderly again. "He has surely directed my paths. I'm so thankful for that."

The two parted reluctantly that evening but with so much happiness and hope.

For the next two weeks, James and John Maund Philpott came at sunup each morning to begin their apprenticeships. John Thomas had decided to continue to farm with his cousin and to also help out the Bowmans when needed. James and Sarah now ate most meals together, and her family drew closer and closer to the young man she loved.

One day, while in the barn watching James put the finishing touches on a beautiful cedar chest, Peter Bowman said to him, "It's quite a wonderful example of woodworking skills, lad. I would like to purchase this from you. I intend to give it to my daughter for her trousseau."

James shot a surprised glance at Peter Bowman. "You know, don't you, sir? If not, I will tell you now. I love your daughter. Sarah is a heaven-sent angel to me. I would be honored if you will allow me to have her hand in marriage."

Peter reached out and embraced James. "And I would be honored to have you as my son-in-law."

James pulled back and wiped a tear from his eye. "If you don't mind, sir, I would like to find her right now and tell her the good news."

Peter nodded and James ran into the house to find Sarah writing in her commonplace book.

James took her by the hand. "Sarah," he said, leading her to the front porch, "I need to talk to you. I have news that you might want to record in your book." After they were seated on the bench, James smiled and kissed her. "Your father has agreed for us to marry!"

Sarah threw her arms about his neck and exclaimed, "Oh, James!" They kissed again and again, three short kisses, followed by a long, deep one that left them breathless.

"Oh, James, when?" she asked.

"I don't know, but I say it can't be soon enough for me!"

Three weeks later James and Sarah were married on the front porch of the Bowman home. Sarah's mother also re-hemmed Miranda's gown and altered it a bit to fit Sarah. Judith also adjusted one of Edward's suits to fit James, who bought a new white shirt and a new pair of dark shoes for the occasion. Priscilla wore her sky-blue gown again and Judith, the pale green. She and Lucy prepared more pastries for the after-wedding party. Father Callahan again presided over this ceremony. Tears were shed by everyone for God's great blessings, but no one shed more tears than Sarah and James knowing the providential way He had intervened in their lives.

Edward and Miranda had offered the use of their new farmhouse as a honeymoon cottage for two nights, after which James and Sarah would occupy Edward's old room in the Bowman house. Edward and Miranda went to stay with Robert and Meggie for those three days and two nights.

When they entered the farmhouse early that evening, James and Sarah were touched by the flowers left in several vases around the house. They found that Miranda had left them fresh baked bread, cheese, and fruit on the table. Past the cozy sitting room, they stepped into the bedroom, finding the bed freshly made with a handmade quilt on top. On a side table were more flowers. Sarah felt tears filling her eyes as she glanced at James whose eyes were glistening as well.

"How sweet of Miranda!" she said. "What a wonderful gift."

James nodded. "The best part of their gift is we can be totally alone with each other. I love you, Sarah."

The setting sun shone golden rays into the bedroom, and James walked over to the one window and pulled the curtains closed, darkening the room somewhat. He was still wearing his new suit and Sarah, her wedding gown. She had worn her long auburn hair up in an elegant way for the wedding, and James had never seen it like that. "My princess," he said smiling deeply into her beautiful green eyes.

He took her hand and pulled her to him, holding her tightly about the waist. Their mouths met in a sweet then hungry kiss. James stopped and removed his jacket and stepped out of his shoes. "Dear Lord," he prayed aloud, "I have been dreaming of this moment since that day in the clearing, and I don't know if I'm quite ready for this." He went to her, sliding his arms about her waist again and kissing her first on her left ear and then her cheek. He found her neck and kissed her there, weakening her as he heard her moan softly.

Then he found the pins in her hair and helped her remove them. Once her hair was down, James ran his fingers through the auburn waves. He gently turned her around and laughed softly. "Let's see. How *do* I get you out of this thing!"

Sarah laughed and shuddered as she felt his fingers loosening the clasps that closed the gown along her back. The gown fell to the floor, and Sarah stood there in her new cotton slip. James pulled the new white shirt quickly over his head and stood there in his black pants. Sarah touched his strong, sculpted shoulders and drew him close. In the next few moves, Sarah's slip was over her head and on the floor by the bed, and James finished undressing. They stood by the bed, their bodies close together as they continued to kiss. James stopped and reached over and pulled the quilt down to uncover the white muslin sheets. Gently, he held her, and as they kissed more and more hungrily, he lowered her to the soft bed and lay over her. James was very tender and gentle at first, and hearing her sighs, he loved her even more deeply.

With the intensity and desire they felt, the act only lasted a few minutes as James satisfied them both much too quickly. He was still over her breathlessly, kissing her. They lay there speechless yet breathing heavily. James finally quipped, "Give me a few minutes, love, and I will be with you again!"

The young couple blissfully enjoyed their night together and were so grateful that this was just the beginning. By early morning, it felt as if they had been together all their lives and never with anyone else. Sarah was dozing off and on, and at one point, she awoke with James kissing her back and neck.

"I have one important concern," James whispered into her ear as he pressed himself close behind her. "How shall I ever work again? How am I ever going to appear normal again to those around us?" He laughed and they were together yet again.

The next time Sarah awoke, it was late morning, and she was facing James's back and was startled to see the still red scars she had forgotten about. It made her do two things. She said a silent prayer of gratitude that those scars represented a past that was not to be repeated. And then she slid closer and gently kissed his back, marks and all. "I love you, James West," she whispered.

In the bright light of midday, they loved each other again. When they were truly awake and feeling spent, they realized they were hungry for nourishment. Sarah put on her slip and James, his pants, and they went into the living and dining area, the only other part of the house, and treated themselves to Miranda's bread and some of the fruit.

James smiled at her over their meal and joked, "Now, Sarah, what happened in that bedroom is *not* to be written about in your commonplace book! And no sketches from that imagination of yours."

"I don't think I imagined that." She smiled back at him. "Don't worry, some things are sacred."

"Speaking of sacred, isn't God's plan for the human race to reproduce magnificent?" He grinned winking at her.

The two of them did not emerge from the house until late afternoon on the third day, and it was with great reluctance that they took their things and headed back to the Bowmans. As they walked over, Sarah commented, "Isn't it something to realize that all married couples feel as we feel. Miranda and Edward, my parents, your parents—all experienced, for a first time, the same things we just experienced!"

James clasped her fingers and leaned over and kissed her cheek as they walked. "I refuse to admit that anyone else has ever experienced anything that incredible."

They quickly settled into Edward's old room, but James was already speaking to her about a place of their own. One morning of many that the couple was late joining the Bowmans for breakfast,

Peter teased James, "When you first agreed to be an apprentice for me, you were here most days before sunrise. Now you live in my house, and you are late getting to work every morning." He smiled and made both Sarah and James blush. But Peter and Judith were so pleased to see their happiness.

Even though Miranda and Edward had married a few weeks ahead of Sarah and James, both women began to experience the same symptoms about the same time. The telltale sign of nausea gave them both reason to think they might be expecting. Even with the misery, they both were thrilled to think that they might have babies together. Judith began to get anxious remembering the stillbirths of her first two children, but she did not choose to share her concerns with the girls.

One morning about a month later, three months after the wedding, Sarah awoke with severe cramping and bleeding and sobbed for James. She had miscarried their first child, and James was as distraught as his young wife. Judith tried to console her daughter with her own truth. "Sarah, I've never told you, but I lost two before I carried the two that died to full term. It is a sad reality of life that when bringing a family into this world, you often must experience grief as well."

That night in bed, James held Sarah close to him. "Do you remember what I said about this magnificent plan of God's to bring more humans into the world? Now we are seeing the downside of this plan. I am so sorry, Sarah. I caused this! I loathe myself for being so demanding of you! I will keep my distance for a while now."

"Well, you will have to, James, until I am able to try again."

"I think even then I will stay away. I cannot bear to see you in pain!"

"James, I *do* want a child!"

"I know, Sarah, but I just can't bear to be the cause of your pain!"

As he held her, she felt his tears mix with hers. She told him, "Mother lost two before she lost the two buried in the cemetery! She just told me today."

"It seems a cruel thing to do to people. I know He is God Almighty, and I revere Him for being who He is, but this is just painful."

Sarah began to regain her strength, but it was made more difficult by the fact that Miranda continued to swell with child. Miranda did not gloat, as Sarah knew she would not. Miranda knew that she risked losing her child even up until birth as Judith and her own mother Meggie had. Miranda tried to downplay her own happiness for Sarah's sake, and Sarah forced herself to express joy for Miranda and Edward.

By the time Miranda gave birth to a healthy son, Sarah was expecting again. She began to grow, and she would sit and hold Miranda's little angel Peter Clark Bowman and project to holding her own bundle of happiness. She was feeling movement now, and often as little Clark squirmed in her arms, she would also feel movement within.

It was about this time that James got a letter from Francis. He had not even told Sarah he had sent a letter just before the wedding to Francis West in Granville County, North Carolina, and by some miracle, it had reached him at last. The response spoke of so much joy to hear from James and to know he was in the colonies and about to be married. Francis and Christian had added a daughter and another son, and the farm was doing well. He said he would gladly help his brother start a farm of his own.

James shared the letter with Sarah but told her that they would wait a bit with a child on the way. Plus, he was still working and saving money; the time was not right just now for many reasons. Sarah was relieved as she felt she needed her mother and Miranda with the impending birth.

Sarah noticed later in her pregnancy, when she was very large and uncomfortable, that two days had passed and she had not felt the baby move and kick within her as she had the last few months. Miranda tried to alleviate her fears. "Clark did that very thing just before he was born. It was like he finally just did not have any more room to move about!" she said with a laugh. Judith, however, was worried about the birth of her second grandchild.

Late one night, Sarah began to go into labor, and after a day and a half of agony, she gave birth to a beautiful daughter. Judith was by her side as was James, shedding tears. Sarah announced to them both that she wanted to name her Hannah. Her mother looked at her and said, "Sarah, do not name the baby just yet. Darling, do you notice the faint blue tint about her mouth? Notice how her chest moves in and out trying so hard to breathe? Will she nurse?"

Sarah had tried to feed the new baby, but she did not seem to be interested.

Judith went down to Peter and fell into his arms. "I am so afraid this little one is not going to make it! She can't seem to breathe well, and she's not feeding. It reminds me of our first baby. Oh, Peter, it grieves me so to see my daughter suffer! I wish I could take away her pain."

Sarah continued to rub the baby's back as she cuddled her, returning her to the breast time and again. She stroked her cheek as she had seen Miranda do when Clark was more interested in sleeping than eating. James did not leave their sides and was there early the next morning when Sarah watched their daughter draw one last, tiny breath. She shook her lifeless baby and began to cry. "No! James, no! She can't be gone!"

James fell to his knees by the bed and sobbed with his wife. "God!" he cried out. Peter and Judith came running to comfort them. Judith held and rocked her daughter as Sarah clutched hers. *There is just no way to prepare a soul for losing a child*, Judith thought. They allowed Sarah to hold her for the next few hours, and James found himself drawn back to the early morning on board the *Tryal* almost two years ago when he had watched poor Alice Roney fling herself over the ship's railing along with her deceased baby. He had never shared that story with Sarah and certainly could not now. He was just as empty and spent as Sarah was; the two were motionless, silent. There was no desire for food, for love, or for anything except for something that could miraculously end this pain. James wanted to be dead with his daughter, and he knew Sarah felt the same.

An hour later, James and Sarah were still motionless on the bed, Sarah lying down cradling the baby in the crook of her arm; James sitting upright beside her, in shock. Sarah did not say a word as her mother came and took the babe from her daughter's arms and stood at the foot of the bed dressing her in a tiny white gown and cap. Judith was weeping softly and kissed her little angel grandchild.

"Sarah," she said, "your father has dug a grave for this little one. Do you have the strength to come with us to bury her?" Sarah looked at her mother as if she were speaking to her from a place miles away. James too looked disbelievingly at Judith. "James," she asked, "do you want to take your daughter downstairs? Sarah, do you want to kiss her goodbye?" She held the baby over to Sarah's arms, and Sarah leaned over and kissed the cold, still face. James seemed to wake as if from a sleep and got up off the bed. He took the baby from Judith's arms, leaned over, and kissed the top of his wife's head. "Sarah," he said, "I'll be back, my love."

He carried his daughter's body down the steps and accompanied Judith to the cemetery where he and Sarah had had their first real conversation. Peter was down there, sweating profusely from digging the grave. James realized that his father-in-law was crying as well as perspiring. "I am sorry, Father," James told him. "I should have done that."

Peter led the three of them in prayer and produced a simple wooden box that he had hastily constructed. Judith had with her a knitted blanket, and she helped James wrap the baby in it and assisted him in putting the small, doll-like figure into the makeshift casket. Peter put the lid into place, and James carefully lowered it into the ground. He stood, and as Peter began to shovel the dirt into the hole, James took the shovel from him, finished the job, and then fell to his knees, crying at the foot of the new grave.

CHAPTER 13

For the next two months, Sarah and James shared the same bed but slept apart, back to back mostly. Sarah seldom spoke to anyone and usually in one or two word responses. James was worried about her, but he knew he wasn't doing well either. He refused to work in the barn with the carpenter's tools, as any contact with wood and carpentry brought to mind the box that held his daughter under the ground. No one heard James mention God at all, and Peter and Judith were both worried about the young couple. At first, Judith was all about just letting them have time to heal. Miranda stayed away; the one time she did come visit with little Clark, Sarah just looked away, too pained to see her dearest friend's child, her own little nephew.

Judith talked to her daughter at last telling her she understood her pain but that it was time to move on and live again, that it wasn't healthy to keep living in this fog of grief. Sarah had not picked up her commonplace book to record anything about this loss, nor did she visit the cemetery to see where the little one was laid to rest. She ate little, and Judith worried she was going to shrivel up and die as her infant had done.

Peter approached James in the fields one day where his son-in-law lived and worked in silence, pounding the earth and digging at it as if he were trying to exact revenge on God Himself. Peter convinced him to go walking with him that day, and they wound up back in the clearing by Cuckold Creek where James had realized he loved Sarah.

"We are concerned about you, son. You *and* Sarah. Believe me, I know. You cannot tell a person when to start and stop grieving. Judith and I lost two babies. But you have to reach a point when you both decide that life must begin again. You must find happiness again."

James looked at him blankly. "I have come to learn that happiness is not real. It is a facade. I'm at the point that I feel almost foolish that I spent so much of my life believing that God really cares. He does nothing but play cruel tricks on humans. He allows evil men to torment good, decent humans. He Himself seems to delight in turning on good human beings, especially those who believe in Him."

"James, I know how you feel. After losing two babies to miscarriage and then having two stillborn children, I felt lost and bewildered as well. I watched my wife grieve, and I was grieving too but from afar. But at last, we made a conscious decision that we did indeed love each other. We knew we still wanted to have a family. And we did! We had Edward and Sarah and Timothy and Priscilla and Hannah!" Here, he paused and his smile faded. "And then we lost Timmy and Hannah! Yes, son, I know about grief! But losing faith in God is not how you handle it! God does not walk away from us, but if we walk away from Him, we will never be happy! I know and believe in my heart that I will be with my children again someday. This earth is temporary, but heaven is our eternal reward! James, you and Sarah need each other. You need to be grieving together, in each other's arms and with God in your lives."

James simply looked at his father-in-law and said, "I cannot love my wife again. I cannot bear to run the risk of hurting her or myself like that ever again!"

"But, James, can you imagine living like *this* the rest of your life? With this emptiness? That is no life! There is no life without risk. Every day is a risk. Life is filled with both sadness and happiness, son. It is part of the human experience, and there is nothing we can do to change that. What we *can* control is how we react to the difficulties life hands us."

James lay in bed that night with his back to Sarah once more. He thought he heard her crying. She had not cried much at all since the baby's death. She had basically just been in shock, not feeling anything. He felt her turn over, and for the first time in months, he felt her slide her arms to touch his back. Without turning over, he whispered almost coldly, "What are you doing, Sarah?"

With more emotion than she'd shared since the baby died, she said, her voice shaking, "I need you, James!" He turned to her and held her close, just to hold her, not for anything else. He felt her tears and felt her body trembling. Before he knew it, she was caressing him, kissing his neck and chest hungrily, and it made him angry.

"Why are you doing this to me?" he cried out, sitting up in bed. "Why do you want more misery?"

"I don't want more misery. I am sick of misery! I need to be loved, and so do you!"

In an instant, they were one and sharing passion as two that had been starving and thirsting and had just found manna and an endless wellspring of good water. They finished with tears on their faces, telling each other how sorry they were that they had left the other to grieve alone.

The first thing they did in the morning was walk out to the cemetery hand in hand. It was the first visit Sarah had made since her baby had been buried there. As they approached the grave marked with a third rock, Sarah's hand flew to her mouth as she saw scattered across the little mound clusters of tiny forget-me-nots. She and James wept and held each other. By afternoon, Sarah was out there again, this time with her commonplace book in hand, pouring out her heart in writing about the little girl they had lost, and she sketched her angelic face as best as she could remember.

That afternoon, Judith told Peter, "I believe our prayers have been answered, husband."

She told him about seeing the two of them holding hands in the cemetery and about how Sarah was out in the cemetery writing in her book.

"They are turning that corner," he agreed. "It is such a hard thing to cope with, as you know, dear. Let us continue to pray, but I think they are on the road to healing."

The next day, Sarah walked to Miranda and Edward's house. She would not tell a soul, but she loved visiting that house and remembering where she and James had loved each other for the first time. Miranda was surprised to see her but welcomed her in. She had little Clark on her hip. Sarah immediately began to cry and apologize. Miranda interrupted and told her she had no need to be sorry.

"Sarah, dear, I understand! I have ached for you! I knew it was the worst kind of pain for you to see me and Edward with our little one!" The two hugged affectionately. Miranda continued, "You should not feel guilty about grieving your daughter. We have been worried about *you*, though. You are so thin. But I knew, I just knew, healing had to begin soon! Praise God that it has! I can see it in your face, even with the tears."

"The worst part of it," said Sarah, "was that James and I turned away from each other. He was petrified to touch me ever again. With the miscarriage and then losing the baby, he did not want to ever see me hurt again. *He* did not want to ever hurt again!"

"But, Sarah, it is part of life. Death is, I mean. Granted I have not had to go through it like you have, also losing your little sister and brother, but I know it is part of God's plan."

"James and I have become one again, but I worry about his relationship with God. He had so much faith before this! It is one of the things that made me love him so much! Throughout his voyage here, the hard times on the plantation, he felt it was all part of God's plan to find me."

"He will find his way back to God. God will see to that."

Within a few months, Sarah recognized the signs again and knew she was with child. She told her mother first and also told her she was almost afraid to tell James. She prayed about it and felt strongly as an answer to her prayer, that this time all would be well. And she felt that the Lord had given her this sweet confirmation of the spirit in order to help James deal with his anxiety over the new baby.

One night after they had loved each other in a very sweet way, she told him the news.

"James, I am expecting another baby."

"I knew it. I have noticed your sickness. But I also knew it here," he said, touching over his heart. "How are you, Sarah?"

"I am at peace. It is time for a blessing, James. I feel it is time for something good to come our way."

"I hope you are right, my love. I need something to restore my faith that I have missed. I have not been a faithful servant, and I have suffered so much with unhappiness. It has been wonderful to feel your love again, but I have lost so much understanding and belief when it comes to God. I have not been a Job, that is for certain."

"You are a husband, James, and yes, a father. You are human. That's what is amazing about God is His power to love and forgive even when we think we don't deserve it."

As soon as Sarah said those words, James remembered Captain Duggar and how he had spoken basically the same message to that poor man. Grieved and troubled by the death of Alice Roney, Captain Duggar was very penitent, and James had been the one who had convinced him of God's grace. Now he felt so far removed from that faithful young man who had helped another to see the light just three years before. Before he knew it, he was weeping and telling Sarah about Captain Duggar, and the story of Alice Roney and her stillborn baby spilled out. Sarah then began to sob.

"Oh, James! I know her pain! I think it was God Himself who kept me from doing something as dreadful! You witnessed that, James? How awful for you!"

"But now, three years later, I know her pain too," said James, "and I understand Captain Duggar's as well. Sarah, I am sorry. I should never have told you about Alice Roney. I never wanted you or anyone to know what happened to that poor woman. It was dreadful."

"James, I'm glad you told me. It's a vivid reminder of how great despair can become. I was on that path these last few months. Feeling completely hopeless. Not wanting to live. I want to live now. I want to have this baby. I feel it is going to be a son. And he is going to be healthy."

"My love, I wish I was as certain as you."

James stayed anxious throughout Sarah's pregnancy, but she seemed self-assured that all would be well. She felt that God had given her this confidence, and she was trusting Him.

When Sarah went into labor this time, it was daytime, and James was in the barn with Sarah's father. James had returned to carpentry, and it had become his love as well. He loved farming and seeing the "fruits" of his labors, but the same thing applied to the trade of carpentry. He had just finished a new cradle for this baby. Lucy was the one who brought word late that morning that Sarah had begun labor, and James dropped everything he was working on and hurried to his wife's side.

What Sarah had not told James was that her pains had actually begun during the night. She had not wanted to ruin his sleep or add to his anxiety any sooner than need be. She had been in labor most of the morning also, with her mother and Lucy by her side. She would only permit them to tell James when she felt she was close so he would not have to endure the extra hours of agony and waiting.

By the time James reached her side, she had begun to push.

"She is doing well," Judith reassured James with a quick embrace.

James was there about thirty minutes when Sarah pushed one last time and out came a red-faced, dark-haired baby with a lusty cry. It was a boy, and James broke into sobs as he saw Sarah take him to her breast and witnessed his son hungrily feed on her.

"Praise God!" he said with tears streaming down his cheeks. He wiped them and kissed his wife and pulled up a chair next to their bed to watch the miracle. Sarah, her mother, and even Lucy were crying happy tears as well.

"He looks so much like you, James," Judith said, getting together things to wash and leaving the two alone. "Congratulations," she added on parting.

"He is well?" James asked his wife.

"I think he is doing incredibly well! His color is good, and his appetite is wonderful," she said, smiling.

"You, my love, are a prophetess," James said, kissing her on the top of her head.

"I wouldn't go that far, James. I felt a little inspiration is all."

"What should we name the little fellow?" her husband asked.

"I know what I *want* to name him," Sarah said.

James gave her a questioning look.

"I want us to call him James, after his father."

James looked at the baby as if he were seeing him for the first time again. "My son!" he said grinning and beaming with pride.

Sarah made a point of asking for her commonplace book and proudly recorded his birth thus: James West born May 2 *Anno Domino* 1769. Underneath that date, she began to sketch his cherubic face and dark hair. Words began to form in her mind later as she was feeding him, and Sarah wrote a poem called "Baby's Breath." She was very proud of it, as it was the first bit of poetry she had written in years.

Baby's breath comes gently from small, pink lips.
Baby's sleep closes tiny, squinched eyes.
Baby's hair is soft, warm fuzz.
Baby's breath escapes in precious little sighs.

Mother's arms are filled with sleeping child.
Mother's eyes and ears guard through the night.
Mother's lips kiss smooth, pink cheeks.
Mother's love fills home with the warmest light.

She shared it with James that evening and watched as he read it and closed the book. "Sarah, you are amazing. What a sweet moment to capture. That's what you do best, you know? You capture moments in words and in drawings that would be forgotten otherwise. What a gift!"

Little James, as he soon came to be known, grew quickly. Sleepless nights and crying spells were exhausting for the couple but so welcome because the baby was very normal and healthy. James became more vocal again in his praise and love for the Lord, especially in gratitude. Peter let James voice the family prayer on occasion, and it was a blessing to hear the young man's faith blossom again in his prayers. It was clear that James had been truly humbled.

Judith and Peter loved both their grandsons, but since this one lived in their household, they became very attached to little James. As he began to crawl and then walk at ten months of age, Peter particularly delighted in chasing the youngster around and hearing him squeal. James too spent every spare moment he could with his son, loving the experience ever so much.

Sarah mentioned Francis in North Carolina from time to time, but James seemed so content there at Swan Point that he did not seem in a hurry to go see Francis. The letter from his brother had brought contentment for him. Life was good. His son was healthy and strong. He was working and saving money, but he was not sure when he would go to North Carolina to see his long-lost brother. He once talked about going on horseback for a faster trip, just him alone, and then returning, but he could never bring himself to leave his new little family.

When little James was about fifteen months old, Sarah felt the familiar signs of nausea and tenderness and prepared herself and James for the possibility that another little West was going to be added to the household. Everyone was thrilled as Miranda and Edward had just had a daughter named Maggie, a variation of her mother's name, Meggie. Maggie was born just before little James's first birthday. Family gatherings became such fun with Clark and little James toddling and running around and now "princess" Maggie in the family.

One night at dinner, the Bowman dining room table was crowded with family and grandchildren. Everyone was laughing and talking and enjoying being together when suddenly, without any warning, Peter Bowman looked as if he were about to address his wife, and then he fell out of his seat at the end of the table and onto the floor.

"Father!" Edward called out. James and Edward both reached him at the same time. There was no heartbeat, and just like that, Peter was gone. In an instant, happiness became shock and sadness. The little innocent ones looked about them and did not understand the immediate weeping and expressions of disbelief.

The girls went to Judith at the other end of the table and helped her to her chair in the parlor. James and Edward moved Peter's body away from where he was half under the table and laid him out closer to the parlor. Lucy and the girls quickly cleared the table of all dishes.

The clinking of plates and the sounds of intermittent crying could be heard all through the downstairs. Lucy retrieved a clean white sheet and covered the table, which would soon become Peter Bowman's bier.

All the members of the family were crying so hard and were in such shock over how quickly he left this earth. With the fresh sheet in place, James and Edward lifted Peter's body and lay him on the table.

"He looked at me as if he were about to speak to me," cried Judith from her chair, still in disbelief. "Then he was gone! It must have been his heart! He has complained some lately of feeling pressure in his chest. I just cannot believe he is gone!" Her sobs continued.

James went over to console Sarah, but she saw that he was in as much need of consolation as she was. "I loved him like a father!" James said in his wife's ear, embraced her, and wept openly on her shoulder.

"I know! He loved you so much, James!"

Lucy left to tell Robert and the rest of the Wades, and soon, they were all in the house. They gathered in the living room not far from where he lay.

"I'm not sure what to do," Judith told them, wringing her hands.

James spoke up, "I will see to his casket, Mother."

Robert and his sons said they would dig his grave in the morning—another grave, a growing cemetery. Edward said he would contact Father Callahan to come perform a ceremony at the home.

James worked on the casket all through the night by lantern light, stopping to cry for his beloved father-in-law from time to time. He was so sad to think that little James would never remember his Grandfather Bowman nor how much the man had loved his grandson.

The next afternoon, on a beautiful autumn day in late September, the Bowmans buried their fifty-two-year-old patriarch. That night after the funeral, Sarah curled up next to her husband in bed and told him, "It is time to go to North Carolina. I have had enough of death."

When they approached Judith about their intentions, Sarah begged her, "Please, you and Priscilla come with us!"

Judith said she could not, that she was not up to the trip. She assured Sarah that she and Priscilla would be fine. "We have Miranda and Edward. Robert and Meggie will help us as well."

"Mother, I feel so guilty going off and leaving you so soon after Father's death."

"Sarah, poor James has put off going to see his brother for years. He came in 1765. It is now 1770. He needs to go see his family. I am going to go ahead and give you your part of your inheritance. Plus, I want you two to take our wagon and our horses. Take the feather mattress from your bed, and you can put it in the back to sleep on while on your trip. It will be more comfortable than just quilts."

James used the skills taught to him by Peter Bowman to build a small canopy over the back of wagon, and he covered the frame he built with an oilcloth. Sarah cried as she packed, but she did not think she could bear to stay there and watch her mother grieve. Her parents had always been such a close couple.

The day before leaving, Sarah and James left little James with Judith and Lucy, and they headed out to see Cuckold Creek one last time. First, they walked to say farewell to the two Johns. James wanted to thank them, especially John Thomas, for helping him escape and gain his freedom and for being the key to his meeting Sarah. "If not for your kinship to the Wades, I would have never come to Swan Point and met Sarah," James told John Thomas. They also paid one last visit to Robert and Meggie Wade, thanking them for all they had done, embracing them both before heading to Cuckold Creek.

The sun was going down as the two stopped and sat upon the flat rock that had been the place they had come to know and love each other. James kissed his wife tenderly and said, "So much has happened here, Sarah. My life has totally changed because I met you."

He placed his hand on her belly not yet beginning to swell again with their new child. "I was so wrong to lose faith. I am very thankful to God for all my blessings. And having you in my life is the greatest blessing of all."

On the morning they were to leave, Sarah took one last visit to the graveyard by the house. She touched the six stones, including the one that marked her father's new grave. She said a last farewell to

Hannah, Timothy and her angel baby. Finally, she plucked a small bouquet of forget-me-nots and pressed them into her commonplace book.

Miranda, Edward, and the children came to see them off, and Priscilla cried as she handed little James back to her big sister. Sarah embraced Edward and whispered, "Please take care of mother." He assured her he would. Next, Sarah gave her mother a kiss and a very long embrace filled with tears. Then as Sarah and Miranda held each other tightly, Sarah knew in her heart that she would never see her sister-in-law or any of these beloved people of Swan Point again this side of heaven.

CHAPTER 14

James and Sarah left Swan Point the first week in October, and they knew it would take six weeks at least to get to North Carolina. The trip would have been much shorter had there been a bridge spanning the Potomac, but there was none. They would have to head up toward Baltimore and then head west and then south. James was not worried. Thanks to the kindness of Sarah's mother and her deceased father, they had extra money, plus what James had saved up for the last few years. He knew that if the weather became too cold, they could stop at an inn, if they could find one.

James was beginning to get excited thinking of being reunited with his brother Francis for the first time since 1758. His thoughts went back to that last trek they took to their uncle's home in Fishguard and how Francis had planted in his head the exciting images of what he thought America was going to be like. James had left in 1764 headed to London, and here it was 1770, and he was finally getting around to going to see his brother. Now Francis had a wife and four children, perhaps another since the letter he'd received.

Sometimes, they let little James ride up front, but a great deal of the time Sarah rode in the back with the baby so he had a little room to play. They did not bring furniture as James knew he could build and buy most of what they needed. They would be staying with Francis until they had built their home on the land adjoining Francis's farm. They did, however, have with them Sarah's large cedar chest that James had built sitting on top of the mattress and off to the side. Inside the chest were their clothing, some quilts, Sarah's commonplace book, and some food. James had also brought many of the tools from Peter's barn that he used for carpentry. There was space for both Sarah and little James to nap. At night, they removed the cedar chest and placed it under the wagon, and all three slept in the back of the wagon under the cover James had crafted. James slept with his rifle close beside him, just tucked under the side of the mattress.

One night, about two weeks into their journey, just as they had started on the main thoroughfare that led south, they found an inn and decided to take a two-day break from the wagon. James got someone to help him bring in the chest, and he took his rifle in so he could keep it safe. They relaxed and enjoyed a few wonderful meals, some of the scenery in the area, and the joys of a comfortable bed.

Finally, they headed back on the road continuing their trek to North Carolina. James promised Sarah that they would do that same thing at least one more time if they could find another nice inn along the way. It helped break up the trip, and little James seemed to enjoy the family time, having his daddy do nothing but play with him. The horses needed the break as much as they did, James thought.

They were blessed with heavenly weather and only ran into a few sprinkles during the first part of the trip. October was a gorgeous, golden month to be traveling out in the open space headed south. Sarah looked over at James a great deal, wearing his black knit cap she'd made for him, his long, dark curls underneath and down his neck. She loved the man so much it almost made her hurt. He would turn and smile at her a lot during their travels, and she would smile back and squeeze his hands as they held the reins. Sometimes, he would just reach over and gently touch her knee. *How blessed I am, Father!* she thought. *It's days like this that You give us that help us deal with the painful memories and deaths of those we love.*

Many days later in Virginia, they found another inn and decided to rest for another two days. They were becoming weary of the riding and bumping day in and day out. Sarah's belly was swelling a little now, and she found herself getting fidgety and restless, as was little James. She had read the entire book *Robinson Crusoe* and read much of the Bible while little James napped. At first, this had been a great adventure, but now they could not wait to finish the remaining third of the journey. They were sad this time when the two-day rest was over, and James was tempted to extend the stay another day and night, but he knew he wanted to hurry and get to their new home and see his brother whom he had not seen in twelve years. Besides, it was beginning to get very chilly nights as November was upon them, and the weather could be very unpredictable, so they headed back out after their two-day stay in Virginia.

One day, James began to observe the markers Francis had told him to look for as he neared the North Carolina border, and they knew they were traveling the last fifteen or so miles. It was getting colder, even during the day with the sun shining brightly, and Sarah and little James were spending many hours cuddled up in quilts in the back of the wagon. James and Sarah stopped one last time, just about two or three miles from where Francis's farm was supposed to be. They had gone as far as they could, and then it grew so dark, James could no longer see the road. That last night out was very cold, and the three of them huddled under all the quilts they had with them, anxious for morning and the last bit of the trip to be complete.

When the sun was barely up, James headed out again, leaving Sarah and little James still sleeping in the back. He found the land marks which told him they had reached the road to the left that led to his brother's farm. About two miles down the lovely road surrounded by deep woods and occasional fields, with the rising sun's rays slanting through the trees, James approached a farmhouse that he knew in his heart belonged to his brother and his family. He pulled the wagon into the yard, bringing the horses to a stop. He pulled his gloves off and rubbed his hands on his wind-chapped cheeks.

"Sarah, we are here!" he called to his wife. He went around to the back of the wagon to help Sarah and little James, whose eyes looked sleepy still, down to the ground. James scooped his son up into his arms, and together, they walked up the four steps and onto the porch of the house. The door opened before they even knocked, and they were greeted by a raven-haired lovely lady they knew to be Christian West. Instead of a smile, her face wore a look of disbelief. She stared at James, then Sarah, before her gaze went back to James, her eyes wide.

"I'm James," he said smiling at his lovely sister-in-law. "Francis's little brother."

At last, she smiled just a little. "Please come in! I would have known you anywhere. You look almost like Francis's twin!" she said. A welcome blaze was in the fireplace, and the room was almost toasty. A young lad about the age of ten came from a room in the back and stopped dead in his tracks when he saw James. He did not speak but only stared.

"Mother," he finally began.

Christian interrupted him, "James! This is your uncle James and your aunt Sarah."

"And *your* little cousin, James," said James, motioning to the child in his arms. James smiled and said, "I think we need to have some new names in this family!" tousling the hair on his nephew's head with his free hand.

Francis's little James was now looking straight up into his uncle's face. He began again, "Mother, he looks just like Papa."

Christian had her hand to her mouth, and there were tears glistening in her large brown eyes.

"Yes, he does, son."

"So where *is* my brother, my twin?" James asked with a grin.

Christian seemed to have a hard time finding her voice. "James, I don't know how to tell you. Francis is—he passed away a few days ago."

James's reddened, chafed face almost blanched with disbelief. "No!" he said. Sarah took little James out of his arms and watched her husband lower himself into a nearby chair. He put his head down and buried his face in his hands. The tears began, and he looked up at his sister-in-law and asked in a broken voice, "What happened?"

"I am so sorry for you to find out this way. I had no way to reach you." She stooped down next to James's chair and placed her arm consolingly around behind his back patting him gently. He looked into her eyes, and there were tears on both of their faces.

He asked again, "What happened to my brother?"

"He was out picking grapes from some wild vines we have in the woods behind us. A large snake, a copperhead, was in the tree where the vines were attached. It struck out and bit Francis on his face and neck. He made it home and was very sick for three days, and then he died. We are still in shock. We buried him just two days ago."

"I can't believe this! I waited too long to come see my brother, Sarah!" he said, looking up to his wife who was also weeping. "If we'd not stopped at those two inns and had those few days of rest, I could have seen him alive!"

"James," Sarah said softly, "do not do this to yourself."

"She's right," Christian agreed, standing up and offering Sarah a seat. The other children came out of the back of the house, and Christian introduced them all. They gathered around James staring in amazement and with sad faces seeing how much he looked like their deceased father.

"I want to see his grave," James said, wiping tears, rising from his seat.

"Of course," she said. "We buried him in Malachi Frazier's cemetery. He is our neighbor. They have been wonderful friends. He and Sally are about your age."

"Sarah, do you mind?" James asked.

She motioned for him to please go ahead with Christian out to the cemetery. She would stay with all the children and get to know them better.

Christian grabbed a heavy shawl, and she and James walked arm-in-arm down a path that twisted to the left onto the next farm over and into a clearing. This graveyard reminded James of the one at Swan Point except there were more stones. He remembered Sarah's words from a few weeks ago. "It is time to go to North Carolina. I have had enough of death." Now Francis was dead. He would never see his brother's face again. Christian walked him over to a new mound of dirt with wildflowers still strewn over the top. There was a large rock to mark the spot. She let James stand there and grieve; she backed off a few paces and stood behind him as he faced his brother's grave. James spoke to Francis in his mind but not aloud. He knew that would happen at a future date.

Francis, I am sorry I did not come earlier! I cannot believe you are gone! Fresh tears spilled onto his cheeks, and he brought his hand up to his mouth to stifle what he knew would be a loud sob, but there would be time for that later as well.

Christian approached him again after a few moments. She surprised him by saying, "You need to know. The children and I are leaving." He turned to look at her, shocked. She went on, "We are going with my brother's family to Tennessee. We leave next week. James, Francis has willed you half of this property, but I must sell the other half, including the house."

"I will buy it from you. We have with us our inheritance money from the death of Sarah's father. He just passed away two weeks before we left Maryland."

"Oh, I am sorry!"

"Yes," James told her with a tone of sarcasm. "We felt the need to go because we were tired of death." New tears slid down his cheeks, and he wiped them away.

She hugged him about the shoulders. "I am sorry, James. But yes, I would love to sell to you. That would be a blessing." She paused then said, "Can I ask a favor? And I know I don't really need to ask."

He looked at his brother's widow. "Anything."

"Tend his grave for me?"

He nodded. "For as long as I am alive."

As they turned to leave, James glanced about and had the sudden question pop into his mind. How many more graves would his family add to this cemetery?

For two weeks, both families lived in tight quarters, but they were busy helping Christian and her children pack. They were leaving all the furnishings behind for James and Sarah. Christian was even leaving a beautiful cradle, which Sarah would need in the spring.

One evening when they had been there a little over a week, Sarah, James, and Christian were sitting around the fireplace, and the children were asleep. Christian said suddenly, "James! I had forgotten! You had a visitor here almost three years ago! A friend of yours stopped by to see if you were here yet."

James looked quizzically at her. "A friend of mine? Here?"

"Yes, he came by and said last he knew this was where you were headed."

"Who was it?"

"His name was Hussey. Yes, John Hussey. He said you met in London."

James jumped to his feet incredulously. "John Hussey is dead! We were told he died!"

"Yes, he said as much. Said he was shot running away from a plantation. He said you and some others escaped, and he and two others were shot and left for dead."

James was pacing the room, running his hands through his hair trying to figure it all out.

"Tell me all that he told you! Did he say where he was going? How did he make it out of the woods after being shot? Why did he not come join us at Swan Point? He knew that's where we were headed!"

"He said the three of them were left for dead and one *was* dead. I believe his name was Roger. The other man was not too severely wounded, but John was unconscious. He had no recollection of it, but was told that the other man, Samuel—I think his name was— flagged down a boat and got them both aboard, and they crossed the Potomac. John said when he woke up, he was in a stranger's farmhouse in Virginia!"

"Dear God!" James said unbelievingly. "John Hussey, still alive! Sarah, can you believe it? We were told the three of them were dead!"

Christian continued, "He told us the whole story—about stealing the red cloak, being in jail, crossing on the ship, going to the plantation. He said he thought of you as his little brother. He could not get over how much you and Francis favored one another. When he left here, he said he was headed west."

"John got to meet Francis," James said, shaking his head. "He saved my life. Kept me alive through all that. I didn't know what I was doing. I regret that, though, you know. The stealing part. I never should have gone along with that plan to steal. But John Hussey was a good man."

"He showed up right after Francis had gotten your letter," Christian added, "and so we were able to tell him about your marriage to Sarah and that you were living at Swan Point. Francis had already responded to your letter, and he meant to send you another to tell you about John, but he never did. Your letter seemed to indicate you would be coming in the near future, so he thought he would just tell you about it once you arrived."

James was silent, letting all this information sink in.

"Once he was in Virginia," Christian continued, "he said he couldn't risk going back to Maryland. So after he healed, he headed this way, hoping to find you. He stayed here for two days. All he told us was he planned to go out west. After he left, about a week later, two of our children got very sick, and we just forgot about John Hussey. And as I said, Francis thought you would be coming and he'd tell you then."

"Life can be so strange," James said, still standing in the middle of the room. "I guess I did tell him several times in great detail about where you and Francis lived. But how will I ever find him again? Heading west could mean Kentucky, Tennessee. He could be still in North Carolina."

James had a hard time sleeping that night and kept Sarah awake as well. He finally turned toward his wife and whispered, "Sarah, would you make me a promise? And this is to be even after my death. I do not want my children to ever know about my time as a thief, being in jail, nothing from that part of my life. I do not care if they think that I was an indentured servant and that I volunteered to come over and work. But I do not want them to ever know that I was a convict servant. It never should have happened, and I am ashamed of it." She kissed him and said she would never reveal it. When James did sleep, he dreamed about John Hussey. If he had not gone too far west, perhaps he would return for another visit.

James and Christian went to the courthouse in the county seat the next day to take care of all the paperwork involving not only Francis's death but also his will and the sale of the house and the land to James and Sarah. The town was called Oxford and was almost five miles from their new home.

The day Christian's brother arrived with his wife and two children, Sarah held her sister-in-law in her arms and thanked her for everything. Once again, Sarah knew she was embracing someone whom she knew she would never see again in this life. Francis's children held onto James, and one even cried, "I want to stay with Uncle James!" As they pulled away, Sarah and James waved and then turned and walked up the steps to the porch where Sarah sat in a chair with her little one on her lap. James stood with his foot in the bottom of the railing, facing away from his wife, watching the wagon disappear around the curve of the dirt road. He was still very despondent over the horrible timing of everything: losing his brother and missing by a few days being able to see him alive. It also grieved him that he had not known John Hussey was still alive. He was punishing himself emotionally knowing now that they should have gone back to see if John, Roger, and Samuel were still alive and needed help.

"We are so blessed, James," Sarah said, trying to lift his spirits. "Winter is coming, and we have a house to live in. A very nice house built by your brother."

He turned to look at her. "You know I would much rather be planning to build my own house with Francis helping me and the two of us being neighbors and growing gray-haired together."

"I am so sorry, James."

"It seems God is not through tormenting me yet."

"James, you've got to stop seeing God as your tormentor," she said gently but firmly.

"It is very hard sometimes not to be angry at my Creator."

"What is that verse," Sarah offered. "'The Lord giveth and the Lord taketh away'?"

"I know it's not supposed to be my place to say, but I think He has taken quite enough from me."

"You're right, it is not our place to say what He can and cannot do."

"Give me some time, Sarah. I'm just still in shock and grieving is all."

He went into the house slamming the door behind him. The next time she saw him, he was heading down the path to the cemetery for the first time since the day they had arrived. He was gone a long time, and she began to worry. After almost two hours, he reappeared.

As he stepped into the house, Sarah said, "I'm glad you are back. All I could do was wonder how many copperheads there are in those deep woods."

"Don't you worry. I will kill every copperhead I run across out there, even if I have to use my bare hands."

He went over and hugged and kissed her gently. "I did not mean to worry you, Sarah. I had a long talk, out loud, with my brother. I felt him there in the graveyard waiting for me. I don't think he'll hang around, but we had to have words. I also spoke to God. And I did an awful lot of weeping. You know what a crybaby I can be." His tone was gentle again.

Sarah said, "You are such a good soul, James. You have a tender heart, just as my father did." Then she went on, "James, I am going to miss your sister-in-law so much! I came to love Christian these past two weeks. I know Francis must have loved her very much. She is such a beautiful woman with a great faith."

"She is lovely. I'm sure he cared for her very deeply—and the children."

Sarah was quiet, and James came up behind her and slid his arms around her expanding waist and pulled her close. "But you are much more beautiful, my angel," he said, kissing her on the nape of her neck. "As a matter of fact, doesn't this house remind you of Edward and Miranda's place just a little? Hmm? What do you think?" He kissed her again teasingly on her neck. "Where is little James?" her husband asked. "Is he napping?" She nodded, smiling. "Why don't we go spend some time together? It has been a while, wife."

She nodded again and turned and led him by the hand to their new bedroom.

Chapter 15

*T*heir first winter in North Carolina proved to be difficult for James and Sarah, and they found themselves thankful for their neighbors Malachi and Sally Frazier. Their respective homes were less than a quarter of a mile apart, and this made for a close association.

The Fraziers, as Christian had told them, were about the same age as James and Sarah, and they had married when Malachi was eighteen and Sally, sixteen. Both couples were now in their twenties; the Fraziers had two daughters, Isabel and Rachel.

Malachi's father William had just passed away the year before, as Sarah's father had. His widowed mother named Martha lived with them on the farm. It was the Fraziers who invited them to their church, which Malachi's father had helped build about ten years before. It was a small Presbyterian church in a beautiful clearing about a mile away from James and Sarah's new home. There were already tombstones in the back of the church of a few of the members who had passed away in the last decade. They were going to build an addition to the small frame church in the spring and do renovations to the sanctuary, and Malachi was glad to hear of James's carpentry skills and his willingness to assist in the planned construction.

For Christmas, the two families celebrated together, enjoying a very touching service at the church and a festive meal at the Frazier home. Some of both Malachi's family and Sally's came that Christmas day. The house was filled with people enjoying the season along with wonderful aroma of hams, roasts, and pies and tarts of all kinds. Sarah and James were made to feel as welcome as family. Except for missing his brother, James felt at peace being here with Sarah and his son.

Sarah was thrilled to receive a letter from her mother with news from Swan Point as well as holiday greetings. Miranda and Edward were expecting another baby. Sarah must have read her mother's letter twenty times in the first two days after getting it. She sent her mother a long letter in response, telling her all about arriving in Granville County and getting settled in. She, of course, told her mother the tragic news of getting there and finding Francis had just died. She shed a few tears knowing her mother was going through her first Christmas without Peter, and she expressed those feelings in her letter, but she did not let James see her cry. Sarah felt very dedicated to trying to keep James's spirits up. His faith had wavered in the past, and she wanted nothing more than his happiness. She was comforted by his faith when he was strong and assured.

It was just after the New Year that little James became very ill. It reminded Sarah of the fever her whole family had endured that resulted in the deaths of Timothy and Hannah, and it put fear in her heart as little James was so small; he would not be two until May. He developed an awful cough that was also reminiscent of the illness the Bowmans had endured. James went to the Fraziers to see what they could offer. Sally and her mother-in-law had herbs that they instructed James how to use to make a steam pot and told him how to cover the baby's head so that he could breathe the moisture. Sarah's mother and Lucy had made something similar for all of them when they were sick, but Sarah could not remember what herbs they had used.

The steam helped little James's cough somewhat, but his fever persisted. Malachi's mother sent word that Sarah should keep using a damp cloth, wet with tepid water, not cold, to bathe the child with so as to bring down his fever. She also sent an herbal tea she had made to give the baby to keep his strength up as he would not eat. Sarah tried not to let James see her fear that came as a result of losing Timmy and Hannah, but it was hard to conceal. She knew that he too was concerned.

One day, however, when she thought James was out of the house, she knelt by little James's bed and prayed in tears. *Father, please, Dear Father, bless my son! Please do not take him from me and*

James! We love him and we have already been through so much loss of loved ones! I know, Father, that it is in Your hands and we ask that Thy will shall be done. With that, she broke into sobs and fell onto his little cot. James appeared at this moment and shouted, "No!" as he came into the room. He rushed to the baby and picked up his warm, feverish body and was relieved to see the boy's eyes open and look up at his father.

Sarah came to her feet, startled and apologetic. "James, I am sorry! I did not mean to make you think—I was just frightened and praying he would get well is all! I have been so worried!"

James moved his son to his shoulder and pulled Sarah to him with his other arm, kissing her face. "I understand, Sarah. You know that I could not bear the thought of losing my son either."

When little James woke up the next morning and indicated to his mother that he was thirsty, Sarah felt his face and knew his fever had broken. *Thank You, Father!* she acknowledged. She continued to tend to his symptoms and made sure he drank broth and continued to drink tea as he completed his healing. He had a little irritating cough that eventually improved, but she knew the worst of it was over. Over their meals for the next few days and nights, James continued to offer his gratitude to God for allowing little James to get better.

At dinner one night, James announced to Sarah that he and Malachi were going to a meeting at the church. A local militia, the one to which Malachi belonged, was getting together to discuss training. They were considered part of the local law enforcement as well, and James was going to attend and decide if he wanted to be part of this group.

He found out at the meeting that this was the same group who would fight if another war came to the colonies. Captain William Burford was in charge. James did not like to think of war, but the talk was very strong that night about all the things King George had done to take advantage of the colonists, including all the taxes he had levied against them. The thing that seemed to make the men angriest was the fact that these things were being done without allowing any person from the colonies to go to Parliament in England and represent the needs and interests of the colonists. James agreed to join the militia that night, signing his name to a roster.

On the way home, he and Malachi spoke as they slowly rode their horses side by side. James asked his new friend, "How much do you share with your wife about the militia? I want Sarah to know I've joined, but I do not want her worrying about my safety."

Malachi said, "Well, Sally's father and brothers are members of other regiments who fought in the last war. I just stress to her that we are not at war and that we are basically peacekeepers."

"I heard a great deal of talk tonight," James said, "from those who own slaves. I don't know how you feel, Malachi, but I am very opposed to any humans being owned and mistreated. That's just the kind of man I am."

"I agree with you. I have no slaves. My father owned some indentured servants, but they became free under him. There is a great deal of division, James, in ways of thinking around here. We have people right here who are loyal to the crown. They refuse to be part of a militia. Then there are those who are slaveholders who feel themselves to be better than those who do not own slaves. They look down on those of us who don't own them, thinking it's like sour grapes, the old fable. They think we are opposed because in reality, we cannot afford slaves. They have had slaves for so long in their families that they truly feel privileged."

"And justified in beating and whipping them," James added.

"Exactly. I know what you are thinking, James, but there is no way to form militias based on philosophies. One thing about humans is we all are different—different religious beliefs, different political beliefs."

"I know," said James. "I, for one, though, pray that one day, all men will be truly free. I heard a gentleman say tonight that the British should set us free as God gave to all men the right to be free. I am thinking, are not these dark-skinned people who are owned and whipped humans who want to be free as well?"

"I don't know how that's all going to turn out," said Malachi. "But right now, they are not viewed by most people as being humans."

"It's sad," James replied. "I think one day, this nation will pay for having the blood of these people on their hands. Just look at the Egyptians who paid for enslaving Moses and the children of Israel."

The two men parted ways. James headed home with a heavy heart remembering the injustices done to him and a young man named Calvin.

Winter continued with two significant snowfalls, but the families managed to keep warm and fed. Sarah was looking forward to April as she had calculated that to be the month this new baby would come. She talked to Sally and the older Mrs. Frazier about possibly assisting her with the birth of this child. They both agreed to help if needed. One could keep the other three children occupied while the other would help Sarah.

Finally, at the end of April, Sarah began to show signs of delivery and sent word by James. James and Malachi both had been in their respective fields planting for days, but on this day, James stayed at home. Both women came in the wagon with the children, and at first, they tried to shoo James back out to the field, but he held firm and stayed at the house. He was concerned with his wife's welfare, and after the death of their first baby, he was not taking any chances of not being there for her.

Sarah told the ladies about losing her first daughter who had lived only a day and a half and explained that as being the reason James wanted to be close by. He ended up entertaining the children, taking them in the yard to play in the spring sunshine while Sarah labored inside with the two women by her side.

Sarah had a very quick, easy delivery of a beautiful girl, rosy and screaming her entrance into the world. James came running with little James when he heard her cries. Sarah was all smiles as she cuddled her new daughter, bringing her to her breast to feed. James and Sarah both knew that a baby's cries and ability to latch on and feed was the key to life. They had had the baby who could not breathe properly, whose color was not good, and who did not want to feed because of that struggle to breathe, and that baby had died in their arms. It was always going to be a relief to James and Sarah to hear the sounds, see the color and vitality, and watch the hunger of a healthy baby.

The ladies took things that needed to be washed, wished them both well, and gathered the children. Malachi's mother had brought dinner for them and a pie. Sarah expressed her gratitude to the two of them before they departed. Sally's mother-in-law was now "Martha" to Sarah, and she had already, in both this birth experience and with her aid in helping little James get well, become a second mother to Sarah.

Sarah was so happy to have James there, and they loved hearing little James say the word *baby* and point to his new sister. As Sarah continued feeding her, James got little James down for a nap. Then he came back into the room and took the sleeping baby in his arms, and he sat in the chair by their bed holding her tenderly. At last, he spoke, "Sarah, I've a confession to make. I am in love with another woman." He grinned at her. "I have another princess in my life. What should we call this little beauty?"

"Husband, since you are so smitten, I will let you decide," Sarah said with a smile.

"I'd like to name her for my mother—Susannah. How's that?"

"I love it. And I love her. And I love you." He stood with the baby in his arms, went over to the bed, and kissed Sarah on the lips, first briefly then deeply.

"I love *you*," he told her, as he stood swaying the baby. "Thank you for blessing me with such beautiful children. I feel guilty, you know. You amaze me. You willingly endure hours of terrible pain in order to bring these children into the world. I do not understand how you do that."

She smiled up at him again. "This is why. They are such blessings."

"I endured seven lashes of a whip and felt it was the end of the world," he said, continuing with his expression of guilt. "You go through hours of agony and count it as a blessing," he told her.

"That is simply because what happened to you was evil and unwarranted. Having a baby, even the pain, is part of God's plan. Kind of like death in an odd sort of way."

"Sarah, do you ever wonder why God's plan is filled with pain, just like evil is?"

"My, aren't you full of questions that cannot be answered today? Perhaps you need to go see Reverend Polk?" Sarah asked with a smile.

"I'm not doubting God, Sarah. I just think it's a point worth discussing."

"I am exhausted, my dear. I will say, though, that I think God wants us to appreciate the good things, and if we did not have the bad things to compare them with, we would not know how *good* the good things really are." Sarah leaned back on her pillow and closed her eyes. Then she opened them again. "James, could you bring me my book? I want to record Susannah's birth while you are here holding her."

He retrieved the book from the cedar chest while still holding his new daughter.

Sarah took her quill pen, dipped it into the ink bottle, and wrote the name "Susannah." Then she looked at James and said, "I don't think I even know the date of today. I know we are in April, near the end."

"Today is the twenty-fifth, my love."

Sarah recorded April 25 *Anno Domino* 1771 after Susannah's name. James lay the baby in the cradle that was next to their bed. Little James was napping too, and James crawled into the bed next to his wife and just lay watching her doze. *Lord, I am so blessed*, he prayed.

Spring was beautiful that year. The farm was flourishing under James's labor, and Susannah quickly became a constant source of joy and delight for the family. Little James was talking now, and he loved his "Sudie." They grew even closer to the Fraziers, and James added them to the list of blessings in their lives.

One hot summer day, James was working out in the fields. He had a small crop of tobacco and an even smaller cotton crop. This was in addition to the garden of corn, peas, and beans that they needed to eat. Malachi had a few hired hands, and they often came and helped James with his work as well. If this crop did well, James was going to begin hiring a few workers, perhaps some of Malachi's nephews. He was blessed as Francis had already established a fairly successful small farm, so James had the barns, outbuildings, and tools he needed.

On this sweltering day in late July, James was alone in his garden working hard and perspiring heavily. He had removed his shirt, and Sarah could see the sweat dripping off his back from where she and the children were on the back porch of the house. His back was also getting red from too much sun. She noticed that his faded scars had a little color again from the sun and stood out, almost as red as they had been when she first saw and touched them. Sarah took the children inside and went in to get some water for her husband. When she came back out, she saw Malachi in the field with James. She walked out with the water and greeted Malachi warmly and handed James the container of water she had drawn. He drank thirstily and expressed his gratitude, "Thank you, my love!" and smiled and winked at her.

A few nights later, James and Malachi went by horseback to another militia meeting. During the meeting, the same vocal member who James knew to be a prominent slaveholder in their part of the county dominated the meeting with a "sermon" about how God had given all men a right from birth to be free and that they needed to use that as a basis for insisting that the colonists should be free from British control.

James had never spoken up at meetings before, but he chose the end of this man's speech to say, without standing, "I am wondering if you truly believe that all men are made by God to be free. Isn't it bothersome that you are speaking for freedom for all men and yet you enslave other men?"

The man who had just seated himself after his lengthy oration rose to his feet again. Malachi looked at James with a worried expression. The plantation owner cleared his throat and said, "Master West, I think you need to be reminded that you are in the colony of North Carolina. I am not accustomed to having to explain the necessity of slaveholding here. You are new here. I don't think you understand that you, as a small farmer, have no grounds for speaking out at our meetings, and you certainly have no right to judge me when I am doing what most successful plantation owners are doing here in the colonies. Perhaps you are filled with envy that you cannot have the wealth that comes from being a successful plantation owner. Perhaps you are one of those men who think they are a better Christian than another. You, sir, with that attitude, will never be successful or very respected in these parts."

James stood. "I feel neither envy nor self-righteousness. I just know that I believe slavery is wrong. I believe all humans should be treated with respect. I have seen with my own eyes the abuse of slaves in the colony of Maryland where I come from. I came to Maryland by way of Wales, and I never saw slavery there. Class division is one thing, but slavery is altogether another issue. I just feel in my heart it is wrong."

The gentleman moved closer to James and was now pointing with his finger not too far from James's face. "There has been slavery on this earth since the beginning of time. Perhaps you should rethink serving in a militia that may one day rise up against the mother country. You sound almost like a loyalist to me. Perhaps you should return to Wales, Master West."

The meeting ended on that awkward note as the room filled with both small farmers and those who owned a few or many slaves began to clear. James and this defender of slavery gave each other one last look of contempt. One could see the obvious division as a few of the men came over and patted James on the back as he and Malachi exited the church. Most stood around the gentleman plantation owner and praised him for being so eloquent.

As Malachi and James mounted their horses, the sun was almost gone from the sky, yet the humidity was still heavy and stifling. The two rode slowly side by side, and James began, "I fear I should not have done that. I am a peace-loving man, and I hope I haven't made any enemies tonight. It was not my intent."

Malachi spoke up, "I am guessing you have a very personal interest in the subject of slavery, James."

James said nothing and Malachi went on, "I don't mean to step into a space I shouldn't be stepping in, but a few days ago, when we were in your garden together, I couldn't help noticing scars upon your back."

Malachi was afraid now that he had said too much as James did not respond at first. Finally, James said, "My friend, just know that I was an indentured servant in Maryland. I ate, lived, and worked with the slaves on a plantation south of Baltimore for a short time. Indentured servants were whipped just as slaves were whipped. I was whipped for trying to befriend a young slave and teach him to read and write. I will never believe that slavery is right."

"I am sorry to hear that, James. I know that must have been hard on a man as kind as you are."

"Thank you, Malachi. Being a servant is how I got to America so I could find my brother. My uncle was living when Francis left Wales, and he knew someone who owned a ship and was able to help Francis get a job on board. When I decided to come here to look for Francis, I did it on a whim, and my uncle had passed, and I had to come over as a servant. But I am educated, and I don't say that to boast, but it has made it more difficult to deal with servitude. From my vantage point, it's the slaveholders who seem the most unlearned."

"I've only known you since last year, but I know you are not a pompous man, James. You are a humble servant of God."

"Now don't be making me sound like a saint. I have had many moments when I lack faith."

"So have we all, James."

"You, Malachi?"

"Indeed. Life isn't easy. We are only human."

James explained, "I seem to have the hardest time when I lose a loved one. The death of my newborn daughter nearly killed me and Sarah. Coming all this way to finally find my brother and discover he died a few days before I got here was torture. Watching a young slave boy being whipped because he wanted to learn gave me enough anger to last me the rest of my life. It's the unjust things that make me waver sometimes. I am certainly no Job."

"I know how you feel," Malachi said. "I just try and remember all the men in the Bible who had failings and weaknesses and wavered in their faith, only to become some great men of God. Think of Abraham who had the concubine Hagar. Or David after Bathsheba. What about doubting Thomas? He became a devoted disciple of our

Lord. Peter *denied* knowing Jesus *three* times and became the rock upon which Christ built His church!"

"For someone who is just a year older than I am, you certainly have a great deal of wisdom." James smiled, as the two of them stopped for a moment in front of Malachi's farm.

"So do you, my friend. Thank you for sharing what happened to you in Maryland. These men need to know."

"I would appreciate it if you would not share it. What you saw on my back."

"I will certainly respect your wishes, James. Good night, friend."

Chapter 16

"Sarah, you've got to see what Malachi just showed me!"

Sarah stepped out of the bedroom holding Susannah whose diaper she'd just changed.

"You know we live here by what they call Mountain Creek? There is actually a mountain, well, a very large hill! We've been here all this time, but we can't really see it from here, and we can't see it from church or the road to Oxford. But if you go back on the road we came in on months ago, it's off in the distance, and we live behind it! The lay of the land keeps us from seeing it from where we are. But just come, get the children dressed. I want you to see it."

It was a Sunday afternoon in October, and the sun was shining and illuminating the beautiful colors on the trees. James helped Sarah onto the wagon seat and handed her Susannah. He swung an excited little James onto the seat next to his mother and sister. Then James climbed up and scooped little James into his lap to let him help him drive the "horsies."

"He showed me the shortcut," said James. "It's called Cooper's mountain. We didn't see it the morning we arrived because the sun wasn't quite up when we passed it, and I still can't figure out why it's not visible from our house. But when you follow this road and then turn and head back the other way, it's off in the distance. It reminds me of Wales."

They drove a little over a mile, and at last, it came into view. With the red and yellow trees on top of the hill, it was indeed a grand sight. James stopped the wagon, and they just sat and stared at the beautiful hill standing majestic on the near horizon.

"You're right," Sarah said. "We live right over there! Why can't we see it from our house? And why do they call it Cooper's mountain?"

"There's a plantation nearby," explained James. "This land is part of it. It was owned by a man named Benjamin Cooper, but now it's owned by that man I told you about at our militia meeting— Master Herbert Stokes, the slave master," said James, his voice full of disgust.

"So how do you get up there?" Sarah asked.

"Malachi says there is a path not too far from us that leads up the backside of it. The back of our land is actually up on it more than halfway, which makes it hard for us to see it. It's hard to explain actually."

"It is lovely," Sarah agreed. "So have you and Master Stokes had any more confrontations?"

"No, I stay quiet at meetings now. But he hasn't been eager to talk about freedom for all men any longer."

They started again driving in the direction of how they came in almost a year ago. Not too far down the road, they could see the Stokes plantation off in the distance. It was quite a view, the large house surrounded by barns and outbuildings and slave cabins, with Cooper's mountain as a backdrop. They sat and looked at the property and then turned to go back in the other direction toward home.

James said, "I think one day, I'll get Malachi to show me the path up there so I can see the view. But of course, part of the view will be the backside of Stokes's plantation, but I'm sure it is lovely. It does remind me of home."

"Thank you for sharing it with us," Sarah said, reaching over and touching him on the arm. "Oh, did I tell you that Sally is expecting number three?" she added.

"No, but Malachi thought she might be."

"She thinks it will be here in late spring. I will be sure to return the favor and help out with her girls when she goes into labor. She will be well taken care of. Martha is a wonderful midwife."

The winter of 1771 came and went and was a mild one with only one small snowfall. In April, Sally gave birth to another girl named Ruth. Sarah kept Sally's other girls for a day or two to help out. With Susannah toddling about, Sarah had her hands full and was tired when the two days were over.

In early summer, Sarah recognized the signs again and knew she was going to have another child. She and Sally teased each other about taking turns and laughing about what poor Martha would do if they ever went into labor together. Sarah and James welcomed Mary on February 15, 1773, in the middle of a snow and freezing rainstorm and in the middle of the night. James bundled up and drove the quarter of a mile to the Frazier farm to get Martha to come help. Sarah was only in labor about four hours and delivered within less than an hour after Martha arrived.

She laughed with Sarah, saying, "I believe you could have done that without me!"

Then as they had predicted might happen, Sarah caught up with Sally. When Mary was only six months old, Sarah became pregnant again. She and Sally were both due in the spring of 1774. The babies were born a week apart with Sally giving birth to her first son, Shadrack, at the end of April, and Sarah and James welcoming Peter in the first week of May. Sarah named him for her father, and he even favored Peter Bowman, they both thought. Four years after arriving in North Carolina, James and Sarah were now parents of four children. James decided to spend part of his time that next year building an addition to their farmhouse.

He and little James drew closer than ever. In addition to being his father's helper with the work on the house, Malachi had shown them the path to the "hidden" Cooper's mountain, and it became little James's favorite thing to do, to hike to the top and look over the valley where the back of the Stokes plantation stood. There was a lovely clearing on top of the hill where James and his son would build camps. James taught him how to pull a sapling sideways, use a vine to tie it to a nearby tree, and place sticks and pine straw to create a "hogan." Little James wasn't old enough to do this himself, but he learned by watching his father. On these treks to Cooper's mountain, James spent a great deal of time talking to his son about nature, God, and the value of all human life. James enjoyed this special time with his son as much as the boy did.

In 1775, James and Malachi became more involved in the militia, which was no longer just meeting to let off frustration with words but were now organizing themselves and training for eventual battle. James lay in the bed one night and expressed his concerns to Sarah.

"I am no war monger, Sarah. You know me. I would prefer peace any day. But it's no longer an issue of 'if the war starts.' The war is already taking place up north. There have been battles between the Patriots and the Loyalists up there. What makes me so sad and a little frightened is that there's not a boundary line. Here, right where we live, we have Patriots and Loyalists living side by side. Where we are, most Patriots are like me, they want peace. But those in charge are going to draw us into battle. I just know it. I'm not afraid. I do want us to be free from British control. I just don't want to leave my family. I don't want to leave you here to deal with everything. I don't want to leave you at all."

The regiments of Granville County were called to fight in the battle of Moore's Creek Bridge in February 1776 down near the Cape Fear River. It was just days after Sarah had given birth to a son named William. It was also wintertime, and James left Sarah and the children with a rifle, ammunition, firewood, and food they had put away. James and Sarah had an emotional farewell, and little James was perhaps the most upset over his father leaving. Little James was a very nervous, anxious child who was chronically worried about things in life. Something like his father being gone to war was very traumatic for him. Susannah, Mary and Peter seemed to adapt quickly to the sudden absence of their father, but little James spent most nights his father was away in his mother's bed being consoled. When James left, the child was nearly seven, and James asking him to be the man of the house while he was away almost did the child in. He took that expectation very seriously and tried hard to be grown-up, but Sarah could see the stress wearing on her son. That kept her motivated to stay positive in his presence. She made a mental note to talk to James about it when he returned.

Sarah was thankful for the end of the mild winter and the arrival of an early spring as this made it easier to stay in constant touch with Sally, Martha and the children just down the road. One day the women were talking about how they hated seeing their men go off to battle in their old hunting shirts and coats they had worn forever. James was still able to wear the light brown surtout, or waistcoat, he'd brought from Wales, but Sarah wanted to surprise him with a new coat on his return. The women kept busy making coats out of some dark blue wool Sally was able to get. Sarah was grateful that Martha was as great a seamstress as her own mother had been. The women were pleased with the final products and couldn't wait to present the coats to their husbands on their return from battle.

Sally and Sarah both had five children now. Sally's son Lewis had been born in the latter part of 1775. Many days, the women would take turns keeping all the children so the other could work with Martha on the sewing or other chores. Those were long days, but the women stayed busy and were tired and missed their husbands very much. Sarah was just grateful she had Sally to talk to. Martha was also a comfort. The thing that amazed Sarah so much about Martha was that though she had lost her husband just a few years before, she clearly had made a conscious decision to continue to be happy and to be a support to her son's family. Sarah hoped her mother was faring as well in her widowhood.

The Battle of Moore's Creek Bridge took place down east en route to the coast of North Carolina. The goal for the Patriots was to prevent the Loyalists or Tories from reaching Wilmington, which was on the coast. The regiments from Granville County and other counties were camped at a place called Rockfish Creek. One day, not too long after they arrived, when James was in line to get food, he heard a voice that made him turn about quickly.

"James West? Dear Lord, we meet again!"

James was face-to-face with John Hussey. They embraced and both young men shed tears.

"You know, I should be punching you in your bloody face for going off and leaving me for dead in those woods," John Hussey laughed through his tears.

James wiped away his own tears and began to apologize profusely, "I wanted to go back for you! We heard the gunfire. John

Thomas said we had to keep moving! I spent days and nights worried about you! We were told by Orr that you had died!"

"You went back to Orr?" asked John.

"No, but he found out where we were and sent word you were all killed! John Thomas's cousin bought our freedom with Orr making a nice profit. He made Robert Wade pay for losing you three as well!"

"That Orr and his men were such bastards!"

"I did not know you were alive until Sarah and I got to Granville County. Francis's wife told us about your visit. I was in shock!"

"So you finally made your way to your brother's!" John smiled.

James said sadly, "Only to find he'd died a few days before."

John drew James to him in an embrace. "Dear God, no! What happened to Francis?"

"He was in the woods gathering grapes, and a large copperhead was on the tree and bit him on the face and his neck. He died three days later."

"I am so sorry, James!" John said sincerely. "I enjoyed getting to know your brother. He could have been your twin."

"His wife and children left two weeks later with her family to go to Tennessee. We bought all the land and house. I have five children now, John."

"I'm not surprised," he said with a laugh. "You and the missus have a very happy love life I take it."

"She is the most beautiful woman on earth! We left Swan Point in 1770. We lost a child, a daughter, and then had little James. He's my oldest. We've added Susannah, Mary, Peter, and William," he said counting on his fingers. "So where are you living now, John? Which regiment are you with?"

"I settled in Orange County, just outside Hillsborough. We have seven different regiments here to fight these damned Brits." He chuckled. "I too have married. My wife is Miriam, and we have three sons and a daughter. Two of my sons are twins! I met her very soon after I left your brother's place."

"We must get the families together, John, once this war is over."

The two old friends ate that meal together and found out where the other was encamped and continued to talk and see each other until the battle began in earnest.

James valued life, but he found himself to be a good shot in the weeks of battle. He knew that he had injured at least one of those Tories in the battle that lasted over two months. James convinced himself that every British soldier he aimed and fired at was Thomas Orr or his henchmen Morris and Walters that had whipped him and Calvin. Thinking that seemed to make it easier to be aggressive.

One day, when he went looking for John at the camp, he found out his friend had been hurt, and he headed for the tents that housed the wounded Patriots. He walked past several of the injured and at last found John Hussey nursing a wounded femur.

"James West," he called out, "wasn't it *your* turn to get shot?"

James went over and sat down on the blanket John was on and hugged him closely. "I am sorry to see you are wounded, my friend. What can I do for you?"

"Put in a good word for me with God. I know you have a strong connection there. Actually, I know I am going to be fine! I will probably be riding my horse back home when this is over."

"I think it's all but over now. Those Tories have turned and run, most of them."

"Those Brits are such women," teased John.

"Hey, John, *we* are from the mother country." James smiled.

"We *were* from the mother country. I am an American now. They are dirty distant cousins. They have no idea what you and I have done to be here."

"I am so glad you survived, John. Here, but in Maryland as well."

"And, James, I am very sorry about the whipping you got. I still have nightmares about that. If I could have stopped it, I would have. Bloody bastards."

James asked, "I know Roger was killed, but what happened to Samuel?"

"I don't know. He helped me get on a boat, and we crossed the Potomac. When I woke up in a stranger's house, he was gone. It was a sweet little old lady and her deaf husband that nursed me back to health. The Pritchards. Angels, they were."

"I've had angels of my own," James said. "John, please write to me. Let's keep in touch."

"James West of Granville County," said John, reciting James's address, "I will do it. I might just show up one day, me and the missus. I know where you live. You would probably have trouble finding us in Orange County."

The two hugged again. "I can't wait to tell Sarah I found you," said James.

"Next battle, it's your turn, little brother," John quipped, pointing to his bandaged thigh.

"I wish I could have taken this one for you," James said. "Take care of yourself, friend."

The victorious Patriots began to head out in late April after all the Tories had been killed, captured, or just run off. The Granville regiments began to regroup and make their way back north. James found Malachi on the route home, and they rode together for the remainder of the trip back to Granville County.

They talked on the way back about the battle and thanked God that they both survived. They both expressed how much they had missed their wives and families. "It's the longest Sarah and I have ever been apart. I don't like it. I pray all is well at both our homes." James then shared with Malachi about seeing John Hussey. He left out the part of stealing the cloak and spending time in jail but told him most of their adventure in Maryland. "I thought he was dead," James said. "He actually came here and visited with Francis and Christian thinking I would be here. I can't wait to tell Sarah about seeing him."

They came down the road to their homes together, ragged and weary. Little James was the first to see them coming and ran screaming into the house. "Papa's home! Uncle Malachi is too!" Then he raced back out to the porch, and James could see his son jumping up and down and waving.

At seeing home, both men broke into a full gallop to greet their loved ones at their respective homes. James jumped off his horse, scooped up little James first, and kissed him over and over. Then

Sarah came out with the son James had barely seen before leaving. He kissed her fully on the mouth, saying, "You have no idea how much I have missed you!" He kissed the baby sleeping in Sarah's arms. Then one by one, he picked up little Peter, Mary, and Susannah, all squealing and clamoring for his arms to hold them. He placed the last one on the ground, and then he scooped up all three at once again and kissed their faces in quick succession. He turned and put them on the ground again and saw little James standing there shyly waiting for more attention. James stopped and saluted his oldest son. "Job well done, son! You've done a superb job holding down the fort!" Little James blushed, beamed, and returned the salute.

Sarah could not stop the tears. She felt as if she had held them in for years, not just a few months, for fear of frightening or worrying the children, particularly little James. Now the floodgates opened, and she wept and held her husband. "Thank God you are home! We have been so lost without you!"

He brushed his lips near her ear and neck and whispered, "I sure hope you are well from your last delivery. I am very much in need of some love." Then he smiled. "I am sorry for the beard and mustache," he said, plucking at his hairy chin. "We have had very little access to razors while down east."

"I rather like the look," she said. "I've always loved your hair long, and I think you look handsome with facial hair." She smiled, tweaking his goatee.

"I look like a scoundrel!" he said laughing. "And speaking of scoundrels, guess who I ran into? John Hussey! He is living in Orange County. He was wounded slightly, but I think he will be fine. We must try and see them. He said he will bring his wife and children to visit sometime. It was so good to see him."

"James! John Hussey? That is wonderful! Tell me about how you first saw each other."

James recounted their reunion with details as Sarah put water on to heat so that her weary husband could have a good bath. While he soaked in the tub, she sat near him and nursed little William. It was hard to get the children to go to sleep, but by the time she finished nursing William, the last one was asleep, including the newborn.

As James dried off and put on a clean shirt that covered his thighs, he turned to see Sarah holding up a beautiful dark blue coat with gold buttons. "Sally and I made them for you and Malachi." She smiled.

"Sarah, it is magnificent. They shall have to make us captains!" He laughed. "The British, last I saw of them, wore bright red coats. Our men just wore regular clothes. We looked like farmers and commoners. But we whipped them, Sarah! They ran off with their tails between their legs! So much for fancy, red uniforms," he said. "This is much more in keeping with what victors should wear! Thank you, my love!"

She hung the coat up in their armoire. As she turned around, James had taken off his shirt. He stood there waiting for her and said, "Tomorrow I shall shave." They embraced by their bed, and the passion they shared felt almost what it was like on their wedding night in Edward and Miranda's "honeymoon cottage."

After they had loved each other completely, as James was beginning to drift off to sleep, Sarah said, "I can imagine reunions like this are taking place all over this colony tonight. Men in battle with no women in sight—that must be difficult for you soldiers."

James thought about the brothels that were set up just outside their encampment. He knew he would never tell Sarah that there *were* women there for the soldiers. He and John had talked about it, and John had joked that the British had set up the brothels and those whores were really spies. Those women walked in and around the encampment, even visiting wounded soldiers in the tents, tempting them to spend some of their money on them. James had seen them and knew exactly why they were there, but he knew he could never be unfaithful to Sarah. He had heard rumors of some men taking diseases home to their wives. Seeing the women had made James think of the intimacy they shared and that he missed, but he vowed he would not betray her trust; however, he knew that many men had weakened and given in.

He slept at last after thanking the Lord in his heart that He had brought him and Malachi back home where all was well. He also prayed that another call to their regiment would be a long time coming.

CHAPTER 17

S arah blessed James with two more sons before he had to serve again in the war. Daniel was born in November 1777, and Abraham followed closely in November 1778. James had built a second addition to the farmhouse before his regiment ordered him and Malachi to South Carolina in April 1780. The war in the southern colonies centered around the city of Charleston at that time, and both sides were suffering losses.

Sally and Malachi had added a son to their family, Guy, born in 1778. And before the men left in the spring of 1780, both women were pregnant again. This time, their husbands would not be there for the births. Sarah and Sally both thanked God for Martha who still had an amazing stamina for helping birth babies and helping out with the care of a household. Sally's oldest girls were twelve and ten, and little James was almost eleven. These children were old enough to help look after the little ones, as well as do many household chores. Plus, some of Malachi's younger nephews had been hired on to handle the farms of both James and Malachi while they were off in battle. A few of Malachi's older relatives were going to oversee the farms, as they were too old to join in on the fighting.

This time when his father left, little James was more prepared to be "man of the house" in his papa's absence. James told him before he left that he prayed this war would soon be over and that little James would never have to be a soldier.

In August, Sarah gave birth to a daughter to whom she passed along her own name. She sent word to James in South Carolina that they now had a little Sarah, but she had no way of knowing if he received word of the birth or not. At the time of this baby's birth, Sarah and James had been separated four months, twice as long as before in 1776. All the women had heard rumors that the troops had moved from Charleston to Camden to King's Mountain, all in South Carolina, and finally to a place called Polk's Mill back up in North Carolina out in the southwestern part of the state. Sally got word in mid-October that the men were headed home for a furlough. At the end of October, both James and Malachi returned home after eight months away.

This homecoming was not as joyous an occasion as the first one four years before. This time, both men had been wounded but were healing. This time, their spirits seemed much more war weary. They were both happy to see their new daughters, however. Sally had given birth to *her* Sarah just before she received word that the men were headed home. Sarah and Sally both noticed how quiet their husbands seemed to be after their long absence.

One night after they had made love, Sarah finally asked James why he was so despondent. "I am worried about you, husband. And James is concerned too. I can tell."

"I just need some time is all. Believe me, I am grateful to be home. You have done an amazing job, Sarah. Having a baby without me. I hate I wasn't here. Let me just say, I was involved in a little more killing and wounding than before. I was wounded in the arm as you can see. It's still not completely healed yet. Malachi's knee injury is hurting him something awful. I hate war. I don't want to have to go back, but this isn't over. We are doing well on our side, but the British can be bloody stubborn."

"You would have been so proud of James," she said. Realizing she was no longer calling their son "little" made James feel a bit sad.

"He's growing up. I am so proud of him. He is not 'little' any longer, is he?" James asked somberly.

She smiled. "He's been my *only* James for so many months, so I just dropped the 'little' part. Plus, he has worked like a man here. He's been side by side with Malachi's nephews out in the fields, tending to the animals, teaching Peter and William how to do chores around the farm. And Susannah and Mary have become such good little mothers helping me with the babies. And I don't know what any of us would do without Martha."

Sarah heard soft snoring and realized she had talked her husband to sleep. She lay there gazing at this man she loved so much. He was now thirty-two years old. They both were. They had eight children, and Sarah could actually see an occasional white hair on James's head and in the beard that he now wore again.

James did not return to the battlefield until March 1781 for the Battle of Guilford Court House. Malachi, it seemed, would not be going. His knee had barely healed and not well. James really dreaded the trek without Malachi by his side. His own wound in his arm had completely healed during these few months at home.

In their meeting before leaving, their regiment was notified that there were going to be units from all over North Carolina converging for this battle. James heard that they would not only be flanking regiments from Orange County but also that some of their own captains would be leading troops from Orange County, due to injuries of some of the captains from that regiment. Of course, James hoped he might see John Hussey again, especially since Malachi would not be there. He had not seen John in any of the battles they'd fought in South Carolina the year before.

When he arrived with his regiment at the encampment in the vicinity of the Guilford Courthouse at a place called Reedy Creek, James was amazed at the number gathered. During his first battle in 1776, there had been over one thousand Patriots participating. This time, there were several encampments, and Granville's Patriots were housed with Orange County and units from Warren and Franklin counties, all three of which bordered Granville. There were over four thousand Patriots united for the battle. James spent the day before the battle began, walking through the camp, hoping to catch a glimpse of John. One soldier from Orange County said he was certain John Hussey was with them. When James turned to head back to his tent, he heard that familiar voice call out. "James West! Remember, lad, it's *your* turn!" He looked back and saw John Hussey's cheeky grin, and the two walked over to each other and embraced.

"My friend! Where were you when we were in South Carolina last year?" James asked. "See? I took one in the arm!"

James pulled up his sleeve and showed John his scar.

"Lovely," John said. "I have a matching one on my thigh. It gave me issues. Healing was slow. It got me out of South Carolina last year. So how many babies have you added to your brood?"

"I have eight at present, John. How about you?"

"We have added two more. I have six now."

James walked with John to his tent to see where he was housed. Then James pointed out where he was staying.

This was going to be a major battle for ultimate control for the Patriots. Nathanael Greene, the head of the Patriot forces, after four subsequent battles in South Carolina, had begun to head north with a ragged Tory army in pursuit. Greene had made it to Virginia and, on the way through North Carolina and Virginia, relayed word that all would be needed to finish off the Brits. At last, Cornwallis had headed back southwest. Greene had headed in that direction as well, and now here they were with over four thousand troops from Virginia, North Carolina, and South Carolina.

In this battle of the Guilford Courthouse, the Patriots stood three lines deep. They outnumbered the British, two to one. The battle, which began in the morning, was brief but fierce. The fighting only lasted a little over two hours, but the British were victorious, with numerous casualties on both sides. The fighting was very much hand to hand, and many Patriots from the front lines had been killed or had simply taken off.

When it was all over and the smell of sulfurous cannon fire was still strong in the air, the Patriots fled back to their camp at Reedy Creek. James and John found each other there gratefully.

"Not hit?" John asked, holding James close for a moment and checking him over. James shook his head.

"Nor you? Thank God we made it. As soon as we get word, I am headed home, but we are told to be on standby."

"I am as well. It was great seeing you again, James. I would like to think that this is the end of it, but I doubt it. Those British women are some kind of stubborn." John smiled.

"I passed Hillsborough on the way in," James told John. "Mind if we ride together 'til we get to your place?"

"I would love for you to stop and meet the missus and the children," John said, grinning. "Perhaps you could stay a day or two, break up your trip home?"

"I would love it. Sarah has no idea the battle is over already so she won't be watching for me."

"She's probably glad you're gone." John laughed. "Give the poor woman a rest, James."

"Who are you to talk? Six? Including twins?"

John and Miriam lived on land adjacent to her parents. James enjoyed meeting John's wife and children, but all it did was make him homesick for his own family. Miriam was a quiet woman and seemed very tired. She kindly fed them and saw to it James had a bed to sleep in, but she did not have much to say. James and John walked his property, looked at the crops, and talked about their past.

James insisted, "I believe it was Providence that brought us together, John."

"And whom do I thank for leaving me in the woods for dead?" he asked.

"Well, perhaps you should look at how blessed you were that Samuel got you aboard a boat and that you made it into Virginia."

"I wish I had your perspective on such things," John said. "I am not much on understanding the ways of our Creator."

"I have had my times of wavering faith," James added.

"Have you? When?"

"Starting with Calvin's beating on the Orr plantation. Then when my first daughter died in our arms. Then when I got to Granville County after waiting years to see Francis only to find out he was dead. I don't handle loss or injustice very well. Seems like sometimes God is a tormentor and not a very loving Father."

"Hmmm. I thought you were a man of solid faith," said John.

"I guess I am. But I have learned I am also human. Now Sarah. She's amazing. I have to borrow from her faith from time to time. I have to. My own gets dim sometimes. Those eight months fighting in South Carolina last year were a real test."

"But you made it," John said.

"Yes, but when I got home, I had a hard time coming back as myself. I feel guilty. Sarah has to work so hard to try and lift me up. I should be lifting *her* up. Eight children."

"Then give the woman a break! Don't you have any self-control?" John smiled, placing his arm around James's shoulders.

"Not where that beautiful woman is concerned. She makes me weak."

"Miriam just tolerates me," John admitted, only half joking. "But it's all right. I know I can be a pain in the arse."

James only stayed a night and left for Granville County the next morning. Sarah was pleasantly surprised not only to see her husband home much sooner than she had expected but also to see him in much better spirits than he had been in since his last return home.

"From that big smile on your face," she greeted him, "I would guess this war is over!"

He kissed her soundly. "I surely wish. They held their ground, but both sides took losses. I think I'll be going back out soon, love. But I'm home for now."

"I am just glad you are in a better mood."

"I think that's because I just spent the last few days with John Hussey!"

"Really?"

"We rode home together as far as Hillsborough, and he invited me to stay at his place for a night, meet his wife and children, see his farm."

"And? Was it a good visit?" she asked.

"It was. He has six children, a set of twins included."

"And his wife?"

"Miriam is her name. She is—she seems—tired."

"I can understand!" Sarah sighed.

"You don't show it, my love!" James insisted. "John says she merely tolerates him. I, for one, am happy to be loved. And to be in love," he added, gently kissing the back of her hand.

"Remember that," Sarah told her husband. "Those last few months when you got home from South Carolina, you were very hard to live with."

"I am so sorry. I know I was terrible. Just too much killing. I came home exhausted. It's such a waste of time. And life. War is, I mean."

"I guess war is what they call a necessary evil," she said.

"Definitely. And those bloody Brits won't take no for an answer. If all wars could be short battles like the one I just fought in, it would be a little more tolerable."

"So not as much killing this time?" Sarah asked.

"Well, we lost lots of men from the front lines, but the Tories lost over a hundred, they say, with many more wounded carried off. It was a ferocious, close-up battle. But I know you don't want to hear of it. If you don't mind, I think I am going to see Malachi today and give him all the details."

In May, less than two months later, James was summoned with his unit for duty back in South Carolina. James was involved in both the Siege of Ninety-Six and the bloody Battle of Eutaw Springs, where his unit lost their commander William Burford. The Patriots suffered a great loss of life and had many wounded. At last, James came home near the end of September, recovering from the sweltering heat and a minor injury to his shoulder. His spirits were low again, but a few months later, word came that Cornwallis had surrendered to George Washington at Yorktown, Virginia, and the war was over. The colonies were free from British domination.

"Do you regret not being part of the final battle?" Sarah asked after word of the victory came.

"No," said James. "I saw enough Patriot blood shed for the cause. I only wish this freedom was extended to all."

He and Sarah lay in bed talking, holding each other. "That may be our next big war, Sarah. I can see slaves rising up someday demanding *their* independence. That may be the war our sons or our sons' sons will have to fight."

"I have news, husband," she said.

"Again? I haven't been around much lately. Are you sure you're not seeing someone else when I ride off into battle?" he asked her with a grin and a wink.

Sarah knew he was teasing, but it hurt a little even in jest. "You are enough for me clearly," she said. "I am probably due sometime in late January or early February. I must have conceived the last night we were together."

"Of course," James smiled. He was quiet a bit and then said, "You're tired too, aren't you, Sarah?"

"I am getting a bit war weary," she said, trying to make light of another pregnancy. "But I guess the good Lord has other plans. I am thankful I have both boys and girls. You have future farmhands, and I have girls to help with the laundry and cooking and tending to the little ones. It makes life easier in some regards."

"Are you still writing in your commonplace book?" James asked. "Or doing any sketching?"

"I have done a couple of sketches, but I need more ink. I recorded Sarah's birth finally when she was six months old." Sarah sighed and moved closer to her husband. "Things were so different when we were young, James. Remember life at Swan Point? Remember Cuckold Creek?"

He smiled and kissed her cheek and took her fingers in his. "I will always remember you and Cuckold Creek, Sarah. To me you will always be that lovely young girl I first saw there. You know, we are only thirty-three now. It's not like we are in our sixties."

"I heard from Miranda while you were gone. She and Edward just had their fifth child. She sounded tired too. And I know she did not want to worry me, but I don't think my mother is doing well. She was also telling me about Priscilla's wedding." Her voice broke off.

"Should I have taken you back home, Sarah, when we came here and Francis was dead? I never even asked you. I just bought the land, and the house, and moved you in here and never asked you what you wanted to do. I am sorry."

"James, do you remember how long it took us to get here from Maryland?" she said with a laugh. "There was no way I was going to turn around and make that trip again! I have been so blessed to be here. I have Sally and dear Martha. I have all my babies. James will be thirteen in May! No, James, I do not regret leaving Swan Point. This war has been a huge distraction, but I still love you as much as I did the day I saw you in the creek cooling off those marks on your back."

"I will never forget these sweet fingers," he said, kissing hers, "that rubbed liniment on my back! How much I desired you that evening on that blanket, Sarah."

She started to laugh. "You ordered me home at once," she said. "You were not going to take my virtue before we were wed."

"And I did not!" He smiled, pulling her close. "And it was indeed worth waiting for, my love."

They began to kiss, and he said as he began to love her, "This, my dear, is why we have number nine on the way."

By December, Martha knew Sarah was calculating again for number nine to arrive in late January or early February. She teased that she would prefer not to be summoned in the middle of the night in a snowstorm. They all enjoyed another Christmas advent season together with the two families sharing refreshments on Christmas Eve after a lovely service at church.

Early Christmas morning, James, Sarah, and the children gathered around the fireplace to open presents. James had spent many hours at night in the barn crafting wooden toy guns for the older boys, wagons for the little ones, and Sarah had taken apart a couple of her old dresses to make rag dolls and painted beautiful faces on them. For Susannah, she used a strip of black velvet that had bordered a dress and added a clasp and a cameo to create a lovely choker. For little James, though, his father gave him a real British pistol he'd gotten from a raid they had done in South Carolina, when a group of Tories had abandoned a weapons cache. The family was having a merry Christmas morning, and the children were happily showing each other their gifts and playing with their new toys.

Sarah stood to go start breakfast for the family and felt a sudden pain that brought her instant concern. As she went into her bedroom to avoid being seen in pain by the children, she felt the sudden gushing forth of water. She walked to the door and motioned to James who sat with little Sarah on his lap. He handed the two-year-old off to Susannah, and he joined his wife in their room.

"You need to send for Martha. I have just passed water. This baby is coming now, and it is much too soon!" Tears sprang to her eyes. James was able to talk to the two oldest children and let them know what was happening. He sent James on horseback to tell Martha. He had Susannah and Mary take the little ones back to one of their bedrooms to play. He was thankful for the two additions that had almost doubled the size of the house and allowed for more privacy.

Martha came with Sally by wagon, and she immediately checked Sarah's progress. She told James, "I don't think this is good news. You may want to go build a small box, James. I am sorry." Such a somber mood settled on the house for what should have been a festive time. James did as he was told. As he sawed and hammered in the barn, he felt tears come to his eyes, remembering his first daughter and the shock and grief they had felt. He prayed as he worked and asked the Lord that Sarah would be spared. She had had such amazing luck with all her babies after that first miscarriage and losing their first little angel who had struggled to breathe for a day and a half. When he finished the box, he went back to his wife and stayed with her only leaving every now and then to check on the children.

After about five hours of labor, Sarah gave birth to a tiny daughter who had already left this life. Her grayish pallor made Sarah cry out, and she knew instantly when Martha placed her in her arms that her child was lifeless. She cried and pulled the baby to her face so that she could kiss her forehead. She was perfectly formed, although a miniature of the last deceased daughter she'd held years ago.

Sally quietly looked through Sarah's baby clothes and found a small dress that her girls had all worn at birth, but even then, it almost swallowed this new little angel. James took her in his arms from Sally who had dressed her. He had tears on his cheeks. He sat next to Sarah on the bed. It felt as if they were at Swan Point in Edward's old bedroom again. But this time, all James could think of was poor Alice Roney. "It was not yet her time," the crewmember had told Captain Duggar. This baby was so like the doll figure that Alice Roney took with her into the depths of the ocean.

Sarah was crying, but James could see strength and resolve on her face and in her green eyes. "James, I am sorry that you will have to tell the children. Don't let them see her. She is too small. Let's put her in the box now. I will let you take her out and bury her tomorrow. I do not want her buried on Christmas Day. Sally, may we use your cemetery?" Sarah asked. "I am feeling too weak to go, even tomorrow will be much too soon."

"Yes, of course! Oh, Sarah, I am so sorry." Sally held her friend close. "Listen, Malachi and I will go with James out to bury her. He won't be alone."

"I am so grateful to you and Malachi and Martha," Sarah said, as James put the baby back in her arms and went to the barn to retrieve the tiny casket. They wrapped her in a blanket that Martha had made for one of Sarah's girls. Both Sarah and James kissed her face and, together, placed her in the box and put the tight lid into place. James put the box on the table in their room next to their bed. He went out and got a sprig of holly with red berries from off their decorated mantle and came back and placed it on the top of the closed box.

James kept the smaller children away from Sarah as she did not want them so see her so sad. Mary and Susannah came in with their brother James, and the three of them hugged their mother and looked at the box, sitting there like an unopened package. They cried together, but little James seemed to have the hardest time.

He and his father sat by the fireplace later that evening, long after the girls had gotten the littlest ones to sleep. Twelve-year-old James gave his father a serious look and said, "I think my mother has had enough children." He was still crying a little.

James looked at his son. "You do not understand, my boy. Your mother and I love each other. Someday, you will know what that means, and you will know more about how grown-ups love each other. She may have more children if it is in God's plans."

"Papa, I know how babies come to be here. I would think you would not want to cause her any more pain. This is in your hands."

James did not want to make his son feel foolish, but he said, "James, still you do not understand what it is like between a man and a woman who love each other and are married. I genuinely appreciate your concern for your mother's welfare, but know this. She loves every single one of her children that God has blessed her with."

He hugged his son and wished him a good night. The boy gave his papa one last look of frustration and then went to bed. James could tell that his son was still upset with him, perhaps thinking he cruelly forced himself upon his mother, but he knew there was no way to help him understand how incorrect he was in his understanding of love, marriage, and having families.

James went and joined his wife in their bedroom. Sarah was lying on her side, awake, facing the table with the box. He climbed into bed and held her close, and they cried and grieved, together.

Chapter 18

*J*ames never told Sarah about his conversation with little James on the subject of having more children. His relationship with his son was never really the same afterward. It was even more stressed when in 1783 Sarah got pregnant again. James just knew his son could not possibly, at his young age, understand a marital relationship.

The younger James West was a loner by nature. He was very meticulous in his manner, and he took life way too seriously. Both his parents knew this about him and worried that life was almost too much for him at times. He seemed to have a double or triple dose of the sensitivity Sarah saw not only in her father and in her husband but also in herself.

His younger brothers, on the other hand, were much more carefree and enjoyed their boyhoods. Peter had a best friend named William Edwards who was actually closer in age to his older brother James, but Peter and William enjoyed fishing together. The three "stairsteps," as Sarah referred to William, Daniel, and Abraham, traveled in a pack with Shadrack and Guy Frazier. That gang of boys loved to play in the woods and hunt. Sometimes, they were hunting rocks, sometimes birds' nests, sometimes birds. They all had slingshots and loved being out in nature doing boyish things. They were loud and rowdy at times but were very healthy and happy boys.

The girls, Susannah and Mary, were usually best friends and also enjoyed looking after their baby sister, Sarah. The Frazier girls were also dear friends of theirs. They exchanged hair ribbons and did needlepoint together, and both sets of girls loved cooking and helping their mothers.

Little James, however, had no best friend. His passion in life was going camping alone at the top of Cooper's mountain. There he seemed to be king of his own kingdom. Through the years, he had built and perfected several hogans or huts up there. He had slept in them and sometimes stayed a whole weekend up there alone. His father used to be his favorite person to camp with, and he had adored the times when it was just him and his papa. Those had been his happiest days. His parents had not noticed, but he had become more and more reclusive with each and every child born. He knew in his heart that his anger over his mother having so many children was not just about his mother's welfare, though he did adore her and worried about her weariness in life, but he knew his prevailing thought had been since he could remember was, "Why did they need to have other children? Why wasn't I enough?" But the boy had kept that bothersome question to himself and let it fester away inside him.

Sarah and James added child number nine with another handsome boy named Joseph in February 1784. Ann came not too long after in October 1785. James thought of adding a second story to their home but instead added a third wing to the one-story farmhouse. Little James helped him with the addition, but they worked quietly side by side.

"Little" James was now sixteen, and James was amazed thinking that his son was the same age he had been when he ran off from Wales. He had told James all the stories of his adventures except the part about stealing and doing time in jail and being a convict servant. He never felt completely comfortable telling his children he was an indentured servant because he knew it was a half-truth, but he had never wanted his children to know he had willfully broken the law, been in jail, and served time as a convict.

All the children knew by heart the story of how their grandfather had bought their father and set him free so he could marry their mother. They had heard stories of Cuckold Creek and Swan Point. They were familiar with the names Edward and Miranda, Grandmother Judith and Grandmother Susannah, and knew all about James's life in Wales in a village called Manorowen.

The children loved to look at their father's Bible and read the inscription from Captain Trenton Duggar, knowing he was the captain of the ship that had brought their father to America. The girls occasionally turned the pages of their mother's commonplace book and enjoyed the drawings she had done of her siblings and the swan and the sketches she had done of them. They knew that Timothy and Hannah were her brother and sister who had died. Sarah had not shared, however, the drawing of James in the creek with the whip marks upon his back. She had removed that sheet from her book and had it hidden on the bottom of the cedar chest under quilts and old clothes. They did not know of Calvin or the whipping he and their father had gotten. Since Malachi had seen his scars, James had made sure his children did not see him without a shirt on. Even on the hottest summer days now, he worked in the fields with a shirt on, hiding his back.

One late afternoon, after finishing in the fields, in October 1785, little James passed through the house with a bag upon his back and told his mother he was going to spend the night on Cooper's mountain. She was in the rocker nursing his newest little sister Ann, and all Sarah asked was, "Have you finished your chores, James?" He responded that he had, and he ran out the door.

James hiked the familiar winding path and reached his favorite clearing. He was proud of the hogan he had just completed. This was not just a sapling tied with vines to a sturdier tree; James had completed what was the equivalent of a cabin. His father had not seen it, nor been invited to see it, but if he had, it would have reminded him of the cabin he had lived in with the two Johns on the Wade property or the cabin he had endured on the Orr plantation. Little James had procured bits and pieces of scrap lumber and had carried them by a small handcart a few at a time. There was a dirt floor, but even his father had slept on a dirt floor on the Orr plantation. James had built a raised wooden platform and had brought an old feather tick mattress and had it on the platform with a goose-down pillow. He loved his little home away from home he had created. He fantasized that he would be allowed some day to build his own real home atop Cooper's mountain. He had to walk quite a ways through thick woods to view the "valley" that revealed the back of the Stokes plantation. His father had warned him that technically Mr. Stokes owned the mountain and that he was actually trespassing, but it had never been an issue.

On this afternoon when he opened the door to his mountain home, he was shocked to find it occupied. Lying on his mattress was a young girl about his age. She wore a ragged shift and was barefoot. She sat straight up and tried to dart out of the building, but James grabbed her by the arm and stopped her. Her thick, light-brown hair was matted in places, and her face showed genuine fear. By the tone of her skin and the texture of her hair, James could tell she was a very light-skinned Negro. Her eyes were a beautiful shade of amber, and tears were pooling in those eyes.

"It's all right," he told her. "Don't be afraid. I promise not to hurt you."

She stood there, not knowing what to do. She did not want to leave this place of refuge she had found, but she did not know what would happen to her if she stayed. She went over to the door and stood by the wall. She was shaking all over.

James spoke again, "My name is James West. This is my house that I have built. It's okay for you to be here. Can you tell me your name?"

She didn't speak at first then barely whispered, "Rose."

James smiled at her. "Rose, do you mind telling me why you are here in my house?"

"I—I had nowhere else to go. I can't take it down there anymore."

"Where is there?"

"Mr. Stokes's plantation."

"So you ran away?"

She nodded. "Please don't tell. Don't turn me in."

"I won't," James reassured the girl. "How old are you?"

"I think about fifteen."

"Do you have family there looking for you?"

"My mama. Her name is Estelle." She paused for a moment and then admitted, "I'm sorry, but I ate some of your food."

James glanced over to the box where he kept things, including food brought from home.

"That's all right. I can bring you more."

He convinced her to sit back down on the mattress. "My father worked on a plantation in Maryland," he told her. He remained standing. "He was an indentured servant. That is how he got to America."

She looked at him and picked at a torn place on the hem of her dress.

James went on, "My mother's father bought him and gave him his freedom. He even let him marry my mother. My father is very much against slavery."

James thought carefully about what to say to the frightened girl. Finally he told her, "Rose, I want you to feel safe here. I know you don't want to go back down there and be a slave. I am going to go home and—"

"Don't tell anybody I'm here!" she said, jumping up again. "They will *have* to send me back!"

"No, it's all right, I won't. I just want to go back home and get some things—some food and drink. I think you could use some blankets. It gets chilly up here at night."

"You'll let me stay? They are searching for me. I am so scared they are going to come up here and see this cabin and come in and get me!"

"I've got protection up here." James went over to the box and dug to the bottom. "Here is a loaded pistol. My father got it from a British arsenal during the war a few years ago. I can show you how to use it if you have to. It's mine now. He gave it to me for Christmas a while back. I can leave it right here on the top of these other things in this box. Or you can put it on the mattress with you." He extended his hand with the gun in it over toward her. She motioned it away as if she were as afraid of the gun as she was of her slaveholders. He placed the pistol back in the box.

He turned another box over and used it as a stool and slid it closer to the mattress. She still looked as if she did not trust him. "You can stay here as long as you like," he told her. "I am not going to hurt you."

"Yeah, that's what they say down there at Stokes's place."

"How do they hurt you, Rose?"

"Well, they just whip me all the time. I'm tired of it."

"I can imagine you are. What does your mama say?"

"What can she say? They hurt her too! Mr. Stokes is a mean man, and he has mean men working for him. And mean sons."

"Rose, I am going back to my house. I will not tell anyone about you. I want to bring you dinner from our table and some more blankets. I will come back tonight. I promise. And the gun is there if you need it."

James left and practically ran down the backside of Cooper's mountain. He got home just as his family was sitting down to dinner. The first addition his father had built included a dining room with a huge table that was just now becoming a bit small for all of them. He could smell the ham the girls had baked and biscuits. He sat down in time for the prayer. The first thing his mother said after the blessing was, "We were not expecting you for dinner, James. You told me you were camping on the mountain."

"I forgot to take any food, and I was hungry." James began to eat. He knew he could convince his mother to let him take extras back up the hill with him when she and his sisters were clearing the table. As soon as they had finished dinner, there was a knock at their door. Peter opened it and welcomed in their "uncle" Malachi, who limped into the dining room apologizing for interrupting their meal.

"We are finished," James assured him. "Come in."

He offered Malachi a seat in the parlor.

"I just got word, James. Word from Herbert Stokes's place. They said to be on watch for a runaway slave. It's a female. A young one. She goes by the name of Rose. She's got to be on foot, they said."

"We'll keep an eye out," James told his friend. "How young? I hate to think of a child out there alone," he continued, thinking of Calvin.

"I think she's about fourteen or fifteen."

"Still she's got to be frightened."

"If you find her, they're offering a reward."

"Yes, I just bet they are," said James with disgust in his voice.

"Now, James, you've managed to make peace with Stokes. Don't be thinking about harboring a runaway."

"Malachi, I am not foolish."

"I can just see your big, tenderhearted self hiding her in a wagon and getting her across a border somewhere."

"Don't I wish! That would be sweet revenge."

"They said she is mulatto."

"That makes me wish I could help her escape even more. There's no telling what her mother has endured from those beasts or what *she's* going through for her to run away like that."

He walked Malachi to the door, and they continued to talk on the front porch. James was not aware that little James had heard every word and was comforted by what he'd heard his father say. He felt he could count on his father to come up with a plan to help Rose, but he would have to convince Rose that it would be okay to tell. He got leftovers from the kitchen as Susannah and Mary were doing dishes and putting things away. He also grabbed a couple of blankets from a chest in his room and made his way up the path that was easy to traverse in the dark as he knew it so very well.

As little James opened the door of the cabin, he was startled to see Rose sitting there on the mattress with the gun in her trembling hand.

"It's just me, Rose!" She sighed and wiped tears from her eyes and placed the gun next to her on the mattress. He handed her a dish of ham and two biscuits.

She began to eat what he brought her ravenously. He gave her a container of fresh water.

She did not say thank you, but he could see the gratitude in her eyes.

He waited for her to finish and then he told her, "They are looking for you. Our neighbor came after dinner tonight and told us to be on the lookout for you. They are offering a reward. Rose, you should have heard my father. He was saying how much he wished he could rescue you."

"But he can't," she said.

"I think he would. I told you how much he hates slavery. How my grandfather bought him so he could be free. Rose, maybe my father could buy you! You could come live with us and be a servant, kind of like Lucy Wade was to my mother's family!"

"I don't think Mr. Stokes would ever do that. I don't think he'd sell me to anyone else."

"If he could make a profit, he might! That's how my father came to be bought from the plantation owner who had him! My father is very smart, and I think he would know what to do."

Rose refused to agree for James to tell his father. That night, James slept on a blanket outside the cabin with his pistol by his side. Rose slept on the mattress soundly for the first time in a while knowing James was out there guarding and protecting her with a gun.

The next morning, they ate and James left the gun with her again as he went to go help his father in the fields. He promised to return with dinner again that night.

For over two weeks, James continued to sleep on Cooper's mountain and feed and take care of Rose. Early one morning, Rose awoke very sick to her stomach. James hated to leave her, but he knew his father would become suspicious if he did not show up to help on the farm.

That very morning as he was getting ready to go to the fields, James said to Sarah that he was concerned about his oldest son. "I think I was much that way just before I took off. Maybe he is planning to leave us. He is sixteen. I don't know if my parents saw it coming or not. He just doesn't seem to be part of us anymore. He is of an age to start thinking of leaving. I guess I am realizing now how much it must have hurt my parents for me to leave like that so suddenly."

"I don't know, husband. He has always been such a private child. I wonder what he does all the time up there on Cooper's mountain."

James said, "He has always had a fixation on the place. I remember camping up there with him once when he was probably about eight. Do you know what he asked me?"

Sarah shook her head.

"He said, 'Papa, if I die before you and Mama, would you make sure to bury me up here on Cooper's mountain?' He said, 'I don't want to be in Uncle Malachi's cemetery.' Then he made me promise that I would have him buried up there." James turned to look at

Sarah and realized immediately that he never should have told that to his wife. She had tears in her eyes.

"How sad to think my young son was thinking about death at the age of eight."

James apologized. "I am sorry. I should not have told you that."

Sarah wiped a tear out of the corner of her eye and gave James a goodbye kiss as he headed off to the fields.

Little James did not show up for breakfast nor to work in the fields. He had gone into the cabin and fixed both Rose and himself food from the night before, hoping it would help her feel better.

Rose was crying softly. "James, I don't know why, but you have been so wonderful to me. There is no reason why you should care about me. I'm just a runaway slave."

"Rose, I think you are beautiful. I get angry when I think of how you've been treated."

"James, I may need to go back," she said.

James looked at her unbelievingly. "Why would you say that?"

"My mother told me something before I left, and now I think she is right. If she is, I am frightened to be alone up here when you go to work."

"What is it, Rose?"

"I think I am going to have a baby."

James looked at her horrified. "How, Rose? We've done nothing."

"Of course not. I was attacked by two of Mr. Stokes's sons. They"—she began to cry—"they took turns with me. I tried not to let them, but I had no power over them!" She was crying hard now. "I didn't want them to!" James sat on the mattress next to her and took her in his arms.

"Rose, I am so sorry!" James touched her face. "That is so wrong! I am so sorry!"

"When my mother told me what might happen, that I might be carrying a baby, that's when I decided to run away. James, I have sat here many days when you are gone and thought about just using this gun on myself. My mother never told me, but I have heard that she was attacked by Mr. Stokes and that he might be my father. If that is true, then I am carrying a baby given to me by someone who is my half brother!" She began to weep again. "I may as well be dead!" she wailed. They held each other, and James kissed Rose's cheek and wiped her tears.

James had been in the fields for about an hour, and there was still no sign of little James. He got an overwhelming prompting to go check on him. Without even telling Sarah, he took off on horseback toward the woods that led to the path to the top of Cooper's mountain. When he finally reached the clearing where he and his son usually camped, suddenly James came out of the cabin with the pistol aimed at his father.

"James! Son!"

"Oh, Father, it's you!" He lowered the weapon, relieved.

"What are you thinking, son? What is wrong with you?" Then his father pointed to the cabin. "Did you build this? This is amazing! But I don't understand. Why the gun?"

Little James held the door open for him, and as he walked into the cabin, James saw Rose sitting on the mattress.

"Dear God, no!" James said, stricken with fear. "James! What have you done?"

Rose began to cry and draw back against the wall.

"Papa, this is Rose."

"I know that, son! But do you realize what you have done? You can't hide a runaway—"

James could not even bring himself to say the word *slave*.

"Father, you've got to help her! I told her how Grandfather bought you and freed you. I told her I was sure you could do the same for her! Surely, Mr. Stokes would sell her for a profit!"

"Oh, James, no, son. It's not the same! Mr. Stokes will have us both put in jail!"

Rose stood and tried to run, but little James stopped her. "Rose, it's going to be all right! Don't go!" He held her close to him and said, "I love you, Rose! I want to marry you!" She looked at James with her mouth open and with terror in her eyes.

"I love you too, James," she said, shaking her head. "But we could never do that!"

"She's right, James. Son, there is not a place in this world where the two of you could ever be together!"

"But, Papa, she is going to have a baby. I must—"

His father began to weep. "James, no, how could you?"

"It's not mine," he insisted. "I would never do that! She was attacked by Stokes's sons."

"Dear God," James said, leaning over and trying to catch his breath.

"James, I am afraid. I think I need my mother," Rose said, trembling.

"But they will whip you when you return!" he said to her.

"It won't be the first time I have been whipped," she said sadly. With that, she took off through the woods heading in the direction of the view overlooking the plantation. Little James went to run after her, but his father grabbed him and held onto his angry, weeping son.

"Why can't you do something?" he screamed at his father. "You hate slavery! Why can't you do something for her?"

"James, son, you don't understand! There is nothing I can do without landing in jail. I will not do that to my family! I just pray she doesn't go tell them she was held by us!"

They stood there just outside the cabin door, not knowing what to do or say. James was still holding his son, afraid he might take off after Rose.

"James, I am sorry for you. It seems you were born a century or two too early. Perhaps in another time, it would be acceptable for you and Rose to be together. But white people and black people now just cannot be married."

James turned angrily and freed himself from his father's grasp. "Then why do they do what they do? Why did that white slaveholder rape Rose's mother? Why did his white sons rape Rose? She gets no say so! She has to walk around part white and part black! Her baby will have to do the same! Why do they get to do that?"

"It is evil, son."

"Like what you do to my mother."

"No! James, does your mother act like she is afraid of me? We love each other. We are married, and there is a world of difference between the two situations. Son, I do not force myself on your mother. She is in love with me, and I am with her. We both want to be together. It is a very natural thing to do. We are blessed to have each other and to love each other."

"Papa, I know Rose loves me too. She is just frightened. I think we could head out west. Even if no one will marry us, I could be a father to her baby. No one would question its color since she is part black and I am white. We could live together somewhere out west. I know we could."

James shook his head sadly. "Son, I know it's going to hurt, but you must forget her."

He shook his head and fought back tears. "No! I will never forget her!"

"James, son, let us go home. We can talk on the way down. You did a very noble thing trying to protect Rose. I am proud of your kind feelings. I know how you feel."

"No, you don't," said James as if from a million miles away. "You got to marry the woman you love."

Father and son were still standing outside the cabin facing each other. "Come back home. We will take the day off from the fields. We can spend today just talking," James offered.

Young James hung his head and said softly, "Yes, Father. Let me get my things." The boy turned and went into the cabin. At the instant James had the premonition, he heard the gun go off.

"No!" he screamed. "No!" He entered the cabin still screaming. "James! My son!" As he slumped to the floor and scooped his son into his arms, he screamed as he'd never screamed before and could not stop.

CHAPTER 19

As James cradled his son's bleeding head in his lap and his screams subsided, he saw the pistol lying on the floor just inches from little James's fingers. Without even thinking, James reached and grabbed the gun with the intention of flinging it as far away as he could. As soon as the gun was in his own hands, the thought came into his brain in a flash. *Here is relief. Your son just proved it. Here is relief from all your suffering and grieving.* Before he knew what he was doing, James raised the gun and pointed it at his own anguished head. A sudden flash of light filled the tiny cabin, and James saw the figure of Captain Trenton Duggar before him. His voice thundered, "NO, LAD! IT IS NOT YET YOUR TIME!" Startled, James threw the gun against the wall over the mattress. He looked again and saw no one. Yet he heard the captain's voice in his heart, "Sarah and the children need you."

Like one in a catatonic state, James stood, picked up James's body, and lay him on the mattress. Then he shut the door to the cabin tightly, and like a man sleepwalking, he headed for home.

On the way down, James wept as he had these thoughts, *How am I going to tell Sarah what just happened? I didn't destroy myself, but now I am going to destroy her? Did I really just see Captain Duggar? Did I really just hear his voice? What words will I use to tell Sarah her firstborn son just took his own life?*

Then again, in his mind and heart, he heard as he kept walking, *Angels will assist you.*

By the time he reached the bottom of the path, he had formulated his plan. He got on his horse he'd left tethered to a tree and rode to Malachi's. Malachi was behind his house on the worn path overlooking his fields. James pulled up on his horse and dismounted, still breathless.

"James! What is wrong?" his friend asked.

"I need your help. I need you, and I need Sally and Martha. Can your girls watch the little ones?"

"Certainly, but what is it?"

"My son James. He is dead. He took his own life up on Cooper's mountain." The words seemed to be coming from someone else. "I have to tell Sarah. She is going to need your wife and mother."

"Dear Lord in heaven, no!" said Malachi, immediately weeping. He embraced James. "How? What happened, James?"

James breathed deeply and told his friend, "He never came back from the mountain to work this morning. He has been spending many nights up there in a cabin he built. This morning when he didn't show, something told me to go for him. Please do not tell anyone, Malachi, but he had Rose, the little runaway slave up there with him. We did not know, but he had been hiding her in his cabin, and he was feeding her and looking after her. He thought I could help." At this, his controlled voice fell apart. "He thought I could fix things!" James sobbed.

Malachi hugged James to him again, released him, and James continued, "When I told him I could not, she ran off to return to the plantation. I thought I'd convinced him to come home with me. He said he needed to get his things, and he turned to go back into the cabin, and just as I had another forewarning and turned, I heard the gun go off. He had that British pistol with him that I had given him. He had been protecting her with that. He shot himself Malachi!" James crumpled again, sobbing. James sat down on the ground holding his knees and crying with his head down. Malachi went to inform the women, and after several minutes, the three of them were in the wagon, and James climbed back up on his horse to lead them to his house.

James did not want to go into his own house. On the brief ride home, he began to feel a huge weight of responsibility for what happened to his son. He had given him the damned gun! He had given the boy no hope when he was desperately trying to help the girl! He might as well have fired the gun at his son!

Malachi had his arm around his friend, and the women were holding each other about the waists as they walked into the house. Sarah had just finished nursing Ann. When they came in, Sarah knew immediately that something was very wrong. She had actually had a heavy heart all morning, ever since she and James had talked about little James and his obsession with Cooper's mountain and his desire to be buried there. She handed the baby to Susannah who was nearby and asked her to take the baby and put her to bed.

James and their visitors did not take seats. Sarah stood and faced them.

"What is wrong, James?" she asked her husband.

"I do not know how to say the words, Sarah." He was already weeping openly.

"Please just say it, husband." She was crying with her hands clasped and to her mouth and did not know why she was bracing herself.

"Perhaps you should sit, Sarah," Sally said, coming over and helping her into her chair.

Even Sally had clearly been crying.

After Sarah was seated, James went over to her and knelt in front of her chair, taking her hands in his.

"Sarah, James is dead. Our son took his own life."

Sarah crumpled into James's arms, and everyone was weeping. Sarah's cries were the loudest and very emotionally painful to hear. "Oh, God!" she kept repeating. Finally, she asked James how it had happened.

"I knew when he didn't show up to the fields something was wrong. I went up to Cooper's mountain, and I found him. He was there with Rose, the Stokes's runaway slave girl. He had been hiding her up there and taking care of her."

"How did they even meet?" Sarah asked, her nose red from crying. Tears were still streaming down her cheeks.

"Apparently, she found his little hut and was hiding out in it. He went up there one day and found her and befriended her and wanted to take care of her. So he's been feeding her and looking after her. He took his gun to protect her. They became very close. He begged me to go see Stokes and offer to buy her. I—I didn't know what to say! I told him I could not do that because Stokes would have us both in jail! He kept saying his grandfather had bought me and allowed me to marry you and wanted to know why I couldn't do the same for Rose! When I insisted this was far different and that there was nothing I could do without going to jail, she became very frightened, and she took off. I kept James there and told him he had to forget about her, that it could never be! I convinced him, I thought, to come home with me so we could talk. So he went back into the cabin to get his things, only he got the gun instead. I was right there by the door, and I heard the gunshot, but I was too late!" James was crying very hard, still on his knees, holding Sarah who was weeping as well.

"Oh, my poor son!" she said again and again. James held Sarah close and they wept pitifully in each other's arms. At last James got up and went to his chair and sat.

Malachi asked, "What would you have us do, James? We will do anything we can!" their friend insisted.

"I do not know. I left his body up there in the cabin. He has always said he wanted to be buried up there. So I must go dig a grave, I guess. If you could assist me, I would be indebted to you. I do not want a church funeral. I want just my family and your family present, those you think should be there. Malachi, if you could say a prayer and a few words over my son, I would certainly appreciate it. Sarah, how does that sound?"

She nodded mutely in obvious shock.

"I am going to go start his grave," James said. Looking at Sally and Martha, he went on, "I would be appreciative if you could stay with my wife." James leaned over and kissed Sarah's cheek.

"James," Malachi said, "why don't you let me and some of my nephews go dig the grave? You need a casket. You are the carpenter around in these parts."

"You are right. I've got to make another casket," James said through fresh tears.

Sarah stood. "I will go get clean clothes for him."

Martha whispered in her son's ear, and Malachi nodded. She was reminding him that they needed to take something to clean him up with. By now, the other children had heard the sobs and had gathered from every direction, and before James left to go to the barn, he gathered them around and told them the sad news. They all began to cry, except the littlest ones. Susannah and Mary ran to their mother and held her close. They went with her to find clothes to bury James in.

Malachi had left to go get help with the digging.

Peter was only eleven but seemed to feel a need to do something. He asked his father if he could help with the casket. "Yes, son. And you can help me get it up the mountain using our old handcart."

Malachi and two of his oldest nephews went up on Cooper's mountain and dug the grave and readied the body, dressing him in the clothes Sarah had sent. They placed a clean blanket over the mattress and lay his dressed body on top. Malachi and the boys looked through James's few possessions in the cabin trying to find the gun. They looked everywhere and did not find it. Malachi fastened the cabin door, and they left. He only told the boys that James had killed himself. He did not say anything about the slave girl.

James and Peter worked quietly together in the barn making a casket of pine. James took the opportunity to teach his second son a few skills. He stopped and they both cried several times. Peter kept asking his father why James would do such a thing, and it was hard to explain the reason so that someone Peter's age could comprehend it. He told Peter that James was not happy and that sometimes life was too hard for some to live.

"Do you think God will forgive him for taking his own life?" Peter finally asked.

James pulled his son down to sit with him on the barn floor. He held his son close. "Peter, I believe that God knows what is in our hearts. I think He loves us and knows us very well. He knows what we really are like on the inside. I believe God knew that your brother was not happy. I think just like you can break an arm or a leg, I think James had a broken heart and a broken mind. I believe that right now, he is in the arms of Jesus and Jesus is holding him just like I am holding you."

That night in bed, Sarah and James held onto each other and wept. "Sarah," her husband told her, "I feel so responsible."

"James, no! We had just talked about how hard life had always been for him. He took life so seriously. As his mother, I had always worried that something might happen to him."

"But I gave him the pistol! I should have known better! James was never a hunter! I wanted him to know I thought of him as grown. Plus, I feel I failed him. I gave him no hope. He said he was in love with Rose. He wanted to marry her. He wanted to marry her the way I wanted to marry you. He thought I could make it happen the way he knew your father helped us be together. Sarah, I am keeping this part just between the two of us. Rose is with child."

Sarah gasped, "Did James tell you that?"

He nodded. "And she confirmed it. She was raped by two of Stokes's sons."

"Oh, Dear God!"

"James wanted to be her hero and be the father of her baby. He wanted to take her out west and get her away from here. I completely took away any hope of that ever happening."

"But, James, you were being truthful!"

"He couldn't see that. You should see the cabin he built. He built it with his own two hands. She sought refuge there. I think over the last two weeks or so, it became like their Cuckold Creek. They bonded together. They fell in love. I told James that he was born a century or two too early. That maybe someday, it would not be forbidden for people who are black and white to fall in love and marry. He was trying to do a noble thing."

"So now what happens to Rose?"

"I am assuming she went back to the plantation. She said she knew she would be whipped but she wanted her mother. She was afraid of giving birth alone. I want to go kill people, Sarah."

"James!" Sarah said, horrified.

"I am just so sickened by the whole idea of slavery, especially when there is a twisted and perverted side to something that is already so morally wrong!"

The next day James and Peter headed up the backside of Cooper's mountain before the others, hauling little James's casket up in the handcart. Together they unloaded it near the newly dug grave, went into the cabin, retrieved the body, put it into the handcart and then wheeled it to the casket, placing the body inside. James and Peter both cried silently through the whole process. Together they stood for a moment and took one last look at the face of their son and brother. James got the lid and sobbed aloud as he put it into place, covering the body of his firstborn son. Then he and Peter held each other for a few moments, weeping together. Sarah had asked that the casket be closed as she did not want to have an image anywhere in her memory of little James's body.

Peter then looked around and saw some asters and brown-eyed yellow daisies growing nearby and began to gather them and place them on top of the casket. James sat on the ground and continued to cry for his son, both of his sons.

They were soon joined by both families, most coming to the top of Cooper's mountain on foot, but the women and babies being led up on horseback. It was a sad, silent procession interrupted by occasional cries of mourning. Slowly they gathered around the handmade pine coffin near the open hole.

Malachi could barely speak as he read from the Bible and talked of life everlasting and the mercy and grace of God. He offered a sweet prayer asking God to bless James and his family. All wept as James, Malachi, and Peter lowered the casket into the ground. The families headed down the mountain, with James and Malachi staying behind to cover the grave. As they were shoveling dirt, James was thanking his friend. "You and your whole family are angels to us," he said.

"We feel the same about you," Malachi said. "James, I wanted to ask you something. The boys and I, when we came up here yesterday to dig, we searched and searched for that gun. Did you leave it up here?"

"I flung it against the wall where the mattress is. I assume it's still there."

"We looked through everything, tore the mattress apart putting a clean blanket over top. It's not in that cabin."

James and Malachi went back into the cabin when they were finished covering the grave. They went through the two boxes that James had up there. They brought around the handcart and threw the shovels in the back. James began to load up everything that was in the cabin: the boxes, the mattress, and the extra blankets. There was no sign of the gun.

The two men headed down the path toward home. James was about to tell Malachi about what happened before he threw the gun, about how he wanted to end his own life, but before he could even start the story, the piercing sound of a gunshot could be heard from above them, back up on the top of the mountain. They stopped pulling the handcart, left it there, and ran up the hill as fast as they could. Malachi's lame knee slowed him down, but James rushed to the top.

"Oh no! Dear God, no!" James cried out. Lying across the new mound of dirt on little James's grave was Rose, bleeding from her head. James found the gun near her hand. The way she had fallen, he could see her legs underneath her worn dress. Her calves and as much as he could see of her thighs revealed fresh marks of a whip. James was already sitting on the ground with his head in his hands weeping. "Malachi! God, help me! I have never wanted to kill anyone more in my whole life!" he screamed.

His friend sat next to him on the ground and held him as he sobbed. "I am done with life!" cried James. "I hate these evil men! I have had my fill of them!"

Finally, James stopped and looked at his friend and said, "Malachi, I can't think straight! What do we do?"

He looked at James and said, "I say we put her body in the handcart and take her straight to Stokes and tell him what just happened."

"But what if he tries to say we killed her? A man that evil? He would lie in a heartbeat and say it's our word against his!"

"We could open up the grave and put her in with your boy."

"No, I want him to know that we *know* how he tormented her!"

"James, I believe being honest is always the best way to go. But maybe I should do the talking."

They decided to take her back to James's and transfer her body to the large wagon. They placed poor Rose in the back of the handcart on top of the mattress and covered her with a blanket. On the way down, Malachi said, "Perhaps we should find a magistrate."

"I have a feeling Stokes is going to do that anyway," James replied.

"We could bury her in my cemetery," Malachi offered.

"No, you're right about the honesty part. Word's going to get out, and I don't want to make it look as if we are trying to hide anything."

James felt so badly for his friend as he could tell that all the walking and digging he'd done had really hurt his bad knee. They got to his house and moved Rose's body to the large wagon and hitched the horses. It was late afternoon, and the two men left without saying a word to anyone in either family. They drove the shortcut to the Stokes plantation. James sat in the front of the house looking up at the imposing front of Cooper's mountain that he rarely got to see. He and Malachi hopped down from the wagon. They were met near the front steps by Herbert Stokes himself. James and Malachi moved to the back of the wagon and uncovered Rose's body.

Malachi told him, "Mister Stokes, we were up on the mountain burying James's son this afternoon. As we were all leaving after the funeral, we heard a gunshot. We found her body lying on his son's grave. A double suicide a day apart. Seems she had been hiding in a hut the boy built up there. None of us knew he was looking after her up there. James went up there because his son didn't come home to work, and he found them up there. She ran off, and James told his son they couldn't be together. His son killed himself. She must have gotten the gun, and she probably watched us have his funeral today, and when we left, she used the gun and killed herself on his grave. That is the whole truth, Mister Stokes."

James's face was pained with grief, and Herbert Stokes could see that.

"What's your boy doing building camps up on my mountain?" Stokes asked.

"He's been going up there for years," James explained. "He's always loved being up there, and he even asked to be buried up there."

"Well, looks like you could have gotten my permission first."

Stokes was not looking directly at Rose's body.

"According to my son, she was scared to be here, and she ran away," James added, looking the man straight in his face.

"You know how it is, especially with the young ones. They don't want any responsibility."

"I can see she has fresh whip marks," James said, his anger rising.

"I know you're not about to lecture me on how I treat my property, Master West."

"She told my son she was carrying a baby, that she was raped by two of your sons."

"That's a damn lie! Sounds like if she was carrying a baby, your son was the father. Sounds like they fell in love. Not surprised, him being your son and all. I know you've always had a soft spot in your heart for the darkies."

James leapt toward Stokes with his fists clenched, but Malachi held him back. "James, don't," he begged his friend. "It's not worth going to jail over. Sarah and the children need you," Malachi reminded him.

"He's right," Stokes said. "And if I hear any talk of anything in the community about all this, I will have the law on you for stealing my property."

James grimaced as he told Stokes, "May God have mercy on your evil soul! May you rot in hell!"

Stokes motioned for two of his slaves to come over and remove Rose's body from the wagon. When they finished, James and Malachi climbed back on, and James gave Stokes one last contemptuous look. Stokes walked over before they left and said to James, "Sorry about your boy. If you've got any more sons, I'd be teaching them to steer clear of other people's property."

When they neared the Stokes's main gate, they both heard a scream: a female was wailing and lamenting back at the plantation. Rose's mother had just been told. James stopped for a moment and put his head down. "God, help that poor woman," Malachi said.

James said no more all the way home. He dropped Malachi off at his house and thanked him again. "I don't think I'll ever be able to repay you, friend," James told Malachi. "Get off that knee. I know it's been hurting you all day."

"I'll be praying for you and your family, James."

"Please do."

James drove home, unhitched the wagon, and put the horses up. It was getting dark.

Sarah met him at the door. "I was so worried! I couldn't imagine what took so long!"

He held her close. He sat wearily in his large chair and pulled Sarah onto his lap. "We cleaned out the cabin and brought all of James's things home. Something happened, Sarah. Malachi and I were a third of the way down the path, and we heard a gunshot. We ran back up, and it was Rose. She'd run away again and had gotten her hands on James's gun. She killed herself on his grave," James told her, his voice breaking.

Sarah wept into James's neck. "What did you and Malachi do with her body, James?" she finally asked.

"We took her back to the plantation. Drove right up to Stokes's front door. We told him about James and having his funeral today. We told him we'd brought Rose home. Told him there had been two suicides on Cooper's mountain. I made sure he knew what James had told me about how she was raped by two of his sons."

"James! What did he say?"

"He called me a liar. He told me if he heard talk about any such things in the community, he would charge me with stealing his property. Sarah, she had fresh lash marks on her legs. What I wouldn't give to be able to tie that bastard to a whipping post and beat him until the blood ran!"

Sarah looked at her husband with concern. James finished with a sneer on his face, "I told him, 'May God have mercy on your evil soul!' I told him I hoped he would rot in hell." James stared off across the room, his thoughts clearly elsewhere, maybe at a pit of fire watching this man burn.

CHAPTER 20

*T*hat night in bed, James could not sleep. Sarah was awake as well, not only because of her husband's tossing and turning but also due to the heartache and tears that kept coming to her.

At last, James said, "Sarah, I know you are awake. I want to tell you something. You may think I am mad. Maybe I am. Perhaps being there when James took his own life affected me somehow." He sat up in bed and pulled his knees up under the sheet and hugged them.

Sarah remained on her back.

"When I ran into the cabin and I was on the ground cradling his head in my lap—"

"That's why your clothes were so bloody. I threw them out, you know. There was too much for me to clean. They would have smelled like blood forever," she said numbly, interrupting him.

He looked back at her. "I am sorry you had to deal with that, Sarah." He paused, collecting his thoughts. "As I was holding him, I saw the gun lying there very nearby. I picked the gun up with the idea that I was going to throw it as far as I could. But when it was in my hand—" he paused to remember. "When I could feel it in my hand, the thought came to me that must have come to James as well, 'Here is relief. Here is the end of your suffering.'" He paused again. "Sarah, I took the gun and pointed it at my own head. I wanted to kill myself. No, I was *going* to kill myself."

He felt Sarah reach out and touch his back with her fingers as she continued to lie behind him.

"All of a sudden, there was a bright light in the room. And it was already daylight, and the door to the cabin was open. It was still late morning, but there was a *really* bright light in that cabin. First, I heard a voice and opened my eyes, and I saw—please don't think me mad—but I saw Captain Duggar! I heard him say, 'No, lad! It is not yet your time!' But it was loud! When that happened, *then* I flung the gun against the wall over the mattress." James was still speaking slowly as if he wanted to remember every detail carefully and in order. "Then I heard his voice again, but when I looked up, he was not there, but I heard his voice saying, 'Sarah and the children need you.'"

Sarah did not speak; she could not as tears had tightened her throat.

"You don't believe me, do you?"

She was nodding, but from where he was sitting in bed, he could not see her.

"You think I've gone daft."

Finally, she found her voice. "No, James, I believe you."

"It was so real," he said.

"I had something similar happen, though not as dramatic," she told him. "Perhaps it was because of what we talked about when James didn't show up to breakfast that morning. You told me about his wanting to be buried on the mountain when he died. But that put such a weight on my heart. I felt all morning as if I was being prepared for an awful thing to happen. I found myself praying, 'Lord, please not another tragedy.' But the promptings were so strong that I *knew* that someone was going to walk in with horrible news, and when you got here with the Fraziers, I could feel that same voice saying, 'Here it is. I told you.'"

He lay back down and took her hand in his. "I had a prompting as well. I was in the field, and it had been about an hour with no sign of James, and I felt a strong prompting that I must go see about him! It felt too urgent to deny. I even went on horseback to the bottom of the path to get there faster. When I got up to the cabin, he came out with the gun aimed at me. Rose was in the cabin, and he was protecting her. So after I completely crushed all their hopes and she ran off, he went to get his things, and the image of the gun flashed in my mind, and I *knew*, but I did not have time to stop him. I did not have time to stop him," he repeated, tormented by that fact. "Why would I get a prompting for that if I couldn't get it in time to stop him?"

They lay silently side by side for a few more minutes, letting the truth sink in that for whatever reason, they were led by a higher power in this whole horrible event of losing their son. They both knew that it was divine intervention, but why?

James spoke again, "I knew a lad who took his own life back in Wales. I was about ten, and he was a few years older. An acquaintance of Francis's. I remember hearing my parents talk of it, and they had heard his parents say, 'We did not see it coming. We had no idea that he was so distraught.' So why were *we* warned, Sarah, especially when we could do nothing to stop it?"

They both were quiet again, pondering.

"And why Captain Duggar?" James asked.

"From what you've told me, he really grew to care about you," Sarah said softly. "What was that you once told me? That he said he knew that angels would assist you. Perhaps he is now one of your angels."

"I have often thought of that moment on the ship when we were saying farewell. It was like a benediction or some sort of blessing from him. He said that he believed angels would assist me in finding Francis, yet Francis was *dead* when I found him." James was quiet for a few more seconds. Then he said, "Do you know what I think? I think this is sure evidence that perhaps God is a marvelous trickster." He chuckled.

Sarah sat up at this.

"James, how could you say such a thing! God has blessed us so much in our lives! I do not think you should persist in your thoughts that God is purposely tormenting you!"

James sat up again and cried out, "Do I need to list for you the people whom I love that He has taken from me?"

"No, you do not! I have lost them as well! I have grieved right along with you!"

"I think by showing me Captain Duggar and the image of the gun, yet taking my son's life, God is mocking me! I can almost see Him laughing and sneering!"

"Oh, James, I cannot begin to tell you how very wrong you are!"

"Wrong? I think I have finally figured it out, my love! Why should I worship one who delights in hurting me?"

"James, you cannot mean such a thing! You have always loved God and read His Word. You have always had such a strong faith that I have relied upon and admired. He brought you home from battle many times and has given us a beautiful family!"

"That beautiful family," said James, now laughing, "is just a result of lust! Did you know that, Sarah? Isn't that the truth? Even little James saw through that!"

"What are you talking about?"

"The night you lost the baby on Christmas Day, James—he was twelve, I think—stopped me in the parlor, angry, and said, 'I think my mother has had enough children.' Oh, I sounded so noble saying, 'Son, you have no idea what you are talking about. Your mother and I love each other.'" James was out of the bed now, pacing and talking. "I told him he did not understand grown-up love. He told me, 'Papa, I know how babies come to be. This is within your control.' I thought, *Foolish child*. But he was right! He was wise beyond his years! I should have stopped, but I lusted! It's through sin and sin alone that we have so many children. That is nothing to be proud of."

"Now I think madness *has* taken over your brain," Sarah said, lying back down and sighing in disbelief and concern for her husband's state of mind.

The next morning, James was silent all through breakfast. Sarah had to ask Peter to ask the blessing on the food. James left for the fields without even saying anything to his wife. She said another silent prayer as she and the girls cleared the table, asking God to help James deal with the hurt of losing his son.

It was with a heavy heart that they all attended their duties that day. James did not return for dinner that night, and Sarah and the children became concerned. She sent Peter and William out into the fields and the garden looking for their father. On their own, when they did not find him, they went to Malachi's to see if he knew where he was. He did not, and Peter and William returned on horseback quickly to tell their mother they could not find their father.

Sarah began to think of sending someone up to Cooper's mountain and was about to send Peter back to Malachi's when James came in very quietly. He went straight to their bedroom without so much as an apology or an explanation.

When Sarah stepped into their room and shut the door behind her, she found him sitting on the bed removing his shoes.

"Hope I didn't worry you. I went to Oxford today."

"Why did you not let me know?" she asked. "I have been worried sick. I have kept your dinner warm."

"I have eaten." When he stood and walked past her, she clearly smelled liquor.

"James West!" she called out. He continued walking into the parlor. She followed him but whispered as two children were nearby, "James, have you been drinking?"

"And eating, as I said. There's a gentleman in Oxford who runs a nice inn with food and drink. Perhaps we should go there sometime, Sarah."

"How much did you have to drink?" she whispered to him.

"Not quite enough," he replied.

He stooped to see what Joseph was playing with on the floor. When he stood, he almost lost his balance. He laughed just a little and sat in his chair. Sarah went over to her husband who now had his eyes closed.

"James West, you are intoxicated!"

"Not really. Just a bit numb. And warm. It's getting chilly out."

"How can you do this? Did you not work out in the fields today?"

"Earlier, I did. But Colton and the boys came and helped. So I just left."

Sarah knew this had everything to do with his talk of insanity the night before. She knew he did this to try and forget his pain. But she also knew that this was not her husband and this was not a good thing.

When he went to bed without saying good night to anyone, Sarah asked Susannah to be in charge of putting the children to bed. She followed James into their room. He was already in the bed in his nightshirt. "Perhaps tonight, I shall sleep," he told her. "They say a good stiff drink will help you sleep. I hope to find out."

"James, we must talk."

"Talk to me, love. Perhaps your chatter will help put me to sleep."

"James! That is rude!" James put a pillow over his head. "James, we need to talk about this. This is not you! You do not drink! This is no solution!"

He removed the pillow from his face long enough to yell at his wife, "Please shut your bloody mouth! I do not want to hear any nagging from you! I am a grown man and will do as I please!"

Sarah got ready for bed and lay next to him. Soon, she heard his deep snoring. He did not hear her soft weeping.

The next morning, he had a severe headache and was sick to his stomach. She did not speak as he suffered. She prayed this would teach him a very serious lesson. He got up and went to the fields but came back by midmorning and got into the bed. "I am not feeling well," was all he told Sarah. By three o'clock in the afternoon, he was off again to Oxford, she assumed. He left on horseback without speaking. The day was lovely, and Sarah left the baby with Susannah and walked over to the Fraziers. She hated sharing this burden with their dear friends but hoped Malachi might be able to share some wisdom concerning James.

She sat at the table drinking Martha's herbal tea and was surrounded by Sally, Malachi, and Martha at their dining room table.

"There is something very wrong with James," she told them. "He came home drunk last night."

Malachi looked stricken. "Not James?"

Sarah nodded. "The night before, he told me he had decided God was still his tormentor, and he was tired of it. He was saying all kinds of insane things. I know he is just having a hard time dealing with James's death. But so am I!" Sarah wiped tears at this point. "When we lost our first child, we made the mistake of grieving separately. It was wrong, and I thought he'd learned. When we lost the baby at Christmas, we grieved together, and we were able to deal with it. You three know my husband as well as I do! He is a faith-filled man! He is a good man! But I do not want him to become a drunk! What should I do? What would you do, Sally, if Malachi suddenly became an infidel?"

Sally look horrified at the thought. Malachi reached over and took her hand. "We've had our times," she said. "All couples have. But I would like to advise you to love him but do not judge him. Continue to love him, but do not nag. I think he will come around. The pain is still so fresh, Sarah."

Malachi nodded. "Good counsel, Sally, my dear. And, Sarah, we shall pray. Would you like for me to speak to him?"

Sarah shook her head. "He would probably take that as nagging."

That night, Sarah braced herself. James came in after they had eaten as he'd done the night before. The children were now concerned for their father, and they could tell Sarah was uneasy.

This night, he went straight to bed. Susannah took charge of the little ones again, and Sarah sat on the bed next to James. She could smell the alcohol again, and by the time she had put on her nightgown, he was snoring loudly.

This happened over two more nights, and then he did not go into town any longer, but he began spending more and more time in the barn at night. She assumed he had purchased bottles of whiskey and had hidden them in the barn. She knew this had to be true as he no longer went to Oxford, so she was certain he must have bought enough liquor to keep on hand. Three nights in a row, he simply drank until he fell asleep and stayed in the barn. She tried to follow the advice of the Fraziers and remain the quiet, attentive wife.

One night, however, James came in from the barn, probably drunker than she had ever seen him. He wasn't loud, and she was grateful for that, but he came into the bedroom and fell into the bed and immediately began to fondle her. She had not been asleep, but she was in no mood to be part of his drunken pleasure. When she tried to push him away as the stench nauseated her, he cursed at her and told her, "So you are going to make me turn to whores as well as the bottle?"

She began crying and turned over. He soon fell asleep and was snoring. It was the first night he had slept in their bed in three nights.

Sally and Martha came to visit the next day to see how things were going. Sally embraced her friend and held her as she wept. James was out in the fields attempting to work. "Malachi is out visiting with James," Sally told her.

"He must have a massive headache this morning," Sarah said. "Last night was as drunk as I have seen him." She sighed.

"No offense intended," said sweet Martha, "but, Sarah, my dear, you look as if you haven't slept in nights."

Sarah smiled a little. "I haven't slept *well*, Martha. I am crying myself to sleep, though. I feel," she said, "as if I have lost my husband *and* my son! I have lost both of my Jameses!" Tears poured anew. "I don't even feel as if I have properly grieved my son for losing my husband!"

The women tried to bring solace to their friend.

"How are the children?" Martha asked.

"Not well. They know there is something dreadfully wrong with their father. I have talked to the older ones, and they know he is grieving awfully for James and that he has turned to drink."

"Poor little ones," said Sally. "Children seem to suffer the worst in situations like this. They hurt here," she said, pointing to her heart. "They do not understand what is going on, and sometimes, they blame themselves."

They were soon joined by Malachi, alone. He had been trying to talk to James out in the field, and he came in and sat at the table with the ladies.

"He is barely speaking to me," said Malachi. "He wasn't hostile, just acting like he doesn't care very much. I tried asking him if there was something I could do to help ease his pain, and he said his pain was being eased, thank you very much. Then he grinned and said, 'Feel like killing some bastards, Malachi? That would help ease the demons by getting rid of them.'"

Malachi shook his head and vowed to continue praying for his friend.

That night, James came in from the barn drunk again, and Sarah was already asleep. This time, for the first time in their marriage, James forced himself upon her, and so as not to alarm the children, she said nothing after the first few moments of quiet struggle. The next morning, he seemed to not even remember what he'd done. He ate a little breakfast, lost most of it, and headed out to the fields to work.

Sarah was not sure how much longer she could hang on. She knew she still loved James and she understood his deep emotional pain, but this time, like after that horrible death of their first child, she was grieving all alone, and it was worse because she was also mourning the loss of her husband.

As December began, she tried talking to James about toys for the children. This was usually when he was sneaking out to the barn, busy with carving and building.

He sighed loudly as she brought up the subject. "I'm not sure what the boys would even like. Perhaps I shall buy them something in town. Maybe you could make them shirts. To be honest, I would love it if we could just forget Christmas this year. It's going to seem all wrong without James anyway."

"I wonder if that is what your parents said in Wales the first Christmas after you ran away?"

He gave her a look that cut into her heart. "How dare you bring that up?"

"What? That you left home? That's never been a sore point before, James."

He turned away. "You do not understand, do you?" he asked. "You have no idea what I'm going through!"

He walked out of the house and headed for the barn. He came back about thirty minutes later, and he was enraged. Sarah had never seen him so angry. His face was blazing red as he came into the house, screaming, "Who has been in the barn?!"

When they all looked up from their play or work silently and with fear on their faces, James screamed again, "Who has been in my barn?!"

"James!" Sarah exclaimed. "Do not scream at my children!"

"*Your* children? Someone has been moving things out in the barn! I am missing some things!"

All were quiet. He screamed again, this time reaching out and grabbing Sarah by the arm. "Was it you, wife? You are the one who has been nagging me! Did you go out there and take it?"

Peter stood bravely and shouted at his father, "Do not touch my mother! Take your hands off her!" James glared at the boy, turned, and left the room and the house, still in a rage. Sarah was crying but assured the children she was fine. She went out onto the porch and found James sitting on the top step. She sat down next to him. They both sat silently for a few minutes. Sarah was hoping James might apologize, but he said nothing.

"I love you, James," she finally said softly. "I cannot bring our son back any more than you can. You have turned to drink to ease your pain, but what am I to do? I cannot drink and look after my family."

"So you think you are so much better than I am?" he asked angrily, not looking at her. "You are not better than me."

"I never said that. I am saying that I am hurting too."

"So why do *I* get to get drunk and you don't?" he asked. "You, woman, were not there! You did not hold your dying son in your arms after he put a bullet in his head!" His voice was so full of wrath.

"No, but I have held two dead daughters in my arms!" she said firmly. "James, you told me about the amazing experience you had when Captain Duggar came to you in the cabin and stopped you from killing yourself."

"I was insane to listen to an illusion! I should have died with my son!"

"You are listening to illusions now! Drink, drunkenness is an illusion. It is a temporary solution. And it is turning you into a monster!"

"A monster? If I were left unto my own, Stokes and his sons would be dead men now! Do you know that? I am not just drinking to numb the pain of James's death. I am drinking to squelch the desire to go kill people. Did you know that, Sarah?"

"James, have you stopped to think that by having all this hate in your heart that you are no better than they are? You are now like them," she said. "To have peace, you have got to learn to forgive and let go."

James did not respond but got up and went to the barn. She watched him leave on horseback and assumed he was off to find more liquor. She wondered who had taken James's hidden bottle. She thought perhaps Malachi did it to help his friend out. She prayed that the truth she just spoke would not send him over the edge.

James rode with tears stinging his eyes. He rode as if he were trying to outrun real demons pursuing him. He found himself unexpectedly stopping at the church. It was very dark, but he slowed his horse and got down and tied it to a tree. He felt as he fumed and walked toward the church that he was about to have a showdown. God was the one with whom he was the angriest. Forgiveness? He was supposed to forgive the evil men of this world? He would tell God what he thought of that idea.

James entered the quiet, dark church and moved quickly down the aisle until he was standing in front of the pulpit that he had built.

For a few minutes, James simply listened to the stillness in the room. The pewter cross on the large table behind the pulpit cast a shadow on the floor from the moonlight that shone through the plain windows.

"I bet You are not even here," James began in a sneering voice. "*You* are nothing but an illusion. You cannot torment me any longer as I have decided You do not exist. Do You hear me?" he shouted. His voice echoed just a little. "But if You *do* exist, if You *are* here, do You know, God, do You *know* or even *care* that my son is *dead*?" he screamed. "With all Your promptings and sending Captain Duggar, *he died*! He died just the same! HE TOOK HIS OWN LIFE!" James was screaming now. Tears were pouring down his cheeks. "WHY DO YOU CONTINUE TO TORMENT ME!" he screamed again. Sobbing, James fell across the altar that he had helped to construct just a few years before.

I know your pain. My Son died as well. It is agony.

"I CAN'T TAKE THIS PAIN ANY LONGER!" James screamed again.

My Son went through agony. And because He did, only He can lift your burdens.

"That can't be all!" James cried. "I have done awful things! I have turned my back on You, on my family! Even now I need to be purged! Please, Dear God, purge me of this awful hatred! It is consuming me! I am sick of hating! I don't want to be like them! I cannot live with this loathing! I need peace, Father!" James wept. "I need peace!" He fell onto the floor and lay on his side still crying.

You are forgiven. I love you.

"But I cannot forgive *myself*! I gave him the gun! I did not even try to give him hope! I have been drinking and showing hate toward my own family! I am broken, Father!"

You are forgiven. I love you. I know your agonies. My Son suffered your agonies.

James was now lying on his back in front of the small altar looking up at the ceiling. Tears were running into his ears. His sobs were subsiding just a bit.

Go ask Sarah for forgiveness. Go love your children. In this, there is true peace and happiness.

James got up from the floor and made his way back to the altar on his knees. "Father! I do not deserve their forgiveness! I do not deserve Your forgiveness! What about all those evil men! They beat me! They beat Calvin! They raped Rose! I want them punished, Father!"

Vengeance is mine. It is not yours.

As he bowed at the altar, James prayed, "Father, forgive me! Forgive this broken sinner! I need your love, and I need your mercy! That is my only hope!"

I do love you. You are forgiven.

"Thank You, Father! But I am so unworthy! Why do you love me? I am so unworthy of Your love!" he sobbed.

My Son died for all. I love you. You are my child.

"Father," James prayed again. "I miss my loved ones so dreadfully! I did not get to see Francis! I have lost two daughters and a wonderful son! Help me get over this awful pain of losing them!"

They are with me. You will know them again. You will be with them forever.

"Can it be? Thank You, Father!" he prayed aloud over and over.

James stayed a while longer on his knees at the altar uttering words of gratitude and continued to weep. His heart felt joy. To feel joy again was so freeing. He felt an immense love washing over his heart, healing him like a holy salve. At last, James left the church with his head bowed humbly. It seemed he could not get home fast enough.

CHAPTER 21

*J*ames dismounted and put his horse in the barn when he got home. He could still taste the tears and felt them dried on his face. He went into the house. The children must have all been in the bed. He wanted to run wake them all up and apologize and hold them and beg them for their forgiveness. But first, Sarah.

His angel wife was sitting in her chair with his Bible open in her lap. She had obviously fallen asleep while reading and probably praying. For him. He felt guilt wash over him suddenly realizing the sleepless nights he had given her. He knelt quietly by her chair and said softly, "Sarah? I'm home."

She awoke and saw from the first glance at his face a changed countenance. His eyes spoke humility and profound sorrow. She was worried perhaps that *this* was an illusion; perhaps she was dreaming.

On hearing her sweet voice say his name "James," his face crumpled into new sobs. "Sarah, I am so, so sorry! Do you think you can ever possibly forgive me?" He laid his head in her lap and continued to cry. She leaned over and caressed his head and joined in with her tears.

When he could speak, he said, "I have been wicked. I have been so lost. Sarah, what was I thinking?"

"I have been praying for you, my love," she told him, wiping her own tears. "Where have you been, James? What happened? When you left here, I was afraid you were heading to find something to drink. I have never seen you so angry."

He sat on the floor next to her chair and kept his face pressed next to her lap, like a small, penitent child.

"I only made it as far as the church. I have passed the church every time I have been to town lately, but tonight, I stopped."

Sarah sat listening. "I stopped to give God a piece of my mind," he continued. "I went in there to tell Him I didn't believe He even existed, so He might as well stop tormenting me. I don't know if I can ever tell anyone what happened in that place, Sarah! Let's just say, I heard the still, small voice. It was powerful. I do not deserve your forgiveness or His, but I'm here to tell you that I have been forgiven by a very real Father in heaven." He had tears on his cheeks. "He is real, Sarah. And He loves us. And He knows us. I was told to come ask for your forgiveness."

Sarah touched his face softly with the back of her hand. "I do forgive you, James. You have been through such a refiner's fire. You have been through hell seeing James die. You are a good man."

"There has only been one good man on this earth—a perfect man, our Savior, and He suffered for us all. I know that now and cannot deny it. But I also know that the adversary is real. He wants our souls. I was giving him mine in horrible ways. I still cannot believe what I was doing to you and the children! You were right, Sarah! I was becoming one of those evil men that I hated so much!"

The two of them went into their bedroom and knelt by their bed, and James offered a very humble prayer and cried a little more. Sarah was so thankful to her Father for this blessing.

James knew she needed sleep, but he needed to talk.

"Sarah, God spoke to me tonight. Not here," he said, pointing to his ear, "but here and here," pointing to his head and his heart. "Have you ever experienced such a thing?"

Sarah nodded. "Yes, I remember when I was in the cemetery one day, not too long after we lost Timothy and Hannah, I wrote about it in my commonplace book. Do you—would you like for me to share that with you?"

James nodded. "Please," he said. She climbed out of the bed and reached into her chest and found the book. She turned to the portraits she had drawn of her younger siblings. "Here it is." She sat back on the bed and began to read her journal account. "Today, I was missing Timmy and Hannah so very much. I went to sit by their tombstones and found myself praying about how hard it was to lose someone you love so much. Words came into my mind and my heart that I know were not my own. The voice that I did not hear but felt said, 'Oh, my daughter, Timothy and Hannah are more alive now than when they were on earth. You will know them again someday.'"

James said, "Read that again!"

Sarah repeated the words.

"Yes!" James exclaimed. "That is exactly how it was for me. He is real, Sarah! He knows us, and He knows our pains. That's something else I had confirmed for me tonight. He knows us individually and loves us whether we deserve it or not. He will say things to our heart to comfort us. But if we do things that the evil one wants us to do, we can drown out those words of comfort. Look at the comfort that comes from those very words you are sharing with me! Look how much comfort that brings over losing James and the babies. That is truth. They *are* more alive now than when they were on earth! And we *will* know them again someday! We will know James again. He is alive right now in heaven."

They embraced and kissed each other. For the first time in weeks, they loved each other wholly and purely. And when they were done and holding each other, Sarah whispered, "James, did you turn to other women as you said you were tempted to?"

"Praise God, I did not. No, Sarah, I have never been with anyone but you. And I am deeply sorry for the times you tolerated my awful behavior here in our own bed."

The next morning at breakfast, James came into the dining room after all the children were seated. He knew he did not deserve their forgiveness either, and as he walked in, they all looked at his face, afraid perhaps of more harsh words. The innocent looks on their faces and the fear he saw made James cry as he took his seat.

"Children, I do not know how to even begin. I am so, so sorry for the way I have acted in the last few weeks. I have been very wrong. I have treated you badly. I have treated your mother badly. I have been drinking. I thought I was trying to get rid of the pain of losing your brother, but that is no excuse! It only made my pain worse! It made me hate myself. Please know that I love you all and I am sorry. I hope and pray you can forgive me someday."

They seemed to be looking to Sarah for guidance on this. She smiled and said softly, "I have forgiven your father. I love him. We both want to be a happy family again."

Peter was the first on his feet to come around the table to hug his father's neck. He had tears in his eyes. "Papa," was all he could say.

Susannah and Mary approached him next. "We love you, Papa." The others joined the family circle around their prodigal father.

That day, James rode over to see Malachi, who could instantly see the happiness on his friend's face that had been missing for so long. James recounted his experience of visiting the church the night before, shedding more tears of joy. Malachi smiled widely and wiped tears of his own. "God is good."

"Something tells me I've had quite a band of angels praying for my soul lately. Both on this side and the other," James told him.

"No doubt, James," said Malachi. "Probably none more than my mother. She loves you and Sarah and your family so much. She is a mighty praying woman."

"Malachi, tell Martha I love her, and I appreciate her prayers more than she will ever know. And, brother, I love you."

The two men embraced. "And I love you, James. Welcome back."

"It does feel like I have been in some other place. And I never want to go there again."

Two days later, James was in the barn, working on some things for Christmas for the children. It was evening, and he had two lanterns lit to work by. He heard someone come into the barn, and there stood Peter. He had his hands behind his back and walked up to James.

"Papa, I have to confess something that I did wrong." James looked at his son, and from behind his back, Peter brought out a bottle of whiskey. "I stole your bottle. I found it here in the barn. I hid it in my room under my bed. I just didn't want you to get drunk anymore."

James felt tears trickle from the corners of his eyes. "Peter, do not apologize, son. That was the best thing you could have ever done. As a matter of fact, why don't we go pour this out together?" They walked down the dark path to the creek holding one lantern to light their way. At the edge of the creek, James stooped down, unsealed the bottle, and said, "Peter, I don't want you to ever forget how evil this stuff is. It can change a man's soul. Do you hear me?"

"Yes, Papa."

"I want you to remember that this almost destroyed our family."

His son nodded. He handed Peter the open bottle and watched as he emptied its contents.

He then looked up at James and said, "You promise, Papa, you won't ever drink again?"

"I can promise you that I have learned my lesson. I love you, son." The two hugged warmly and headed back to the barn.

In spite of losing little James, that Christmas was one that James knew he would never forget. The spirit of the season that year reflected the joy he had felt in the small sanctuary a few weeks before. Celebrating the birth of the Savior meant more to James than it ever had, in that, through Christ, he felt newborn. He talked to Reverend Polk the Sunday before Christmas after services were over. They sat in the empty sanctuary as James shared what had happened in that room a few weeks before. "I was christened as a child, but could I be baptized again?" James asked. "I feel such a need to be baptized anew so that I can enjoy it."

Reverend Polk said he would be more than happy to baptize James the following Sunday, which would be the day after Christmas.

Christmas Eve was spent with the Wests hosting a party at their home. All the Fraziers were there. There were sweet treats and a fire blazing. There were evergreen boughs and red holly berries upon the mantel and on a table or two about the room. To the children, the weeks before now seemed like a bad dream. They were all so happy that James had found peace and was himself again.

On Christmas Day, there were presents to open, and James, though he had gotten a late start on the toys, did not disappoint. That morning around the dining room table for a Christmas breakfast, James offered a prayer, and in it, he said, "Lord, we are thinking this morning about all our loved ones whom we miss. Some are still living, and some have passed on. Please let them all know that we love them. Bless us, O Lord, that we may be with our loved ones someday as we gather around Your holy feet. Bless us that we may never forget the birth and the death of Thy Holy Son, Jesus Christ. Bless us that we may ever be in Thy service. In Jesus's name, amen."

These days, James's prayers were so heartfelt that they brought tears to Sarah's eyes. Her own silent prayer was deep gratitude that God had heard her prayers and brought her husband back to her and the children. In James's prayers, Sarah never detected a hint of self-righteousness, just deep humility.

The next day at the worship service, James's baptism was celebrated by all present. James felt such a cleansing, even though the baptism was by christening and not immersion as some churches did. Reverend Polk surprised James and asked him if he would like to speak to his fellow parishioners on this day. James walked up to the pulpit, which overlooked the altar on which he had wept and asked God to change his heart. As he looked out and saw his family and Malachi's family, he got choked up. He loved his whole church family and felt that love burning in his heart. Then his eyes went to Sarah, and he was not sure if he was going to be able to speak.

Humbly, he began, "Some of you may not know, but we lost our son back in October. He was my namesake, and I loved him as I love all my children. I have always had a difficult time with life's trials such as death and injustice. In the past, it has led me to question God and His purposes. I was brought up in Wales, in a home where I was taught to love the Lord. My parents were good, hardworking Christian people, just as you are. When I lost James, it was very difficult. He took his own life with me standing just feet away. I was horrified, though both my wife and I felt we had been prompted to know that something was about to happen. I saw it as a sign that God was a cruel tormentor. It is amazing what the evil one can put into your heart to make you lose faith, for that is what the evil one wants is for us all to lose faith. For weeks, I became a different man. I began to drink for the first time in my life. I became angry and filled with hate. I think I hated myself most of all. One night, I came to this very building and walked in to talk to God whom I had begun to think did not even exist. I began to rant and rave, and then I began to confess my sins, and I told Him I needed peace! That led to a great deal of crying."

James was wiping tears as he related this story. "Many of you know I am quite a crybaby." He smiled. "As I poured out all the anger and hatred in my heart, all the doubt, I began to hear the still, small voice. He told me of His love for me. He told me of how His Son had already suffered all of my agonies. He replaced the hate and anger in my heart with an overwhelming sense of love. I am here to tell you humbly, my brothers and my sisters, that our Father is very real. He loves us. He loves you. The most important thing you can do in this life is to love God and love your family. He let me know that I will see my son again someday. I am so thankful for this mighty change in my heart that He has blessed me with. I am also thankful for the mighty prayers offered up in my behalf by those who love me and never lost hope." James gave a smile in the direction of both his wife and Martha.

After the service, many came up and hugged James or shook his hand or patted his back. Reverend Polk thanked him for sharing his story. He felt that those were the words needed for everyone here at the beginning of a new year.

James was now spending many days and nights around the fireplace reading the Bible to the children and just to himself. He told Sarah that as a child, he loved the stories of the Old Testament but he wanted to make sure his children knew the stories of Jesus. He thought of how Captain Duggar had remembered from his childhood his grandmother reading him the story of the man with palsy who was lowered through the roof of the building where Jesus was teaching. James would sometimes shed tears as he shared the stories from the New Testament with his family.

He also started a second go round of reading *Robinson Crusoe* aloud to his children. The boys especially loved it, and though he was rereading the tale for the little ones who had never heard it before, he noticed that Peter, William, Daniel, and Abraham always made sure they were close by when he started reading.

Sarah continued to work with her children, as she always had to make sure they could read and write. She told the children about teaching their aunt Miranda to read and write when they were both teenagers. She even taught Lucy, their servant, to read and write a little. Lucy learned her letters and numbers and could write her own name. She remembered how proud Lucy was that she could do that.

Sarah noticed that Mary had inherited her talent for art, and she spent a great deal of time studying her mother's drawings in her commonplace book. Mary drew a wonderful sketch of little Ann that Sarah thought was better than anything she had ever drawn. Mary even took the portrait of her father that Sarah had done and did another as he looked now, about twenty years older. Mary also shared some poems she had written that really pleased Sarah.

Susannah loved sewing and doing needlepoint. Susannah actually did most of the sewing for the little girls, Sarah and Ann, these days. Ann was just toddling about and brought so much joy to her parents. James had always had a soft spot in his heart for his princesses as he called them. Susannah was princess number one; Mary, princess number two; Sarah, princess number three; and Ann, princess number four. Sometimes, he would substitute the title "Your Royal Highness."

There was peace and comfort in their home, and both Sarah and James always made sure to acknowledge the Lord's grace and mercy for making that possible. It was at the first of the year, 1786, that Sarah received word that her mother Judith had passed away. When she got Miranda's letter, she wept but she immediately smiled knowing that her mother and father were together in heaven. Even in death now, she and James could find joy. What a blessing that was to both of them!

James and Sarah talked about wanting to take a trip somewhere together. James thought of taking her to the coast, but part of him wanted to head to Hillsborough to see John Hussey. He felt a need to see his old friend so that he could share with him the spiritual things that were in his heart. They felt that Susannah and Peter could easily take care of running the household and seeing to the farm chores. James had hired some of Malachi's many nephews to help with spring planting. Sarah became excited thinking of going away with her husband for a little over a week in late May! She was glad she had weaned little Ann, and she knew even the young ones would be in good hands with Susannah as "mother" and the Fraziers close by. They discussed it and decided to visit the Husseys. James was so happy Sarah had agreed. They decided they would stay at an inn while there. James rigged the wagon again as he had done fifteen years ago on their trip to North Carolina so that there was a cover and they could sleep in it at nights on their trip. Hillsborough was much faster to reach on horseback, but they wanted to take a little extra time and enjoy the scenery and each other's company.

James and Sarah had both just turned thirty-eight years old, but on this little journey, they felt like teenagers again. They had been married for twenty-one years. While riding along, James would give her a very sweet smile and let her know how much he loved her. Watching him as he drove the horses, Sarah remembered years before when she was pregnant with Susannah and little James would sleep in the back. She felt such a sweet desire for her husband as they traveled along, and at night in the back of the wagon, they would pretend they were on a blanket again at Cuckold Creek, only this time, they gave in to the passion they felt. James joked about how their lovemaking had gotten so much better with a little age and experience. But most of all, he had this new gratitude in his heart that he had been forgiven and had been given a second chance to be a good husband.

They found a lovely inn just outside Hillsborough. James had not sent word to John Hussey that they were coming, but he assumed they would be welcomed just the same. Besides, all his encounters with John Hussey had been unexpected.

James was fairly certain he remembered the way to the Hussey farm and was pleased to see that he remembered correctly. He and Sarah pulled up about one o'clock in the afternoon. John was out in the fields with some of his sons, including the twins. He greeted James with a big smile and embrace. He turned to Sarah, removed the wide-brimmed hat he wore, and bowed low in his typical dramatic fashion.

"Oh, my dear! James, you were telling no tales! She is indeed a beauty! Sarah, it is a pleasure to finally meet the queen of my little brother's heart!"

"James," Sarah said, "you never told me how charming John Hussey was!"

James grinned. "No, but I told you true—he is a con man and a thief!"

John acted as if he were grieved, pretending to stab himself in his chest. "Please do come in. I have someone I'd love for you both to meet." Before he opened the front door to his farmhouse, John stopped and looked at them both. "My Miriam passed about a year ago. I have remarried. Her name is Sophia."

They were not even given an opportunity to offer their condolences. They stepped into the room and met a girl who looked to be about Susannah's age, though she was almost twenty. She was obviously expecting a baby in about two or three months. She was a pretty girl, but she was a young girl. She spoke to them shyly and offered them seats. John sat as well and explained, "Sophia is Miriam's niece. She came to help out when Miriam became ill, and after my wife died, I asked Sophia to stay, and we wed not too long after. She has been a blessing."

"I am sure," James said to his friend. "We are sorry to hear of Miriam's death, John."

"Thank you. I am glad she is no longer suffering. So how many have you added to your brood since I last saw you?" asked John.

"We have ten children. Since the war, we have added Joseph and Ann," James told him. "We lost our oldest, though. Little James died in October."

John sat forward in his seat. "I am so sorry to hear that. You have *my* deepest sympathies."

"Thank you," Sarah said.

James chose not to go into the details at this point. Sarah knew at some point in the visit that James would talk to John about the suicide.

"We are adding our first, but Miriam had no more children after the war," John explained. "So I assume you know, Sarah, the story of how James and I met."

"Yes, you rescued him at the shipyards in London," she said with a warm smile.

"He looked so much like my brother Stephen who had passed. And he looked so lost!"

"I *was* lost." James laughed. "I thought I was going to walk up to a ship and ask for a job on board and get hired immediately."

John smiled. "I had to set him straight and show him the better way. I said, 'No, my boy, we must go break into a clothing shop. We must get arrested. We must sail to America in a cargo hold that stinks to high heaven!'" John laughed. "And then on board the ship, he gets in good with the captain because he has a book and can read! I'm left to my own devices day in and day out down below with some really upstanding criminals! It seems that I was always getting bloody noses and lips in jail as well as in that cargo hold!" John was carrying on in his usual jovial way, but James wondered for the first time if perhaps John really had issues with that. He'd sensed while on the *Tryal* that John was a bit jealous of his partial freedom, but now, even years later, he could still feel it.

"I am sorry, my friend," James said, "I could not help being singled out in that way. I did bring you extra bread each day."

"I know. You are blessed. It was easy to see that God had his hand on you, especially since you were allowed to escape the Orr plantation and not left for dead in the woods."

It was another almost humorous yet stinging comment about the past. James felt guilty again and said, "As I told you when we later saw each other, I am sorry. I wanted to go back for you. John Thomas insisted we move on. I was grieved and so worried about you. You did so much for me, John."

"Oh, I am fine with the way things turned out. Things equaled out. You took a bullet in the arm against the Brits!" John smiled. Finally getting serious, he said, "Truthfully, I would have taken on all that again plus more if I could have stopped the whipping he got for helping that little boy."

"I know all about that too," Sarah said. "I am thankful, as I know James is, for all the things you did for him, John." John's last comment made James feel a little better.

"So do you do as I do and entertain your children with our stories of adventure?" John asked.

James replied with a grin, "I have a version of the truth that I tell. I leave out the part of the red cloak, our time in jail, our trial at the Old Bailey, and the fact that we were convict servants."

"Oh, so you've cleaned it up a bit?"

"Yes, they think I was an indentured servant who worked on a plantation for a short while. They love the part about their grandfather buying my freedom so I could marry their mother."

"Do they know of the whipping you got?"

"No, I do not share that. I keep my shirt on so that they won't see."

John frowned. "You still have scars?" he asked.

Sarah and James both nodded. "They have faded a bit," said Sarah, "but they are still there."

"I do show them my scar from that British round I took in the arm." James smiled.

Soon, Sarah and Sophia went off to talk about the baby she was expecting and to exchange recipes, and James and John wandered off to the front porch.

As they sat in chairs, John again offered condolences on the passing of the younger James.

"It was awful," James said. "He took his own life with a gun I had given him as a gift."

"Oh, Dear God! I'm so sorry, James! How old was he?"

"He was sixteen. Same age as I was when we started our adventure. He had a hard time with life, John. He was always a very serious child. I think he had thoughts in his head we did not know he was having. He looked at things differently. We have a mountain near our house; it's just a very large hill, really, but James loved it so much. He and I would camp up there. It became his favorite place to go. He and I built little hogans, and he even built a cabin up there from scraps I'd given him. One day, he went up there, and there was a young runaway slave girl hiding in his cabin. Her name was Rose. We knew nothing about the fact that he was hiding her and feeding her. They fell in love. I walked up there and found them together, and he told me he had a plan. Since he knew how much I hated slavery, he wanted me to buy Rose from her owner, the way Sarah's father bought my freedom. He wanted to marry her. She was a light-skinned mulatto girl, very pretty eyes. She was pregnant. Two of the sons of her owner had raped her. James wanted to be her hero and a father to her baby. I told them both it was impossible. I already had bad blood with her owner. He was in my regiment, and we had had words on the topic of slavery. There was no way I could help the girl. I knew he would make sure I, and probably James, went to jail. When I shot down their hopes, she ran off back to the plantation. The poor girl was scared out of her wits about having a baby. She knew if she went back, she'd be whipped, but she wanted her mother. When she ran off, James yelled and screamed at me a bit for not helping. Then I talked him into coming back home with me, or so I thought. He turned to go into the cabin to get his things, and I heard a gunshot. With me standing three feet away, he put a bullet into his head."

"I cannot imagine your pain. I know you were devastated!"

"He had told me when he was about eight that he wanted to be buried up there. So we all went up to the top of the mountain to bury him. After his funeral, a friend and I were covering his grave. We had walked a third of the way down the hill and heard a gunshot. We went back up and found out Rose had come to his grave with his gun and killed herself right there. Malachi and I took her body straight to the plantation, and I told that bastard what had happened. She had fresh whip marks where she'd been lashed when she went back. I told him I knew that she was carrying a child from when his sons had raped her. He told me if he heard any talk in the community of what I'd said, he'd notify the law and charge me with stealing his property. Orr isn't the only sorry plantation owner out there."

James was shocked that just talking about it had stirred up so many of his feelings of hatred he thought he had put behind him. But he wanted to share his spiritual turn around with John and knew he needed a basis for doing so.

"I wanted to kill people, John. Losing my son like that was bad enough, but the hate I felt for this man—I lost my faith. You know me as a man of faith. But I tell you, I became quite the infidel. I was so angry at God. Sarah and I both were prompted something might happen to James, yet we could not stop it from happening. I decided that God was an illusion and, if He did exist, He lived to mock me and torment me. I started to drink."

"You, James?"

"Yes. This all just happened in October. I hated myself. I was angry at God, so angry at my children and Sarah. I was so wrapped up in my own pain I totally forgot the grief she was going through! I told her I was drinking, not just to numb the pain of losing James, but I was trying to drown out the desire to kill people. Finally, she told me that with all the hate in my heart, I was becoming as bad as the people I hated. That I had to learn to forgive and let go."

John was listening quietly.

"I went to our church one night, ready to go in and let God know, if He existed, what I thought of Him! I went in there screaming and yelling at God for taking my son, but something happened in there, John. God spoke to me, not in my ears but in my heart. Before I left there, I was sobbing like a baby and knew I was forgiven and blessed. He told me to go ask Sarah for her forgiveness and the children's. I am a new man, John. I am humbled by what happened. It still hurts that I lost James, but now I can deal with it because I know I am loved and I know that my Savior has atoned for my sins. I know I will see my son again one day. I am so thankful for that. It has changed my life."

John had tears in his eyes. "I am so sorry for you, James, for going through so much pain. I cannot imagine enduring such an awful thing! I am not surprised to know, though, that you had such a turn around. I have always known you were a good soul. I am glad our paths crossed. I have been blessed to know you. You are probably right. The last time you were here, you said you thought Providence had brought us together in this life. I believe you are correct. I needed this today. My new wife is a very devoted girl. She loves the Lord.

My Miriam had a quiet faith, but Sophia wants more of God in our home. Do you think I could ever be as close to God as you are?"

"I think you are, John. Even with your silliness at times, I think you have always been a good soul. I know He's close to you. You did so many things to help me. But if you do not know how to draw closer to Him, all you have to do is ask Him. He is very real, my friend, and He will answer your prayers. He surely answered mine. And His forgiveness is sweet."

At the end of their visit, James and John held each other, and James told him, "I do not know if we'll ever see each other again in this life. I hope we do, but if not, I hope we will meet in heaven. I love you, my brother."

"And I love you, my little brother. Thank you for coming and blessing me."

James and Sarah headed home. They missed their own children so much. After they had been home for a few weeks, Sarah realized she was having symptoms again.

"Husband, I have news," she told him.

CHAPTER 22

*E*lizabeth West was born March 12, 1787. She was to be James's last little princess. It seemed he sensed that, and he and Sarah relished the idea of one more little girl in their household. Sally and Malachi were blessed the year before to have twin girls named Judith and Michal.

James continued to study the Word of God more in depth than he ever had before. He often met with Reverend Polk, and they spent a great deal of time discussing points of doctrine and tenets of their faith. James found comfort and understanding from his pastor in terms of life's difficulties. Reverend Polk helped James understand that he was not the only person to pose the eternal question: "Why does God allow terrible things to happen to good people?" Perhaps it was physical maturity or maybe the experiences of life, but James progressed in his comprehension, both mentally and spiritually on this topic.

James made so much progress in his spiritual development that even when lightning struck a large tree that fell onto Herbert Stokes's huge barn filled with cured tobacco, burning the entire crop, James did not gloat even once.

In late 1789, Sarah experienced symptoms once again, and in May 1790, she gave birth to their last child. James wanted to name this son John, for his friend John Hussey. They now had eleven children in their home, and every corner of James's additions was filled with growing boys and girls. When John was born, Susannah was nineteen; Mary, seventeen; Peter, sixteen; William, fourteen; Daniel, twelve; Abraham, eleven; Sarah, nine; Joseph, six; Ann, four; and Elizabeth, three.

Susannah was of a marriageable age, yet she showed no interest in courting. She loved being her mother's right arm. Mary seemed to feel much the same way. Mary spent much of her time writing and drawing, as well as helping with the smaller children. The boys were content to assist their father on the farm, and James's crops continued to provide enough money to live on. He was able to purchase more and more land, which other farmers leased or James sold for a profit. Some of his land he was saving for his sons as their inheritance.

In 1792, when they were both forty-four, James took Sarah on a trip to the coast of North Carolina. They had been married for twenty-seven years. The love between them was stronger than ever. They had survived James's temporary lapse of faith caused by his son's suicide and had come back with more love and endurance than they ever thought possible. They acknowledged the Lord's hand in this.

James found an inn near Wilmington, and they enjoyed walks along the sandy shore and the time they had to be together, just the two of them. They remarked how blessed they were that they still felt like the teenagers who met on Cuckold Creek.

At sunset one evening, near the end of their weeklong trip to the ocean, James held Sarah about the waist as they listened to the crashing surf. "I still love you, my angel, more than you will ever know. You are the greatest blessing God has given me. We are both blessed that we are still passionate lovers, as well as servants of God. And Lord willing, we still have many, many years ahead with grandchildren and great-grandchildren."

"I wonder about that." Sarah smiled. "Susannah and Mary do not seem to be in any hurry to court, marry, and move away! We were married when we were their age!"

"And why they are not in any hurry to leave is a tribute to you. You have given them a home where they are loved and cared for. We both teach them about what is really important in life."

Sarah said, "Maybe we have done too good a job. Perhaps it will be difficult for them to find spouses who love them and the Lord as we do."

"I would think they have to look no further than our neighbors, Malachi and Sally. Their children are much like ours—strong in their faith, hardworking people."

"I mentioned the Frazier boys to both Susannah and Mary one day, and they both were horrified! 'Mother,' they said, 'the Fraziers are like our siblings! We have grown up together.' I think because they have always called Sally and Malachi aunt and uncle they feel related to them."

"Young people today marry first cousins all the time," James laughed. "They will marry, Sarah. They will marry. Let's just enjoy the years they are with us. I just pray they can find spouses who are from nonslaveholding families. But I realize I do not have much control over that."

"James, thank you for this trip. I don't have many pleasant memories of the ocean in Baltimore. I only went twice, and I just saw busy shipyards. This has been wonderful."

"Well, it's only fair. I took several trips, and you have had none, except the trip to see John Hussey and his wife."

"What trips have you taken, husband?" she asked.

"Well, I did see many parts of North and South Carolina," he replied.

"But that was during the war! That cannot have been relaxing!" Sarah laughed.

"No, it was not. But I did get to see other places," he said grinning at her.

"It is wonderful that we have peace now," Sarah said, clasping James's fingers in hers.

"I pray we can keep peace. I still worry about a war *within* our country—an uprising—when these slaves have had about all they can take of being abused and beaten. But I guess we will have to leave that for another generation. We've planted good seeds in our children. It's all we can do," said James.

"I still am so thankful that *you* are at peace, James. It was very hard to deal with when you were at war with God."

"That was not a good place to be. I was so lost, Sarah. It was losing James that caused that. And not just losing him but losing him the way we lost him. And being there. Having him die in my arms. Not being able to stop him from taking his own life. I know now that God understood my anguish. He *knows* my anguish. And I believe now James knows my anguish and probably regrets it. But I am comforted. I had a dream about a year ago, Sarah. I have never shared it with you or anyone as I wanted to treasure it up just for me. I consider it a sacred thing." James paused before going on. "One night, I dreamed I saw James. I was back on Cuckold Creek, and I saw him, sitting there on the rock we used to sit on. He was smiling. He was at peace."

"Oh, James! How wonderful! What else?"

"That was the whole of it. But it was enough. It was all I needed."

"Wonder why Cuckold Creek? He was only there as a baby," said Sarah.

"I know why Cuckold Creek. That place was heaven to me. Meeting you there. Falling in love with you there. It was a perfect place to see my son."

He leaned over and kissed Sarah's lips tenderly. They strolled back into the inn and to their room where they enjoyed another night of sweet passion. As they began to doze after their lovemaking, James asked, "Do you think you might conceive again, Sarah?"

"I do not think so, James. I have stopped having my cycle. I have weaned John, and I have had no other monthly cycle. I am forty-four. I believe I am done."

"I love you, Sarah. It has been a wonderful life with you."

Sarah, at hearing those words, had a terrible premonition of the time that would one day come when they had to say farewell for this life. She began to cry softly.

"I do not know what in the world I would ever do without you!" She wept and could not be consoled.

"Now, wife, we have years ahead together. Weddings to enjoy. Grandchildren! I did not mean to make you cry!"

"It just hit me that one day, one of us will leave the other. I pray I go first so I do not have to endure life without you."

"Well, that's not very kind! You would leave me to suffer alone?" He smiled, teasing her.

"James, I think you could handle it better than I ever could!"

"I tell you what. Let's not waste a moment of our time together worrying over something which we cannot control."

James and Sarah returned home in the next few days. They were met at the door by Susannah, and the frantic look on her face made them both feel instant fear and concern. She stood in front of her parents. "I am glad you are home. Aunt Martha is asking for both of you. She is about to pass."

The couple immediately got back into the wagon and drove back the quarter of a mile to the Frazier home. Martha was in her bed, raised up on pillows. Sarah had never seen this amazing woman look so frail. It seemed as if someone else had taken over her body.

Her voice was still strong, however. "Sarah! James! I am so glad to see you both! Sarah, I think I have birthed my last baby! How is little John?"

"He is very healthy, Martha." Sarah tried not to tear up at the thoughts of losing this dear friend.

"Well, I am not," she sighed. "It's my heart. I can tell it grows weaker. But I cannot complain. I have lived a very full, blessed life, Sarah. I just wanted to be able to say farewell to you and James. I love you both. You have been like my children from that first winter you moved here."

"Oh, Martha, you have been such a mother to me! Thank you for everything you have done for us!"

Sally and Malachi were back in the room as were some of the children. The room was full, yet all were talking softly. Martha grew quiet. Near the end, she began to breathe a little heavier. Then without warning, she all but sat up in the bed and exclaimed, "There is William! He has come for me!" With that, she lay back upon the pillow and closed her eyes taking her last breath. They all watched as her face softened and became smooth and filled with radiant peace.

Sarah could not quit thinking about Martha's final exclamation of seeing her deceased husband. It was such a reassuring thing to witness. It strengthened her belief that she and James too would be reunited someday after this life. Sarah was also calmed by the peace on Martha's face. No doubt, she was not only greeted by William, but together, they were now in the presence of their Savior.

James and his oldest boys dug Martha's grave as a final act of service for this beloved matriarch. The funeral took place two days later at the church that William Frazier had helped build. She was laid to rest in the Frazier cemetery where William was buried. Susannah and Sally's two oldest daughters sang a lovely hymn at the graveside.

James was the first to notice his daughter Susannah standing in the Frazier home after the funeral talking to Martha's great-nephew who had come from Person county for his aunt's funeral. He had been a pallbearer. His name was Jedidiah Coley, and he was handsome but seemed humble. He and Susannah had become instantaneously attracted to each other. Susannah was now twenty-one, and Jedidiah was twenty. They ate lunch together and continued to talk after the family gathering. He was staying the night with Sally and Malachi, and he and Susannah talked until bedtime. James and Sarah kept giving each other these knowing looks.

The next day, James went over to Malachi's to speak to the young man. "I did not have the chance to get to know you yesterday. Something tells me, I must!" James smiled. Jedidiah was farming with his father in Person county but was also in school in order to become a schoolmaster. Some people in this next county over were thinking of establishing a school and wanted Jedidiah to be the new teacher. Needless to say, James was very impressed. Jedidiah confided in James that he was thinking of being pastor as well. He was not sure where the Lord was going to lead him, but he was pursuing his education in any case. This made James very happy.

Two weeks after Martha was buried, Malachi developed a swelling in his calf, just below that irksome war-wounded knee. He could not walk at all, and Sally became concerned. They now had a doctor in the area, but he had to serve such a large area, including parts of Virginia. So by the time Malachi was seen, it was too late. The doctor was certain a blood clot or at least infection had gone into his heart. The doctor opened up the calf, but it was clear that infection had spread.

Malachi was very feverish and became incoherent at times. James was upset by the thought of losing his best friend, indeed this brother whom he had grown to love through the years. As he got home late one night after sitting with Malachi, Sarah met him at the door.

"Sarah, I don't know if I can take losing Malachi!" He held his wife and wept on her shoulder.

"I know, husband! And so soon after losing his mother!"

They lay in bed that night holding each other.

"I can see Martha waiting for him to come over. But surely, she must know that Sally needs him!" James lamented.

"James, I don't think Martha can will him over. This is in the Lord's hands."

"Malachi is only two years older than I am. He is not yet fifty! He is young still."

"Your son was only sixteen. The babies died in a day. The Lord's will is the Lord's will."

"I surely know that. It just doesn't make it any easier losing them."

The next morning, James immediately went to check on Malachi. He had survived the night, but by morning's light, he seemed to be slipping away.

James grasped his hand as he sat next to his friend's bed. The two of them were alone for a few moments.

Malachi whispered, "James, please do me a favor and keep an eye on Sally and the children."

"Of course, brother. Anything. I will make sure they always have what they need."

"Would you tend my mother's grave? I don't really care about my own, but women care more about these things than we do."

"I will." James drew his chair closer to his friend's bedside. "Thank you, Malachi. You have been my rock these many years! In the war, you were my strength in ways you do not even know. I love my wife so much, but having you with me kept me away from the brothels, did you know? I have never told Sarah that there were always women near the encampments. There were times I was tempted, especially in those eight months in South Carolina when I was wounded and the women came around to tend to us and to offer their services. Having you right near me with your knee injury, you were my guardian angel, you know that?"

Malachi smiled. "And you were mine. Not that I would have seen much action with the ladies with my poor knee!"

"And, Malachi, when James died, I do not know what I would have done without you. Please continue to pray for me on the other side, brother."

"I will. I expect to see you there someday."

"Aye. I look forward to it, my friend. Malachi, one last thing. If you see little James, please give him a hug from me and tell I love him and miss him still."

"Indeed, I will."

Malachi dozed off, and while he was sleeping, with his loved ones gathered around, he went peacefully to his home on high.

James cried as he knew he would, but even with the tears came peace. "How can one not feel peace," he told Sarah, "when a man such as Malachi earns his reward?"

Jedidiah Coley returned for his cousin's funeral and decided to stay a few weeks to see what he could do to help Sally. James and Sarah felt, though, that he was staying to see more of Susannah. By the end of his visit, they were engaged to be married.

Jedidiah returned home, but Sarah, Susannah, and the girls began to plan this first family wedding. Susannah wanted Ann and Elizabeth to be her small attendants and her sisters Mary and Sarah would stand with her. The wedding would be at the church with Reverend Polk performing the ceremony. James would be walking his daughter down the aisle.

Sarah, though busy with wedding plans, made sure she checked on Sally frequently. Sally was grateful to have Sarah to cry with, but she offered to do some of the food for the wedding feast and help Sarah with the gown, as she said it would occupy her mind. Sally also had such wonderful, attentive children and was grateful for them as well.

The wedding took place the first weekend in September 1792. Susannah was such a beautiful bride, and Sarah and Sally had worked on the gown, finishing it just two days before the ceremony. James and Sarah bought new clothes, and Sarah didn't think she had ever seen her husband so handsome. He got a haircut, perhaps the shortest he had ever worn it. He had gray mingled with his dark hair, and Sarah thought it made him that much more attractive. They both were so happy over Susannah's choice of a mate, and it seemed like Providence had brought them together as He had done for Sarah and James.

As the reception ended, James and Sarah watched as Susannah and Jedidiah kissed and left by wagon to go to stay at an inn in Oxford. James whispered in Sarah's ear, "I hope they will be as happy as we have been. Do you remember, Sarah, those two nights in Edward and Miranda's home? Remember how new and wonderful it was to experience love for the first time?"

"Indeed, I do. I have been thinking of that a great deal these last few days. I think of it every time we love each other. As wonderful as it was, it has only gotten better, James."

"I love pleasing you, wife," he said, kissing her near her ear.

"And you do it so well," she whispered.

Chapter 23

Jedidiah's family lived just on the other side of the Granville County line, so it was not too far for Sarah and James to visit. On the very first visit, they found out that Susannah was already expecting their first grandchild. Sarah now knew how *her* mother must have felt when she was first pregnant. She felt anxiety for her daughter as she remembered her first miscarriage and her first baby who passed away. The passage of years really did not diminish the memory of the pain she and James had shared, the way they had grieved separately, the way he had feared ever loving his wife again. These were the things they had to work through and deal with. She prayed Susannah would not have to even consider these issues. Perhaps her firstborn would come easily and effortlessly.

The second visit was for the delivery. Susannah wanted her mother there, and she was thrilled when her papa came along also. They were welcomed into the Coley home, given a guest bedroom, and treated like family. Susannah called Jedidiah's mother, Mother Coley, and they seemed to have a very warm relationship already. Sarah found the woman a bit overbearing but in a friendly way. They were good Christian people, and James and Stephen Coley, Jedidiah's father, became fast friends. The baby came on the third day of their stay. Sarah and Becca Coley assisted Susannah in the birth, and Sarah could not remember a birth that was more routine. Stephen James Coley was born screaming but latched on quietly to his mother's breast and, when fed, slept ever so peacefully. James and Sarah offered a prayer of thanks for the blessing of a beautiful, healthy grandson.

They only wished they lived closer so as to be with the little one more frequently.

Sarah was quiet on the trip home. James reached over and touched her hand, which she knew after all these years meant, "Tell me what you are thinking."

"I am just feeling grateful, James."

"Did you watch them together?" he asked.

"I could see it, yes. They love each other very deeply. He is very attentive of her. She looks at him as if he is the only person on earth. For that, I am grateful also."

"Prayers answered, Sarah. I talked to him about his schooling. He is still feeling the leaning to go into the ministry. I told him Reverend Polk can't be in the pulpit much longer. Perhaps they could move here, and he could take on our church."

"We shall see. I am almost afraid to pray for much else."

Little John, James and Sarah's youngest, grew much too quickly, and they both doted on the child, as did Mary, Sarah, Ann, and Elizabeth. Sarah began to think the others would be with them forever. The boys—Peter, William, Daniel, Abraham, and Joseph—worked hard with their father. James not only farmed with his sons but also taught them the craft of carpentry. He even opened a little blacksmith shop. Together, they learned the trade, and they took in some business in that area. Peter seemed to have found his love with smithing. James was always doing carpentry work and getting paid for it, but he began to include wagon wheels and started another fairly lucrative business, which combined blacksmithing and carpentry.

Occasionally, Peter and his younger brothers escorted young ladies in the community to various functions at church or elsewhere, but they seemed to be in no hurry to marry. Peter was still close friends with William Edwards and was even his bondsman and witness at his marriage to Mary Moseley.

Several new families moved into the growing farming community, and friendships grew. Sarah remained close to Sally and the children, and both families did many things together. James had seen to it that tombstones were placed at both Malachi's and his mother's grave. He had put a carved stone on Francis's grave years ago and tended all the plots in the cemetery. He even purchased a little granite angel and placed it on the grave of the Christmas baby they lost.

One family that moved into the area was Aaron Pinson and his family of mostly daughters. James kept encouraging his sons to get to know the Pinson girls and visit with them at church, but James realized he could not force his boys to court certain girls. He remembered that Susannah showed very little interest in young men until she met Jedidiah, and then love blossomed quickly.

By the end of 1798, Susannah had added two daughters to her growing family. They visited when they could, but it was difficult. Jedidiah was pastor of a small church in Person County, and they stayed very busy. They had a parsonage to live in, and Sarah and James had been to stay with them and spend time with their grandchildren. Little John enjoyed going with them on these trips as well.

About this same time, Reverend Polk's health took a turn for the worse, and he died. James was asked to fill in for him until they could find a replacement. James took this temporary calling very seriously and began to double up on his Bible study, in addition to farming, and helping with the blacksmith shop and his carpentry work.

Sarah was very humbled yet proud of seeing James in the pulpit offering up his spiritual counsel week after week. He was not a thunderous hellfire and brimstone sort of preacher but one who stressed love and peace. James always encouraged the members of his beloved church family to seek to know God on a very personal level because he believed that was how people were seen by God. He touched his fellow members, and each week, he received comments about how blessed they were to have heard his words and his testimony.

By the middle of 1799, a young pastor named John Matthews was sent to be their new ecclesiastical leader. He was single, aged twenty-six, and seemed to have a constant flush about his face. One could sense his nervousness in front of the congregation, but in getting to know him, James felt the Lord had sent the right man for the job. James loved his humility most of all and did everything in his power to build up the young minister's self-confidence. John Matthews spent a great deal of time at the West home, eating dinner and learning more at the feet of James, whom he saw to be an embodiment of one who had been through the refiner's fire. He had heard James's story and was touched to know of the mighty change of heart that had taken place in a man so traumatized by the suicide of his oldest son. James felt most of the young man's schooling had been perfunctory, but he knew behind that training lay the heart of a true pastor. John Matthews, through the questions he asked, exhibited a spiritual quality that most importantly revealed a love and a concern for each individual member of his congregation. As James told Sarah, "That young man truly cares about the worth of a soul."

James also noticed that during meals and in his free time, John Matthews was spending more and more time conversing with their daughter Mary. One day, he and Sarah spied Mary and John walking down the path toward the cemetery a good distance and then turn and head back. They were laughing and enjoying each other's company very much.

James turned to Sarah and said, "Do you think it's possible we could wind up with two ministers in the family?"

"That would be a blessing indeed," Sarah agreed.

John Matthews came to see James one afternoon with his face flushed a little more than usual. "Mister West," he began, "I have grown to respect you very much. You and your family have welcomed me here warmly. I have learned so much from you. I appreciate that more than you will ever know. But, sir, I have come to realize that what I am missing in my life most is a wife. I would be so pleased if you would allow me to marry your daughter, Mary. I love her, sir."

James smiled and remembered when Peter Bowman had bought the first chest that James had built and said he wanted to give it to Sarah for her trousseau. James had taken that opportunity to ask for Sarah's hand in marriage. Peter Bowman had embraced him and said the same words James now said to John Matthews, "I would be honored to have you as my son-in-law." The two men hugged, and James thought he saw a glint of tears in the young man's eyes.

Their wedding took place in the spring of 1800. The year alone gave everyone a sense of a fresh start, a new beginning, and a sense of curiosity about what a new century would bring. The wedding was performed by John's father, a pastor from Orange County. James and Sarah enjoyed getting to know Reverend Matthews and his wife. Susannah and Jedidiah and their family of five with one more on the way came for the ceremony, and Sarah and James loved having all the family under one roof again.

The wedding was on a sunny spring day, the last Sunday in March at their church, but the reception was held on the lawn of the West farm. All the young men looked so handsome, and the ladies were so lovely in their pastel gowns. Sally had helped Sarah with the food again, and everyone enjoyed the pastries, pies, and cakes they served. Mary, Sarah's emotional writer and artist, seemed a bit teary about leaving home, but she assured her mother that she was fine. The wonderful thing is they were going to live in the parsonage, which was less than a mile on the other side of the church. Sarah and James knew that when the children started to arrive, they could be closer to these grandchildren.

In the summer of 1802, not too long after Mary had given birth to their first child, a daughter whom she named Amelia, Sarah was sitting on the front porch with the new baby on her lap, talking to her daughter about all their blessings. Sally came over to see the new little one.

"Sarah, I know you are in a grandmother's paradise! I am so glad all of mine live nearby! She is a sweet little thing! I can see both you and James in her!"

Sarah just smiled and played with the baby's feet and kissed her face. "There is nothing like a newborn grandbaby, especially when they start crying or dirty themselves, you can hand them right over to their mother!"

"Speaking of children, if you are missing two of your young men tonight, they will probably be at our place," Sally said. "Both William and Daniel are spending more and more time over there."

Sarah looked at her curiously, but Mary smiled knowingly.

"Since the twins have turned sixteen, we have had more young men courting them!"

"I have not heard a thing!" exclaimed Sarah. "Daniel and William are twenty-five and twenty-six years old! The girls are only sixteen! Well, I guess they have finally decided to go in search of wives! Judith and Michal are such pretty girls."

"Wouldn't that be something," Sally said, "if we finally get some of our children married to each other!"

Mary remarked, "Mother, you might be having several weddings soon. As I understand, Abraham is seeing Nancy Pinson. I think she is one of their oldest daughters. She is closer to Abraham's age than the others."

Sarah was not aware of Abraham's interest in the Pinson girl either.

"So tell me, Sally, which of my boys is seeing Michal and which is seeing Judith?" Sarah wanted to know.

"Assuming they can tell them apart"—she laughed—"Daniel seems to be spending time with Judith, and William with Michal. As I said, there are other boys coming round some, but my girls seem smitten with your older ones. They are very handsome lads!"

"Now if I can just get Peter interested in someone!" said Sarah. "Joseph and John still have time."

"Peter has always just enjoyed spending time with William Edwards and his wife. They have two daughters and a son. William has been trying to get Peter to court his younger sister," said Mary with a laugh. "But you know Peter. I think he is just a little too persnickety."

The conversation the ladies had that afternoon turned into reality, with three whirlwind weddings of Sarah's "stairstep" boys, who had always been close, taking place in less than a year. She and Sally both stayed breathless with William and Michal marrying by the end of the year in December 1802, Daniel and Judith marrying in February of 1803, and Abraham and Nancy Pinson wedding in November of 1803. Just like that, James and Sarah were down to six children at home. James had helped his sons build their homes on land which he deeded to them as wedding gifts, so now they all had farms within three to five miles of the West farm. James was thankful he had purchased land from various people through the years and could give his sons nice places to get a start with families of their own.

It was New Year's Eve of 1805, and since those three weddings, it was almost as if James and Sarah could hardly keep up with the grandchildren they came in such rapid succession. They lay in bed that night naming them all one by one.

"Now let's see," began James. "Susannah has Stephen, Martha, Mary, Andrew, and Thomas. Mary has Amelia, John, and Mark. William and Michal now have Ida and Hardy, with number three on the way. Daniel and Judith have Paul with number two on the way. And Abraham and Nancy have Susan and Peyton. My children have been busy procreating, Sarah."

She smiled holding her husband closely. "In just a few short years, we now have more grandchildren than we had children."

"Life couldn't be any sweeter, wife," James told her, kissing her gently. "And we still have more to marry! The Lord said to be fruitful and multiply, and we can honestly say we have done our share!"

Peter knocked suddenly on their bedroom door with urgency. "Father!" he called from the other side of the door. "The smith shop is on fire!" James jumped out of bed, and in spite of the cold, he slipped on just his boots and an extra shirt and ran to assist his son. Sarah got out of bed and woke the girls, and they began to draw water from the well.

James was glad he had not attached the blacksmith shop to his barn, though it was in close proximity. With all his carpentry materials in the barn, he knew there would be a great fire hazard. Part of the shop was brick, so that helped delay the consumption of the building. But by the time they got out there, the top parts of the walls were ablaze. The first thing they used was water from the barrel that was always available in the blacksmith shop for cooling the heated, formed metal. James, Peter, Joseph, and John automatically channeled their energy into saving the barn. This was where James's most profitable business was outside of his tobacco crop. He had been after Peter to purchase extra bricks to make the blacksmith shop more fireproof, but he was not about to fuss at his son about that now.

There was a cold, brisk wind blowing, and it took everyone working on that side of the shop and barn to get the fire under control. At last, the fire was out, but the blacksmith shop was gutted from the top of the brick walls upward, with much of the roof gone as well. The barn thankfully had been spared. Peter was going to sleep in the barn to keep an eye on the shop for the remainder of the night. He and Joe were going to tend to any hot spots.

Sarah and James walked into the house with the girls and John. Everyone was smeared with soot and coughing from the smoke they had inhaled. James stood and looked at his family.

"God blessed us tonight. Thank you all for your help."

Sarah told them all to go change and bring all their smoky, blackened clothes and put them in the middle of the floor of the dining area. "Tomorrow, I will decide what can be salvaged. I hope all of our clothes can be washed and worn again, but we will see. Girls, I will need your help tomorrow." She hugged them all good night.

James embraced his three youngest princesses: Sarah, Elizabeth, and Ann. "Happy New Year to you all. I love you." He hugged John who was now almost as old as little James was when he died.

"Papa," John said, "I'm afraid this fire might have been my fault. I was trying to help Peter finish up a batch of nails. I think some of them got away from me and rolled over in a corner. I never went and picked them up."

"John, that's probably not what happened. The floor is dirt, and the walls around the floor are made of brick. I can't imagine that would be it. Perhaps the wind got into the building and stoked up some of the coals. Don't worry about it, son. Peter is going to get more brick and rebuild the smith shop."

"I just don't want him to think I can't learn the trade."

"Learn the trade? John, you are almost as good at blacksmithing now as Peter is. I'm sure he will let you continue working with him. You and Joe both. I've got an order for wheels coming up soon, and I will need all your help. Go to sleep now. Happy New Year, son."

He kissed the top of his son's head, though he was almost as tall as James.

James slipped into the bedroom with Sarah, who had changed into a clean gown already. She had enough water left for both of them to sponge bathe with to help get rid of some of the smoky residue.

"I hope this isn't some sort of bad omen for how 1806 is going to be," Sarah said smiling as she watched James change into a clean nightshirt. He stepped to the door and tossed the dirty one out into the parlor.

"Sarah, my love, we don't believe in omens," James said, kissing her and helping her into the bed and underneath the quilts. "I love you, Sarah. 1806 is probably going to be the best year yet."

CHAPTER 24

O ne of the first projects of the New Year was rebuilding the blacksmith shop since it was necessary to make the wagon wheels someone had ordered from James. Peter purchased more brick, and the entire structure was hopefully now more fireproof. James was certainly grateful for his sons and their assistance, and by the end of the reconstruction, James commented on how they could add masonry to their list of trades. God had been good to all of them, enabling them to make a nice living off not only tobacco but also the trades they had learned as well. James felt Francis would have been proud of how he had taken the farm and turned it into a successful place. He knew he had to credit Malachi also for helping him learn many things that he now knew how to do.

James still missed Malachi very much. He and Sarah both thought perhaps Sally would remarry, but she insisted she had no desire to do so. Her boys helped her out so much, even the ones who had married and moved away were still close by just as James's sons were.

One cold night in March, Sarah and James lay in bed talking, and he asked her to take out her commonplace book. "I want to read what you have written throughout the years. I guess it is kind of a book of our lives, isn't it?"

She went and got the book. Together, they lay propped up on pillows with the book open between them. They started at the beginning looking at Sarah's girlish writing and read her simple journal entries about the beautiful scenery of Swan Point. They then read the sad accounts of Hannah's and Timothy's deaths and looked at the drawings of the two. There was another drawing of Priscilla at the age of four. James chuckled as he read the two short entries Sarah had written about Garrett Matthews. "Poor Garrett! He had no idea he was done for as soon as you met me!"

James stopped at the entry Sarah had written about the night he first kissed her at the edge of her property after they had first talked at Cuckold Creek. He read aloud, "'This evening, I was at my rock on Cuckold Creek. James West, that young man who is staying with the Wades, showed up! He told me our timing was better this time than the last (the last time I had accidentally intruded upon his bath!) We had talked some at the wedding. This evening, we talked for quite a while! He told me some things about himself that were very sad. He ran away from Wales and came here to find his brother who left home years ago. He is an indentured servant and came over here in a ship with a friend named John Hussey. John was shot and probably killed running away from the plantation they were working on. James is educated and has a copy of *Robinson Crusoe* with him. He told me that this book (my book) is what his teacher called a commonplace book, I guess being one common place to record one's thoughts and one's favorite quotes, scriptures, and just words in general. He walked me home, and we kissed!'"

James looked over at Sarah with a big smile on his face. "I remember that! It had gotten dark quickly, and I had to move pretty fast to kiss you. You were headed home like lightning! You were so, so pretty!" He kissed his wife. They continued to read.

James found the entry where they had gotten married and Sarah had tastefully recorded, "'I am James's wife! What can I say, but I love to be loved by my husband. He is my world.'"

James grinned at Sarah. "Very nicely done. I was worried you might have written down all the lurid details of our first night together."

Sarah turned and kissed his shoulder. "Those memories are here," she said, pointing to her head.

The next entry James found and read aloud recorded the death of their first daughter, three months after it happened. "'I am still numb with grief. I carried our daughter for nine months, and she lived a day and a half. She struggled to breathe and never fed. She was so beautiful, and it was so hard to let her go. I was not able to write about this when it happened. It hurt James as much as it hurt me. He and my parents buried her in our cemetery here at Swan Point. I am sitting by her grave as I write this.'"

James stopped for a few seconds to let that hurt wash over him anew. Sarah just snuggled next to him and touched his hand, as she was reliving the pain as well. Then he said, "I did not know you wrote about this!"

"What is that?" asked Sarah.

"About Alice Roney! I never intended for anyone to know that story. It was so sad."

"Read what I wrote," she requested.

"'James told me today a story about a woman named Alice who was aboard the ship he came on. She was a convict servant sentenced to fourteen years in America. She gave birth while on the ship to a stillborn child whom she asked to bury at sea. James was with the captain, and together, they watched as she flung herself and her baby overboard! I know that woman's pain. Life stops, or you want it to, when you lose a child.'"

James was silent. He was remembering every detail about that morning. The way the sea lay flat and glassy with almost no breeze. He could recall the gray of the sky, the smell of the ocean. The sound of Alice Roney's voice as she ordered Captain Duggar and the other woman to "stay back!" He remembered his own sense of horror as the last he saw of her was her feet beneath the white shift she wore, going over the railing. Captain Duggar had shouted, "No!" He had wanted to save her, but the other woman had grabbed his arm and asked him, "Save her for what?"

James continued to read. Sarah had recorded entries about her father's death, entries along the way to North Carolina, the births of their babies. In an entry dated December 31, 1781, Sarah had written about their loss on Christmas Day. "'We had a Christmas angel visit us this year. She never drew a breath, but she came from us and our love. She was tiny, and she arrived too early. We held her, and then James buried her in the Frazier's cemetery. What profound sadness.'"

James read on, moved by the day-to-day things he never gave a second thought to that Sarah had written about: the change in the seasons, the beauty of the earth, the love in their home, her love of the Lord, many of the firsts of all their little ones, the times he was away in battle. Then he came across this and read it silently.

I cannot breathe. I still cannot grasp it. My firstborn son, our first angel whom we watched every single movement he made from his birth, has taken his own life. We have often remarked about how seriously Little James has viewed life on this earth. He always got emotionally hurt easily. I think we were not aware how deeply some things bothered him. He loved Cooper's mountain, and he spent many of his last days and nights up there in a cabin he built. He was only sixteen. He wanted to help a friend and could not. Feeling helpless and I guess useless, he took his own life. I am so worried about my husband as he is the one who was there. He is most grieved that he could not stop it from happening. I am praying for my husband that he can have some relief from his anguish. If only we all could. No mother or father should ever outlive a child.

James read this entry to himself, but Sarah knew where he was as she saw his face crumple into tears and sorrow. He used the bedsheet to wipe his face.

"Sarah!" he sobbed aloud. "I had no idea how powerfully you captured these moments from our life! What a gift. It hurts so much to read this, but now it will not be forgotten! I love you. Thank you for this marvelous gift of our life. You have written a book about us!"

With one arm, he pulled her close and kissed her face.

He continued reading: the weddings, the births of the grandchildren. When he reached the end, he said, "You must get another book! There are only about six pages left in this one."

As he turned to one of the last pages on which she wrote, he said, "Here's a poem. You wrote this? This isn't one you found and copied?"

Sarah now looked at where he was. "Yes, that is mine. I wrote that when we were returning from a trip to Susannah's. I sort of wrote it in my head and then finished and recorded it here. Very simple, but it so expresses how I have always felt about being remembered."

James read it out loud.

Forever Loved

The seasons change—
the earth becomes warmer, then colder.
The seasons pass—
I am full of life, I grow older.

I need to know—
my life has bearing on those yet to come.
I need to leave—
more than a name, more than a hard, cold stone.

I yearn to etch—
on someone's heart my story to be told.
Please, Dear Father—
let someone remember I was a breathing soul.

This is my song—
I sing it to the blue sky above.
As I have lived life—
I must know that I will be forever loved.

—SBW

James shed fresh tears and held his wife close. "Sarah, it is beautiful! When you pass away many, many, *many* years from now, someone must read this at your funeral."

"I will let you do that!" She smiled. "Remember you agreed to let me go first so I do not have to bear living without you."

They put away the book of memories and made love sweetly that night.

They celebrated John's sixteenth birthday the first week in May, and that night, James went to bed feeling sick. Seeing him so nauseous made Sarah think back to when he was drinking and could not keep anything on his stomach. She prayed he would be better soon, and in a day or two, he was.

By midafternoon, however, on the second day, he came into the house and got into bed. He told Sarah about having an awful pain in his abdomen, and they both assumed it was the residual effect of the stomach ailment he had suffered through. By that night, he was burning with fever, and the pain had grown more intense. Oddly, two days later, the severe pain had lessened and then stopped all together, but his fever raged on.

Sarah stayed by his side and feared the worst. James all but ordered her not to come so close as he might be contagious. She leaned over the bed and kissed him. She had tears on her cheeks seeing his wan face and his weak eyes. She told him, "I hope it is contagious, and I pray I catch it."

By early afternoon, he told her, "Sarah, my love, I fear I am dying. I have no strength left. Come closer," he told her almost breathlessly, as even his voice was weak. Sarah climbed into bed next to her husband. She did not want to waste a second of whatever precious time was left to them to send for any of the children. She wanted the remaining time with her beloved husband for herself.

She curled up next to his right side, the side that had hurt just a couple of days before. She lay her right hand on his chest and could feel his heart racing. She had sent word for the doctor two days before, but he had not yet shown up. Sarah was not ready to lose her fifty-eight-year-old husband.

She lay there listening to his breathing as it changed. At last, he whispered, "Sarah, my love, thank you for being my wife. I love you. You have been so special to me." Sarah kept her hand over his heart, and he clasped that hand with his. She prayed that if he left her, she might go with him, and that was why she stayed there in place by his side. In a few moments, as she felt his heartbeat diminish, he suddenly turned loose her hand, and with his hand pointed upward, his eyes opened, and he said, "Sarah! Look! Do you see?" Her eyes followed the path his hand pointed out, but she saw nothing but the ceiling of their bedroom. She turned to see him lower his arm and draw his last two breaths and felt his heart as it stopped its beating. She closed his eyes completely, as they were still open, seeing the glory he must have beheld.

She curled up next to his still warm body, crying, "James! No! Oh, James, you did not take me with you! I wanted to go with you!" She wept into his nightshirt, clutching it, and her soul ached for him.

She envied the peace on his face, and it comforted her to know he was now at last with Francis. He was with little James again, and she felt that her own mother and father must be close by as well. She knew his own parents must have been rejoicing to see their son they had not seen since he was sixteen. She lay there as he grew cold, not knowing what to do but knowing she did not want to leave him.

At last, Peter came into the room and found his mother curled up next to his father. She said, "Peter, your father is gone!" She was still weeping softly.

"Mother! Why did you not come find me?"

"I could not leave him," she whispered. "You must see to his casket, son."

"Mother"—her son had tears on his face—"I will go tell the others."

"Thank you, Peter. I will see to his clothes."

"The girls can do that, Mother."

In a few minutes, Elizabeth, Sarah, and Ann were in the room. They began to cry, and their mother cried with them. Then Joseph and John entered the room as well, and they continued to weep and mourn their beloved father. Joseph and John left on horseback to notify all the other family members who lived nearby.

Mary and her husband, their pastor, arrived first. Sarah was up helping the girls gather their father's clothes. She heated an iron to press his shirt. She was already amazed at what she could accomplish with only half a heart. Sally came in soon and embraced her friend. "Sarah, I was not aware James was even sick!"

"He was hurting in his side for a few days, then that the pain went away, but he had a fever. He slipped away almost two hours ago," Sarah told her wiping tears.

"How are you?" she asked Sarah.

"You know exactly what I am feeling, Sally," said Sarah, taking her friend's hand. "I wanted to go with him."

Sally blinked away tears. "I know."

"He is not alone," Sarah said, tears streaming down her face again. "He is with Malachi and Martha and Francis and little James."

"He is with Jesus," Sally said, also weeping.

"Sally, tell me, how do you go on? How do you live day to day without your heart?"

"I wish I could give you some sort of secret, Sarah. Your life is now going in a different direction. First was your life with James, now comes your life without him. It is not the same. You will amaze yourself at the things you can do and still ache for him. It surely makes heaven a daily goal." The two hugged again. Sally told her, "Know that I am here for you."

"For that, I am thankful."

His body was still in the bed, his head propped up on pillows. When she had his clothes ready, she went to her older sons—Peter, William, Daniel, and Abraham—and asked if they could please help her to dress their father. The men were shedding tears as they helped undress his body. It was Abraham, standing next to the bed, propping up his father's body after removing his shirt, who asked, "Mother, what are these scars on my father's back?"

Sarah could not speak at first. "He never wanted you boys to see those," she finally said.

They were all now looking at James's back at the whitish marks, and it was Peter who asked, "Did his father do this? Is this why he left home?"

"No, son. He was an indentured servant to come over here to America. You know that. What you never knew is that indentured servants were treated just as slaves were treated. Your father was whipped on the plantation he was on. That is why he ran away."

They were all wiping tears. "Why would they whip my father?" Daniel asked.

"He was caught trying to teach a young slave how to read and write. He did not know it was a whipping offense to do such a thing. The boy's name was Calvin. Your father thought of him all his life." She was touched at how moved they were by this knowledge. "This is just one reason why your father has always hated slavery."

They very tenderly completed the task of dressing him and lay him back on the bed. Peter went back out to finish working on the casket. Malachi's sons and nephews were already digging the grave in the Frazier cemetery. They were going to bury him next to his brother Francis.

Sarah found a few moments to sit with John Matthews, her son-in-law and pastor, to talk about the service. He was very grieved. He did not apologize for openly crying.

"Mother West, I shall be weeping at the pulpit, I will tell you now," said John. "I loved my father-in-law."

"May I share with you his last words?" she said softly. "His heart had slowed down, and I was lying next to him, when he suddenly opened his eyes and he lifted his arm and pointed upward. He said, 'Sarah! Look! Do you see?' Then he lowered his arm and took his last two breaths. His spirit just emptied out of his body. His eyes were still open, seeing glory. I closed them."

"I know what he saw," John said with tears on his face.

"I am sure I know as well," Sarah said smiling. "There was a look of awe and wonder on his face and in his eyes."

"Praise God," breathed John. "Do you mind if I use that in the service?"

"By all means. I know he would want it told."

She gave John some of James's favorite verses, many of which he already knew were his favorites from their previous talks. Then she remembered the poem she had written, "Forever Loved," and told John about it. "I will write it out for you. He really loved it."

Over the next two days, Sarah came to understand how when others mourn with you, they help bear your burdens. She was surrounded and uplifted by sons, daughters, in-laws and precious grandchildren, and friends. The funeral service could not have been any more special, and she felt that James's spirit was allowed to be at that gathering to witness the love of his family and to be at the place where he was laid to rest, next to Francis, the one he sought for so many years. Perhaps they were there side by side at last.

That evening after all the visitors had left, Sarah and the children who lived with her were quietly straightening the house when they heard a knock at the door. It was the doctor who had been summoned days before. Sarah heard Peter talking with him at the front door.

"You are too late. My father has passed." He welcomed him in anyway, and Sarah joined them in the parlor. The doctor was still standing when she entered the room, and he removed his hat.

"Missus West," he began, "you have my deepest sympathies. All I can say is we need more physicians in the area."

"Thank you. I could not agree more."

"Do you mind telling me your husband's symptoms?"

Sarah explained the nausea, pain, and fever.

"It sounds like a ruptured appendix. Surgery would have been the only thing that could have saved his life. You have my condolences. I am sorry for my delay. Good evening."

That night as she was in their bedroom alone, a thought came to her mind that she needed to send a letter to John Hussey to let him know of James's passing. This was the first of many times Sarah would feel a thought come to her mind that would make her feel certain that James was never going to be very far away.

CHAPTER 25

*T*he day after the funeral, Sarah wrote a letter to John Hussey telling him about James's death. In spite of tossing and turning and weeping half the night, she felt nervous and anxious instead of exhausted. Peter interrupted her as she was finishing the letter.

"Mother, how did you sleep?" he asked.

"You can imagine, Peter."

"Yes. Mother, I am not sure how much you know about Papa's financial arrangements. Do you mind if we talk?"

"Yes, Peter. What is it? I do know he did not leave a will."

"Exactly. But the house and this land are already mine. When he went and deeded the other pieces of property to my brothers, he deeded me this place. I guess he assumed I would never live anywhere else. But without a will, we must have an estate auction, not for the house and land but for his personal property. I have talked to my brothers, and we will take care of everything. We will buy what you need. The county will also provide you what they call 'a widow's portions.' But we must auction off his personal belongings. It is a formality really. You will stay here, and I and the others will look after you. If we can sell some of his things, it will give us extra money until the next crop. Mother," he said, "I don't want to tell things that aren't mine to tell, but Joe is talking about leaving."

Sarah looked up, surprised. "What do you mean?"

"I think he has our father's sense of adventure and wants to head west."

Sarah felt tears come into her eyes.

"I know I shouldn't be telling this the day after Papa's funeral, but I wanted you to prepare yourself for one of your chicks leaving the nest."

"I appreciate that, son. And tomorrow is your birthday. We need to do something to celebrate even though we are in mourning still."

Elizabeth walked in on that and agreed with her mother and offered to help plan a dinner for her brother. Peter, however, insisted that they did not need to worry about doing anything for his birthday. Elizabeth hugged her mother and held her close.

Sarah felt tears surface and said, "I just want things to be as normal and routine as possible. It's the only way I know to cope." Then Sarah cried, "But things will never be normal again!"

Both of her children encircled her in an embrace. They all three wept.

The estate auction was held on the twenty-sixth of the month. Each of the boys purchased things and gave many of the items back to their mother, such as their father's books and other personal belongings. Some of his things were purchased by those not in the family. The day after the auction, Joseph found his mother in her bedroom, looking through James's Bible.

He tapped on the open bedroom door. "Mother, I need to speak with you."

She stood, went over to him and held him about the waist. He was the tallest of her sons, and he reminded her more of Peter Bowman than any of them. "Yes, Joseph."

"Mother, I hate to do this so soon after Papa's death, but I am leaving. I am headed out west. I don't know if I will stay in the western part of North Carolina or go further into Tennessee or Kentucky, but I have to go. They say there is so much beyond our border—land just for the taking. I don't know if I will farm or what. I have many skills that Papa taught me that I can use to make a living. But I don't think I will be truly happy until I go see what is out there. Do you understand?"

"Yes, and knowing your father, I am sure he would be very supportive of your wanderlust," she said smiling through tears.

"It's funny, though, Mother, Papa's sense of adventure stopped right here. He came from the mother country, across the ocean, to Maryland and then here. And then he was content. I would think once he knew Uncle Francis was gone, he would have kept moving."

"It just felt right to be here, Joe. We felt right at home here with Malachi and Sally. And I think it was almost his way of staying close to Francis by being here, carrying on his legacy. But you have my blessing, son, and I know you would have your father's. I pray you will know when you have found *your* place to stop."

Joseph left two days later, and a week later, William and Michal had child number three, a son, whom they named James. Life, it seemed, was going to continue even without Sarah's beloved James walking upon the earth. Sarah tried to think of Martha and what a noble widow she had been. She had seemed happy and determined to be useful to the family she had left. Some days, Sarah was just not sure how dear Martha did it.

Sarah tried to save her weeping for the nighttime for indeed that was when she felt James's absence the most. The empty place next to her in bed was almost too much to bear most nights. She would hold onto what had been his pillow and sob into it trying to imagine his arms were still about her. She missed his smile, his voice calling her "my love" in his sweet Welsh brogue, and she ached for his tender loving.

When Sarah got a response to her letter to John Hussey, it was written by Sophia, his young wife. John sent his deepest condolences and said he knew that heaven had gained "an extraordinary angel." Sarah realized that John probably could not write but was touched that Sophia had answered the letter. Sophia wrote that John had wept for his friend, and she included her personal gratitude for their visit in that John was now "closer to God" and attending church with her, and she felt it had everything to do with that visit from James. This made Sarah tear up, as she knew how deeply James had wanted to influence his dear friend that Providence had sent him many years ago. It touched Sarah to know that even the awful experience of losing little James and how it had eventually solidified James's faith was still changing lives, like the rippling effect of a stone into water.

The next monumental change affected both families, the Wests and the Fraziers. Daniel also revealed a desire to wander, and he and Judith packed up their little family of four and headed southwest toward Alabama. Sarah and Sally shed many tears over the grandchildren leaving, and Michal was very distraught over losing her twin sister who was also her best friend. Sarah had the feeling, as did Sally, that Judith was not very happy about her husband's decision as she kept insisting that perhaps they would come back this way if things did not work out. She and Michal had a very tearful farewell that almost made Daniel change his mind about leaving. Peter bought Daniel's house and property from him to lease for now and perhaps for a profit down the road. Sarah had a feeling that Peter just wanted to make sure it was still in the family for their eventual return.

In August 1809, Elizabeth married Timothy Russell, an older man she had been courting for just a short period of time. His wife had died leaving two children that his mother was caring for. They moved in with his mother and father and became an instant family. She seemed very happy and lived only four miles away. Sarah and Ann soon followed suit, marrying two local men. Sarah wed Thomas Harris, whose father owned a shop in Oxford, and Ann married Arthur Short from a farm that was just east of them on Grassy Creek. Sarah was now left alone with only Peter and John. The home that once needed three additions now felt much too spacious.

In 1811, Peter more than surprised his mother by telling her *he* was planning to marry. His friend William Edwards had passed away from pneumonia the year before, and though he and his wife were older than Peter, Sarah assumed that her son would marry Mary Edwards, his best friend's widow. She was shocked to learn that her thirty-six-year-old son was betrothed to William's fourteen-year-old daughter, Susan. He told his mother that he had loved the child all her life, that there was something special about her from the time she was a baby. It seemed the marriage had the blessing of Susan's mother and her sister Judith who both absolutely loved Peter. Sarah realized that she just had had no idea how close Peter had been to this family most of his life.

Peter and Susan married in a very small ceremony at the Edwards' home. Mary's John performed the marriage rites, and it was the last service he performed in his capacity as their pastor. He had been called to preach at a church in Orange County, his father's church since his father had become ill. Sarah braced herself for losing Mary and the children to whom she had become so attached.

Sarah felt more lonely now, even though she had John with her and still had Peter, William, and Abraham's families not too far away. Many mornings, John would take her by wagon to Sally's, and the two would spend the day together, cooking, mending, or just visiting. They spent a great deal of time reminiscing about the days when Martha was with them sharing her wisdom and assisting them, not only with the births of their babies but also helping with their care. Of course, the women loved to talk for hours on end about their beloved husbands. They would still get emotional thinking of how much they still loved them, how sorely they missed them, and how much they had been loved by them. Both men had been humble with immovable faith, at least James was after the life-changing experience that took little James from them.

Peter lived close by in the Edwards' homeplace. He had thought of moving his new family to the West farm, but Mary Edwards begged them to stay there with her and Susan's sister Judith. Judith was a special young lady who had been emotionally and physically handicapped since birth. She was sometimes hard to deal with, but she loved her "uncle" Peter as she had always called him. He spent time with the girl, and taking her on horseback rides was a favorite way to pass the time. Susan gave birth to James Peter in 1812, about ten months after they married. Seeing Susan and Peter together always made Sarah think of John Hussey and Sophia, as they looked much more like father and daughter than husband and wife. They had a daughter they named Mary in 1814, and in 1818, a son was born that they named Thomas William after Susan's father and grandfather. Their last child was Lucinda, born in 1820.

Sarah loved all her grandchildren, and she used most of the last six pages in her commonplace book to record James's death and then continued her list of each grandchild born. It grieved her not to hear from Daniel and Judith nor from Joseph. She prayed the Lord and James would keep an eye on them.

One day in the summer of 1822, John found his mother mending one of his shirts, sitting in her favorite chair. He leaned over and kissed her on top of her head. "Mother, I have decided to marry!" he announced.

Sarah looked up at him. Having heard this from all the other children had not surprised her. It did not surprise her coming from John either, except with this marriage, provided he went to live with his wife's family, meant this was her last child to leave. It would mean Sarah would be all alone.

"I have asked for Ann Walker's hand in marriage. You knew I had been courting her?"

Sarah nodded. She also knew she had another reason to be bothered by this marriage. Ann's family owned a plantation with many slaves. She knew nothing about them personally, but she knew they were slaveholders. Two of Sarah's girls had married into families who owned black servants and a few slaves, so this was not the first time, but Sarah knew this was different.

Sarah stood and asked her youngest son to follow her. They walked back into her bedroom where Sarah opened her cedar chest. "John, you were not with us in this room the day your older brothers helped me dress your father's body. I do not know if they ever told you what they saw." She reached under several quilts and pulled out a folded piece of paper. "This is what I saw the first time I ever laid eyes on your father. He was seventeen."

She showed him the drawing she had never shown anyone except James.

"I was by Cuckold Creek, and out of the water came the backside of a young man I did not know. I saw his back with these marks. They were whip marks. He was bathing and cooling them in the water. He was an indentured servant, but they were treated just as badly as the slaves were. He was whipped with seven lashes that left scars that he had until the day he died for trying to teach a young slave to read and write. The young man was named Calvin, and he was whipped as well. Your father never forgot about Calvin. This is why your father ran away from that plantation, and it is why he was so against slavery."

John was quiet, and Sarah saw him wipe his eyes. "Mother, I know what you must be thinking. I will never treat the slaves on Ann's father's place like that. Perhaps I can show them a better way."

"Are you planning to live there and work for him?"

"Yes, that is the plan."

"Then I pray you will remember this and think of your father and never, ever use a whip on any human being! They are humans, John! They are not animals!" John could not think of a time he had heard his mother so vehement on an issue. He leaned over and kissed her on the cheek.

"I promise you I will never forget this. Mother, you are welcome to come live with us. I am sure there is a great deal of room on their plantation."

"No, son, I could never go live on a plantation. I must stay here in my home. I feel close to your father here. I will be fine, I promise."

With John gone, Sarah's visits with Sally became less frequent. Some days, one of Sally's children would bring her to Sarah's to visit. Sarah found herself sitting in her chair alone reading or mending most days. The day came, however, when Sally grew very ill, and Sarah was sorely grieved to learn her friend had passed away. She wept harder than she had since James had died. She was envious too that Sally was now with Malachi as Sarah wanted to go be with James so badly. After Sally died, Michal came to visit Sarah more often since she missed her own mother so much.

There were days, Sarah told Michal one day, when she felt that James was perhaps just in the next room. "Sometimes, I feel like if I just open the front door that he will be standing on the other side of it! Even with as many children and grandchildren as I have, it seems I have so many more loved ones on the other side just waiting!"

In April 1828, the family celebrated Sarah's eightieth birthday at her home. She now had several great-grandchildren through Susannah and Mary, and when she saw her reflection in a mirror, she laughed and said that she was glad James could not see how she had lost her beauty. Her children reassured her she was still a lovely woman.

It was at this time that the family decided Sarah should be living with one of them, and it was William and Michal who extended that invitation to Sarah. Sarah was actually grateful for the invitation, but she made a personal vow that she would not be a disruption in their lives. Sarah would never have told a soul, but Michal was her favorite daughter-in-law. She loved them all, but Michal was so much like her mother Sally that being with her was such a sweet reminder of her dear friend. Michal did not simply tolerate her mother-in-law, she genuinely loved to hear Sarah's stories about Swan Point and her early years with James. Michal ached when Sarah talked about losing her first child and then losing little James. She knew the stories by heart about Cuckold Creek and was truly touched by the memories Sarah shared of falling in love with James. With Michal, she even shared about Calvin and the whippings that James and Calvin got, and she told her about little James and Rose, though she asked her not to tell anyone. The only thing she never told Michal, nor her sons and daughters, was what she had promised her husband she would never tell, even after his death, and that was the fact that he had gone to jail for stealing a red cloak and had been convicted of larceny and had come to America as a convict servant.

Moving out of the homeplace was necessary, but it grieved Sarah so. Peter still owned the house, though she was not sure what he would ever do with it. She made the boys promise to tend to the graves as their father had done. She walked through her home one final time, hours before William and some of the grandchildren came to get her in the wagon. In each room, she thought of her children when they were small, and their laughter echoed in her mind. The fireplace in the parlor brought memories of Christmases that were so joyous and reminded her of all the times James read to them from Captain Duggar's Bible. But saying farewell to their bedroom was the most painful of all. She stood there in the doorway, remembering babies being conceived and babies being birthed and fed, and in her mind's eye, she could see her husband there, loving her and loving them all. She said a silent prayer, thanking God that except for losing little James and losing big James for a time, she had had such a blessed life. In her life, she had truly been loved by her husband and by her Father in heaven.

William's family never considered Sarah a burden but thought of her time with them as a blessing. Until she approached ninety, she was able and willing to do chores about the house, mostly mending and minding the smaller grandchildren, her great-grandchildren, when they would visit. Sarah loved to take the little ones on her lap and study their sweet faces and kiss them tenderly. She wished her vision were not worsening because she wanted so much to sketch them for future memories. The children, grandchildren, and great-grandchildren loved to have her take out the commonplace book from her cedar chest, though the pages were worn and the ink faded. She would hold the book and read to them from it, parts that she felt were important for them to hear. She showed them the pictures she had drawn of her little brother and sisters. She wanted them to know that their grandfather and great-grandfather James West had been a man with a strong faith in God, as was her own father Peter Bowman. She shared with them all about Manorowen, Wales, and how James had traveled across the ocean, arrived in Baltimore, and how they met at Swan Point.

She was visited at William and Michal's by all her children at various times, and she loved seeing them. On one occasion, Peter came to see her alone without Susan.

"Mother," he said, as he pulled up a chair next to hers, "I do not know if you have heard, but I wanted you to hear it from me. John has been taken to court. You know Ann's father died and left him as executor of his estate, being his oldest son-in-law. Her siblings, particularly her brothers-in-law, have brought a suit against him. It seems when he divided the property, he kept most of the slaves for Ann and himself."

Sarah sighed deeply. "I knew this was not a good thing for him to marry into a family with such a large plantation. But I do not know what I can do for him at this point, Peter. It is something he is going to have to work out for himself."

About a week later, John came to visit his aged mother and found that she was in the bed. He took a seat in a chair next to her bed. He thought he would have to explain all this from the start, but Sarah startled him by asking, "What does your attorney say about the suit against you, son?"

"Mother, I am sorry. I guess you heard then. I came today to tell you why I did what I did. Mother, at Ann's father's death, I became the executor. Let me just say that I did not equally divide up the slaves. I kept most of them for us. But is there is a reason why! My father-in-law was a decent slaveholder. He does have overseers who are somewhat harsh out in the fields, but Ann's father was fair and decent. I know that some of my wife's brothers-in-law are probably not going to be fair and decent slaveholders. I am also worried about splitting up families. But I have been ordered to divide them up in a more equal manner."

He got quiet for a moment but then went on, "Mother, you were right. It has been difficult being part of a plantation. I have told Ann that perhaps we need to just take our land we have been left and raise our sons to farm with me. I think I am going to relinquish control of the entire place to one of Ann's sister's husbands. I want to make my father proud. I want to have a clear conscience."

He leaned over and kissed his mother's wrinkled cheek. "I love you, mother."

"I love you too, son. I hope you will be able to do just that."

The day came when Sarah was no longer able to leave her room, and she smiled as she lay in the bed with the sheet pulled up to her chin, her snow white hair in a braid over her shoulder. One of William and Michal's granddaughters named Elizabeth was twelve. She adored brushing and braiding Sarah's hair. She loved to keep the water pitcher next to her bed filled. She would bring Sarah her meals and talk to her when she was there visiting. Sarah always smiled more when Elizabeth would come spend time with her.

One day, Elizabeth asked her great-grandmother, "Why do you smile so much? I would think being in bed most of the day and all the night would be tiresome. What makes you smile?"

Sarah reached out with her shaking hands and took her great-granddaughter's hands in hers.

"I will be leaving soon, Elizabeth! One of these days, I am going to go to that place that your great-grandfather saw and told me about just before *he* left."

"But I don't want you to die! I am going to miss you!" The young girl's eyes filled with tears.

"Oh, but, child, it is going to be wonderful to be in heaven! Just before my James died, he pointed up to the ceiling, and he said to me, 'Sarah! Look! Do you see?' And then he took his last breath and died. He saw heaven, child!"

"But I am going to miss you!"

"I want you to stay close to the Lord, Elizabeth. I want to see you in heaven when it comes *your* time to leave this earth."

It was Christmas Eve of 1838, and most of the family had gathered for a holiday party at William and Michal's. Sarah had turned ninety that year. As the party was going on, her family members were in and out of her bedroom visiting as the evening wore on. Sarah was just too feeble to even be taken down to where the family was gathered. Nancy, Abraham's wife, had just stopped in to say her goodbyes to Sarah. The old woman did not respond. Nancy could tell she was still breathing but in a very shallow way. She slipped out of the room to get Michal.

"I think Mother West is about to leave us. I thought you'd want to know." Michal went into Sarah's room while Nancy went to inform Sarah's children who were still there. Quietly whispering to each other, they began to fill Sarah's room and surround her bed. There was a small lamp burning on the table next her.

William, Abraham, Peter, and John gathered around their mother. They watched as her lips moved, her breathing growing more and more faint. Then all that were there heard Sarah say, "James! Look at you!" as a smile formed on her lips. Thinking that these were her last spoken words, they began to cry softly but were stunned when she said clearly—almost in the voice of a young girl—"I, Sarah, take thee, James, to be my wedded husband."

Sarah reached to take James by the hand, and he led her through the veil between earth and heaven, and as he did so, she could see an amazingly bright and warm light. She instantly knew its Source, and she could feel it all the way through her being.

"Remember how golden the sun would get on Cuckold Creek?" he asked her. "This is so much more beautiful. You are even more beautiful here, Sarah." Sarah was so glad to see James but not startled in the least.

"I have missed you so much, James," she told him.

"I have never left your side, my love. I have been waiting for you."

Sarah turned toward the direction from which this Light was emanating.

"Sarah," said James, "look! Do you see? Just look who's here!" She had never seen James with so much happiness on his face.

"It's our son, little James!" she said smiling.

"And do you know this lovely young lady who looks so much like you?"

"Yes, that's our daughter that we held for several hours at Swan Point!"

As Sarah gazed ahead, she realized that there was a line of familiar faces that continued out of sight, nothing but row after row of people to greet, and everywhere the brightness which was already filling and embracing her soul.

"Mother! I have missed you so! Father! I love you both so much!" she said, greeting her parents.

Sarah realized then and rejoiced to know that James was going to walk by her side and be with her as she greeted each and every loved one. She felt such joy as she knew that this time he was going to be with her forever.

EPILOGUE

*R*everend Ken Clark knocked on the door of the old farmhouse. He was greeted by a woman in her early sixties who reminded him of his own mother back in Virginia. The lady welcomed him into the neat, small living room where she offered him a seat.

"Mama's in the kitchen. I'll bring her right in."

She disappeared into the next room, but Reverend Clark could hear her speak loudly.

"Mama, that young man who wrote to you is here." He watched as this woman carefully helped her white-haired mother into the living room. The older woman was using a cane to help her walk into the room and take a seat.

He stood politely while she found her way to what was clearly "her chair."

"Please, have a seat," she greeted him. "You've met my daughter, Joyce. I'm Cornelia, but everybody calls me Nealie."

"It's a pleasure to meet you, Nealie. I believe we are cousins, distant cousins."

"From what you told me in your letter, I believe you are right!" She smiled. She was a little winded as she finally got comfortable in the chair.

"James West was my third great-grandfather. His son William was my great-great-grandfather," he explained.

"James and Sarah were *my* great-great-grandparents," said Nealie. "William was my great-grandfather, but I never knew him.

My granny was Michal Frazier West, William's wife. She was my great-grandmother, and she lived with us when I was a little girl. She lived to be very old as Sarah did. I was almost twenty years old when Granny died. I loved listening to her talk about James and Sarah, her in-laws. She told me a lot about her own parents, Malachi and Sally Frazier, too, though. The Wests and the Fraziers were neighbors and close friends."

Reverend Clark smiled. "I think you can help me then. I am trying to find out all I can about James and Sarah. Your great-grand-mother knew a lot about them, I take it?"

The old woman nodded.

"Were they from here in Granville County?" he asked.

"Oh no. James came from over in England, or near England. He was from a place called 'Mnorway' or something like that. He came over in 1765 on a ship and landed in Baltimore. He apparently had to work on board the ship then had to work as a servant for six months or so before he was free. I think he worked on a farm or a plantation. My granny talked like he ran off. While he was in Maryland, he met Sarah. They got married up there and then came down to North Carolina. He had a brother here he wanted to find, but when they got here, he was dead. My granny talked like James just left home in England suddenly. Ran off from his home. Said he used to talk about how he was out slopping the hogs or pigs one day and just decided that he was going to come to America and find his brother. So he just dropped his slop bucket and walked to the nearest port and took a boat to come over here."

"Do you remember if she said anything about his family back over in England? Did he ever contact them or mention their names?"

"No, I don't believe he did. We know about Sarah's family because of the book she wrote in."

"She wrote a book?" he asked.

"Yes, it is sort of like a diary, with drawings and all in it." Nealie nodded to her daughter, who got up to go get the book. Reverend Clark could see into the room across the hallway that Nealie's daughter entered. He watched her lean over and open a very old-looking chest. She brought out a large brown paper sack. She carefully slipped the volume out and placed it gently into Reverend Clark's lap. He was stunned. He had not expected to see something that belonged to his ancestor Sarah West, but here he was with a very old book that was clearly falling apart. The pages were almost crumbling, but most were still intact within the binding.

As he turned to the first page, he could clearly read in faded brown ink, "Sarah of Swan Point." There was a drawing of a swan floating on water. Most of the writing was still legible.

"This is a treasure!" the minister exclaimed.

"Yes," Nealie agreed. "My great-grandmother Michal told me she remembered her mother-in-law Sarah reading from the book and entertaining the grandchildren and great-grandchildren with the stories."

Reverend Clark opened the notebook he brought with him and asked, "May I take notes?"

"By all means. I will also tell you what I remember, not only from what my Granny told me but from what I've read in that book over the years."

"That would be wonderful! Did Sarah do the drawings herself?" he asked.

"Yes. Seems she was a wonderful artist *and* writer. There are even some poems in there that she wrote. Granny said she and James both were educated and loved to read. I remember her showing me a Bible that James had. But I don't know what happened to that."

Reverend Clark was taking notes listening to Nealie but was also jotting down dates and names from the book.

"James and Sarah lost a baby girl while they were still in Maryland living with her family. Then they had a son they called little James. He died when he was young, a few years after they got here and after they'd had other children. Little James loved the local mountain, which we call Cooper's mountain. Some call it Daniel's Mountain now, and apparently, that's where he told his father he wanted to be buried. He died young, as I said. Sarah wrote in the book that he took his own life. I've heard rumors, stories people in the family have told, that young James fell in love with a slave girl. And when he realized they couldn't be together, well, they say it was like a Romeo and Juliet kind of story. They buried him up there on the mountain, but I don't think anybody knows where his grave is."

"Is there a family cemetery?"

"Yes, it belonged to my granny's people, but the Fraziers let the Wests bury their people there too. I know James and Sarah are buried there. It's way back in the woods near the old Frazier homeplace, but it's overgrown now. But you can still get to it."

"She writes here that James fought in the Revolutionary War! These dates! These entries are dated in the 1700s. This book is almost one hundred and seventy-five years old! Here are drawings of Sarah's younger brother and sisters." He jotted down names and dates. "Looks like they died young. It seems she really wanted them to be remembered."

"Granny said that Sarah was very interested in telling those stories so that people would know about them. That's what one of her poems is about, wanting to be remembered. Sarah lived with my granny and her husband William for about ten years. Sarah died in 1838, almost a hundred years ago. She died in their house. Granny told me that just before Sarah died, she recited her wedding vows!"

Reverend Clark stopped writing and just looked at the woman. "No!"

"Yes, she apparently called out, 'James!' And then said, 'I, Sarah, take you, James, to be my husband.' Then she held out her hand and had a big smile on her face and took her last breath!"

Reverend Clark wrote all this down.

"James died way before she did, so she was a widow for many years. She drew a picture of James, what he looked like when they first met."

Reverend Clark turned back some pages and found the drawing she spoke of. "He had long hair," he said. "Seems he was a handsome young man."

"See if you can find that loose page in there. I keep it stuck in the back."

He turned until he found it. "This is odd. Who is this?"

"Sarah told my granny that that was how she first saw James, coming up out of the creek near her house."

"It's hard to make out, but are those stripes on his back?"

"Yes. She said that's why he ran away from that plantation. He got whipped. Him and another boy."

"That is very sad. That must have been difficult."

"As far as I know, James and Sarah never owned slaves. I guess that's why."

"It must have also been difficult if their son fell in love with a slave. Even now that would be unheard of—interracial love and marriage."

"Well, I don't think many people knew about it. I'm not even sure that it's true. It *is* true he took his own life. Sarah writes about it in the book."

Reverend Clark searched until he found the entry. He read it to himself. "Hmmmm. Such hurt and pain in her words. Sounds like James was very grieved as well."

He continued to listen to Nealie and write down notes. By the time he left that afternoon, he'd copied most of what was written down in Sarah's book. "If only all my ancestors kept such good records. Bless you for sharing this with me." He gave his cousin Nealie an embrace and left.

Granville County
1984

"Is this Reverend Clark?" the woman asked over the phone. She had been given his name by a fellow West researcher.

"Yes, it is. To whom am I speaking?"

"My name is Cynthia Abbott. I have gotten copies of your notes from Anne Kline. She and I are both interested in the James West family history."

"Yes! Anne is descended through Abraham, son of James. Which of James and Sarah's children do you come through?"

"I am descended through Peter and Peter's son Thomas. I live right here in Granville County."

"So you know where Cooper's mountain is?"

"Yes, I think they call it Daniel's mountain now. Have you found the cemetery yet?"

"No, I never found it. I meant to get someone to show it to me, but I never did. I also wanted to go to the top of Cooper's mountain but never did that either. It seems little James had quite an attachment to that place and was buried up there."

"In the notes I have of yours, I see you've got the children listed with birthdates. So did you see the family Bible?"

"No, there was a book that Sarah wrote. She listed her children, wrote journal entries, and drew sketches."

"Do you have that book now?" she asked.

"No, but I held it in my own hands back in 1938. One of Sarah's great-great-granddaughters showed it to me."

"That must have been amazing!"

"It was a genealogist's dream! It was her personal journal in her handwriting with sketches she drew."

"I wish I could have seen that! I have copies of a family Bible. It was a Bible kept by son John's family. It's copyrighted 1851. It lists the children of James West."

"I would love to have copies of that!" he told her. "I did not know that it existed." He gave her his address so she could send copies.

"There is something you might want to know that I have never written down as it may not be true. Young James, their oldest son, committed suicide," he told her.

"You hinted at that in your notes. Do you know why?"

"It is true he took his own life. Sarah recorded it in her journal. But why he did it was just rumored. Some in the family say that young James fell in love with a slave girl. They couldn't be together, so it ended much like a Romeo-and-Juliet-type situation."

"That's so sad! I'm sure it was very forbidden back then."

"The ones I talked to seemed to think most people did not know it."

"Thank you so much for sharing all this with me, Reverend Clark."

Granville County
2016

Via the internet, Cynthia Abbott found a distant cousin from Virginia, a retired school teacher, another descendent of James West, who was researching and blogging about James and Sarah. With the aid of modern technology, this researcher, Pattie Neal Hunt, found court records of the trial of James West and John Hussey held at the Old Bailey Courthouse in London, January 1765. It contains all the words spoken by the plaintiffs and the defendants. The sentencing and transport records were also found. Immediately, these two cousins felt that James West and John Hussey intended to get arrested. They wanted this free ticket to America. They both believed the two young men intended to escape as soon as they got to the plantation where they were sentenced to work out their seven years. Soon came the proof. A newspaper account in the *Maryland Gazette* gives notice of the escape of James West, John Thomas, and John Maund Philpott from a plantation in Lower Cedar Point Maryland, just a couple of weeks after landing in Baltimore, offering a reward for their capture. It gives such a vivid description of James that one could almost draw a portrait. It was Hans Christian Anderson who wrote "The beautiful and the good are never forgotten. They live always in story and in song." At last, the story of James and Sarah feels complete, and now these ancestors of many will live on and be loved forever.

What Is True about the Novel?

*J*ames and Sarah West were my fifth great-grandparents. James really did come to Baltimore from London, and he really did steal a cloak with a young man named John Hussey. What their relationship was before that, I have no clue. I have copies of the court records, including James's actual words spoken in court in his own defense. (And I use them in the novel!) James and John were sentenced to seven years in America and were sent on board a ship called the *Tryal* that landed in Baltimore. There is never another mention of John Hussey. James and the two Johns escaped from the Thomas James (not Orr) plantation in Lower Cedar Point in Charles County, Maryland. I have a copy of the newspaper advertisement telling of their escape on May 17, 1765. James is said to be fifteen or sixteen when he ran off. I aged him and Sarah a year or two in the novel. Based on the oral family history that was written down by Rev. J. Kenneth Clark of Halifax, Virginia, a descendant of William, son of James and Sarah, James told his family he came from a place pronounced "Mnorway." A fellow researcher wrote to an Atlas maker in the 1980s to help her find a village that would be pronounced like that, and he sent back that the only village in all the United Kingdom that would be pronounced similarly was a small one in Wales called Manorowen. It would have been pronounced like "Mnorway" only with an *n* on the end: "Mnorwayne." If anyone questions whether that James of the court records/newspaper escape record is *our* James West, I refer to the oral history, which clearly states he arrived in Baltimore in 1765 and married Sarah Bowman while still in Maryland.

Sarah is completely fictionalized. I know very little about her except that James met her and married her in Maryland. No marriage record has been found (fire burned marriage records?). After doing lots of research, I am wondering if her last name was actually "Boarman," as there were more Boarmans than Bowmans, though I did find a Peter Bowman from that area in a later census. I think it is just a variation of name spelling that often happened with names such Robertson, Roberson, Robinson. Many people were illiterate then through no fault of their own, and name spelling was just not a priority for most people that far back.

I thoroughly enjoyed finding a very real place called Swan Point (now an exclusive coastal resort) that was indeed named by Captain John Smith for the same reason given in the book. I do know Sarah's children were important to her, and somewhere along the way, she recorded their names and birthdates that were later transferred by one of her grandchildren into a Bible from 1851. I also know she lived to be very old, maybe about ninety. I know she lived in her later years with her son William and his wife Michael Frazier West. I know what she purchased at James's estate auction in 1806, and one of those things was a book. I am guessing she bought James's Bible, but again, my guess. The fact that she passed along and kept the story of James going let me know that she was a "rememberer."

Speaking of the estate auction, Rev. Clark wrote that he could never find a will or any settlement of an estate for James, but after hours on the old microfilm, I found in loose estate records the actual record for the auction of James's estate. The most amazing thing about this auction was the presence of nine books. In all my research, I have never had even one book recorded as being a possession of an ancestor, though I am sure some had books. This was a virtual library! It, to me, was proof positive that James was literate! This fueled the whole *Robinson Crusoe* part of the story.

Also true is that James never owned slaves, and once I found out he had been a convict servant, I assumed that that was possibly why he never owned slaves as he had once been treated as one. His son John married Ann Wilkerson, and when her father died, John was named executor of his father-in-law's estate. When John, who had never been part of a slaveholding family, had to divide up the estate, he was a little unequal in his distribution of said slaves and was taken to court by his in-laws to force him to equally divide the slaves. I choose to believe (in my account anyway) that John did this to protect the slaves and to try and keep them out of the hands of those who would have abused them. According to the 1850 Slave schedule, John owned four slaves after the death of his wife. He is listed as age sixty and his youngest child is nine years old. He had two or three children who lived with him without marrying, and one of them, probably daughter Sarah, entered the data into the Bible. It is exciting to know that I actually held John's Bible (b. 1790, youngest son of James and Sarah) in my own hands and made copies. I know the approximate location of the place he raised his family. Also interesting is that in the 1850 census, it lists a young man living with John and his family, as a carpenter's apprentice.

I have the novel set on what is now known as Cornwall Road near where the Fraziers and the Eakes lived. This would have been near Grassy Creek and Mountain Creek in northern Granville County just behind what is known as Daniel's mountain. James's sons who stayed here spread out just a little. William's family lived just a few miles northwest in what was known as Young's Crossroad, and Peter, Abraham, and John were in Goshen/Oak Hill, a little north of Grassy Creek/Mountain Creek. Joseph left and was never heard from again. Daniel and Judith either moved down east (there are census records of a Daniel West whose age and family's ages could be a match in Sampson County, North Carolina) or to Alabama. Some descendants of Peter and William moved to Kentucky and Tennessee. Peter's son James Peter West and *his* son James Reuben West settled in Butler County, Kentucky. William's son Hardy West married Abraham's daughter Susan West, and they moved to Rhea County, Tennessee. They had William Thomas West who became a Baptist minister. Peyton West, whom we assume was Abraham's son (by process of elimination since we know from census records that Abraham had eleven children), moved west to Person County, still very close to the area.

Cooper's mountain was mentioned by name in the written down oral history (the Rev. Clark history from Cornelia West Vaughan). It tells that little James asked to be buried on Cooper's mountain. I can't find anyone who ever remembers a place called Cooper's mountain, but there is a Daniel's mountain very near where they lived in the Grassy Creek/Mountain Creek area. It is the highest elevation in North Carolina between Granville County and the coast, and it is clearly visible on Highway 96. But once you are on Cornwall Road and in that area where I have been told James and Sarah lived, the mountains are not visible, probably due to the lay of the land and the thick woods.

There was a Francis West who married a woman named Christian, and they lived in Granville County. Francis died in 1783, not 1770, and Christian really did move to Tennessee with family members. I created this fictitious relationship between James and Francis to give a viable reason why James would have left Maryland and moved to Granville County, North Carolina.

James's sons William and Daniel really did marry the daughters of Malachi Frazier (Michael and Judith) which is why I made them neighbors in the book. And speaking of the Fraziers, I have William, Daniel, and Abraham close friends with Guy and Shadrack Frazier. While doing research toward the end of the book, I found the marriage record for one of them, and Shadrack Frazier is the bondsman!

James was in Capt. William Burford's regiment on the 1771 roster. As far as I know, this is the earliest proof we have of James in Granville County, which is why I have them arriving in 1770. The battles of the Revolutionary War mentioned in the novel are the actual battles that regiments from Granville County fought in. I have no idea in which of these battles James was involved. There are documents, however, verifying his enlistment in 1771, 1777 and 1782.

What is kind of amazing, and maybe even a little creepy, is I decided, though there were no subsequent records of John Hussey after Baltimore, to make him reappear in the book. First, Christian tells James that John escaped and visited them looking for James. Then James runs into John while in his first battle of the Revolutionary War. I decided to make John with an Orange County regiment since they were together so often with the Granville County regiments. I also just decided to have John reside in Hillsborough. That was totally fiction, or so I thought. After I originally submitted this manuscript, I found a compendium of all the soldiers from North Carolina who fought in the Revolution. In the index, I found James West, of course. Then I just decided to check out to see if there was a John Hussey who fought for North Carolina in the Revolutionary War. Imagine my surprise (and the goose bumps that went with it!) when I saw that there *was* a John Hussey (only one!) who fought and that he was with an Orange County regiment *and* he resided in Hillsborough!

Abraham's son Elisha Battle West moved to Morgantown, Kentucky. Elisha's son James Larue West had a daughter named Anne West Kline with whom I had the pleasure of corresponding in the 1980s. It was she who gave me so much information including the letter and map from the atlas publisher who found Manorowen. Some still believe maybe James was really from London, but my question still is where did the name "Mnorway" come from in oral history? And speaking of the oral history, with Sarah living to be as old as ninety and her daughter-in-law Michael with whom she lived living to be so old, it is clear to see how the details of James and Sarah's lives would be preserved, as Michael knew James and Sarah as in-laws and then had Sarah live with her for many years. The stories seemed to spring from William's descendants, but someone in John's family transferred the names and dates of all of James and Sarah's children into a Bible copyrighted 1851. Surely, Sarah had them written down elsewhere? Maybe in a commonplace book?

I was inspired to include the commonplace book when just a few months before starting this novel in earnest, I was visiting an older woman who was related to a friend of mine. She said she had letters that my friend's great-great-grandfather had written to her great-great-grandmother. When I went to see this lady to borrow the letters and to make copies, she said, "They are in this book!" The letters must have been rough drafts as they were still attached inside the old book! The letters were dated in the 1880s, but as I looked through the book, I realized it was actually owned by my friend's great-great-great-grandmother and there were all kinds of writings including some original poetry dated in 1846! Just having that book in my possession for a couple of weeks transferred me to the past of an *actual* young school girl named Bettie. I held that book, which was about 170 years old. It helped me create the whole idea of Sarah keeping a journal or a commonplace book. Google commonplace book. Just as I was starting the novel, a friend posted an interesting article on Facebook about the commonplace book. It's fascinating!

For years, all I knew was that I was descended from Thomas West, a blacksmith from northern Granville County. I knew we came from both his sons Fleming and David West whose children, first cousins Joe and Mollie, married. Ironically by 1976, I had the record from the family Bible when my future brother-in-law brought me the Bible in possession of his aunt Christine and uncle George West (who descended from John West, to whom the Bible clearly belonged). I made xeroxed copies of all pages but had no idea how my Thomas connected to this James West. Years later, my father got a letter from researcher Anne West Kline, and in her letter, she listed all of James and Sarah's children and said Abraham was her great-grand-father. Imagine her thrill when I responded with copies of the John West family Bible! All she had to go on was Rev. Clark's written down oral history. Even so, I still did not know how my Thomas fit into the family. I somehow got the name of a Don Shelton from Winston Salem, North Carolina, who had done research, and after scaveng-ing the Granville County Courthouse, he had uncovered an obscure record, a suit against the estate of Peter West. Peter had left a will, but he only mentioned his wife, his wife's sister, and his mother-in-law (and a bay horse). There was no mention of children. But the suit brought against the estate for money owed lists Peter's four children, two sons and two daughters: Thomas West (m. Mildred Currin), James Peter West (m. Nancy Currin, sister to Mildred), Mary West (m. James Eakes), and Lucinda West (m. Joseph West). We still do not know who that Joseph West's father was, but he is more than likely, through a process of elimination, the son of Abraham, so first cousin to his wife. That was a great day in my life when I finally had the connection with the James West of the Bible and the Clark

History! Peter was the missing link between my Thomas and James West!

And what about Little James and Rose? I had the privilege of talking on the phone with Rev. Clark (an older gentleman by the 1980's), and he, when talking about little James's death, said that though some thought he died as a child, some people he talked to said that the younger James was possibly a teenager when he passed away. He said that there were family stories, which he did not record, that James had fallen in love with a young slave girl in the area. (He practically whispered that part to me over the phone!) He interpreted it to be kind of like a Romeo and Juliet scenario where they knew they could not be together and that perhaps they (or just he) had done themselves in very tragically. I decided to use this in the book, though there is no proof other than whispered family lore.

My obsession with James and Sarah began long before 2017 when I first held that Bible belonging to one of John's family. That, along with the Clark History and the story of James dropping his slop bucket and walking to a fishing village, strengthened in me a desire to tell their story someday.

But the thing that recently triggered the beginnings of this novel was finding a cousin online, Pattie Neal Hunt of Virginia. She is descended through my great-great-grandfather Fleming West's brother Robert West (who both fought in the Civil War). When she found the court record of James's *conviction* and *transport* on the *Tryal* to Baltimore, and then she found the newspaper account of his escape in a May 1765 copy of the *Maryland Gazette* is when I thought, *This story is already partly written, and it is a great story!* Cousin Pattie has a wonderful blog on James and Sarah at mypassagethroughtime. blogspot.com. The West family information (including some great photos!) is archived in her April-June 2016 blogs.

Interesting is the fact that Anne Kline had found the name James West on the *Tryal* coming to Baltimore in 1765 (which verified Clark's history), but we did not know that it was a convict ship! We assumed, as James seemed to want his family to think, that he was indentured, that he worked on board the ship, and then he indentured himself to a farm or plantation in Maryland.

And what of poor Alice Roney? She was a real convict, sentenced to fourteen years in America and was with James on the *Tryal*. According to her court record, she was a very big part of a theft ring, dealing mainly in handkerchiefs! Her husband testified in court he knew nothing about it. She went to America alone, or did she perhaps leap to her death in the middle of the Atlantic Ocean?

Herbert Stokes and his plantation and evil sons are all fictional. That is not to say there weren't plantation owners in Granville County who abused their slaves. I would be shocked to find that out. In my opinion just owning slaves was abuse! After years of teaching slave literature as part of the American literature curriculum, I detest slavery as much as I detest the horrors of the Holocaust. Both historical realities epitomize man's inhumanity to man. Though most of my West ancestors did not own slaves, I had many ancestors who did own slaves. I feel sad knowing this, but I know that I had no control over the choices they made. It was a different time period, and I am all about harmony in these days for my descendants. I pray that this book will bring about peaceful feelings in those who read it, as well as be a boon to my readers' personal walks of faith. I have a very personal testimony of my Savior Jesus Christ.

A special thanks to another West cousin I found through technology. His name is Charles "Ted" Pendergrass, and our grandfathers were brothers. He is a gifted photographer, and he allowed me to use one of his awesome sunsets that I feel reflect what the golden rays on Cuckold Creek must have looked like as James and Sarah met and fell in love there. The artwork was done by my extremely talented daughter-in-law, Holly Abbott. I think her artistic gift adds a special touch to *Forever Loved: Sarah of Swan Point*.

I thought of my father Morris Wheeler West so much when writing about James. My father was a tenderhearted man who wept easily and freely, especially when singing about or sharing his faith with others. He and my mother were sweethearts just as James and Sarah are in my novel. They also taught me from birth about the love our Savior Jesus Christ, and they exemplified Him in every step of their lives. My mother lived only a few years after my father's death, and we have often said she died of a broken heart. It is to them I lovingly dedicate this book.

Cover photo credit:
Charles Thomas Pendergrass, Jr.
PenTed Photography Moments
Artwork credit:
Holly Nicole Abbott

The children of James and Sarah West, names and dates recorded in the births section of the Bible belonging to their youngest son, John West. Names and dates probably transferred from a record Sarah had, possibly recorded in this Bible by Sarah West, daughter of John and his wife Ann Wilkerson, granddaughter of James and Sarah.

RAN away from the Subscriber, living near Lower-Cedar-Point in *Charles* County, the 17th of *May* last, Three Convict Servants, imported in the *Tryal*, Capt. *Errington*, from *London*, viz.

John Thomas, a stout swarthy Man, about 32 Years of Age, upwards of 6 Feet high, has black Eyes, and dark brown Hair. Had on an old Jacket lined with Country Cotton, a red Cloth Cap, an old Check Shirt, old black Worsted knit Breeches, and 3 Pair of Yarn Hose.

John Maund, alias *Philpott*, about 21 Years of Age, 5½ Feet high, has dark brown Hair, grey Eyes, and Lisps in his Speech. Had on a Snuff colour'd Coat and blue Breeches, ribb'd Worsted Hose, a Check Shirt, and old Shoes.

James West, about 5 Feet high, 15 or 16 Years of Age, has dark brown curl'd Hair, and grey Eyes. Had on and took with him, a *Scotch* Bonnet, a white Linen Shirt, two Coats, one a dark Cloth, the other a light colour'd Surtout, a Pair of Leather Breeches, ribb'd Worsted Stockings, and a Pair of Pumps.

They took with them two new Osnabrigs Shirts, one Pair of Pumps, one Pair of Shoes, and one Pair of old Shoe Boots.

Whoever takes up and secures the said Servants, so that their Master may have them again, shall have Three Pounds Reward; or Five Pounds if brought home, beside what the Law allows, and in Proportion for either.

(1f)   THOMAS JAMES.

N. B. All Masters of Vessels are forewarn'd not to carry them off at their Peril.

Advertisement for the escape of James West, John Thomas and John Maund Philpott. They ran away from a plantation in Lower Cedar Point, Maryland on May 17, 1765. This verifies the oral/ written history that James arrived in Baltimore in 1765. At some point after this, James met Sarah and married her before they arrived in Granville County, North Carolina about 1770. Note: the real captain of the Tryal was Captain Errington.

ABOUT THE AUTHOR

*C*ynthia West Abbott is a veteran high school English teacher and an avid genealogist who has been planning this story for years. It is only with the latest finds through technology that she knew the story, which was already half written, had to be told. The author lives about five miles from where James and Sarah settled in Granville County, North Carolina. She is a wife, mother of two sons, and grandmother of three grandsons.

CPSIA information can be obtained
at www.ICGtesting.com
Printed in the USA
LVHW020435131118
596826LV00007B/261/P